FIND THE BODY

CHAPTER 1

THE NEW PEOPLE

MILDRED CASTLE watched the removal van as it backed slowly towards the front door of 'Spindles.' Loud-voiced men called advice to the driver; she could see three of them, and judging from the sounds there were at least two more behind the van. She was smiling, but her expression was thoughtful, for she envied no one who came to live at 'Spindles'; already she felt sorry for the new people, who had arrived several hours before the van and had been walking aimlessly about the house and grounds, apparently too shy to ask if they could come into the vicarage to wait in comfort. They had, in fact, declined an invitation to come in, but that was probably because Agnes had conveyed it. Agnes was too bad; she took an instant dislike to anyone who came to live at 'Spindles,' and invented the most absurd reasons for her hostility. The truth was that she wanted to live there herself, longed to go back to the house where her husband had died and in so doing had cast the malign spell over the home he had built with such eager pride.

"Whoa, Tom!"

All the men bellowed in unison as the platform at the back of the van touched the pillar of the porch. No greater volume of sound had been heard in the village since the departure of the troops billeted there a year before. 'Spindles' had been taken over by the military, and about fifty men had lived there; by all accounts they had left the house in a most dilapidated state. Agnes said that it was positively disgraceful; she had written a scathing letter to the authorities about the behaviour of the men. As she had constantly harassed the Commanding Officer while the men had been there, and he had doubtless sent an unfavourable report about Mrs. Agnes Blackshaw, she had received a polite rebuff: the condition of 'Spindles' was a matter for the owner of the property to raise, but the authorities appreciated her interest in the matter. Agnes had fumed for days over that.

"Forward a foot, Tom!" called one of the men.

The engine of the van had stopped, and the grating noise of the self-starter and the snort of the engine as it spluttered, were more unfamiliar, disruptive noises. Disruptive, that was, for Agnes; Mildred Castle rather liked the excitement. It was monotonous to lie in bed month after month, to see nothing but the trees in the grounds of 'Spindles,' and to watch the garden going to rack and ruin. Had it not been for the birds that made their nests and reared their young in the bushes, and the rabbits that played about the lawn, ruining a stretch of grass good enough for a cricket pitch, as Harry would say, it would have been unbearable. Except for Harry, too, of course; dear, patient, harassed Harry!

The wind was blowing from 'Spindles,' enabling Mildred to hear every word spoken in a normal voice. The new people had talked in subdued tones, although the man looked rather flamboyant, 'loud,' as Agnes had already said. The woman, presumably his wife, was well-dressed, tall but too thin, and gave Mildred the impression that she was subdued. That was not surprising in anyone who came to live at the 'Spindles' in its present condition; Agnes was certainly right when she asked whether any sane people would come to live at the place before it was thoroughly redecorated. According to Agnes, it was crawling with dirt.

The only time, until then, that the new people had raised their voices enough for Mildred to hear, was when Maude had taken them some tea and biscuits. Mildred and Agnes had battled for an hour before Agnes agreed, with bad grace, demanding to know whether Mildred thought she had suddenly become a millionaire and whether Maude hadn't enough work to do already without spending time gawping at the new people. The struggle had tired Mildred, but she had been rewarded by the look of pleased surprise on the young woman's face, and her spontaneous:

"Oh, how kind!"

"Jolly decent of you," the man had said.

"Please do thank your mistress most warmly," the woman had added, while Maude, who hated meeting strangers, had gone red, shuffled her large feet and hurried away, promising to collect the tray later. The tray was now standing on a wicker garden seat, with the neglected look of all dirty crockery; all the biscuits had gone. That was really rather funny, because when Agnes had finally given way she had rung for Maude and given the order, adding:

"And of course, send *all* the biscuits we have in the house!"

Maude always took her literally, as she took everyone, and when Agnes saw that empty plate she would fly into another rage. Happily Harry would be back as soon as she was, and he would bear the brunt of her ill-temper. Happily? Or unhappily? It was not really fair to add to Harry's burden. How strange it was that a good-living, sincere and entirely unselfish man like Harry should be so troubled over money and other things. It was really time that something was done to increase his stipend; how *could* the villagers really respect a vicar whose clothes were so patched and who always accepted with such eagerness any little gift of eggs or rabbits or home-made jam? Harry was a big man with an enormous appetite, and she knew that he was often hungry.

On the bedspread, itself patched and darned, were Harry's socks and shirts, which needed darning and mending in half-a-dozen places. Thank God she had the use of her arms and hands, and could perform that service for him. Before this paralysis had gripped her legs—it would one day kill her, she believed, but probably not for ten or twelve years—she had been a good and loyal wife to Harry, although not until she had been struck down had she really appreciated his qualities. She often thought how sharp-tongued she had been in the days when Agnes and her husband had been wealthy and she had envied her sister. Looking back, such envy was comic, but there was nothing amusing in the recollection of her dissatisfaction as the wife of an unambitious country vicar. The truth about the first fifteen years of their married life was that it had failed because they had no children. Harry had wanted children very much indeed, and so had she for that matter; the fact that she was barren had not helped her to sympathize with Harry and try to make up for the disappointment; troubles were no easier to bear because one was responsible for them oneself.

"Be careful!" roared one of the men near the van.

"All right, Jack, keep yer 'air on," said another.

They had taken a number of things out of the van; Mildred had hardly noticed what they were, and that would vex Agnes, who would be full of questions when she returned. Although she had said she was glad that she had to go out that afternoon, she really regretted that she would not have the opportunity of judging from the furniture what kind of people the new owners—or tenants—of 'Spindles' were.

Now Mildred saw that four men were carrying a grand piano out of the van, and turning it on end, to get it through the doorway. It looked a beautiful thing. Mildred eased herself up on her pillows to get a better view. The flamboyant-looking man, who wore red corduroy trousers and a green shirt, was superintending this operation and getting in the way; the woman was not in sight.

The man's fair hair was untidy and blowing in the strengthening wind. His face was red, as if with anger which he was trying to repress. Suddenly one of the men slipped and a leg of the piano hit a pillar; the strings gave a deep, clanging note which was drowned in a bellow from the man.

"You clumsy idiots; what are you trying to do? Ruin the only good piece of furniture I've got?"

"Now, Guv'nor, that ain't goin' to do any good," said a large man who was wearing a cap and a green-baize apron; he appeared to be the foreman. "We can't 'elp a little accident, and it ain't done no 'arm."

"Ain't done no 'arm!" mimicked the man in a tremendous voice. "No harm! You've probably ruined the thing; it won't give a correct note until it's been tuned again. No harm! You get here four hours late and pretend you had a breakdown! The truth is you wasted your time in some ruddy pub. Now you're here you're crawling about as if you had all day to work in, and you start throwing the furniture about! Why, I——"

"If yer don't mind, mister," said the foreman, with commend-able restraint, "we can't get the pianna in until you've moved aht of the way." So saying, he backed into the fair-haired man, who disappeared for a moment, but soon returned. The piano was taken safely into the house and the men reappeared. Before they went on with their work all of them—there were six—deliberately stood about the porch and lit pipes and cigarettes. The fair-haired man fumed but said nothing more until they started work again. One after the other they appeared from the van with small pieces of furniture—cake-stands, chairs, towel-horses and the like, and carried them with exaggerated caution into the house. The last man, very old and small, swaggered up the steps and failed to see a piece of sacking which one of the others had dropped. He caught his foot in it and went sprawling, saving himself from falling heavily by thrusting a cake-stand against the pillar. The frail stand broke with a loud rending sound.

"*Strewth!*" gasped the little man.

The new owner—or tenant—of 'Spindles' stared speechlessly at the broken stand, and then rushed forward, picked it up and looked as if he were going to belabour the unfortunate miscreant.

"Why, you—you clumsy lout!" he roared, words suddenly bursting forth. "You did that deliberately, you ruddy scoundrel! I'd like to break your neck! You——"

"Now 'arf a mo', arf a mo'," said the foreman, appearing on the scene. "That's enough o' that, mister. Who do yer think you are, leadin' orf like that at one o' my men? You made 'im nervous, that's wot you did—made 'im nervous, starin' at 'im the way you did."

"I'll make him——"

"Arf a mo', arf a mo'," repeated the foreman, firmly. "I'm haccustomed to working for *gentlemen*, I don't take kindly to this kind o' treatment, that's a fact. Do yer want yer furniture left *hinside* or aht?"

"You insolent swine!" roared the fair-haired man. "I——"

"Julius!" called the woman, and she appeared from the house. She looked distressed, and Mildred Castle, her own cheeks aflame with embarrassment, felt extremely sorry for her. "Please don't lose your temper," said the woman, appealingly. "The men are doing the best they can."

"If you call this their best," said the fair-haired man in a taut voice, holding up the broken stand, "it's time——"

"Julius! Please!" She silenced him and turned to the foreman. "Please go on with the work," she said, "we are very tired, we were up all night packing. Julius, come and sit down in the shade for ten minutes, you look tired out." She led him away and they sat on the bank of the drive, still in sight from the vicarage, the man scowling and sullen, the woman pale and distressed. The foreman had a consultation with his men, and then they began to move heavier furniture. Mildred was chiefly interested in the couple, who were talking in undertones, but she noticed that the furniture seemed old-fashioned. Some pieces took the six men all their effort, but the rhythm of the work seemed faster.

The man and woman got up and walked back to the house. Mildred thought they looked distraught, and was heartily glad that

Agnes had not been here. She would have received a very bad impression of the man, and Mildred, who now took a charitable view of most people, felt uneasy and sorry for the woman. She did not think she herself would like the man. Agnes, who was tone deaf, pretended to hate all music, and the news that a piano was installed would not please her; already she had made gloomy prognostications about loud radio music blaring forth all day.

"Why, there's Harry!" exclaimed Mildred.

Her husband was walking along the drive of 'Spindles'; striding would be the better word, for he was walking swiftly, his head held high and his long legs carrying his big frame with easy grace. When she had married him he had been the most handsome man in her circle of acquaintances, and there had been much heart-burning among her friends when she had carried off the handsome curate. No troubles could spoil Harry's good looks, it seemed, although he was too thin now, and at times, when he sat in a shadowy corner, he looked positively gaunt. To the world, and most of the time to her, he showed a smiling face, and that was helped by his genial, genuinely friendly manner. If Harry had a fault, it was that he was too trusting, too ready to believe the best of every man and woman whom he met.

It was like him to walk into the house without knocking. Even though he was out of sight, she could hear him.

"Is anyone about?" he called.

Mildred laughed; she could hear the noises of furniture being moved and footsteps on the uncarpeted staircase.

"Oh, hallo!" boomed Harry, obviously espying someone. "Please don't think that I have come to be a nuisance. I simply want to find out whether there is anything I can do."

The woman answered him, but Mildred could not catch the words. Harry spoke more quietly, and she had to strain her ears to hear what he said.

"Are you quite sure? I live next door, and nothing would be any trouble, Mrs.——" he broke off.

"*Miss* Stafford," said the woman, with some emphasis.

"Miss!" echoed Mildred, sitting up again.

"Nothing would be any trouble, Miss Stafford," Harry repeated, extravagantly.

Mildred knew that he meant it; if he were asked to help them shift furniture from one room to another, lay carpets or do any of the hundred-and-one jobs inseparable from settling into a new house, he would take off his coat and set to work with a will. He would smoke his old, charred pipe—he had not had a new one for three years, and was now reduced to one which had been discarded—and keep up a cheerful conversation. Bless him; *bless* him!

· · · · ·

"Of course, you don't believe me," said the Rev. Harry Castle, his blue eyes twinkling. "I can see that in your face, Miss Stafford,

9

but I assure you that I mean what I say. After all, we are to be neighbours. I must create a good impression!''

Anne Stafford, little though she felt like smiling, managed to do so successfully.

"You're very good," she said, "but my brother and I can manage very well, and we mustn't impose on even such friendly neighbours. The tea and biscuits were very welcome, thank you so much.''

"Did they send some in?" asked Castle. "That would be my wife. She is confined to her room, unfortunately, or she would have been here in person to offer help, I know. Have you got everything you need? Tea—milk—sugar? I believe that the necessary foodstuffs are always the last to be found when you are moving.''

"I think I know where to lay my hands on them," said Anne, "I really—oh, there is one thing. If you've a small loaf of bread to spare, or could tell me where to get one, I would be grateful.''

"Gladly, gladly!" declared Castle. "I'll fetch it myself—no, it's no trouble. In fact you will be doing me a favour by allowing me to do so. Life gets very monotonous in a small village, you know.''

Anne saw him to the door, and Mildred heard him say with a laugh in his voice:

"If you don't mind I'll take the short cut over the hedge. We'll have to have that fence repaired when you get settled in. My brother-in-law used to live at 'Spindles,' and it saved us such a lot of time having a short cut. I won't be many minutes, you can rely on me." He waved his pipe and hurried off, and Anne stood watching him, unaware that her brother had approached.

The removal men, who were being deliberately pig-headed, had laid the drawing-room carpet in the large hall. The carpet was hardly large enough for the hall and would be lost in the huge drawing-room of 'Spindles.' It was almost as if the removal men had wanted to express their opinion of people who moved from a four-roomed Chelsea attic to a large country house.

"Who the deuce was that?" demanded Julius Stafford.

Anne started. "I didn't hear you come. He—he was the vicar, and I thought——''

"I hope you sent him off with a flea in his ear," said Stafford roughly. "We don't want meddling parsons in and out of the place.''

"Julius, can't you be more sensible? It was very thoughtful of him to come, and he's going to bring some bread.''

"You ought to have bought some," said Julius.

He was not a bad-looking man, but he was too fat. An unkind observer, at close quarters, would have called him bloated. He was florid and looked as if he drank too much, and yet there was a hint of boyishness about him, chiefly due to his surprisingly clear blue eyes. The only likeness between brother and sister was in the eyes.

They were of equal height, but because she was so thin, Anne looked taller.

"I wonder how much longer these brutes are going to be," said Stafford. "They're being as awkward as they can. If they'd put their backs into it we would have got rid of them a couple of hours ago." He glared towards the stairs, down which came three of the removal men, who returned his glare. "I'll be damned thankful when we're on our own," muttered Julius, easing his tie. "You're sure Tony and Gillian won't come to-night?"

"They said definitely that they couldn't get here until Friday," said Anne. "You read the letter. We've two days to—to clear up and get everything—everything settled."

"Shut up!" hissed Julius. He stalked away as the men came back carrying a bundle of bedding, and went to the door. The van was practically empty, and two of the men were coiling rope slowly and methodically. Julius went into the van, without speaking to them, and scanned every inch of the floor. When he left, one of the men said audibly:

"Thinks we've took something, do 'e?"

Julius turned round in exasperation, but his sister approached him and he restrained himself. "It's all right in the van," he said in a whisper, and then went upstairs, past oddments of furniture which had been left at the nearest convenient place to the door, and leaving a little cloud of dust when he walked near the walls. Two men were putting up a bedstead; they had chosen to erect it in front of a window, the last place it should stand. Another was sitting on a blanket box placed near the fireplace, pulling at a clay pipe.

"If you don't get off that box, I'll——" began Julius, in a low-pitched voice, "I'll——"

"What will yer?" demanded the man, truculently. "I've moved some people in my life, but I ain't never met a cove like you. *And* I don't wanter meet any again," he declared. "Come on, you blokes, let 'im do the rest hisself. If I was Bert," he added, in a loud aside, "I wouldn't take a cheque from 'im, I'd hinsist on cash."

Julius glared at their departing backs before going slowly to the blanket box. He stared down at it fixedly. He was sweating, but it was not because of his exertions; he had done very little in the last hour. He seemed unable to tear his gaze away, but swung round when the foreman came in with his bill. Anne was with him. Julius paid the bill in cash, watched the foreman receipt it, and then snatched it away.

"Now get out," he snapped.

"I'm going, *just* as soon as I can," said the foreman, with calculated insult, "and if you want to move agen, mister, don't come to my firm; they wouldn't touch it for a fortune."

"*Get out!*" screamed Julius, and he shook off Anne's restraining hand and rushed at the man. "I'll knock you down those stairs if you——"

"Come on," said the foreman, with a gleam in his eyes. "Come

on, then, knock me dahn—or try to. Come on, yer said yer would.''
He put up his hands for battle.

''Julius!'' cried Anne. She squeezed herself between the two men, facing the foreman. ''Go away, please,'' she said. *''Please!''*

''I don't mind obliging *you*, ma'am,'' said the foreman.

He turned and went downstairs. The others were waiting for him, and presently the front door slammed. Anne and Julius stood in the bedroom, Julius trembling from head to foot, his sister's face colourless except for her bright eyes.

''Julius, you must keep your nerve,'' she said.

He did not speak, but turned to the window and stood looking into the dilapidated garden. It was a long time before he stopped trembling. At last he looked up at her with an apologetic smile, and his voice was maudlin.

''I'm sorry, Pet, it was that swine of a foreman, he nearly drove me mad. You should have seen the way they dropped the——'' he broke off, looked at the box, and then took her arm and led her out of the room.

CHAPTER 2

A VISITOR AT 'SPINDLES'

THE Rev. Harry Castle would have returned to the house in time to hear the outburst upstairs had it not been for his wife. He went upstairs to see her, carrying a loaf of bread wrapped in a piece of tissue paper, and saw that her pillows needed shaking up and her sheets smoothing out. He performed the little services neatly; she could not get up by herself, but once someone sat her up she could remain in an upright position.

''You've been too interested in the new people,'' he said with a smile. ''You're getting as bad as Agnes! My dear, I wish you could see inside, I really do!''

''Why?'' asked Mildred. ''Thank you, darling. Sit down and talk to me for a minute.''

''I don't suppose they're dying of hunger,'' said Castle, sitting on the foot of the bed. ''It was a good idea putting the bed this way, wasn't it? What was I saying?''

''About the inside of 'Spindles'.''

He threw up his hands.

''I've never seen such a mess! They haven't cleaned it out, there's dust everywhere, cobwebs at some of the windows, and carpets put down without even a broom being drawn over the floors. I must stop Agnes going over there until they've had a chance of putting the house shipshape, or the story will be all over the village. No, I've never seen such a mess, and the removal people seem to have made it worse. Bedroom furniture is downstairs, and goodness knows what's upstairs! I felt like taking my coat off and sending for a bucket of good hot soda water and half a dozen bars of soap!''

"What are the people like?" asked Mildred.

Castle looked at her thoughtfully.

"Well, my dear, I took to the girl at once. There's something very nice about her—clean-limbed, nice eyes—rather like Agnes was before she got soured." His voice was quite free from bitterness. "The man is rather a different type, I think. I should hate to jump to conclusions, but he gave me the impression that he was rather—well, wild. I didn't see him at close quarters, but he was looking at me from a doorway. I don't think I was very welcome," he added, with a laugh, "and I don't think we're going to see him in church very often. Well, I mustn't stay here, they might want this bread at once. I offered to help them, but I don't think they'll accept the offer, so I'll be back very soon. Are you comfortable now?"

"Perfectly," said Mildred.

When he had gone, she watched the path next door, so that she could see him the moment he appeared. She was puzzled and surprised. Only a short while before she had been reflecting that Harry was too ready to believe the best of anyone; he must have formed a very poor opinion of the man next door; it was unlike him to voice such sentiments even to her. She saw him swinging along the drive with the paper fluttering about the loaf of bread. He had to ring the bell and, as he expected, he did not stay long; in fact Mildred thought that they kept him on the porch. He did not take the short cut, either; that was an indication of what he felt about the man.

She heard a car change gear; it was a familiar sound, for cars and tradesmen's vans often turned into the drive of the vicarage. There was a squeal of brakes, followed by Harry's hearty voice: he sounded a little scared.

"Well, *that* was a close shave!"

"I'm terribly sorry," said another man, "it's the hedge, you can't see past it. But it was my fault, I shouldn't have swung in like that. Are you sure you're all right, Vicar?"

"Oh, yes," said Castle, "you didn't touch me. Er—I suppose you've come to the right house, Inspector."

"I think so," said the other man, and Mildred, recognizing the voice, nearly managed to get to a sitting position without help. Inspector Foster, of the Milshire Police, was a rare visitor to the village; in fact they would probably never have met him but for the inquiries he made after Agnes's husband's death. What on earth was he doing at 'Spindles' on the day the new people had moved in?

. . . . .

Anne Stafford was standing in the front bedroom which over-looked the drive when the car turned into it and nearly knocked the vicar down. She heard her brother's footsteps on the stairs.

13

By the time Julius joined her, the brief conversation near the gates was over, and the car was coming towards the house. Julius heard the engine, and demanded:

"What's that?"

"We've a visitor," said Anne.

"What does anyone want here?" snapped Julius, angrily. "Why can't they leave us alone?"

"Julius, if you don't take a firmer hold on yourself we shall be in serious trouble," said Anne, in a low-pitched voice. "This is probably a tradesman come to solicit orders."

"I don't believe it!"

"Oh, stop being a fool!" said Anne. "You're telling everyone as plainly as you can that you are frightened out of your life! First you upset the removal men, then you're rude to the vicar——"

"I wasn't rude!"

"Don't you think common politeness required you to ask him in and thank him for his offer of help?" demanded Anne. "Instead, you were hardly civil and you banged the door, probably in his face. Julius, do you understand what we have to do—*have* to do?" she repeated. "We've got to hide——"

There was a loud knock on the front door.

"If that were a tradesman he would go to the back," muttered Julius. "Of course I know what we've got to do, but it's a terrible strain, a terrible strain. I've gone all to pieces."

"I don't need telling that," said Anne. "I've never known you as bad as this, no matter what scrape you've got yourself into." Her voice had hardened, and there was no softness in her eyes. "Stay up here and keep out of sight. I will speak to the man downstairs. And listen to me——"

The heavy knock came again.

"Oh, *I'll* go," said Julius.

"You will stay here," said Anne. "Julius, listen to me. I have helped you a dozen times when you were in serious difficulties. I have never reminded you of the fact before and I have never asked anything of you in return. This time I want your help."

"Aren't I doing everything I can?" muttered Julius.

"You're doing it very badly," said Anne. "Stay here, and don't move out of the room until I've got rid of him."

She hurried out, closing the door behind her. The man knocked again. She hurried down the stairs, her footsteps clattering on the bare boards, and opened the front door.

She felt quite sure that the caller was not a tradesman. He was well-dressed and he had an air with him; in different circumstances he would have created an excellent impression. He was good-looking in a rather severe way, but the severity of his features was off-set by a charming smile. He took off his hat and smiled more widely.

"Good-evening," he said. "I know you have only just moved in and I'm really sorry to worry you just now, but I feel sure you will forgive me. You are Miss Stafford, aren't you?"

"Yes," said Anne. "Who——"

"Is your brother in?" asked the caller, pleasantly.

"He—no, he's just gone out," said Anne.

"Oh, that's a pity, I wanted a word with him particularly," said the caller. "May I wait until he returns?"

Anne said: "I don't know how long he will be. I—but please come in."

She was angry with herself for keeping him standing there for so long, thus behaving in the way she had reproved Julius for doing. The caller unnerved her; she felt more jumpy than she had all day, and she had some idea of what Julius was feeling like. It was hard to explain why the caller had such an effect; his composure and the fact that he knew their name and that they had just moved in, contributed to it.

He stepped over a rug rolled up near the front door, and smiled pleasantly.

"Moving is a terrible job, isn't it?" I always think it takes a month to get top-tidy, and my wife says that it takes a year to get everything in proper order." He was taking a card from his waist-coat pocket. "But I must introduce myself," he said, and handed it to her.

There *was* something unnerving, almost threatening, in his manner. His eyes seemed to take in everything, including the chaotic state of the hall and the rooms which could be seen through open doorways, and the fact that she had gone pale; she could feel the blood receding from her cheeks. She stared at him as she took the card, and then glanced down at it.

For some reason, it was not a shock. She was becoming highly sensitised, she supposed; it was hardly a surprise to read: *Inspector Mark Foster, Milshire Constabulary*, on the die-stamped card. A policeman in the flesh, standing and smiling at her as if he knew everything; and he must have some information or he would not be here.

She stared at the card for what seemed to her a long time. At last she faced him.

"This is rather unexpected, Inspector. I didn't know that the police inspected all newcomers to the county." She tried to sound flippant, but her voice sounded toneless in her own ears. "How can I help you?"

"I think your brother can do so," said Foster. "Is he likely to be very long, do you know?"

"I don't think so, but——"

"I mustn't stay *too* long," said Foster, glancing round as if looking for a chair.

Anne flushed and said: "Come this way, please." She led him into the great drawing-room, where there were a single bedstead, a tallboy and a dining-table, with a miscellany of small furniture. It looked lost in that room, and the high windows through which the sun was shining showed up the thick dust, the cobwebs and the soot which had fallen in the hearth. Paper was peeling from one wall, hanging down in various lengths. There were three drawing-room chairs, one of which she pushed forward. "I do hope you will excuse the muddle," she said, "our staff hasn't arrived."

"It does rather look as if you came in a hurry," said Foster.

"What do you mean?" she demanded, sharply.

Foster looked startled. "Simply that, Miss Stafford. What else should I mean?"

'I'm making a fool of myself,' thought Anne, 'I might as well have let Julius come down.' She glanced towards the ceiling; her brother was in a room immediately above this one. "I'm afraid I'm rather touchy about the state we're in," she said, and hoped that sounded plausible. "Please tell me why you have come. I feel sure that I can help you as much as my brother."

Then, suddenly, it occurred to her that Julius had done something on his own which had sent the police after him. This man's insistence on seeing Julius was an indication of that; she was foolish to think anyone had the remotest idea of *her* particular trouble. Julius was always in difficulties, she had bailed him out twice for motoring offences committed when he was drunk. His own nerves had gone to pieces so completely that she should have suspected there was something else the matter with him, not just that he had lost his nerve about the other thing.

Then she thought: 'But if it were a motoring offence an Inspector wouldn't come.'

Foster was looking at her steadily; she supposed it was his calling which gave him that almost menacing look and gave the impression that he was watching for the slightest slip. He seemed faintly puzzled, too; in a sudden, wild moment she wondered whether his expression would remain like that if he knew that in a blanket box upstairs there was a dead body—of a man who had been murdered; *murdered!* She clenched her hands, fiercely reminding herself that she must keep her composure. If she went on this way she would blurt out some incriminating word, and precipitate the police investigation she feared so much.

"I wonder if you can?" said Foster at last. "It would save me a lot of time if you are able to manage it. Do you know where your brother was yesterday afternoon between three and five o'clock?"

"No," said Anne, involuntarily. A great wave of relief passed through her, and she felt weak. "That is, I believe he was at his club—Inspector, what on earth are you driving at?"

"I know it must sound absurd to you," said Foster, "but Scotland Yard telephoned me this afternoon and asked me to send a man out to see your brother. When I learned that you were moving in to-day, I thought it might be better if I came in person— I like to know everyone in the larger houses, and it seemed a good opportunity. Did your brother say anything about seeing an accident in Whitehall Place?"

"Why, no," said Anne.

When Julius had come home, about half-past seven, she had

16

been in no mood to listen to him, but had talked swiftly and without ceasing for ten minutes. Her story had shocked him; had he been wholly sober, it might have horrified him. It had sobered him up pretty quickly, and he had behaved very well until the start of the journey, when they knew that the blanket box with its grisly contents was on the removal van. The waiting here had been frightening for them both, and Julius had begun to crack; she should have known that he was not the man for such a conspiracy as she was attempting, but there was no choice.

Foster was saying: "There was a rather nasty accident in Whitehall Place, which was seen by two or three people, including, it is thought, your brother. Scotland Yard told me that the porter of the National Club said that your brother left only a minute before the accident. There was a fatal casualty, and you know how necessary it is to get all possible evidence in such matters."

"Yes," said Anne, faintly. A fatal accident, presumably to someone whom neither of them knew; what a fool she had been to work herself up into such a state. "He certainly told me nothing about it, and he probably would have done had he seen anything at all serious."

"You would think so," said Foster. "I'll have to wait for him, I'm afraid. Don't let me stop you from doing anything. Look here"—he smiled again—"can I help you? If you've no staff——"

"No, thank you, we can manage perfectly well," said Anne. "We shall probably just make up the beds and leave everything until the morning." She looked round desperately for something intelligent to say. "Is there a decent hotel in the village, do you know?"

"There's 'The Angler'," said Foster, "and you can get a good meal there. It's a fisherman's haunt, mind you, and you will probably get very bored. Do you know the district well?"

"Hardly at all," said Anne.

"Unless you fish, you're finished socially," said Foster, and added with a gay laugh: "That's an exaggeration, of course, but fish is to Bray what bridge is to a cathedral town. I'm told that the man who built this house came here because he was a fanatical angler. He——" Foster paused, and looked a little discomposed. "He came before my time," he added, quickly. "It's mostly trout in the Mille, Miss Stafford—good sized fish too, I'm told."

"Is—is the river very deep?" asked Anne.

"Deep? No, only a few feet in most places. It's a tributary of the Ord, of course, and that gets pretty deep a few miles from here. Are you thinking of swimming or boating?"

"Er—yes," said Anne.

"The best boating is just outside Milton, the county town," said Foster, "and that's very popular, too." He was sitting back with his legs crossed, and somehow managed to look quite at home in spite of the surroundings. She thought that he would be a difficult man to embarrass, and now that she was beginning to think more clearly she came to the conclusion that Foster was rather

17

enjoying this *tête-à-tête* with an attractive woman. It was some time since Anne had thought of herself as attractive, and it helped her to recover her poise. "Then at the other side of the town we have our lido," went on Foster, "but I don't recommend it unless you want large crowds of urchins ploughing through the water. There's rather a good pool between here and Milton where you can get some good swimming: it's a private club. I will gladly recommend you for membership, if you like."

"That's very good of you," said Anne.

She felt almost light-headed now. Here was a police inspector flirting mildly with her, while upstairs, probably not twenty feet away from his head, there was the body of a murdered man. What a fool he would feel if he knew!

Her thoughts changed. In a few minutes she would have to leave him, tip-toe upstairs and tell Julius to come downstairs and pretend to have entered through the back door. It would give her time to prepare him for the questions, too, and it would steady his nerve. Perhaps she would tell him to wait for five minutes; a breathing space would do him good.

"I don't know how you will get on in Bray," Foster was saying. "There aren't many young people in the neighbourhood, not of the kind likely to appeal to you, at all events. You might find the Carvers interesting, but perhaps you've got friends in the neighbourhood."

"No," said Anne. "We—we bought the house because it was cheap and there was good room for all of us. My married sister and her husband are going to live here," she added, "and we shall probably entertain quite a lot. It isn't too far from London. There's the big room upstairs which will just suit my brother, too."

"The studio," said Foster. "I've heard about that. Does your brother paint?"

"Oh, no—he is a composer."

"*That* Stafford!" exclaimed Foster, with lively interest. "I had no idea that the village was so favoured!"

Anne laughed. "He isn't as famous as all that. I——"

Then she swung round, for Foster started as the door was flung open and Julius, who had obviously been drinking, barged into the room and approached the policeman aggressively.

CHAPTER 3

JULIUS MAKES A FURTHER BAD IMPRESSION

"HAVEN'T you the ordinary politeness to choose a better time than this to call?" demanded Julius, in a thick voice. "Who are you, sir?"

It happened so quickly that Anne was almost taken off her guard.

Foster had jumped up and eyed Julius with astonishment which was rapidly changing to mild disgust. Julius, emboldened with Dutch courage, was prepared to be unpleasant, and there was a bullying air about him. If Foster used his title, however, if the word 'Inspector' were uttered before Julius was warned, all that pomposity would ooze out of him and there was no telling what he would say.

"My name is——" began Foster.

Anne made a surreptitious kick at a chair, and then pretended to fall over it. Both of them turned to her in alarm, and she straightened up with a red face.

"I'm sorry," she said. "I didn't see it. Oh, Julius, did you see an accident in Whitehall Place last night, just as you left the club? The police want to find witnesses." She spoke lightly, and prayed that Julius had the wit to see why she had mentioned the police. For a moment she was afraid that the very word was going to upset him, but he took a hold on himself; it was possible that Foster did not see the way his eyes narrowed.

"Accident?" he repeated.

Foster grew much more formal as he explained. He did not know that he was giving Julius time to recover, and to do her brother justice, Anne thought, he was putting up a very good front. He frowned throughout the narrative, and was scowling when Foster had finished.

"I did hear something of it," he admitted, "but I didn't get a clear view of it. I'm no good as a witness, I'm afraid."

"That's a pity," said Foster.

"It's a fact. I was behind a stream of parked cars when it happened," said Julius. "I'm not a rubber-neck, and didn't wait to see what happened. I don't even know what cars were involved. You haven't come all the way from London to ask this, have you?"

"Good heavens, no!" exclaimed Foster, and explained again why he had preferred to make the inquiry himself; he went on to say that he had been to inspect the village police-stations between Milton and Bray, a tour which was long overdue.

It was already quite clear that Julius had made another bad impression, and he did not improve on it after Foster finished.

"Ever since we arrived we've had nothing but curious visitors," he declared, rudely. "If it goes on like this I shall be sorry we ever bought the place."

"I hope I don't have to trouble you again," said Foster, formally.

Julius flushed; but for the fact that the policeman turned to smile at Anne, as if to ask her not to include herself in his obvious censure, he must have seen it. To cover the awkward pause she said:

"I'm amazed that you knew so much about us, Inspector."

"There isn't anything amazing in that," said Foster. "Scotland Yard sent a man to see Mr. Stafford this morning and got your new address from your ex-landlady—landladies are notoriously garrulous." He smiled again and looked back at Julius. Thus he gave Anne a badly needed reprieve, for the murder had been

19

committed in the attic and she had been terrified in case the land-lady should come up and see anything to arouse suspicions. Because they were moving there had been every excuse to scrub the attic out thoroughly and remove all traces of blood.

"You're quite sure you saw nothing of the accident?" Foster asked.

"Absolutely," said Julius. "A *subpoena* would be a waste of my time, yours, and Scotland Yard's." He opened the door with a flourish. "Sorry I can't be of assistance, Inspector," he added, sarcastically.

Foster went out, after giving Anne a formal little bow and a faint smile. Julius saw him off the premises and waited in the doorway until the car had disappeared. His eyes were bloodshot, the clear blue spoiled. When he returned to the room his hands were trembling and his voice was unsteady.

"I don't believe he told the truth. He suspects something. He——"

"Don't be absurd," said Anne. "How can he suspect anything? We're making a hell for ourselves when there's no need to. No one even knows that Lovelace is dead, and probably no one ever will know how he died. If we can only get rid of——" her voice trailed off.

"The body," said Julius, roughly. "We needn't keep up the pretence between ourselves." He was making a great effort to regain his composure, and managed to smile tremulously. "I know I've been a pretty foul companion to-day, Pet, but it's really un-nerved me. I don't think I realized what we'd done until I saw that van move off and knew the body was in it. If they'd opened the trunk——"

"It's locked and padlocked," Anne said, "they couldn't have opened it even if they'd wanted to. Julius, we've only got to keep our nerve and everything will be all right. No one knew that Lovelace was back in England; he certainly couldn't have been recognized from his looks. I've never seen a man who'd altered so much."

"You almost make me wonder whether it was Lovelace," Julius muttered.

"Don't talk nonsense!" The sharpness of Anne's voice was the only thing which betrayed her taut nerves. "He'd altered as anyone would alter after four years in a concentration camp."

"His voice was the same," admitted Julius.

"Of course it was. So was the scar on his neck; so were his hands, with those short little fingers." She was speaking very quickly. "Julius, he's not been in England since before the war. Everyone thought him dead. No one dreamed he would ever turn up again, and he told us that he had seen no one else. The body of an unknown man will—will be found, but there'll be no connection with us. Even if he were recognized, no one would know that he had come to see us."

"Except that blasted landlady!"

"Who heard him call himself Smith," said Anne.

"I suppose you're right," Julius conceded, grudgingly.

"Of course I'm right!"

Julius said: "There's one thing you forget, Pet. He was killed at the flat, there isn't any doubt about that, he *was* killed there. If no one else knew he was in England, what made the murderer come to the flat? He wouldn't kill an unknown man named Smith who had only just arrived in England. It just isn't reasonable."

"It happened!" cried Anne. "Don't you believe me? Do you think I killed him? Do you——"

"Now, Pet, calm down," said Julius in a steadier voice. "Of course you didn't kill him, I'm quite sure of that. Why, you wouldn't hurt a fly! What I want to point out is that he must have been killed because he was Lovelace, and therefore someone knew that he'd come back to England. That someone followed him to our flat and killed him—ugh!" He grimaced. "I've never seen anything like his face."

"Don't!"

"I'm sorry, I'm sorry," muttered Julius. "I *am* talking sense though, aren't I? No one broke into the flat to see a Mr. Smith who had called casually, they must have known it was Lovelace. I—I'm beginning to think we were wrong, Pet."

"Wrong about what?"

"Not to tell the police."

"With everything against us?" demanded Anne. "With *our* breadknife used, with——"

"*Don't!*" cried Julius, in turn.

"Then for heaven's sake don't talk like a fool," said Anne. "If the truth had come out, if all that beastly muck were raked over in court or in the newspapers, do you think Teddy would still contemplate marrying me? *Do you?* Of course he wouldn't! He would back out, which would be easy enough, and if that happened where would we be, either of us? Where would we be?"

"I know. I know what you mean," said Julius.

"It's so much better this way," Anne said. "They can't trace it to us, they won't be able to identify the body. It was the only thing to do. As soon as it's dark we'll take the body out." She gave a little, mirthless laugh. "The Inspector kindly told me that the River Ord is quite deep, and we've only got to row along the river at the end of the garden and get near the Ord and—and throw it overboard with some stones tied to it. Why, it will probably never be discovered, no one will ever know, no one will look for Lovelace. If we took any other course we would be ruined. Julius! I'm not doing this only for myself, I'm thinking of you. If we don't get some money soon we shall be in serious trouble, we're inundated with debts, *your* debts. Teddy was the only hope, and his family is trying desperately to make him break the engagement. If the body had been found at Chelsea, if we'd told the police, the family would have been too strong for him. Why, you agreed to all this last night, when you were only half sober!"

"Perhaps that's why I agreed to it," said Julius.

Anne said, coldly: "I see. You're too frightened to go on with it. All right, Julius. *I'm* not enjoying it, you know. We haven't disposed of the body yet. We can tell the police everything and explain that we were in a panic and decided to come down here early. We'll tell them why and say that we couldn't carry on with it. On the whole, I think it would be better. I don't particularly want to marry Teddy," she added, with another short, mirthless laugh. "I don't particularly want to see you in jail for obtaining money on false pretences, either, but that would be better than hanging, I suppose."

"Pet, don't talk like that!"

"I thought it was what you wanted me to say," said Anne.

"You know it isn't. I won't let you down."

"I'm not a bit sure that I can trust you," said Anne. "I don't like the way you keep harping on not letting me down. You think I killed him, don't you?" When he did not answer immediately, she raised her voice: "*Don't you?*"

"Now——"

"Stop calling me Pet!" cried Anne. "What a fine specimen of manhood was wished on me for a brother! I've done everything for you, I've brought you up, I've sheltered you from every kind of hardship. If it weren't for me no one would have heard of Julius Stafford, the rising young composer. I've saved you from prison more than once, I've often kept you when you've squandered your money right and left, I've played Martha all my life because I thought you had a spark of genius. And what do I get in return for it? What do I get? You look at me as if I were a pariah and your eyes tell me the truth—you think I killed Lovelace. All right, let's send for the police at once. I don't mind sacrificing what there is left of my life to Teddy for you, but I'm not going to go on while you think that I killed Lovelace."

"It isn't true!" protested Julius, but would not meet her eyes. "Don't lose your head now, Anne. You're quite right, there won't be any reason for the body to be connected with Lovelace, and even if it were no one would know that he had come to see us, except——" he broke off.

"Go on," said Anne.

"Except the man who killed him," mumbled Julius. "That's what you seem to forget, and that's what I can't understand about it. If you didn't kill him——"

"*If* I didn't?" Her voice rose to a scream. "That's the end of it, I can't bear any more!" She flung herself towards the door, half-sobbing, and he stared at her, too startled to think. Then he rushed after her. He stumbled over a mat, and was not in time to stop her from opening the front door, but he caught up with her in the drive. He put a hand on her arm, but she flung it off. He grabbed her waist and half-ran alongside her, not knowing that Mildred Castle was watching the scene in astonishment.

He had the sense to keep his voice low.

"Pet, don't lose your head, I'll stand by you, I don't really think you killed him; it's just that I can't understand it, that's all. Don't lose your head, for both our sakes."

"For yours, you mean!"

"No, I'm not such a beast as all that," said Julius, with a catch in his voice. "I'm not such a beast, Pet, I'm thinking of you as much as myself. Come back and be sensible. We'll get everything done to-night—look here, come and see the boat at the end of the garden."

They were standing facing each other now, and Julius still had his arm about her waist. There was a long pause, until Anne gave way and let him guide her back to the house. By that time Harry Castle had hurried upstairs to his wife's room, summoned by a tapping on the floor with a stick, to which course she only resorted in emergency. Together they watched the Staffords, and then Harry Castle looked at Mildred, his face a study in bewilderment.

"Do you know, my dear, those people are in some kind of trouble, serious trouble. I'm sure of it. I couldn't understand why they had moved in in such evident haste, and the man's manner, to say the least, was abrupt. Then there was Foster's visit, a remarkable thing. I wonder if I can help them?"

"Harry, it's no business of yours."

"I don't know, my dear. If I can help, I should do. After all they are human beings, and they have come to live in my parish. I wonder what is the best thing to do," he added, with a frown. "It will be useless to call on them, of course, they will admit nothing. I must watch for a chance, that is all, and if you see anything which might help, tell me at once, won't you?"

"If you really insist, my dear."

"I do insist," smiled Castle. "I hate seeing people in torment, and I believe those new neighbours of ours are. It's a very good thing that Agnes has been delayed. If she had seen that——" he broke off. "I don't think we'll say a word to her about it, do you?"

"Most decidedly not!" declared Mildred.

Castle laughed. "Poor Agnes! We needn't worry about Maude, who can't see anything from the kitchen, and even if she could I don't think it would convey anything to her. The gentry have such funny ways!" He laughed again, and then heard footsteps in the garden. "I wonder if that's Agnes? For once I shall be really pleased to see her, I'm getting hungry. You know how she carries on if I start my supper before she is in."

"You let Agnes domineer too much," said Mildred.

"You're a fine one to talk! Remember, now, not a word to her about the strange behaviour of the new people. There's one good thing, after all this excitement you should have a good night's sleep, my dear. I—*what on earth is that?*"

He turned towards the window, startled. From 'Spindles' there came music, wild, frenzied playing of some strange melody, which sounded loudly through the grounds and clearly in the bedroom.

As they listened, it became obvious that it was not so frenzied as at first it had seemed, but there was a wildness about it which exerted a strange fascination.

"Imagine playing the piano with the house in that condition!" gasped Castle.

"Harry, go down and talk to Agnes or she'll be going next door and protesting about it. We mustn't let that happen to-night. Hurry, dear!"

Castle bolted from the room and Mildred listened to the strains of the music which was so out of place in that quiet village and, even to her, was disturbing, as if the tormented spirit of the player were struggling for freedom through the reverberating chords.

CHAPTER 4

INTO THE RIVER

JULIUS opened the back door of 'Spindles' and peered into the gloom of the night. Only the stars broke the darkness, except for a gleam of light from a window next door and, in the distance, the glow from uncurtained windows in the village. He could not see more than twenty feet in front of him.

"Is it all right?" asked Anne.

"Yes, I think so."

"Then let's go," said Anne.

"All right—I'll take him, Pet."

He returned to the kitchen, which was lighted by a single candle. On the floor was a sack, and by the side a small suit-case, filled with bricks which would be put in with the body of the murdered man. They had walked down the straight garden path to the edge of the little river several times, twice when darkness had fallen, to make sure that they could reach the river without stumbling. The boat was tied to a small, rotting landing stage.

Julius hoisted Lovelace's body to his shoulder, grunting with the effort, and then went out. Anne followed with the case of bricks; the body and bricks together in the sack would be too heavy for them to carry. The walk seemed interminable, and by the time they reached the unruffled surface of the stream, which reflected the stars so vividly, Julius was breathing heavily and Anne was nearly exhausted by the case; she was holding it in front of her with both hands. There was a soft lapping of water against the boat, which they could see swaying gently.

"Rest a minute," Julius said.

He put the sack down, and Anne straightened up with a gasp which sounded loud through the quiet. "*Hush!*" breathed Julius. He could not see her angry expression as she glared at him.

Soon he bent down. Anne went on her knees to steady the boat which rocked perilously as the heavy sack fell into it, and water splashed into her face. That too sounded very loud, but Anne made no comment. Julius wiped the perspiration from his forehead, blew his nose softly, and then picked up the case and put it in the stern, to balance the weight in the bows. Carefully they stepped into the little boat, and Anne took the rudder-rope. Julius pushed off from the bank carefully, then lost his grip on an oar; it was held secure in the rowlocks, but the splash made their nerves quiver.

"*Be careful!*" hissed Anne.

Even the noise of the oar in the rowlocks sounded loud, and Julius said:

"It's no use, we'll be heard if we go on like this. We'll have to tie rags round those rowlocks."

"We haven't any."

"I saw some old sacking in the kitchen," said Julius. "I won't be a minute."

He left her alone with the corpse in the swaying boat, which made little creaking noises when it touched against the landing-stage. The house was just visible, and a square of light from a window in the vicarage was bright and lurid. The village was visible from the river, and it seemed to be all light, the yellow glow stretched almost as far as the river itself. There were sounds distinguishable now, footsteps in the village streets, voices from the inn, the music from a radio. The lights and noises came from both sides of the river, for there was a small bridge further upstream; they did not have to pass under it to reach the Ord.

Julius was a long time gone.

Anne sat still, with her hands gripping the sides of the boat. Suddenly her body went tense. There was a light coming *along the river*. At first she thought that it was a boat being rowed towards her, but as she saw the way the light wobbled from side to side she realized that it was a cyclist. So there must be a path running alongside the stream on the opposite bank. She watched the light as it drew nearer, hardly daring to breathe. Sometimes the beam shone on the water and seemed to stretch to the opposite bank. Now she could hear the bicycle, little tinny noises and the soft sound of tyres on the path. Nearer and nearer it came, and suddenly the light shone towards her; she put her hand to her mouth to stop a scream. Then it turned away again. The cyclist went past; she thought he was a policeman. As she watched the red glim of the rear light recede, her breathing grew shallow. She jumped when she heard Julius's voice just behind her.

"What was that?"

"A cyclist."

"It nearly made me jump out of my skin," whispered Julius, hoarsely. "It's all right, I've got the rags."

It took nearly five minutes to tie them on to the rowlocks and leave room for the oars to move freely, but at last they were ready. Julius pushed off, got to mid-stream, and then began to row steadily; he was an accomplished oarsman, and once on the water he seemed to have more confidence. The oars made little noise, for he was extremely careful. The lights receded; he could not see them, only Anne could see the village gradually disappear. Then they turned a bend in the river, with high ground on either side, and only the stars lighted their way.

"How long will it take us?" breathed Anne.

"About half-an-hour, now."

"Half-an-hour!"

"Perhaps a little less," said Julius.

It seemed an age. Sometimes they passed near other villages and hamlets, and lights seemed to be everywhere. The stream broadened, and Julius strained his eyes to see the landmark which would tell him they were near the Ord. He had been to the spot after a scratch supper, and seen a white bungalow close to the river's edge. At last he saw the faint blur of its walls.

"We're nearly there," he said.

They were in a swifter-running current then, where the two rivers met, and the little boat swung wildly. Julius steadied it when the bungalow was behind them. Suddenly light blazed from an opened door and spread across the water not a yard behind them. It seemed that they must be seen. There were voices and a burst of laughter: then the door closed. Two people were walking from the bungalow, shining a torch. Their footsteps soon sounded on the hard road which ran along the course of the Ord for a little way. The two in the boat waited until the last sound had gone, and then Julius spoke swiftly.

"Now we won't be long. Open the case, Pet."

Anne's fingers fumbled with the catches, and at last she had it open. She handed him the bricks one at a time, and he put them into the sack. When all the bricks were there, he tied the neck with stout string, and said:

"Sit quite still. Don't move, or we'll capsize."

He lifted the body and the bricks, grunting with the effort. He could not lift his burden high, but he managed to lean forward so that he could drop it into the water without making too much noise. The boat was dipping sharply, and the reflection of the stars seemed on a level with the side.

"Now!" grunted Julius.

He pushed the burden over; it did not make much of a splash, but it did not go easily; something was catching it close to Anne. The weight on his arms was almost unbearable, and he was gasping helplessly.

"Shift it your end—shift it!" he gasped.

She put her hands beneath it and heaved until the sack went over, with a dull splash; almost immediately afterwards, came a louder splash which sent the water into her face and drenched her chest. The boat swayed wildly to and fro, and Julius balanced himself precariously while Anne leaned over the side trying desperately to get at something in the water.

"What is it?" gasped Julius. "Sit still, for God's sake!"

"It's the case!"

"What?"

"The suit-case, it caught against the sack, it—Julius, I can't get it!"

"Be quiet!" he hissed.

He sat down, fuming, pushed out an oar and, seeing the suit-case floating a little way off, he tried to draw it within arm's length. It was just out of reach and floating away rapidly. The Ord flowed swiftly there, and he had to turn the boat in order to follow the case; when he could row again, it was out of sight. He peered in one direction, Anne in another, but although they rowed on for half a mile they saw no trace of it.

"It must have sunk right away," Anne said, in a strained voice.

"What case was it?"

"That cheap fibre one you borrowed from Tony."

"Was our name on it?"

"It wasn't inside, but there was a label."

"A sticky one?"

"Yes."

"It'll come off in the water," Julius said. "We can't stay any longer. It will be the devil rowing against the current."

She did not answer, and he turned the boat again and began to row. They went nothing like so swiftly, and it seemed an age before they turned into the Mille. Even that gently-flowing stream was a serious bar to quick progress, and as they drew nearer the village, which was still lighted up, Julius was breathing harshly, making no attempt now to subdue the sound. Anne said:

"Can I take over."

"No, we're nearly there."

It took them twenty minutes to reach the landing-stage where, for the first time, things went smoothly. They tied up the boat and walked back to the house, Julius breathing heavily and muttering under his breath; she heard the word 'case' and walked on tight-lipped. He reached the back door first, and turned the handle and pushed.

"Why don't you open it?" Anne demanded.

Julius said: "It's stuck."

He vouchsafed nothing more, but put his weight against the door, which still held. He drew back, muttering again under his breath. Anne tried to open it but with no greater success. It was a wooden door, enclosed in a little porch. They pushed together without avail, and at last Julius muttered:

"We'll go to the front."

"Have you got the key?"

"Yes."

They walked quickly to the front of the house, no longer trying to hide their presence, and that in itself was a relief. Julius said that he had noticed the door was tight when he had opened it to go back for the rags, and that something might have become jammed in it. Anne did not answer.

They turned the corner of the house, and then stopped dead in their tracks, staring at a patch of light which shone onto the neglected lawn. The pale eyes of rabbits seemed to stare at them, and they saw the little creatures turn and scamper away.

The light was coming from the front room!

"What on earth——" Anne began.

"*Be quiet!*" hissed Julius.

He crept forward, keeping close to the wall. Anne could hear her heart thumping as she went a little way behind him. He reached the window and peered through cautiously, ready to dodge back at any moment. No one was in sight. Emboldened, he went further forward, but could see no one; the light from an unshaded lamp showed the empty room—and the fact that part of the floor was wet! The furniture was in different places from where they had left it. The single bed had gone, and there was some sort of order at one end of the room. Anne watched wide-eyed, and saw that there the floorboards were damp but nearly dried out, although at the sides they were still very wet.

"Who on earth——" she began.

"It's that damned vicar! I'll wring his neck!"

"Don't be a fool, he wouldn't break in. Someone must have a key." She gasped. "You did lock the front door?"

"Of course I did! I—look out!"

They heard footsteps inside the house and dodged out of sight. A tall man entered the room in his shirt-sleeves; he was smiling with evident satisfaction. He carried a bucket of water and a mop. Lighter footsteps followed, and a girl appeared, young, fair-haired, looking thoroughly happy. She was comely and a little plump, and there was an infectious gaiety in her manner as she spoke to the dark-haired man, whose laughter sounded clearly to the ears of the watching couple.

"Well, I'm damned!" exclaimed Julius, "Tony and Gillian!" He glared at Anne. "You said they wouldn't get here until Friday!"

"You read the letter!"

"Well, at least it could be worse," growled Julius. "We'll tell them that we've been out to dinner."

"But we're both wet through—at least I am, and you're not much better." Anne stared at her brother, holding her clenched hands in front of her. "Everything has gone wrong, everything possible has gone wrong!" Her voice, although thin and low-pitched, held a touch of hysteria. "Look at them, making fun of it—fun! Julius!"

"Now who's losing her head?"

"Never mind that!" Anne gripped his wrist tightly. "Julius, did you scrub out the trunk?"

"The——" he began, and then he turned pale and stared back at her. "No," he muttered, and gulped. "No, I didn't think I need worry about it then, I was going to do it as soon as we got back. It—it wasn't very stained, I took particular notice. They can't have seen anything."

"We must go in," said Anne, "it doesn't matter what we look like, we must go in and you must get upstairs and lock the trunk before they look into it, you know what they are, they'll pry everywhere, and—*and it's their trunk.*"

"It—it was Tony's suit-case," Julius muttered.

"Fancy using that when we'd several of our own!"

"No one could have foreseen this," muttered Julius. "I did keep asking you if you were sure they wouldn't turn up—they're your particular friends, I haven't got much time for either of them, even if Gillian is my sister, the pi little brat. Come on, we'll put a bold face on it and tell them that we stumbled into the river by mistake; they'll believe anything, that's one advantage."

"But it's obvious you haven't fallen right in!"

"We'll tell them we only just went into the edge and got splashed a bit—I tell you they'll believe anything. We must get that trunk, don't you understand? You said so yourself. Come on," he added roughly. "I'm getting cold."

Anne said: "I'm chilled through. I—just a minute, Julius! Let's bang on the window. It will scare Gillian, she's always nervy, and then they won't have their wits about them when we get in."

"That's a good idea," said Julius, casting her a glance of approval. "You've got your wits about you now, I will say. Won't I be glad when this is over!"

"Don't waste time," said Anne. She went forward, keeping to the side of the house, and then clenched her fist and banged loudly on the window.

CHAPTER 5

TONY AND GILLIAN

TONY and Gillian Abbott were enjoying themselves in their own particular way. Gillian, sister to Julius and Anne, had always been light-hearted and gay, with a serious streak in her which she never allowed to gain the upper hand for long. She did not approve of Julius, but she admitted that there were times when she was fond of him. She was fifteen years younger than her brother, who was thirty-nine, and twelve years younger than Anne, of whom she was really fond. She had often told Anne that she made too much fuss of Julius, who traded on the fact that he had been hailed in some quarters as one of the most promising composers of the day. Both Julius and Anne would have been the first to admit that she was loyal, and it had been chiefly due to her influence—exerted with some reluctance, for she was by no means sure that it would work out successfully—that they had bought 'Spindles,' mostly with Tony's money.

When he had agreed to put up the lion's share of the capital required—and that was very nearly all his own capital, nearly two thousand pounds with legal fees and agents' fees—he had been quick to declare that they must look on 'Spindles' as belonging equally to each couple; he wanted no more rights in it than Anne and Julius. Gillian knew that he was sincere in his eagerness not to create a situation which might give rise to jealousies and petty quarrels: Tony disliked pettiness and triviality above all things. He was not particularly fond of Julius, but he liked Anne, who was the business head of the family. He knew that not only had she nursed Julius skilfully, but she had guided Gillian through difficult days of school and adolescence. Perhaps the truth was that he admired more than he liked Anne, who always seemed reserved, as if she had not yet admitted him completely to the family circle.

He had tried, unsuccessfully, to buy a small house in the country. He disliked London except for business visits and occasional holidays, and the small suburban house in the outskirts, where he and Gillian had lived since he had been invalided out of the Air Force, had become anathema. After his failure, Anne had suggested buying a large house where they could all live, as a practical way of reducing their expenses, for they were both paying rent. If Gillian's reluctance had been marked, his own had been even greater, but once he had realized that it was the only reasonable hope of getting away from London, he had agreed whole-heartedly.

'Spindles' had attracted them both. They could see beyond the dirt and the dilapidations, which were not really excessive in view of the fact that fifty men had lived in it for a year. It was well built, the quaint plan of the three floors interested them, and the large studio in the roof was fitted with special doors to keep out sounds. It would be equally effective in keeping the sound of Julius's piano from the rest of the house. His own small study, he had decided, would be in the wing furthest away from the attic windows, a little morning-room where he could work unmolested to his heart's content. Gillian said that he was a novelist; he said that he wrote a bit—not from modesty but because he did not think his novels were any better than the small circle of readers he had obtained suggested. His publishers were content to go on publishing his books, and he made a living with the help of occasional articles and short stories. One day, Gillian said, he would write a really *great* novel. His reply was always the same.

"I don't think I've got it in me, and it certainly isn't showing any signs of coming out yet."

"If you only had more confidence, darling."

"Confidence doesn't make literature," Tony would say.

"You're so sure of yourself in every other respect."

He would laugh at her, and dismiss the subject.

In the middle of that morning they had gone to see Anne and Julius in their Chelsea attic flat, and learned with surprise that they had already left for 'Spindles.' The landlady made a great song of it; they had been up all night packing, and had telephoned the removers just after eight o'clock, to get the van that morning instead of the following day. The landlady just didn't know what had come over them; they had lived in her house for two years, you would think they could bear it for an extra day.

Had it been anyone else they would have been surprised and perhaps piqued, but it was impossible to guess what Julius would do next. There were times when he left London, declaring that the atmosphere stifled him. He would hide himself in a little village pub, usually drinking heavily, for a week or more, until he ran out of money, usually borrowed, and returned truculently; he refused to answer questions if Anne put them to him. Gillian had long since learned that it was a waste of time to reason with Julius; he merely got offensive, and afterwards, when he was half-drunk again, would apologize in maudlin fashion and call her Sweetie Pie or his little angel. In such moods Julius was revolting.

At 'Spindles,' however, they would have their own apartments, and meet only for meals, perhaps not even then. The house was quite large enough for two families. The two sisters could run it with daily help, and the men could concentrate on their work. Tony would plug away steadily, always doing his quota each day, while Julius would sometimes work like a crazed creature, hardly sleeping for days on end, and then do nothing for a month. If Julius had Tony's application to his work, or Tony had the touch of genius which many people saw in Julius, either of them could become celebrated. Gillian thought it unfair that a measure of fame had been given to her brother; Tony *would* refuse to admit that he was capable of great things, whereas Julius took it for granted that he was the best composer in England.

Tony had been before a tribunal about his pension, but why a tribunal had to consider his claim no one knew. He had lost his left leg from the knee, and although he managed remarkably well with an artificial one, there could hardly be any argument about the cause of the amputation, injuries following a crash after being severely hit by flak in a Mustang. He had attended one sitting, and been told that he would be called to another that Thursday, which was why they had not been able to plan to travel to 'Spindles' until Friday. Then they had received a curt notification that the pension had been granted and that no further appearance before the board was necessary. It was that which had sent them hurrying to Chelsea, to say that they could, after all, travel on Thursday. Their own few oddments of furniture had been warehoused by the firm which had done the removal, and all they had to take with them were their personal belongings. Most of those, in fact, had been taken to the Chelsea flat, to save the van going to Hendon and then through London to the south country village of Bray.

They had not really been surprised, on arriving at 'Spindles,' to find it deserted and in such a state of dirt and disorder. Doubtless Julius had grown tired of work, and carried Anne off to the nearest inn for a meal—and to see what the local beer was like.

Had they been left on their own, the Staffords would probably have slept in this mess and waited for Tony and Gillian.

They had been at 'Spindles' for nearly two hours. Two small bedrooms were reasonably clean and tidy, and inroads had been made on the drawing-room, Tony's favourite room; it was odd-shaped, with two red brick fireplaces and enormous windows overlooking the village and the wooded hills beyond. The worst part of the job was the mopping. Tony forbade Gillian to get down on her knees and scrub that night—and every other night, if he could manage it—and they had decided to wash the floors with disinfectant mixed with water. The smell was penetrating but more pleasant than the musty smell which had met them when they had opened the front door.

"Every square yard wants a fresh bucket of water," Tony said, as he walked with Gillian to the kitchen, "and the mop wants washing out every five minutes. I'm beginning to wish we hadn't started on the sitting-room, sweet; we haven't done so badly upstairs."

"We can't very well stop now," Gillian said, practically. "As for those lazy beasts, I'll tell them what I think of them when they do come in!" In spite of her words, she laughed. "I suppose this is how it will work out. Anne will have to mother Julius like a hen with her chicks, and——"

"You'll do the donkey work," said Tony, frowning. "I've always been a little afraid of that."

"Ass! I'm not serious, and *Anne* isn't afraid of work."

"No, that's true."

"As for Julius, can't you imagine him sitting at the piano surrounded by dirt and cobwebs and indifferent to spiders and mice, banging away as if he were possessed by a thousand demons?" said Gillian.

That had started the laughter which had annoyed Julius. They had set to work with a will, unsuspectingly, and then suddenly the quiet was broken by a great bang on the window. Gillian, busy with a wet duster, jumped nearly a foot, and Tony swung round towards the window.

"What the—the *fools!*" he exclaimed.

"What—what was it?" Gillian gasped.

"Anne and Julius. I thought Anne had more sense," said Tony, angrily.

"I expect they thought it was funny," said Gillian, who had gone white. She had not fully recovered from one or two nasty experiences in London during the last weeks of the war, and she was more than ordinarily nervous. "Don't let's start off with a tiff with them, darling."

In the hall, Tony kissed her.

"I won't," he said. "I——"

"Hallo, hallo!" boomed Julius, flinging open the front door. "Oh-ho! The turtle doves are at it already, Pet! Look at them! You'll get the house a bad reputation if you go on like that,

Sweetie Pie! Well, well, well! What gluttons you are for work. Look, Pet—they've been swimming!''

Had it been anyone else, the greeting would have struck them as remarkable, but it was only Julius: anything could be expected of Julius. Anne looked contrite.

''I'm sorry we banged like that, Gill, I forgot for the moment that you were so jumpy.''

''That's all right,'' said Gillian. ''Well, you're a fine couple, I must say. The place looked like a pigsty. Why on earth didn't you tell us about the change of plans? And what have you been doing, you look as if you've fallen into a pond!''

''No pond, a river,'' declared Julius, heartily. ''We took a wrong turning—it was Anne's fault, she's got no sense of direction at all—and I nearly fell into the river. No damage done, though, but I must go up and change. So should you, Anne.''

''Yes,'' said Anne. ''I——'' she looked at the room, the mop in Tony's hand and the duster in Gillian's, and to Gillian's surprise she stepped forward and kissed her, although she was notoriously undemonstrative. ''You're too good to be true,'' said Anne, ''and so are you, Tony. I won't leave it all to you. Sit down and have a cigarette until we come down again—*Julius* is going to pull his weight until we're settled, or I'll know the reason why.''

She hurried after her brother, who was whistling as he went upstairs.

''You can always tell when Julius knows that he's done something he shouldn't,'' said Gillian, half laughing. ''He always whistles the 'Donkey Serenade.' Shall we relax for ten minutes?''

''It's a good idea,'' said Tony.

The rest of the night—they worked until nearly twelve o'clock—went smoothly. The success of their trick had reassured Julius and Anne, and a further inspection of the trunk had shown that there were only one or two brown stains, which did not come off when washed but became very faint. They locked the trunk again, and went downstairs. Julius was in his best mood, and on such occasions he was likeable and amusing. A surprising amount was put straight before they cried enough. They had made beds in three rooms, Gillian and Tony's at the back of the house, just across the landing from Anne's; Julius had selected one further along the passage.

He was coming out of Anne's room, when he heard Tony say:

''Gill, do you know where I put that old fibre suit-case?''

''No,'' said Gillian. ''Why?''

''I think I had my pyjamas in it.''

''They're in the canvas case,'' said Gillian.

''Oh, so they are. It's funny about the other one, though. I can't imagine where it is.''

Julius stood quite still, listening. When they had changed the subject, he turned as if to enter Anne's room again, but changed his mind and went to his own. He looked very thoughtful and preoccupied, and the tell-tale signs of strain were still at his eyes and lips. It had been a severe effort to keep boisterously cheerful for several hours, and whenever he thought of the missing suit-case he had a shivering fit. Of all the damned fool things to let happen, that was the worst. True, it was Tony's, and he appeared to have forgotten that he had lent it to Julius, but the name Stafford and the Chelsea address had been on the label. If by some freak of chance the case had been washed to the river bank and the writing on the label was still decipherable, there were bound to be inquiries, and the police were likely to hear about it.

He mixed himself a night-cap, smoked two cigarettes, and then got ready for bed.

When he woke up it was broad daylight, and he could hear movements about the house. He was filled with a curiously buoyant sense of security and satisfaction; nothing had happened during the night, and this lulled his fears and put him in a good humour when he went along to the bathroom, whistling 'Marigold.'

Gillian, drinking morning tea with Tony, smiled at him.

"Do you hear that?"

"What is it?" asked Tony. "Not 'Donkey Serenade'. "

Gillian laughed. "Sometimes I think you must be tone deaf," she said, "it's as much like the 'Donkey Serenade' as your books are like Bernard Shaw's. No, it's 'Marigold,' and Julius always whistles that when he's in a good humour. It looks as if we're off to an auspicious start. I suppose I had better go down to the village this morning and try to get a daily woman. Anne and Julius will be anxious to get the studio ready, and you can put your study shipshape, darling. I want you to be able to start work by Monday."

"I hope to start on Saturday!" declared Tony, "but I'll put it off for a week if it will help to get a scrubber-in-chief; your knees are too pretty to become a housemaid's."

"It is generally accepted that the knee is the least attractive part of the human anatomy," said Gillian. "I've never heard anyone call knees pretty before."

"But then," said Tony, airily, "yours is a heavenly body!"

She left him, obviously pleased and humming cheerfully. To complete the genial circle, Anne was downstairs preparing breakfast, or rather sorting out a hamper of various foodstuffs, with some put on one side for immediate use. Gillian made no comment and set to work, but when she met Tony alone just before breakfast, she said:

"It looks to me as if 'Spindles' has worked like a charm, darling. I've never known Anne quite so lively and chirpy in the morning before. I suppose no one has looked at the garden," she added, glancing out of the window, "it's enough to depress anybody."

"Depress? That garden? Great Scott! I'll have it looking like a flower show in a few months; there are beds and borders which only want weeding, and I've come across a rose bed which will be the envy of the village. We could do with someone for the heavy digging," he added, with a slight frown; anything which reminded him of his incapacity worried him. "I daren't ask Julius to lend a hand with that."

"Let's see if he offers," said Gillian.

At breakfast, Julius was in great form, chiefly on the subject of the vicar and, he presumed, the vicar's wife. He made great fun of Agnes Blackshaw's sour face and her harsh, obviously reluctant invitation to rest in the Vicarage, and of Maude's red face and shuffling feet. He even tried to make fun of the vicar, but found it difficult, and Anne said:

"I thought he was charming, and really sincere when he said he would like to help us. If the other woman was his wife, I feel rather sorry for him." She frowned. "But it wasn't his wife; he told me that she was confined to her room."

"Poor soul," said Gillian. "I wonder if he can preach?"

"You'll have to let me know, one day," said Julius, grinning.

"It wouldn't do you any harm to find out for yourself," said Gillian, unruffled. "Here and now I declare that Tony and I are going to church on Sunday mornings, whether he can preach or not. I don't greatly mind about that," she added, looking at Tony, "I like the chanting and the singing, it's old Mutton Head who likes to be soundly rated from the pulpit."

"I can never understand anyone taking that seriously," said Julius. "Honest. No offence meant, Tony, but religion always strikes me as being a sop to one's conscience, or else a matter of form."

"Well, we've all got something to learn," said Tony, with a quiet smile. "That appears to be a part of your quota." He looked thoughtfully at Anne. "If the vicar was so helpful, he might be able to suggest a daily woman."

"I shouldn't get too friendly with the old boy," said Julius, "or you'll have him wandering in when you're trying to write, and I'm driving myself crazy trying to get the genius to spark!" He laughed. "I can just imagine him assuming that a musician and an author have nothing to do all day but entertain him. I'll lay you an even fiver, Tony, that within twenty-four hours of learning what you are, he'll say that he always wanted to write a book."

Tony laughed. "Half an hour will probably be enough."

"And another half-hour for you to offer to help him," said Anne, with an unexpected tribute to Tony. She seemed to have lost much of the sobriety which characterized her, and seemed younger and quite gay. "You two had better call on him. We created a poor impression yesterday, and you can put it right. If you can fix up with a charwoman it will be splendid. I think Teddy might come down for the week-end, and you can never be quite sure that he won't drag one of his relations with him."

"Oh," said Gillian, her face falling, "I'd hoped we'd have a week or two to get really tidy. Still, Teddy on his own will be welcome enough," she added quickly, "he rather reminds me of the vicar."

"He reminds you——" began Julius, and then roared with

laughter. "Sweetie Pie, what a girl you are! I can't imagine anyone less alike than your vicar and Teddy. That's a good one." He went off into another roar. "I'll tell Teddy the minute I see him, it's too good to keep!"

"The genius has spoken," said Gillian, looking slightly flushed.

"I'm going to look round the garden," said Tony, breaking into the conversation quickly and side-tracking a clash between brother and sister. Julius's laugh had not been altogether free from malice. "Coming, sweet?"

"Yes—and we'll go next door afterwards," said Gillian.

She did not refer to the incident, but paid attention to what Tony said about the garden. He had only seen it from the windows, except when they had looked over the place before deciding to buy it, but she saw that he was quite right about the flowers. The garden had been kept in order until fairly recently, and it only needed clearing to put it right. The one exception was the lawn, which was a mass of rabbit heaps and holes.

They heard sounds from the house next door, and suddenly a voice hailed them from a window. They looked up, to see a man whom they immediately assumed to be the vicar. His grey hair was untidy, his brown, leathery face, rather too thin, was creased in a smile, and he attracted both of them immediately.

"Good morning! I've been telling my wife that I must have been blind yesterday; you don't look the same people."

Tony laughed. "We're not. Are you the vicar?"

"The Reverend Harry Castle, at your service," said Castle.

"I wonder if we can come to see you for a few minutes?" asked Tony. "We'd be very grateful for a word of advice and——"

"My dear sir, I'm delighted, delighted!" declared Castle. "Come round at once—or take the short cut through the hedge, that's what I usually do."

He pointed to the gap a little nearer the house, and disappeared. When they reached the front door of the vicarage he had brushed his hair, but his coat collar was rucked. He wore a loose-fitting tweed suit and both Tony and Gillian—quick to observe little things—saw that the knees of his trousers were patched, that his cuffs and collar had been darned, and that he needed a hair-cut. The garden of the vicarage looked neat, but the house needed painting nearly as badly as 'Spindles.'

"Come in," said Castle, offering his hand. The hall where he led them was furnished with heavy Victorian furniture, and needed papering. He bustled ahead of them into a room on the right. "This is my study," he said, "I must apologize for the mess—I'm the most untidy creature imaginable!"

There were grounds for his statement. His roll-top desk was littered with papers and the waste-paper basket was overflowing; Castle appeared to have dropped paper to the floor wherever he was standing. It was a dingy room, and looked at its worst because the morning sun was shining through a large bay window. An assortment of broken pipes was on his desk, and he picked one up;

the stem was bound with adhesive tape, and the bowl had burned down to little more than half its original size. There were a few prints on the walls, mostly sporting, and two shabby leather armchairs by the side of the littered fireplace.

"Sit down, do," said Castle. "Don't think me curious, but are you living next door too?"

"Yes," said Tony. He introduced himself and Gillian, and explained the situation at 'Spindles.' Then he asked about a daily woman, and Castle frowned.

"They're not easy," he said, "but I think I know one woman who might do for you. She's got three children, one of them not yet at school, and wherever she works she has to take the youngest child with her. Quite a well-behaved little chap, on the whole, but boys will be boys, you know."

"That wouldn't matter a bit," said Gillian.

"Good! I'm going down to the village this morning, and I'll have a word with her—she's a Mrs. Kelly. If she's willing, I'll tell her to come along and see you. No trouble, no trouble at all," he added, quickly. "I don't mind admitting that I'm very glad that 'Spindles' is occupied at last, and I want to create a good impression, as I told your sister, isn't it? So you see my interest is quite selfish."

He asked few questions; Gillian got the impression that he was anxious not to appear inquisitive. He did tell them about Mildred, and said that his sister-in-law lived with them. And he told them that her husband had built 'Spindles.'

"I knew it wasn't very old," said Tony, pleased.

"Only about twenty-five years," said Castle. "It was designed to look older, of course, but give me a new place all the time—this vicarage is just an invention for collecting dirt."

"I've been intrigued by the name 'Spindles' ever since I saw it," said Gillian. "Do you know why he chose it?"

"There isn't much mystery about that," said Castle. "He was a Lancashire mill-owner, a self-made man and originally a cotton-spinner. By spindles he made his fortune and in 'Spindles' he proposed to live. He was rather handy with a paint brush—quite a good amateur artist, I believe. He——"

Castle broke off, so abruptly that Gillian was puzzled. There was a forced heartiness in his voice when he went on to say that after it had been sold several people had rented the house, but none had stayed for long, and that because it was empty the military had taken it over. Then, perhaps in explanation of his change of tone, he added a little awkwardly, after glancing at the door to make sure that it was closed:

"His wife, my wife's sister that is, has a rather curious fixation about 'Spindles.' Her husband lost his money, and she had to sell soon after his death, but ever since she has been rather—well, intolerant of people who have lived next door. It's only fair to warn you. She may appear to be rude, and cut you in the village. I do hope you understand."

"Perfectly," said Gillian.

"Yes," smiled Tony.

"You encourage me to say that she is tone-deaf and rather hostile to musical people," said Castle, with a rather uneasy smile. "I heard——"

"Was Julius playing yesterday!" exclaimed Gillian.

"And he played very well," said Castle. "My wife and I were entranced. I do hope you understand that what I say goes only for my sister-in-law, and I beg you not to take her too seriously. In the circumstances I thought it only fair to warn you."

"You're very thoughtful," said Tony. "Now we mustn't take up too much of your time."

"At least Tony won't worry her," said Gillian. "He works in his study all day, and——"

"Now, Gill!"

Gillian laughed. ".We may as well get all our confessions over while we're at it, Mr. Castle. Tony is a novelist. So you will see that a very queer bunch of people have come to live next to you."

Castle stared at Tony with glistening eyes.

"Queer, Mrs. Abbot? Certainly not! I've often wanted to write a novel myself. As a matter of fact," he added, half-eagerly, half-shyly, "I've got one nearly finished. It's rather—what shall I say—tinged with biographical detail, of course, and I haven't dared to show it to anyone, not even my wife. I wonder if——" he broke off, abruptly. "I wonder if I shall ever finish it?" he added with a gay laugh, but it was obviously not what he was going to say.

Tony said, quickly:

"I'm no expert, but if you would care to let me have a look at it one day, I might be able to give you an opinion."

"Would you really?" Castle looked delighted and almost crowed. He turned round to his desk and pulled open a drawer, while Gillian hid a smile and Tony grimaced at her. "Here is the *magnum opus!*" He laughed as he held up a thick bundle of papers covered with close hand-writing. "I spend half an hour touching it up in parts most days," he said. "It's—well, it's like a day-dream, one of those things which we hug to ourselves and which always seem as if they might prove the *open sesame* to a better world. I haven't even mentioned it to anyone else; I don't know why I should have started to talk about it to you."

Tony stood up cautiously and stretched out his hand.

"Let me take it with me."

"You're *very* kind," said Castle.

"Nonsense! I shall probably be a week or two," warned Tony. "In fact if I bring it back in a day or two, I'll have a depressing opinion to give you!"

"Then I'll expect it back to-morrow," said Castle, gaily. "I don't seriously think anything will ever come of it. It must have been the fact that you're a professional author, Mr. Abbott, which made me lower my defences. I don't mind being told that

38

I've written a farrago of nonsense by someone who should know, but amateur opinion frightens me. When I said it wasn't finished, I meant that I haven't licked it into the shape I would like, but it's all there.''

"Leave it with me," said Tony.

"I will, gladly." Castle went to the door with them, and as he strolled along the hall, he said: "Oh, there's one thing I should mention. I don't think it amounts to anything, but I think your boat was taken out last night."

"Boat?" ejaculated Gillian. "We haven't got one."

"Yes we have," said Tony, "it's tied up at the landing-stage at the foot of the garden."

"My sister-in-law was in the garden last night—she has a friend who lives in a cottage a little way along the river—and when she came back she told me that she thought she had seen someone in the boat, just pushing off. I thought it was her imagination, but I had a look—you can see the landing-stage from the garden here—and I saw that it was wet and that the oars were shipped differently and free from dust, which is a rare thing for them these days! Probably some youngster decided to have a jaunt, as it was a fine night. Still, I thought you should know."

"Yes, thank you," said Tony. "We'll keep our eyes open."

CHAPTER 6

MRS. KELLY

THEY elected to go along the drive, ostensibly to see the front of the house in the morning sun, but when they had turned into the road Tony said that he was short of tobacco and that it might be a good idea to see what kind of stock there was at the village shop. The road to the village green was narrow, with high hedges on either side. There were attractive thatched cottages along it and there was even a small duck-pond. Beyond it was the river bridge.

Tony bought some tobacco and placed a regular order for his favourite brand, and they started back.

"It's a queer thing," he said, abruptly.

"What is?" asked Gillian.

"That boat business," said Tony. "It would be different if it had been stolen, but it isn't likely that anyone would take it for a spree by night and return it—in the day time it would be more understandable. Anne and Julius said that they had been to the village, but it was quite late before they got back——"

"Julius probably insisted on staying at the bar," said Gillian.

"I don't think he'd been drinking," said Tony. "You can usually tell with him, and his eyes were clear. He gets fuddled quickly and recovers quickly I know, but he hadn't come straight from a drinking session. Then they said they'd fallen into the river, or stumbled into it, rather. I noticed last night that their heads and shoulders were wet, and there were damp patches on Julius's trousers and Anne's skirt, but their shoes looked dry. If they'd stumbled into the river they would have been wet from the knees downwards.''

''I suppose you're right,'' said Gillian, a little troubled. ''I didn't notice as much as you did, but I thought it funny that their shoes weren't very wet. So you think they went out in the boat?''

''Well, it does rather look like it,'' said Tony. ''There's another thing, too. I was thankful that Julius was in a good mood last night, but it was so good for such a long time that it wasn't natural.''

''It was his 'I-am-about-to-ask-for-the-loan-of-a-fiver' mood,'' said Gillian. ''I noticed it. I thought it might have been because he felt guilty at having left the place in such a mess and not telling us that they'd decided to move yesterday. Tony, if you're right, why on earth did they want to take the boat out at night? Julius is fond of boating, but there wasn't even a moon. Even he isn't as eccentric as all that.''

''No,'' admitted Tony. ''I suppose it's foolish of us to worry about it; we'd better not say anything. If they want to tell us they need no prompting, and if they don't want to, then we'll only precipitate trouble.''

''Yes,'' said Gillian. They walked on in silence for a few minutes, and then she shot a quick glance at him.

He appeared to be in a brown study. His profile was good, and his face had been untouched in the crash; only the fact that he walked slowly betrayed that there was something the matter with his leg. He had a good chin, a mouth which smiled readily, and a short, tip-tilted nose.

''I wonder if we have been wise,'' she said at last. ''We're both very conscious of the need for—well, studying Julius's feelings. It isn't going to make a very healthy atmosphere.''

''We came into it with our eyes open,'' said Tony. ''When we've settled down we won't see a great deal of him, remember. If he runs true to form, he'll go off from time to time for a week or two, and the atmosphere will be clear enough then; Anne on her own is a very different proposition. I wonder why she mothers him so much?'' he added. ''I think she's going to marry Teddy Barr because it will enable her to help Julius financially. Teddy isn't the man for her.''

''I've often thought the same,'' said Gillian. ''Anne is a different person when she isn't worrying about Julius. I think she really believes that he is brilliant, and is afraid that if he is left on his own, he'll just run wild and never do any work. She's probably right, too.''

''Yes. Well, we'll say nothing about it,'' said Tony.

''And say nothing about the vicar's manuscript,'' said Gillian, meaningly. ''If you let Julius know what you've done within ten minutes of meeting him, you'll never live it down.''

40

Tony laughed.

"The old chap was so keen and yet so obviously anxious not to look as if he were," he said. "The worst part of offering to do a thing like that is telling the truth if the stuff is hopeless," he added. "You know, sweet, I often think that I would be wiser to stop writing and take up reviewing or editing."

"Don't you dare!"

"We'll see," said Tony.

When they got back to the house, Julius and Anne were busy in the studio. They had managed to make the removal men take the piano there, and it was standing in one corner, highly-polished, like a thoroughbred among cart-horses. Julius was brushing down the walls, which were covered with dust and cobwebs, and Anne was sprinkling water over the floor to lay the dust. Gillian and Tony went to the morning-room, which would be much easier to clean up because it was smaller, but they had only just started when there was a knock at the back door. Gillian went to answer it, and found a short, fat woman, wearing a man's cloth cap with her untidy hair pushed under it. She had a broad smile and a fat, red face, and she was breathing heavily.

"Morning, mum," she said. "The vicar sent me, mum."

"Oh—for daily work?"

"That's right, mum. Kelly's me name, but don't make any mistake, I'm not Irish—Lunnon's my 'ome town, mum—Londoner, I am. Got evacuated in the bombing I did, mum, and back I'd go this minnit only Archibald needs the country air, like the doctor says, so I suppose I'd better stay on fer a bit. I ain't afraid o' work, mum, that's a fact—good work for good wages, that's wot I always says." She looked at Gillian hopefully.

"What do you call good wages?" asked Gillian, restraining a laugh with an effort.

"One-and-a-tanner an hour for odd days, mum, one-an'-fruppence for reg'lar work every day eight to twelve except Sundays—come Sundays for special occasions, like, I wouldn't mind doing that, an' I wouldn't charge you any more."

"We certainly want someone every day," said Gillian, "and this week we could do with you for more than four hours a day, the place badly needs cleaning."

"Don't I know it!" declared Mrs. Kelly. "Took a look through the winders I did, as I come in—crikey, it ain't arf a mess, I thought, I dunno wot they was a doing of, coming before it was cleaned aht. It ain't as if you could be bombed aht these days, is it, mum? Still, it's no business o' mine, I said to meself, and I ain't afraid of work. I'd 'ave to bring Archibald, mum."

"Is Archibald your son?"

"That's right, the one I told yer abaht—don't you get me wrong, mum, he ain't ill, it's just that he's a bit delikit, like the doctor says—he come early, mum, 'e's a n'eight munce baby, my Archy is. Them bombs done it. Ain't it a good job we beat them Nassis, mum? It don't seem the same world, do it? Yer'd like me ter start ter-day, I s'pose?''

"If you can," said Gillian.

"I dessay I can," said Mrs. Kelly. "S'arternoon, it's a bit late fer this mornin', now. Like me ter work mornin's an' arternoons this week, would yer, mum?"

"Please," said Gillian.

"Yer got everything, I s'pose?"

"What kind of everything?" asked Gillian.

"Floorclovs and fings," said Mrs. Kelly. "Crikey! I've worked for some people, I 'ave, expect yer to do blinkin' marvels with yer bare 'ands, they do. I'm hecomical with soap, I will say, but I likes plenty o' soda, an' that's cheap enough, ain't it?"

"If there's anything you need that we haven't got, you can get it from the village store," said Gillian.

Mrs. Kelly's blue eyes sparkled.

"Well, that's 'andsome, I will say—usually I as to manage some'ow; I was only warnin' you that I couldn't do everything wiv me bare 'ands. 'Ave you got a vacky, mum?"

"A vacky?" asked Gillian, puzzled.

"Yes, that's right—a vacky. One o' them electric cleaner fings, mum, a vacky."

"Yes," said Gillian, "it's rather small, but——"

"I was afraid o' that," said Mrs. Kelly, sadly. "I don't mind admittin' I don't like them vackys, mum. I never 'ad one in my 'ome, gimme the good ole brush and pan, that's what I say. But if yer've got one I'll 'ave ter use it, I suppose, only I can't do no fixing. I 'ad a shock once when I was tryin' ter fix one, an' all the missus did was to larf. Larf," repeated Mrs. Kelly, grinning as if it were a huge joke. "I taught 'er to larf, I did—she was three munce wivvout 'elp in the 'ouse arter I left that day. I wouldn't treat no one who treats me decent like that, mum, but she was a real ole cat—no names, no pack-drill, yer understand."

"Yes," said Gillian, faintly.

"Then that's settled, mum," said Mrs. Kelly, with satisfaction. "There's one thing I will say for meself, I'm a worker and I don't talk like some people—I gets on wiv me work. I likes ter do it me own way, mind yer—I don't mind *trying* your way, but I've found me own way's usually the best, mum."

"We'll have to give both ways a trial," said Gillian, struggling to keep a straight face.

"Well, yer couldn't say fairer than that, mum, I will say," declared Mrs. Kelly, with a beaming smile. "Two o'clock suit yer? I'll be along at two o'clock, then, wiv Archy. Good-mornin', mum!"

"Good-morning," said Gillian, "and thank you."

As soon as Mrs. Kelly had disappeared, she started to laugh, and was startled when Tony's laughter echoed hers. He had been in the hall, listening. Their laughter reached the couple upstairs, and Julius came to the landing to ask what the joke was about.

"You'll see," called Tony. "We've got a daily woman."
"What?"

"We've got a daily," repeated Tony.

"Then that's finished me," declared Julius, after a short pause. "I'm parched, and I'm going to see what the local's like!"

Tony stopped smiling, and exchanged glances with Gillian. The same thought occurred to them both; Julius would not have said that he was going to see what the local inn was like if he had been there the previous evening. By mutual assent, they made no comment, and they were busy in the study when Julius banged the front door and strode along the drive, whistling 'Marigold.' The sun caught his fair hair as he disappeared into the road.

In the morning-room there was a legacy from one of the previous tenants, a piece of linoleum which covered the floor. It was particularly welcome, because they would have a lot of staining to do, since their carpets were not nearly large or numerous enough. Anne volunteered to prepare lunch, while Gillian defied Tony and scrubbed the linoleum. By lunch-time the morning-room was thoroughly cleaned, and with the walls carefully brushed—they were distempered—it did not look at all bad. From the window they could see the window of Mrs. Castle's room, not knowing that by sitting up she could see into the study-to-be.

Mrs. Kelly came promptly at two o'clock with a piece of sacking tied about her ample waist to serve as an apron and Archibald by her side. He was tall for his four years, and he looked delicate. There was something appealing about the child. He was quiet and reserved, and although Gillian knew better than to assume that his behaviour on the first day was a criterion, she was surprised that he was the son of Mrs. Kelly. There was an air of refinement about him too, until he opened his mouth, when he spoke in a slow, country voice. Silent, he looked unusually intelligent; speaking with his slurred voice, he seemed almost simple. He came to the morning-room, which in a few hours would become a study, while his mother received instructions from Gillian, and stared wide-eyed at the array of books, some in packing cases, some already unpacked and piled on Tony's desk.

"All right, mum, I'll start on the 'all," said Mrs. Kelly. "Come along, Archibald. 'E'll be as good as gold," she confided, "I got 'im a comic. 'Ere you are, Archy, 'ere's yer comic."

"Does he read already?" asked Gillian, surprised.

"Read, mum? Bless yer 'eart, 'e don't do nuffink else, 'e's a bright boy, my Archibald, aren't you, Archy? Percoshious, that's 'im," declared Mrs. Kelly. "Archy! Don't stand there starin' at the gentleman, that's rude!"

"Odd little chap," said Tony, as Archy went obediently to the hall, holding his comic. "Mr. Kelly must be a remarkable man."

Whatever her husband was like, Mrs. Kelly proved herself a remarkable woman. She worked with concentrated fury and while she was working she hardly said a word. Between jobs she talked so much that Gillian could hardly keep pace with what she said.

manuscript thoughtfully. "Shorn of its wilder criticisms, it's the story of a man who has one great desire, to see Christianity brought to the masses, a man who wants a sound, practical religion based on the New Testament teachings, and I think a lot of people could learn a great deal from it. I know one thing," he added with a smile, "only a really lovable man could have written it."

"Have you told him what you think?" asked Gillian.

"No, I thought I'd rather see what Snub says."

"But darling, you've had it for nearly ten days and the vicar will be eating his heart out! Now I know why he's had a wistful look in his eyes whenever I've met him—he's been stopping himself from asking me about the book."

"I hadn't thought of that," said Tony. "I'm so used to waiting for a month or two before I get opinions on my own stuff. I'll go over and have a word with the old boy now, I think. I mustn't raise his hopes too much," he added, "for I might be wrong."

"I think I'll come with you, if you'll wait ten minutes," said Gillian. "I promised to pop in to see Mrs. Castle again."

"All right," said Tony.

He sat at his desk, pushed the manuscript away from him, and looked at the book-case. He was not thinking of that, nor of Castle. He was remembering the blind rage which had taken possession of him when he had come into the study. In such moments he felt capable of anything, and the moods frightened him. Sometimes it was over trifling things which had not gone as he thought they should have done. Anything in the way of injustice affected him deeply, and had always done so, but he knew that there was nothing normal about the spasm through which he had passed. He had not mentioned his worry to Gillian, but he had talked to Snub Savory, a lifelong friend and a literary agent of acknowledged acumen. Snub had agreed that a spell in the country would probably put him right, and had encouraged him to put his money into 'Spindles.'

"Ready, darling?" called Gillian.

He smiled and stood up. Gillian's companionship was the most soothing thing in his life; she more than made up for hard knocks, for the rudeness of her brother and the curious manner in which Anne sometimes behaved. Whenever he was alone with her he felt content, and the knowledge that she was in the house was always satisfying. He felt quite normal as he walked with her along the drive. The fence behind the hedge had been repaired at Julius's insistence.

There was the sound of digging from the back garden of the vicarage, where only Castle ever worked. They decided to walk past the house and call him, but as they passed the front door it opened and Agnes Blackshaw called out harshly:

"What do you want?"

Tony turned, and Gillian said quickly:

"I think Mr. Castle is at the back, and——"

"You might have the common *courtesy* to knock," said Agnes, angrily. "Just because you've bought 'Spindles' that doesn't give you the right to wander at will over other people's property!"

"Oh," said Tony. "I'm sorry."

"I don't know what manners are coming to," snapped Agnes. "The language I hear from next door is a disgrace, do you hear me, a positive disgrace!" She glared at them, and Tony felt himself colouring, though this woman did not affect him like Julius had.

It was not their first encounter with Agnes Blackshaw, and they knew the 'language' had come once or twice from Julius.

"I am sorry," he repeated.

"So I should think," said Agnes. "I'll tell the vicar."

She flounced off, leaving the others staring at each other. They heard her stamping down the garden path, and then a quiet voice called from a window:

"Is that Mr. Abbott?"

"Hallo, Mrs. Castle!" called Gillian.

"I'm so sorry about such rudeness," said Mrs. Castle, "you will never know how it vexes me. Please do forgive her."

"That's all right," called Tony and Gillian in unison.

Soon Castle came hurrying up, smiling. He knew nothing of Agnes's greeting, and insisted on taking Tony upstairs with Gillian. Mildred Castle said nothing more about the incident, and soon she was smiling amusedly as Tony went into detail about the antics of Mrs. Kelly and Archy. Neither Gillian nor Tony mentioned the story of the hanging.

"Well, Abbott," said Castle with a conspiratorial wink, "let us go downstairs and smoke a pipe in peace, and leave the ladies to their chatter, eh?" He laughed roguishly, and led the way downstairs, while Mildred protested that she did not know what Mrs. Abbott would think of him for such rudeness.

In his study Castle picked up his old pipe and began to fill it from a jar which, Tony saw, was nearly empty.

"Try some of this," said Tony, handing the vicar his pouch. "It's good stuff, although not everyone likes it."

"No, I——"

"Go on," said Tony, smiling.

"Well, if you insist." Castle filled his pipe carefully, talking about the weather, the village, and the fact that the lot of a country vicar was often hard. He could not afford a man to do anything in the garden. How were they getting on in the garden next door? The man's anxiety not to broach the subject of his book was almost pathetic, and Tony fought against the temptation to plunge into it too enthusiastically. He veered the conversation round to his writing, and then said, as if it had only just occurred to him:

"Oh, that reminds me, Vicar—will you mind if I send your manuscript away for a second opinion?"

Castle's eyes lighted up.

"Have you read it?"

"Yes. I think it might have possibilities," said Tony. "My agent will gladly read it, and he's a better judge than I."

rustling in her grandmother's satin! Now they've come to accept me, but they don't come to church."

"Have you ever thought of trying stunts?" asked Tony.

"Stunts!"

Tony laughed. "Don't sound so shocked, I don't mean anything outrageous. Why not try to get a well-known singer to sing solos at a special afternoon service, and give it a good publicity beforehand? Then, perhaps, tea in the vicarage grounds, and——"

He could have kicked himself for the last sentence. Castle's face clouded, and he stood up and went to the window. He looked out for a few seconds in silence, and then spoke in a muffled voice.

"I know, Abbott, I know, but I can't *afford* to dispense teas, and I haven't a single member of the congregation who will come up to scratch. We have a garden party once a year, and since my wife has been laid-up that has been a failure. You've got to have a hostess for these things, and you've got to give a good spread. What point is there in inviting the villagers to tea when you have to go round a fortnight beforehand and beg contributions for the table?"

Tony said nothing.

"There are six hundred souls in Bray, including the farms and hamlets," said Castle, "and with the exception of the five farmers, only one of whom is a church member, there isn't a man who earns more than four pounds a week, even to-day. The wealthier people can be counted out. As a matter of fact," he added, swinging round angrily, "I won't beg from them! I've tried. I don't mind humbling myself, it isn't that, but they just won't play. If my wife were well I would try to find another parish, but I can't move her. I'm anchored here for the rest of her life, and, please God, that will be for a long time yet." He paused and then smiled, as if he were much more confident. "Abbott, you've been a greater help than you know. I've wanted to get these things off my chest for a long time."

"Good!" said Tony. "And who knows, my wife and I may be able to help from time to time. What kind of a village is it for social occasions? Is there a cricket club?"

"No. There was before the war, but we lost one or two of our best fellows, poor chaps, and no one has started it up again. I haven't had the heart to. There's quite a lot of work attached to it, you know, and I don't think there's a man in the village who would be prepared to accept the secretaryship."

"Yes there is," said Tony.

Castle stared. "Who? D'you mean *you* would?"

"Gladly," said Tony. "I used to play a bit, but I can't get about well enough now, but once a cricketer——" he laughed. "The posts of secretary and scorer are filled, you see. All you need are a dozen men and some gear."

"We've got some gear," said Castle, suddenly eager. "I keep it upstairs. It's a bit late for this season, and yet I know there are several clubs in the district that would like to get more fixtures.

Everything is beginning again, and Bray isn't the only village making a slow start. Shall I call a meeting, and see how many we get? I'll have a word with old Tom Pickett, too. He's nearly sixty, but he'll be playing cricket until he's a hundred! Littlejohn, out at Mitching Farm, would probably help, too—he plays for Milton, but he finds it difficult having to travel to every game. The pitch isn't bad. Pickett has cut and rolled it every year, and the outfield doesn't matter all that much these days. Abbott, you've put new life into me! When can you come to a meeting?''

"Any time,'' promised Tony.

"Good fellow! Do you know, I think the spell over 'Spindles' has gone at——'' he broke off, dismayed. "What a clumsy oaf I am!'' he added, angrily.

Tony smiled. "Don't worry; Mrs. Kelly told me all about the tree with the gruesome past.''

"Well I'm——'' began Castle, and his voice trailed off. "Well, I should have expected it,'' he said. "It doesn't worry you?''

"Not seriously,'' said Tony. "If ever it did, we could have the oak cut down, but at the moment I'm against that. It would give the place a sinister touch which it hasn't got at the moment. I don't know how the others feel, mind you, I can only speak for my wife and myself.''

"It's the sensible point of view,'' said Castle. "I haven't heard the piano much lately, by the way.''

"The spark of genius isn't working,'' said Tony.

The conversation recalled the incident in his study, and he was glad when he heard Gillian coming downstairs. In the domestic regions someone was banging pots and pans about; it was not the maid, who came down the stairs after Gillian. Maude was a tall, ungainly girl whose footsteps were shuffling, as if her shoes were too large for her, and whose hair was remarkably untidy. The little lace cap on her head looked out of place. She bobbed to Gillian, and smiled sheepishly before hurrying to the kitchen.

Castle looked pleased.

"You've scored a hit with Maude, Mrs. Abbott, she doesn't usually pluck up the courage to smile at anyone until she has known them for months. I've never known a more nervous child.''

"Mrs. Castle has been telling me how good she is,'' said Gillian.

She and Tony walked back to 'Spindles,' and Tony did most of the talking. At the word 'cricket' Gillian pricked up her ears. She had not known Tony when he had played, before the war, but occasional comments had proved how wrapped up he was in the game. If he could interest himself in a local club it would probably help him a great deal. She knew the effect of the sudden moods of rage, and although he had not discussed them freely with her, she had talked to Snub Savory, and got a clear idea of what effect they had on Tony.

Not until they were out of earshot of the vicarage did he go into the rest of his conversation with Castle, and he mentioned the few grains of tobacco in the vicar's pouch, his eagerness to know how much the book might earn.

"I hope I haven't raised his hopes without cause," said Tony. "I'll pack that manuscript up and get it off to Snub to-night." They were walking round the house to inspect his afternoon's work on the garden, and were immediately beneath the attic window. They heard Anne's voice, sharp and angry.

"Don't be a fool!"

"Be quiet!" said Julius, in a voice equally loud. "Why on earth you have to go into a panic over a paragraph in a paper, I don't know!"

Nothing else was audible. Gillian and Tony looked at each other in surprise, and then shrugged their shoulders and went inside. Tony packed the parcel and walked to the post office while Gillian prepared tea. She shared meal-making with Anne, each having a day on duty.

The post office was a little general store which sold everything, including newspapers, and Tony bought the last remaining copy of the *Milshire News*, a local evening paper. It was filled mostly with local news, and he was thinking that there would probably be scope for some articles on the Bray Cricket Club, if it were re-started. The thought of the club had put new heart into him. He walked along the road to 'Spindles,' glancing at the inside headlines, and eventually turned to the stop-press, a habit which he had started during the war. There were some racing results, some county cricket scores and, badly smudged at the foot of the column, the words:

BODY IN THE ORD

The body of a man which had obviously been in the water for some days was found by two boys bathing near the lido at noon to-day. The face was mutilated. The police, it is understood, suspect foul play.

CHAPTER 8

THE BODY

CHIEF INSPECTOR FOSTER had a good reputation in Milshire. It was a small county, and he was second in command to Superintendent Mellor at police headquarters. Mellor had been on sick leave for some weeks and was likely to be away for at least another month. The Chief Constable of the county, Colonel Harrington, had a soft spot for Foster and a deep respect and regard for the sick Superintendent. Police headquarters, in fact, was generally an efficient, well-oiled machine, in which the relationship between senior and junior officials was excellent. Mellor had put down petty jealousy and rivalry with a heavy hand. There was only one black spot; the only other Inspector on the C.I.D. section was a man much older than Foster, and one who resented the younger man's promotion.

Foster refused to allow himself to be seriously affected by Inspector Garth's hostility, however. At most it gave rise to a series of pin-pricks which Foster, happily married and conscious of success in his chosen vocation, hardly felt. In fact Garth gave him grounds for mild amusement, which he hid from everyone but his wife.

Now trouble might flare up in a more serious manner.

There was no doubt that the section of the town which included the public lido was in Garth's domain. It was south of the river, and Foster looked after everything to the north, which included all the villages on the way to Bray. That day, however, Garth had been giving evidence in the County Court, and had gone straight home to lunch. Consequently only Foster had been on duty when the body was reported. The story came from a reporter on the *Milshire News*, a go-ahead young man who was friendly with Foster and had little time for Garth.

Foster hurried down to the lido, getting there soon after twelve o'clock.

The chief attendant of the lido, which was fairly empty at that time of day, especially as it was not school holiday time, had been called by two excited but rather scared boys who had seen something floating in the river. He, in turn, had telephoned the *Milshire News*, knowing that he would receive a useful payment if he gave them the story. When Foster arrived the body was in the attendant's dressing-room, a cold stone-floored room containing a bench used for massage, for the attendant gave massage for a small fee. On this bench lay the body, covered with a large bathing-towel.

Lancing, the reporter, looked round at Foster with a grin.

"I'm glad it's you, Mark! Garth would have raised a stink because Sam telephoned me instead of you."

"Reprehensible of Sam," smiled Foster. "You haven't lost any time, I hope?"

"As soon as Sam rang off, I called you," said Lancing.

"Good! Well, let's have a look at it."

Foster, as Anne Stafford knew, was a crisp-mannered man with a disarming smile. Murder was unusual in Milshire, but not unknown, and bodies were found in the river half-a-dozen times a year. Usually they were suicides, but one glance at this bloated, disfigured face convinced Foster that there was no question of suicide here. In an incautious moment, he gave that as his opinion; the *News* printed 'Foul Play Suspected.' Lancing and Foster, however, were not thinking of the news angle at that moment.

The body was naked. About the neck was a piece of cord, with pieces of sacking adhering to it. Another piece of cord, and more sacking, were tied about the ankles; the feet were inside the sacking. No clothes had been found.

"Looks to me as if someone tied him in a sack an' pushed him in," said Sam, the lido attendant.

"It might be that," said Foster. "Ugh!" The body and the face were enough to nauseate most people. "How long has it been in the water, Sam?"

"About a week," said the attendant.

"No longer, don't you think?"

"Not much," said Sam.

As he spoke the little dressing-room was invaded by more police, including a photographer. When they had finished their work the body was removed to the mortuary at the police station, and Sam left his room with Lancing and Foster. Half a dozen people were having a pre-lunch bathe, and Sam sniffed.

"They'll be around like flies when this gets known," he said. "Some people beat me!"

He went off, leaving Foster and Lancing smiling after him. The other policemen had gone back by car, but Foster chose to walk. There were bowling greens and a recreation ground near the lido, between the river and the town itself. Milton was a small market town with about twenty-five thousand inhabitants, and although it was the county town of Milshire there were three larger towns within the county borders—all of them seaside resorts, thirty or forty miles to the south.

"You aren't very talkative," said Lancing.

"No policeman is to the Press," said Foster, with a grin. "Don't overdo this, Lancing."

"I'll be good," said the reporter. He was a short, sturdy man with curly hair, a snub nose and a pair of merry blue eyes. "When can you tell me some more about it?"

"I'll see what I can do in the morning."

Lancing grimaced. "Nothing for a special edition?"

"I doubt it. For one thing," went on Foster, "I can see parochial trouble brewing over this. If the body had been brought on this side of the river it would have been all right. You may have to deal with Garth."

"Not if I know you," said Lancing. "This is your murder!"

"Don't be too sure about murder," said Foster.

"I couldn't be too sure," said Lancing. "A man doesn't tie himself up in a sack and throw himself in the river, you know that as well as I do. Is there anyone missing?"

"Not locally," said Foster. "I'll have a look at the records when I get inside."

There were several reports of missing men, information about whom was required by Scotland Yard or by the authorities of other counties. Foster, who had used a tape-measure in the dressing-room, shook his head when he saw the details. The body which they had found was that of a man below medium height, five-feet-five, and broad in proportion. It was impossible to give a description of his face, and there was little else to go by. The police-surgeon, Dr. Anderson, would be with him when he made a closer examination, and until then he would not waste time in speculating. He did send reports to Scotland Yard and neighbouring counties, giving the height of the body, and then he telephoned Colonel Harrington. The Colonel, said a maid, was in Milton, and would probably be found at the White Horse, which was the one good hotel. Foster telephoned his wife to warn her that he might be late for lunch, and went round to the hotel.

Harrington was in the dining-room with two men whom Foster did not know. He caught sight of Foster and beckoned him. Foster went over and did not wait for introductions before he said:

"There's a nasty business turned up, sir, and I'd like your advice as soon as possible."

"What kind of nasty business?" asked Harrington.

"Murder, I think," said Foster, "and not a lunch-time murder, either."

"Nonsense!" said Harrington. "Sit down and tell me all about it. Have you had lunch?"

"No, sir."

"Then join us," said Harrington. "My friends won't be put off by the grisly details." He introduced them, briefly, but beyond conforming to ordinary courtesy, Foster paid them little attention. He talked at some length, and the Chief Constable listened attentively.

Harrington was a tall, leathery man, with sharp features and a whippet-like face, and the brightest grey eyes in Milshire. There was nothing handsome about it, but he was striking, and renowned for his caustic tongue. Those who knew him well ignored it. He believed in letting his men get on with their work and interfered as little as possible, prepared to trust them to report anything that he should know immediately. In spite of his sharp tongue and his reputation as a martinet, he contributed a great deal to the unity which reigned at headquarters.

"Well, you haven't got much to go on," he said.

"That's my own opinion," said Foster, with a grimace. "Identification won't be easy. The body might have been put into the river anywhere between the lido and Grasling. It isn't likely to have been put in north of Grasling Lock, nor very near the lido, or it would have been seen before."

"It could have been put in the Mille," said Harrington.

"Yes, possibly." Foster cut his meat, and went on slowly: "It looks as if it had been tied up in a sack, and the sack weighted to make it sink. The ends near the cord are badly worn. I think the body wanted to float and the bricks or whatever was in the sack wanted to stay on the river bed, and both of them won."

Harrington glanced at his friends.

"A police inspector with a pretty wit," he said, and the others laughed. "Yes, Foster, go on."

"The sack was probably badly worn in places," said Foster. "The lido attendant thinks the body has been in the water for a week. Allow him a margin of three days, that means between a week and ten days. The attendant isn't unused to these things

57

at the man's back. Badly though the immersion had treated it, there was no doubt that the back had once been lacerated dreadfully. There were even ridges where the flesh had healed.

"That's a nasty piece of work," said Anderson.

"A flogging," said Foster.

"Something worse than a flogging," said Anderson. "Something more brutal than a cat-o'-nine-tails was used, too. A *very* nasty business," he repeated.

"How long ago was that done?" asked Foster.

"There's no way of telling. Within the past few years, probably."

"Have you ever seen anything like it before?" asked Foster. He stared at the dead man's back; it was easy to imagine the dreadful state of it after the thrashing.

"Not actually on a body," said Anderson. "I saw some photographs which came out of Germany and were taken after men had been flogged, as they called it, in concentration camps. It is the same kind of thing. Those marks were made by a beating-up of calculated savagery, don't make any mistake about that, Foster. It just isn't conceivable that he received such treatment in this country."

"Oh," said Foster, heavily.

"Why that grunt?"

"If he's a foreigner it's going to make it ten times more difficult," said Foster. "There's been a constant traffic to and from the continent and we no longer keep a close watch on aliens, provided their passports are all right. You haven't given me a lot of encouragement yet," he added, with a grimace.

"If I were you I'd pass this baby," said Anderson.

"What do you mean?"

"Ask Harrington to consult the Yard," said Anderson.

Foster smiled. "He is doing. That doesn't mean that I wouldn't like to have identified the body by the time they arrive, or find out where he was put into the river. There might be something on the rest of the sack," he added, hopefully. "I've got a river patrol looking for it. If it comes to a point, I shall ask for some dredging to be done. I wonder where his clothes are? We won't get much help at all until we know who he is and when he died," he continued, with a touch of irritation. "It would turn out like this, wouldn't it?"

"Turn it over to Garth," said Anderson, laughing.

"That's another headache brewing," said Foster. "How long will you be here?"

"Several hours, as presumably you want to make sure that he died from the wounds and not from drowning," said Anderson, "and I may as well do a thorough job of the post mortem while I'm at it. You go away and play. I don't need you. You might tell them to open a window," he added, and made a wry face.

He had finished soon after five o'clock, and went to Foster's office to report. Death had been caused by the knife wounds; the primary cause was the severed carotid artery, and death had been almost instantaneous. There must have been a great deal of blood on his clothes and in the room where he had been killed—or, he agreed, when Foster interrupted sharply, wherever he had been killed, in or out of doors. He could give Foster no further definite information.

The Chief Inspector sat at his desk and studied the reports he had already received. They could hardly be less encouraging.

Then Garth came in.

The older Inspector was a handsome man, much larger than Foster, with a face marred by a perpetual frown and eyebrows which he allowed to grow bushy, giving him a forbidding appearance. He was dark, with an olive complexion and very fine brown eyes. He went to his desk in the office which he shared with Foster, and after looking through some papers, he said:

"I see you're not above poaching, Foster."

"Don't be an ass," said Foster, testily. "I was on the spot and you weren't. I reminded Harrington that——"

"Knowing quite well that he would prefer you to handle the matter," said Garth. "It is a great asset to have better table manners and a public school education, as I well know."

Foster snapped: "There's no reason why you shouldn't improve your manners!"

Garth's mouth closed like a trap. They worked in an uneasy silence for half an hour, and Garth was the first to leave the office. He walked like a policeman on beat duty. Foster sat back, with the end of his pencil between his teeth, and then his eyes brightened. Although relations between him and Garth were often strained, his wife and Mrs. Garth were on good terms. It would probably help things if Mrs. Garth were warned what to expect. Garth lived several miles out of Milton, and there was time to set the wheels of peace-making going. He called his home, and was relieved when his youngest daughter, aged four, answered him. She was always with her mother.

"Listen, Laura," he said when he had finished talking to the child, "Garth has got a sore head over this business, like the ass he is. Have a word with Mrs. Garth, will you, and warn her to be prepared for a sermon on the evil deeds of his fellow inspector?"

Laura laughed. "All right, Mark . . No, don't *shout*, Wanda—sorry, Mark, she wants to say good-bye." Wanda said good-bye. "What time will you be home?" Laura asked.

"Unless something turns up, about seven," said Foster. "If I'm not there by half-past, you carry on and assume that I won't be in until after dark. 'Bye—good-bye, Wanda!"

He was smiling when he replaced the receiver, but the smile soon faded.

There was a curiously depressing influence exerted by the discovery of the dead man. That lacerated back, the possibility that Anderson was right and that the man had been tortured in a German prison camp, added to it.

The telephone rang as he was about to leave the office, and he was surprised to hear Anderson.

"I didn't tell you before," said Anderson, "I know you of old, Foster, and I wanted to be quite sure of my ground. I took Lumley round to see the *corpus*."

"Lumley—oh, the dentist. Yes?"

"He agreed with the impression I got of the state of the jaws," said Anderson. "His teeth were removed by an amateur. Proper dental instruments weren't used."

"Oh," said Foster, heavily. "You're backing your theory hard, aren't you?"

"Well, people in concentration camps did get beaten up and did get their teeth pulled with pliers and pincers," said Anderson. "You would be quite safe in putting it up as a possibility. You needn't give me any credit, let the Yard think you worked the miracle all by yourself. Good-bye!"

Foster replaced the receiver. Facts were facts, and reluctance to accept them was a fault in a policeman. The man had been tortured; there was no reason to assume that it had happened in Germany, but it had happened somewhere not so many years before.

"Years," said Foster, aloud. "It can't have anything to do with his murder."

The telephone bell rang as he was going out of the office. It was then a little after seven. He was looking forward to talking to Laura, whose calm common sense was invaluable, and he hoped this caller would not detain him for long.

"P.C. Grimes, of Riversmeet, would like to speak to you, sir," said the operator.

"Put him through," said Foster.

Riversmeet was a little hamlet where the Mille ran into the Ord, about four miles out of Milton. Grimes was a reliable man, and there was little doubt that this was the first story to come in response to his telephoned instruction to all village policemen; the flood of volunteered information from the general public would not start until the next morning.

"Hallo, Grimes," he said, "what have you got for me?"

"Some sacking floating on the river surface, sir," said Grimes, promptly. "It's anchored to summat, sir, I don't know what. I thought you would like to come along and see it yourself."

"I would!" said Foster. "Well done, Grimes."

"Thank you, sir. Will you bring some waders with you, or will I get some for you, sir?"

"Waders?" repeated Foster. "Oh, I see. Borrow a pair for me if you can, Grimes." He replaced the receiver and then lifted it again and was put through to the sergeant's office. He would have to take a man out with him, and he arranged for Sergeant Sharp to go home, get a bathing costume, and then join him outside the police station. Sharp was a worthy man, probably the only sergeant in Milton who would bring a bathing costume along without asking questions.

'We might get something fairly quickly after all,' mused Foster as he went to the garage at the back of the police station for his car.

CHAPTER 9

THE RIVERSIDE BUNGALOW

RIVERSMEET was a charming spot, one of the loveliest in Milshire. Where the shallow stream of the Mille flowed into the Ord, itself only three to four feet deep, there were meadows on either side. Near the confluence was a little hamlet with old, thatched cottages resplendent in new cream colour-wash, and only one modern building within sight, a white creeper-clad bungalow, with a red-tiled roof and a well-tended garden. The bungalow was a café, but the sign hanging above the rustic woodwork of the gate was painted attractively, and fitted into the general scheme. Beyond the rivers, on either side, was rising land, some fields already high with green corn, others newly-ploughed. In the distance tractors were working, and from a field near the little hump-backed bridge which spanned the Ord came the refreshing scent of new-mown hay. It filled the air with its perfume, heady and penetrating.

A little crowd was gathered on the bank of the Ord, a hundred yards or so from the point where the two rivers met. There were eleven children of all ages, six dogs, an old man bent with rheumatism leading a goat on a frail-looking piece of string to the annoyance of a fat, dumpy woman who kept edging away from the frisky creatures. She was Mrs. Kelly. Two or three middle-aged couples also watched with interest as Sergeant Sharp emerged from the riverside bungalow with a mackintosh over his swimming costume, and his thin, bare legs covering the ground at a good speed.

Foster and P.C. Grimes, a burly man of few words, stared at a piece of sacking floating on the water. It looked like part of a torn sack. Grimes said that it had been there for two days, several people had noticed it. A boy bathing in the river had tried to move it, but it was tied to something on the river bed. Grimes himself had remembered it when the request had come through, had cycled over to make sure it was still there, and telephoned Foster from the bungalow, the owner of which was watching from his garden.

Foster drew on a pair of waders which the efficient Grimes had borrowed, and was ready when Sharp came up. Grimes also wore waders. Sharp took off his coat and plunged into the river, which was flowing fairly fast because of the recent spell of rain. The sacking was about ten feet from the river's edge. Foster waded until he was knee deep, half-way between the bank and the sack. Sharp reached the sacking, and stood upright; he was up to his waist in water. He took the sacking carefully in one hand and tugged gently, and after a pause, he called:

"It's fast all right, sir."

"Can you see what's holding it?" asked Foster.

"I'll try, sir," said Sharp.

A ragged cheer followed as he jumped up and then dived. His feet waved in the air for a few seconds, and then disappeared. He seemed to be under for a long time, and Foster was getting agitated when the water swirled and Sharp reappeared, gasping, and holding something aloft; it was a brick. A louder cheer greeted him.

"Coming, sir!" he called, elatedly, and tossing the brick past Foster to the bank. "Shall I get them all, sir?"

"Yes, but take a breather. How many are there?"

"About a dozen, I'd say—it looks as if they're in the bottom of a sack, sir."

"The sack is as important as the bricks," said Foster. "Look here, Sharp, you'd better have some help. I—what was that?"

A splash not far away was followed by a second and a third, and suddenly he saw the lithe figures of youths, little more than boys, swimming rapidly from the opposite bank; they wore only loin-cloths. Sharp coloured, but the little crowd cheered heartily, and Foster hid a smile and left the situation to the sergeant. The boys trod water about him, and he took this unexpected interruption good-humouredly.

"All right, try your luck," he said, "but don't go and drown yourselves, and leave the last brick to me—understand? If you let that bit of sacking float away you'll all come up before the magistrates."

As he finished one of the lads heaved himself out of the water and flopped down again, sending a great sheet over the sergeant, who almost lost his footing. The crowd roared, but Foster kept a straight face. One after the other the boys went down and brought up the bricks, tossing them to the bank as if they were playing water-polo. Sergeant Sharp grew agitated as they worked with a speed which left him standing. Suddenly something floated to the surface—another piece of sacking. Sharp roared and went after it, but he was passed by all three lads, who took it with a hand apiece and swam with it towards Foster, holding it up in front of him.

"Thanks very much," said Foster. "Take it to the bank for me, will you?" He waited for Sharp to come out. "They did save you a lot of trouble, Sergeant. It's been good work all round."

Mollified, Sharp hurried ashore, put his mackintosh round his shoulders and went to the bungalow. Grimes and Foster examined the bricks which, as far as Foster could see, were ordinary yellow bricks, perhaps rather better in quality than most. Grimes took the pieces of sacking and, spreading them on the grass, proved that they were part of the same sack; the bottom was missing, and obviously that was what they had found about the dead man's feet, and the top was torn off completely, where it had been pulled away by the cord about the corpse's neck. Foster had brought a piece of the sacking from the morgue, and a comparison proved beyond all doubt that it was the same material; it even fitted to the torn parts taken from the river.

"Satisfied, sir?" asked Grimes.

"I'm very satisfied indeed," said Foster, "although I wish we'd found the clothes. There isn't any doubt that the body was dropped in here. Have you made any inquiries?"

"I thought I would leave that to you, sir," said Grimes.

"Good. The bungalow is the nearest place, isn't it?"

"Yes," said Grimes. "I've asked them to put a room at your disposal, sir, and there'll be some supper, if you'd like it."

"You're very good," smiled Foster.

Symes, the owner of the bungalow café at Riversmeet, was a one-legged, powerful man. He ran the café with the help of a manageress and two girls. Foster knew that it had a good reputation for food and service. By the time he got there the woman was bustling about the kitchen, through which he passed after taking off his waders. A small sitting-room had obviously been made tidy for him, and a gateleg table with ink, paper and blotting-paper was in the middle of the room. Foster looked at it all appreciatively, and Symes asked him whether he would have supper.

"Yes, please," said Foster.

"Then it won't be ten minutes, Inspector."

"Thanks. Well, you've a fair idea of what I'm after, I suppose?"

Symes smiled. He was a big, slow-speaking man, running to fat, and he used a crutch. There were noticeable scars on his cheeks and forehead.

"I'd rather you told me," he said.

"You've heard about the body we found further up the river," said Foster, and when Symes nodded, went on: "It was in a sack, and the sack was almost certainly dumped in the Ord about the spot where we found the bricks." One of the bricks and a small piece of sacking were on the table. "I think it was put there within the last ten days. It would almost certainly have been by night. You live nearest to the spot; have you any recollection of hearing a boat within the last ten days?"

"It isn't a thing I could be certain about," said Symes. "There wasn't a moon ten days ago, and there was a lot of rain. That always makes unusual sounds here—it beats on the river and when there's a bit of wind with it you can't tell one noise from another."

"That's true," said Foster. "I don't want you to invent anything, but if you can recollect the slightest thing out of the ordinary and tell me on what night it happened, I would be grateful." He thought Symes had something to report but was making sure that he was not called upon to swear it on oath.

"Well," said Symes, "there was a little thing, exactly ten days ago, Inspector. It was the night that you'd been in to see P.C. Grimes, I remember him telling me."

"Oh," said Foster. "What was it?"

"I'd had some friends in from Milton," said Symes, "and they stayed till supper and an hour afterwards—it would be about nine o'clock, I suppose. It might have been earlier, I don't remember exactly. It was well after dark, I do know that."

"Yes," said Foster.

"When I opened the door to let my friends out," said Symes, "I *thought* I heard a boat on the river, and I *thought* I heard whispered voices. I couldn't be sure. Voices and sounds travel clearly over the water especially if the wind is blowing across the Mille, and I think it was doing that night."

"What makes you think so?" asked Foster.

"I'd a garden fire burning earlier in the evening," said Symes. "It wouldn't burn very well because the stuff was so wet, but it had been hanging about for several days and I had a go at it. Then I had to put it out, because the smoke came back into the house something awful. I started it about six and it was out by seven, so unless the wind changed it was blowing straight from the Mille where it joins the Ord. Perhaps you can check up with the meteorological people, sir?"

"I can, with your information to give them a good start," said Foster.

Before he went on, the woman bustled in with a tray and an appetizing meal; there were sausages, bacon, fried tomatoes, a fried egg, and a heap of crisp, golden-brown chipped potatoes in another dish.

"Why, this is magnificent!" exclaimed Foster.

"We do our best," said Symes, with a gratified smile. "Shall I come back when you've finished?"

"No, I'll eat and listen at the same time," said Foster.

Grimes was standing by the door, and it opened suddenly to admit Sharp. He was dressed and his damp, fair hair was brushed tightly down on his head; it made him look rather like a schoolboy washed and brushed up for a special occasion. Sharp had many qualifications, including shorthand-typewriting. He was an unimaginative officer, however, and Foster would have much preferred his regular aide, but he had to bring Sharp right into the investigation now. He saw with approval that the sergeant had a notebook and pencil ready.

"Grimes," he said, "give Sergeant Sharp a *résumé* of what Mr. Symes has told me, will you?"

He made inroads on the meal while Grimes was doing so, and was dallying with chipped potatoes in the creamy tomatoes when Grimes finished. He had been thinking deeply during the interval, and recalling everything that had happened on his tour of the village policemen. The one thing which stood out in his mind was his interview with the Staffords at 'Spindles.' At the time he had noticed that there was an atmosphere of strain in the house. He had put it down to annoyance on the part of Anne Stafford at receiving a caller when the house was in such a mess. At the time he had not blamed her, and had formed the impression that she was an intelligent, good-looking and rather serious-minded woman. While waiting for her brother, he had amused himself trying to draw her out. He had seen the many changes which had come over her expression, and now that he thought back he wondered if there had been any unusual significance in her manner. There was a risk of imagining too much, of course; at the time he had not been particularly impressed, although it had certainly left its mark.

"Well, now," said Foster. "You think you heard voices and a boat. Did you mention it to anyone?"

"Yes, to my friends," said Symes. "We all looked towards the river, but we couldn't see anything—that is, I couldn't be sure we did. We thought we saw a dark shadow on the water, but it might have been imagination. There wasn't much sound, that's a fact. The voices could have come from someone on the opposite bank, too, and I think that sack was dropped overboard from a boat."

"So do I," said Foster. "Did your manageress think she heard it?"

"She was with me at the time," said Symes. "We stood waiting for five minutes after our friends had gone, but we didn't see anything for certain. There *might* have been someone there."

"I see," said Foster.

"It's rather a lonely spot here," said Symes, slowly, "and there were some burglaries a few months back. Grimes always thought the thieves came from the river, sir. Do you remember them?"

"Yes. We never caught the beggars," said Foster.

"They stopped working when you got busy," said Symes, with a faint smile. "Well, I thought they might have started again and I kept looking out of the window and opening the door, to make sure that they didn't come into the garden. I suppose it was about half-an-hour later, but it might have been a bit less, when I *thought* I heard a boat pulling upstream."

"Up the Mille?"

"Yes," said Symes. "I stood at the door watching. It was pretty dark, but clearer than it had been earlier. I think it's certain that there was a boat then, but it needn't have been the same one, sir."

"No. Do you often notice boats at night?"

"Not very often. You get them on moonlight nights, of course, and sometimes couples take a boat out after dark, if they know the river. None of the boat-house men will let a boat go after dark unless the people *do* know the river," said Symes. "You'll be able to check up on that, sir, won't you?"

"Yes," said Foster, smiling. "You're very careful!"

"A man's life might depend on what I say, sir," Symes reminded him.

"You're very wise," said Foster. "I wish everyone told a story as well as you do, Symes. Well, now—did you discuss this with anyone apart from your friends?"

"No," said Symes. "I didn't forget it, but no one else mentioned it and so I didn't see that there was any point in starting a rumour that the thieves were busy again."

"Good!" Foster looked at Grimes. "That's a job for you, Grimes. I think you'd better start now, and ask everyone in

67

Riversmeet if they heard anything that night. If two or three people genuinely think they did, that is as good as one man saying he's certain he did. There aren't any buildings on the other side of the river, are there?"

"There's old Martin's cottage," said Grimes.

"A cottage—oh, yes, in the hollow, you can't see it from the river. He isn't likely to have noticed anything; he couldn't see, and he's pretty deaf, isn't he?"

"Yes," said Grimes, "but he's often at the river bank o' nights. He stays there at the end of his garden and smokes his pipe. I think we ought to have a word with him, sir."

"All right."

"If you don't mind me saying so, sir," went on Grimes, stolidly, "it wouldn't be a bad idea if you and the sergeant saw old Martin. He hasn't been very friendly t'wards me lately—not since I had him up for poaching last Autumn. You'd probably get more out of him than I would. I shouldn't take much notice of his deafness, he's not so deaf as all that."

Foster laughed. "All right, I'll tackle him. Let me see——" he looked in his diary. "It was Wednesday week, May the 12th. You get started, Grimes. Oh, Mr. Symes, may I use your telephone?"

"Gladly, sir. It's in the corner."

"Thanks," said Foster. He stood up as the manageress bustled in with coffee. "You know, you're spoiling me," he said. "Sharp, Sergeant Willet is still outside, isn't he?"

"Yes, sir," said Sharp.

"Tell him to take those bricks which are still by the river, and call on all the builders in Milton—there's enough for one apiece— and ask if they can identify the bricks. I want to know where they were made, and in what houses they've been used in this district for the last few years. Don't tell them what part of the district or they might start imagining that a few odd ones were used in all the houses this side of Milton!"

Sharp smiled dutifully, and went out. Foster frowned, wondering if the sergeant had had his supper. He forgot that as he telephoned the station and asked them to check on the direction of the wind on the evening of May 12th, between seven and ten o'clock. When Sharp came back, he asked him about supper; Symes, it appeared, had prepared a meal for the sergeants and they had already finished. Grimes had eaten before he had telephoned headquarters.

"Well, Sharp," said Foster, as they walked over the bridge to the opposite bank, and then climbed a sharp rise, "what do you think of things now?"

"They aren't going so badly, sir, are they?"

"I don't think so. Do you know this man Martin?"

"I've come across him," said Sharp. "A surly old customer, if I know anything about a man. He's got his knife into Grimes."

"Grimes is a bit of a tartar, is he?" asked Foster.

"I wouldn't say that," said Sharp, without a smile. His earnestness would soon get on Foster's nerves. "No, I wouldn't say that, sir. He's let Martin have the benefit of the doubt for a long time. Martin's a poacher, all right, and it was time he was stopped. No one round here mind's a fellow getting a rabbit or a pigeon for his own table, but Martin was doing a trade in rabbits and skins. He said he caught them all on his own bit of land, but it's a remarkable thing if he got so many on half-an-acre."

"I see," said Foster.

The door of the little cottage in the hollow was open. Smoke was curling up from one chimney, and the firelight was flickering inside a front room. It was getting dark, and the sky in the west was a glorious golden red with the setting sun catching little fluffy lines of clouds. The light spread over the whole countryside, softening the hedges and the trees; it even made the dilapidated cottage with its huddle of outbuildings look picturesque. Old Martin kept his garden well; there were vegetables, sturdy and healthy-looking, at the front and sides. A little bed of wallflowers and forget-me-nots made a splash of colour beneath one window.

There was no movement as they reached the door, and Foster called out:

"Is anyone at home?"

"He's seen us, all right," said Sharp.

There was no response, and Foster called more sharply. At last an old man came from the kitchen at the back of the cottage. He was short and bent, but his weather-beaten face and clear blue eyes had a look of health, and there was a hint of strength in his wiry body; he gave Foster the impression that he pretended to be more frail than he was.

"What do 'ee want?" he asked in a querulous voice.

"I am Chief Inspector Foster," began Foster.

"I know 'ee," said Martin. "What do 'ee want?"

The hostility in his voice and expression made Foster thoughtful. It might be due to his quarrel with Grimes, but long experience of questioning witnesses had taught Foster that many had little guilty secrets which worried them and made them hostile when they were questioned about an entirely different matter. Then he saw Martin dart a glance towards the window of the little room, and look away quickly.

He stepped inside the small, low-ceilinged room. It was crowded with oddments of furniture. On a small table was a cloth of red chenille and an aspidistra in a flower-pot covered with crêpe paper, once red but faded to a dirty pink.

"'Ee've no right to come in wi'out bein' asked," said Martin angrily.

"Now, come, Mr. Martin," said Foster, with a broad smile. "We haven't come to make trouble for you, we only want a little information." He saw Martin glance towards the window again, but affected not to notice it. He stepped across the room and sat in an old saddle-back chair, facing the window, so that he could see where Martin was looking, hoping to find the cause of the man's anxiety. Nothing struck him as remarkable. "I'm told you have a very good memory," he went on.

"It's none so bad," agreed Martin, grudgingly.

"Do you remember the evening of May 12th?" asked Foster.

"Oh, *dates*," said Martin, scornfully. "I don't hold wi' *dates*. What night o' the moon were it?"

From the glint in the old man's eyes, Foster thought that he considered he had scored a triumph. When he had looked at the diary, however, he had seen the period of the moon; it had been three days past the last quarter and had risen about half-past four in the morning.

"It was nearly down," he said. "The last quarter was May 9th."

"Oh, aye," said Martin, nonplussed. "Well, what about un, mister?"

"Do you remember what you did that night?"

"If that theer Grimes——" began Martin, heatedly.

"Now don't be foolish," said Foster. "If you've been doing something you shouldn't, Grimes will deal with it. I want to know whether you were in the cottage or at the river that night about nine o'clock?"

"Maybe I was, maybe I wasn't," said Martin.

Foster smothered a sigh of annoyance.

"It was a Wednesday," he said. "A fine night, with the wind blowing across the river towards the café bungalow."

"Oh, *that* night!" said Martin, with sudden eagerness. "The night Symes lit a fire an' it blew back into his place." Martin actually grinned. "Fool of a man!" he declared. "What be a townsman doin' in the country, mister? *That* night! It were the night when theer was someone on the river. Late it were. I was watching, standing by my gate, the one ye came past, mister. I recalls it clear. Two people there was in the boat, and it come downstream."

"The Mille?"

"The Mille or the Ord, I couldn't be certain," said Martin, who now appeared convinced that his own petty offences were not the subject of the inquiry, and had livened up considerably. "Two theer were, I see them."

"Men?" asked Foster, quickly.

"I couldn't see as well as that," said Martin. "It hung about for haff an hour, mebbe more, that's what I remember, an' then off they went again."

"Do you know what time it was?" asked Foster.

"It'd be 'tween half-past eight an' nine o'clock," said Martin. "That's true, mister—'fore the nine o'clock news it were. I always listen t' the nine o'clock news winter or summer, peacetime or war-time, mister."

"You've been a great help," said Foster, warmly. "Have you ever seen anyone on the river before at that time of night?"

"'Ee be thinkin' o' them thievin' varmints," said Martin, with a cackle. "Earlier, they always was. If Grimes had done what I told him, an' watched about seven o'clock, mebbe ye wouldn't have lost them thieves, mister. I told him often enough, he wouldn't listen to me. He's nowt but——"

"We'll talk about that another time, shall we?" asked Foster, standing up.

He walked across the room.

Until that moment Martin had been quite happy, his fears all gone. Sharp had stood by the door without speaking, writing occasionally, a fact which had not worried the old man. Now, however, Martin stiffened. He even put out a hand as if to stop Foster, and then he stood watching with his eyes rounded.

In front of the window was a sofa, and behind the sofa was a fibre suit-case.

CHAPTER 10

INSPECTOR FOSTER PAYS A VISIT

FOSTER was silent as he drove back to Milton with Sharp, dropped the sergeant at the station, and then drove to the Chief Constable's house on the outskirts of the town. It was on a hill, one of many houses built among trees, and friendly yellow lights glowed in a dozen places. Glancing over his shoulder, Foster saw the lights of the town, and rejoiced at the absence of black-out. When he pulled up outside Harrington's front door he stopped the engine and sat for a moment looking over the town. The neon lighting of the new cinema cast a red glow over the centre of Milton, and just at the edge of the glow, to the north, was a little row of street lamps. Almost immediately in front of one of the lamps was his house, and he could just see the faint light from behind the curtains. Laura would be listening to a symphony concert, while knitting or sewing for the children. Wanda and Iris would be asleep in the nursery, each in a little cot; Iris was three years older than the four-year-old Wanda. Kathleen, aged ten, was probably reading in the little room she had to herself; she was allowed to read until nine o'clock, when Laura would go up and say good-night and turn out the light.

Foster gave an involuntary sigh; three better children it would be hard to find, but there were times when he felt almost sad because there were three girls and no boy. Laura was thirty-eight, and she had not had an easy time with Wanda; was it fair to hope?

"This won't do!" he exclaimed aloud, and hurried to the Chief Constable's door.

He had telephoned for the appointment from the bungalow, and was expected. A maid showed him to Harrington's study, a pleasant and homely room, with a store of books which he greatly envied.

71

There was a single table-lamp, by the light of which Harrington had been reading; a book was open on the book-rest by his side. A wood fire gave the room a cheerful look; it was chilly for late May, and Harrington, who had spent most of his life in India, could not get used to cold out of season. He wore a smoking jacket over dinner clothes, and his feet were in pumps. The firelight shone on cut-glass decanters, glasses and a syphon of soda on a table by his side.

"Hallo, Foster, what will you have?" The Chief Constable's hands hovered hospitably over the decanters. "Whisky, brandy, or——"

"A tot of whisky will suit me nicely, sir, thanks." Foster sat down in a chair already pulled up for him, and accepted the glass. "Thank you," he said again.

"To the triumph of Chief Inspector Foster," said Harrington, raising his glass. "You've got some good news for me, I gather?"

"I know where the body was dropped into the Ord," said Foster, "and there are one or two things of interest, sir—I'm not dissatisfied with the night's work." He sat back and, feeling pleasantly tired and mellowed by the warming drink, he told his story. Harrington nodded from time to time, and interrupted with pertinent questions. Foster finished with the river work and the talk with Symes, and went on:

"I took Grimes's advice—incidentally, sir, I think Grimes should be in the running for promotion, he is a keen man and he's very thorough—and saw Martin myself. He confirms the story of people on the river that night, but he says that he didn't hear anything drop into the water. I doubt whether he's telling the truth, because I think he picked something up from the river bank and failed to report it."

"Not the body!" exclaimed Harrington.

Foster laughed.

"No, sir. A suit-case." His eyes were bright and it was obvious that he still had something up his sleeve. "I found it behind a sofa in Martin's parlour. First, he denied having taken it out of the river at all, and then he said that he took it out months ago, but I don't believe him. The case had floated to the river bank from the boat, I think: there were water-marks on it outside, but it looked all right inside. It's an ordinary fibre suit-case—not the cheapest kind, worth about thirty shillings pre-war. A label had obviously been torn off it, and Martin denies having seen it, but I fancy he tore it off and burned it. However, there was something else." He put his hand to his waistcoat pocket. "In the first place the case hadn't been dusted out; it had been shaken, I think, but there was brick dust, and a small chipping of brick lodged in a torn part of the lining. The chipping is of yellow brick, rather good quality, I fancy, and probably the same kind as the bricks which were used to weight the body."

"Hum," said Harrington. "You're building it up well, Foster. You think the body was taken in the boat, and the bricks from the case were transferred to the sack before it was thrown overboard."

"That's right, sir. And then the case went over the side. Old Martin picked it up, thought that he might make a bit on it—he could sell it on the market in Milton for ten shillings, any time—and held on to make sure that no one claimed it or looked for it. It isn't the kind of case one could trace easily," he added, "but——"

Harrington laughed: "You look positively smug, man!"

"I suppose I feel it," said Foster. He held a little metal strip towards his Chief. "That was fastened to the top of the inside of the case. It's one of the metal strips which before the war you could punch out on machines at railway stations; some of them are going back into service again now, I think. It's a bit rusty, but the name is clear enough."

"Abbott," said Harrington, reading. "A. J. Abbott, but there's no address."

"That isn't going to give us much trouble, sir, at least, I don't think it is. A man named Anthony John Abbott is living at 'Spindles'—old Blackshaw's place."

"Abbott?" repeated Harrington, in surprise. "Didn't you tell me that some people named Stafford were there? You told me an amusing story of how you'd caught them before they had even dusted the rooms."

"Yes," said Foster, "but the Staffords are brother and sister, living there with Abbott and his wife, née Gillian Stafford. I learned that from Dr. Anderson a few days ago; Castle had told him—Castle lives next door, of course. By all accounts the Staffords are a queer couple in some ways, the brother particularly. He's the composer, as I told you. Abbott is an author with a moderate reputation. I took one of his books out of Boots two days ago. Sound, careful stuff, not brilliant, in my opinion. It's asking rather a lot to think that we might have found a case belonging to another A. J. Abbott, isn't it? Symes—that's the owner of the bungalow café—is sure that the boat went up the Mille, and 'Spindles' is about three miles from Riversmeet. It all looks as if it's working in nicely."

"Very nicely," said Harrington. "I half wish I hadn't taken your advice to ask the Yard for help."

"As the Staffords and the Abbotts had moved from London that day, I think it's a good thing that we did, sir, even if the Yard handles only the London side of it. It's a curious thing that I called there that night. Looking back—and making allowances for wishful thinking—it's safe to say that the Staffords were very much on edge. That wouldn't be surprising if they knew that the Abbotts, who showed up later that night, were getting rid of the body, would it?"

"No," said Harrington.

"I was thinking of seeing Castle to-night," said Foster, "but I didn't have to trouble—I'll have to see him later, of course—as I had a slice of luck. A woman now working for the Abbotts and the Staffords was at Riversmeet to-night. She prefers the pub there to the one in Bray, and cycles down most evenings, I'm told. You should see her on a bicycle! She must weigh eighteen stone, and

73

she's short! However, sir, she was at the river, and before we'd finished I think all Riversmeet and half of Bray and other villages were there. I had a word with her—casually, of course."

Harrington smiled. "Yes, of course!"

"I found out that the Abbotts arrived some time after the Staffords," said Foster. "Apparently Agnes Blackshaw—you remember her?"

"She was rather affected by her husband's suicide, wasn't she?"

"Yes, and she's still very sour. At all events she makes a confidant of the Castles' maid. She was watching 'Spindles' that night, and saw the Abbotts arrive after dark, probably about half-past nine or ten o'clock. That would be just right, if they had come off the river. The Staffords had been there for several hours—since mid-day, in fact."

"I see," said Harrington. "As far as I can make out, Foster, you're working up a rather peculiar situation. The Staffords were touchy and on edge, but the Abbotts did the job."

"They might all four have been parties to it," said Foster. "Mind you, I'm taking nothing for granted yet, but at least we've plenty to go on. Very much more than I thought likely a few hours ago," he added.

"What do you propose to do?" asked Harrington. "See the people at 'Spindles'?"

Foster smiled enigmatically.

"I nearly went there straight away, and then I thought it might be a good idea if I waited for a day, at least. Mrs. Kelly, the daily woman, will be there to-morrow morning. I think she's certain to talk about what happened at Riversmeet and she'll probably tell them that I asked questions about what time the Abbotts got there. They might get scared, and leave in a hurry. If they do——" he broke off, and grinned.

"So you've got men watching there, have you?"

"Not yet, sir—except that I've told Grimes to keep his eyes open, and I think he will probably plant himself outside 'Spindles' all night. He sees this as his big chance. I don't expect any move until after Mrs. Kelly has gossiped, so I thought we would leave it to Grimes to-night, and send other men out there in the morning."

"Is it wise to assume that Grimes will keep an eye open off his own bat?" asked Harrington.

"I think so, sir, or I wouldn't have taken the chance. It certainly gives him an opportunity."

"Hum, yes. All right, Foster. You'll go out there to-morrow, I suppose?"

"I thought I might go in the afternoon, see Castle—and park my car near 'Spindles,' so that it will be seen—and then see what the position is next door. That's if they haven't flown," went on Foster, smiling again. "It would be almost too easy if they did run away, I'm afraid. I don't really expect that."

"It's worth trying," said Harrington. "Yes, do that. I—but

haven't you forgotten something? To-morrow is Sunday, not a good day for seeing Castle.''

''To-morrow's Saturday, surely,'' said Foster. He picked up a newspaper lying near him. ''Yes, to-day's Friday—by George, sir, you gave me a scare, for among Mrs. Kelly's confidences was the fact that she doesn't work on Sundays!''

Harrington said: ''I'm getting mixed up. What about the Abbotts, Foster? Do you think you'll have enough for an arrest?''

''A great deal depends on what transpires when I see them,'' said Foster. ''I think the best thing is to go in a friendly way and just ask general questions, sliding in a sharp one now and again. By to-morrow I should have expert opinion on the bricks which were in the sack and the brick dust and chippings in the case. If they're definitely the same, then we can say for certain that Abbott's suit-case was used, but that in itself wouldn't be strong enough as grounds for arrest, and I don't think it would be wise to let them know how much we know. Don't you agree?''

''Yes,'' said Harrington.

''Of course, they might precipitate trouble by leaving hurriedly or they might break down under questioning,'' said Foster. ''In either case we might make a move and charge them, but if they hold their ground we shall need a lot more before we can talk about arrest.''

''You're quite right,'' said Harrington. ''I was a little too anxious. After the work you've done I would like to see you make a real break through and clear it up quickly.''

''So would I, sir!'' declared Foster.

''Good!'' said Harrington. ''Will you have another whisky?''

When Foster refused and stood up, the Chief Constable walked to the front door with him, and for a moment they stood watching the lights of the town. ''I come out here for ten minutes every night,'' said Harrington, ''and thank God that the lights are on again!''

''My sentiments entirely, sir,'' said Foster.

''It was like a bad dream,'' said Harrington, ''but I mustn't waste your time talking platitudes; you want a little rest. How is Garth taking it, by the way?''

''He hasn't said anything,'' said Foster, untruthfully.

''Good,'' said Harrington. ''I wish we could find a way of getting round his dislike of you. Do you share it? Be frank with me, Foster. I know that antipathy can be an unpleasant thing, and they've asked for an Inspector at Milsea. It might be a good thing to transfer Garth.''

''Oh,'' said Foster. ''I shouldn't like to think I'd been responsible for anything like that, sir. His home is here, and he's a Milton man. I hope you won't do anything on my account.''

''All right, try to work it out,'' said Harrington.

Foster drove home in a thoughtful frame of mind, and overran the traffic lights at the bottom of the hill. No one saw him. He was smiling when he put his car into the garage, but his wife found him uncommunicative; she did not press him for information, knowing that he would talk freely enough when he felt it would help him. Although he had once wanted to talk the affair over with her, his mind was so crowded now that he felt it wiser to sleep on the events. There were moments of elation when he shared Harrington's optimism, and thought that he might be able to make an early arrest. Before he could prove a case, however, he had to have a motive and to know the identity of the dead man. He wondered if there had ever been a murder charge arising from the finding of the body of an unknown man. He set that thought aside, and asked Laura how she had got on with Mrs. Garth.

Laura, dark, slim and tiny, laughed.

"She telephoned half an hour ago—Garth had gone out for his usual constitutional. She says he is a bit down, but she's often known him worse. Can't you get him to help you?"

"The trouble is that he would think I was dispensing charity," said Foster. "He's so confoundedly proud. If something turned up for him to work on himself, behind my back, for a day or two, it would be a different matter. I hope it doesn't!" He laughed, and they went to bed.

He was talkative at breakfast time next morning, and although he mentioned few names Laura had a fair idea of the situation and the extent of his hopes. When she watched him drive off, she was frowning thoughtfully. She knew that although he had not said so, he was buoying himself up with the hope that before the day was out he would make an arrest, but was a little scared of acting too soon. If he failed to take decisive action, it would disappoint him; the case, which had been so shrouded in mystery at first, seemed now to be very much clearer, but he had worked too fast for his own peace of mind.

Foster himself was trying to face up to the same facts; he must not be over-anxious. It was difficult to wait until mid-morning, however, before sending Sharp and a detective-constable to watch 'Spindles.' He told them that they need not hide; it would do the Abbotts and the Staffords no harm to know that they were being watched.

He had an early lunch. No reports came from Bray, and he felt that if any one of the four people showed any inclination to run away, word would have reached him by now. He was fractious at luncheon, and drove out to Bray soon after half-past one. He pulled up in the middle of the village when he saw Grimes cycling towards him from the direction of 'Spindles.' Grimes dismounted, saluted, and leaned on his saddle to talk through the open window.

"Anything doing?" asked Foster.

"There's been a quarrel," said Grimes rather portentously.

"Between whom?"

"The brother and sister—the Staffords," said Grimes. "I heard a part of it, sir, but I couldn't hear it all. I think Mrs. Abbott managed to soothe them down, but I can't be sure. Then Mr. Abbott went out looking like death."

"*Did* he!" exclaimed Foster.

"I followed him," said Grimes. "I thought something might have happened to make him run, sir. I was there most of the night," he added, "and I got my son to keep an eye on the place while I had a few hours sleep; I didn't want to take any chances."

"Good!" said Foster. "Put that in your report."

"Yes, sir. This Mr. Abbott—he's very well-liked in the village already, sir, and there's some talk of him starting the cricket club again. Old Tom Pickett was telling me about it—he got it from the vicar."

'Cricket' was a magic word to Foster; Milton had no fixture that afternoon, for many clubs were not yet at full strength, but he played whenever he could. In his opinion there was always some good in a man who was keen on cricket, although he admitted that it was not a rule for a policeman to follow.

"Well, where did he go?" he asked.

"To the cricket field," said Grimes, and he sounded puzzled. "He looked as pale as death, and real mad with it. He's got an artificial leg, sir, and can't hurry, but he walked pretty fast for a while, and then he slowed down and went into the field—you know where it is, just behind 'The Angler.' He strolled up and down the pitch several times, and when he came away he looked a different man. He went straight back to the house, and I heard him talking and laughing with his wife. I didn't stay any longer, sir—now that Sergeant Sharp is on duty there isn't any need, is there?" He spoke a trifle wistfully.

"There'll be plenty for you to do before this is over," said Foster, encouragingly. "I'll see you later."

If love of cricket were deep in a man, it was surprising what anything associated with the game could do to him. When he himself had been worked up over a case, or when Laura was lying-in, or at other times of crisis, a walk across the Milton field and five minutes swinging a bat in the pavilion with no one to hear or see him had often worked like a charm. If Abbott's mind was in turmoil, there was nothing surprising in his jaunt.

He pulled up outside 'Spindles.' Sharp was sitting on a barred gate not far away from it, and Foster waved him away when he got down. The other detective was out of sight. No one appeared at the windows of 'Spindles,' but he thought he saw a curtain move. He got out and pulled up the bonnet of his car, so that he was in plain view of the house. Then he replaced it and walked along to Castle's gate.

Castle saw him from the study window, and opened the door to him. He caught a glimpse of Agnes Blackshaw's sour, twisted features; the woman always gave him the creeps. Before her husband had died she had been a cross-looking, spoiled creature, proud and vain, lording it over the village and displaying her wealth ostentatiously. Then Blackshaw had lost all his money and, in despair, had hanged himself. His wife seemed to change over-night. Foster had been in charge of the inquiry, and it had hurt him to talk to the woman. Before the inquiry was finished, however, he had come to dislike her; he did not think she grieved for the loss of her husband, but for the loss of money and position. He always felt sorry for Castle because he had to put up with his sister-in-law, without any help from his wife. He was equally sorry for Mildred Castle. That the Castles were desperately hard up was generally known—he knew, for instance, that Anderson deliberately forgot to send in his bill because he had learned that to pay the previous one, Castle had sold some of his only treasures, a few rare books.

"I can't say that I'm surprised to see you, Inspector," said Castle. "I've seen your men in the village, and I know what you found further along the river, of course. A very bad business, and I'm extremely sorry about it. How is it going?"

"Slowly," said Foster, carefully. "All these things are slow, you know."

"I suppose so. Look here," went on Castle, bluntly, "do you suspect my neighbours?"

"Suspect is rather too strong a word," said Foster.

"Which means that you do," said Castle. "I'm sorry. I don't know them well, of course, but Mr. and Mrs. Abbott are a most charming couple. They'll be great assets to the village, but inquiries like you are making—and you have made them rather obviously, haven't you?—won't be lived down easily. You know what villages are." Castle's manner was a little cool, as if he thought that Foster was going the wrong way about his inquiries.

"I must do my job," Foster said, reasonably. "I can tell you one thing, vicar—in confidence, of course."

"You know I will respect it," said Castle.

"Thank you. Well, the body was put into the river on the evening that the Abbotts and the Staffords moved in. There isn't any doubt about that." He would not have gone so far with many people, but he believed he could trust Castle. "I'm wondering if you noticed anything unusual that day?"

"It was a most unusual day," said Castle.

Something in his manner worried Foster. He was a man for whom the truth was part of life and would never make an easy liar. Now he gave the impression that he had something to hide. Had Foster known of the manuscript and Tony's work on it, he might have understood more clearly; he might have understood even more had he known what a difference to Castle Tony had made by talk on the previous day. As it was, he knew only that Castle was unusually reserved and lacked something of his usual frankness. He wished he had not made the confidence, and felt a little hot under the collar. Castle might become an important witness.

"I understand it was unusual," said Foster, "but I'm thinking of something even more than ordinarily unusual, if I can put it that way. Do you know if the boat was used at all? There is a boat at the end of the garden, isn't there?"

"I believe so," said Castle, with feigned indifference. "I can't imagine them moving in, and being in such a muddle as they were, and leaving it all for a spell on the river, can you?'' He was filling his old pipe, and did not look up.

"I'm seeking facts,'' said Foster, quietly.

"*I* noticed nothing unusual,'' said Castle, deliberately. "*I* saw nothing on the river. I——''

He stopped abruptly, for the door was thrown open. Agnes came into the room, her face livid. She was a tall, thin woman, and since her husband's death she wore old-fashioned clothes, always black or dark grey, with skirts which swept the floor. She wore her hair drawn tightly, almost painfully, from her forehead, and twisted in a bun at the back. Her skin was pale and lined, and her lips were sunken because she needed dentures; that made her lips look very thin. Now there were spots of colour on her cheeks and her eyes were glittering.

"Henry Castle, I never thought *you* would be a liar!''

Castle gasped: "Agnes! What do you mean by forcing your way into my room when I am engaged.''

"I never thought it of *you*!'' she cried. "I thought you were a God-fearing man, not a *liar*. Of course the boat was used!''

"Agnes!'' Castle's voice grew hard. "Go out this moment. I will not allow you to interfere. Inspector, Mrs. Blackshaw has a bitter dislike of anyone who lives next door, and——''

"Who *wouldn't* dislike them?'' demanded Agnes, fiercely. "A wicked, blasphemous lot they are; I wouldn't be surprised at anything they did, murder or worse. The boat was used that night, and I told you so. You went out and had a look at it, you even mentioned it to that man Abbott! Yes you did! You can't deny it!''

Castle had gone very pale. He sat down heavily, but did not meet Foster's gaze. Agnes stood trembling on the threshold, and her voice must have been clearly audible in the garden next door.

"Perhaps you are thinking of a different day,'' said Foster, calmly. "Mr. Castle would hardly——''

"He has taken a liking to the Abbotts, he'll do anything for them,'' cried Agnes. "Aye, *anything!* He would turn himself into a liar, he would deny his Maker for them. He must be mad!'' She pointed a quivering finger at the vicar, who sat very still, fingering his pipe. "I've heard everything you've said, and I knew what you found last night, I don't go about with my ears closed, nor does *he*. That boat was used the night of the murder. And tell me this! Why should they wait until after dark before they washed the floors? Eh? Why should they? They didn't touch a spot of water until after dark, and then I saw the Abbotts scrubbing and mopping as if their lives depended on it!''

Castle said: "I think you have said more than enough, Agnes. What were you doing next door, to see anything of the kind?''

"I have every right to go, it is *my* house!'' cried Agnes. "No one should live there but me, it's mine, mine!'' She was beside herself, and her thin, twisted features were flushed with a rage that was not far removed from hysteria. "I'll go there when I want to, Henry Castle, and you can't stop me! And it's true, they washed the floors after dark, I saw them."

Foster said: "What time, Mrs. Blackshaw?"

"As late as ten o'clock—ten o'clock at night, washing floors! I saw them with my own eyes. I thought then that there was something wrong, I couldn't understand——"

"Agnes, I have never been so ashamed of my own sister."

The words, uttered in a frail voice, came from the hall. Castle uttered a horrified exclamation and jumped to his feet, pushing past Agnes. Foster, torn between the desire to get everything he could from the half-hysterical woman and the need to help Castle with his wife, did neither, and just stood by.

"Mildred!" Castle gasped. "Oh, my dear, you should not have come downstairs, how——"

"Be quiet, Harry, please. Agnes——" Mildred Castle supported herself against the door, ashen-faced, her hair dishevelled. She stood framed there, trembling so that her voice quavered, and yet her words were clear. She had on a dressing-gown which gaped open and revealed her white flannelette night-dress. "Agnes, you know very well that you are making this up because you dislike Mr. and Mrs. Abbott. It is sinful, *sinful!* I wish you to go to your room at once."

There was a moment of tense silence. The appearance of her sister seemed to have shocked Agnes, who stared at her with lips parted and her hands trembling. Before Foster could speak she moved to the door and went along the passage. He heard her walking heavily up the stairs.

"Mildred——" began Castle.

Then his wife swooned, and her legs crumpled up.

CHAPTER 11

A WELCOME AT 'SPINDLES'

It was Foster who telephoned for Dr. Anderson, while Castle carried his wife up to her room. After Anderson had promised to come at once, Foster hurried upstairs. Castle was pulling the bedclothes over his wife. She was unconscious, and seemed hardly to be breathing; her face now looked waxen. Castle stared at Foster distractedly, but did not speak, until suddenly words were wrung from him.

"It is eighteen months since she walked. Eighteen *months!*"

Foster said: "She—so she can use her legs."

"But at what terrible cost!" cried Castle. "I——" he pulled himself up, and unexpectedly rested a hand on Foster's arm. "Please don't disturb yourself, Foster. The blame is not yours—

80

it is mine. I lied to you." He ran his fingers through his hair, and his gaze did not move from his wife. "Agnes told the truth about the boat—it was used. I—I had no desire to do anything to injure a man and woman for whom I have a great regard."

"Did you see them in the boat?" asked Foster.

"No. Agnes told me it had been used. I knew nothing of the house-work that was done at 'Spindles' that night. I know that lights were on quite late, that is all." He stood looking down at his wife for a long time without speaking, and his lips moved as if in prayer.

Foster waited for several minutes, then turned and walked softly from the room.

He did not think this was a time to try to interview Agnes Blackshaw. That she held the Abbotts in a bitter hatred was obvious; in her hysteria, she might as easily tell lies as the truth, and that was not the kind of evidence he wanted. In any case, the incident had shaken him. He knew the devotion of Castle to his wife, and he felt—as he knew Castle did—that the result of this might be fatal. He lit a cigarette as he waited in Castle's study. His indirect approach had brought results more swiftly than he had dared to hope, but the results now gave him no pleasure.

It was some time before Castle came downstairs.

"Have you telephoned for Anderson?" he asked.

"Yes. He should be here any time."

"Thank you. Inspector, I know you understand the situation. I will gladly put myself at your disposal at any time, but just now——"

"There is no hurry," said Foster. "Is there anything I can do?"

"No—no, thank you. Perhaps—perhaps you will telephone when you are coming again."

"I will," promised Foster.

He left the house and walked slowly along the drive. He felt in no mood to press his inquiries at 'Spindles'; until he knew what was likely to happen to Mildred Castle, his thoughts would wander. The utter unexpectedness of the outburst from Agnes Blackshaw had precipitated a situation which might have distressing consequences for the Castles.

Sharp had left the barred gate, and was standing by his car.

"Did you hear anything?" Foster asked.

"I couldn't catch what was said, sir, but I heard some shouting," said Sharp. "I think it was something about a boat."

"It was," said Foster.

"Have we got 'em, sir?" demanded Sharp, eagerly.

"We're getting them," said Foster. He looked dispassionately at his man. He knew that the time when he would find Sharp tiresome was nearer; his own sergeant would have known that this was not a moment to badger him with questions. He had to restrain himself from speaking sharply, although he had the fairness to admit that Sharp was hardly to be blamed for showing eagerness.

In fact the round, fresh-complexioned face of the sergeant, with its guileless expression, looked more intelligent than usual; contact with murder was probably sharpening his wits.

Sharp obviously noticed nothing amiss.

"I know one thing, sir," he said. "The people there heard it." He nodded towards 'Spindles.' "Stafford was leaning out of a window, and the Abbotts came to the front door. I don't think they missed much. It ought to be a good time to have a go at them, didn't it?"

"As good a time as any, probably," admitted Foster, cursing the man. "Keep your eyes open, Sharp."

"Yes, sir." The sergeant was obviously disappointed at being left behind, but he did not say so. Foster walked slowly to the gateway of 'Spindles,' surprised by his own mixed feelings. He saw a face at a window at the top of the house, and thought it was Anne Stafford's, but was not sure. He was half-way along the drive when Sharp called 'Sir!' in a curious half-tone, suggesting that he wanted to attract his attention but not that of the people in the house. Foster turned. Cycling at a good speed along the road was P.C. Grimes waving with one hand towards Sharp and looking towards him. Foster's heart leapt hopefully as he turned to go back to the gate, but he took himself to task. If he went on like this, it would be better for Garth to take over; at least he would not be affected by sentimental upsets and a vivid imagination. As Grimes jumped off his bicycle Foster had a vivid mental picture of Abbott—whom he had seen once only and that at a distance—walking pensively along the cricket pitch behind 'The Angler.'

"Well, Grimes, what have you found now?" he asked, forcing a smile.

"I thought you ought to know this at once, sir," said Grimes, a little breathlessly. "Mr. Stafford rang up just now, it proper took my breath away."

"What did he want?" demanded Foster.

"He *said* he wanted to complain about the boat here, sir—he *said* people have been taking it out at night, and he wants them stopped, sir."

Foster stared at the man, a completely new emotion taking possession of him.

"Did he, by George! That's very smart of him, Grimes."

"That's what I thought, sir."

"Do you mean he knows we're on to him and he's trying to find a way out of it?" asked Sharp, incredulously.

"As we know boats have been used by thieves along here, it isn't a bad get out," said Foster, judicially. "I see. I think I'll be very careful with Mr. Stafford—you're sure it was Stafford, not Abbott?"

"Quite sure, sir. I wouldn't make a mistake about his voice—he nearly always shouts, and Mr. Abbott is a quiet-voiced gentleman."

"Good!" said Foster. "All right, Grimes, you get back. You

wait here, Sharp.'' He heard a car coming along the road, and waited when he recognized Anderson's Humber. The doctor pulled up, and asked for the latest news of Mrs. Castle. Foster told him what little he knew. As he reached the door of 'Spindles,' Anderson's car drew up outside the vicarage porch.

The door of 'Spindles' was standing open. Foster knocked, and after a pause Tony Abbott appeared from a room on the left.

It seemed to Foster, as Tony approached slowly, that each was taking the other's measure and was aware of it. His own impression was good; in that queer, undefinable way which always puzzled him, he knew that Abbott was a man whom he could like. There was an air about him, partly self-confidence, a mixture of pride and friendliness, too; it was not the look of a man who was trying desperately to cover up the traces of an evil deed. He did not even try to show surprise or to pretend that he did not know the caller.

''Good-afternoon, Inspector,'' he said.

''You're Mr. Abbott, aren't you?'' asked Foster.

''Yes. If you're wondering how I come to know you, you have been pointed out by my brother- and sister-in-law in the past half-hour.'' He seemed genuinely amused. ''How can we help you?''

He stood aside in silent invitation, and Foster stepped into the drawing-room, which was on the right. He was surprised to find it looking so well although there had been little redecoration. A touch or two of paint in places, and a dark stain about two small Persian carpets, made a world of difference. Every polished surface shone.

Tony offered cigarettes.

''Thank you,'' said Foster. ''I'm not a bit sure that you can help me, Mr. Abbott. I am investigating——''

''A murder,'' Tony said, calmly.

''You're well-informed.''

Tony laughed. ''Mrs. Kelly works here, and if you know Bray well you will know that she is a fountain of information. I think I know everything that happened when you were at Riversmeet last evening, and I have seen the early edition of the local paper. Two and two make four. The coincidence of our arrival and the dumping of the body in the river is puzzling you, isn't it?''

''It is,'' said Foster, a trifle sourly.

Although the good impression remained, he felt on the defensive and a little aggrieved. This was not at all the kind of interview he had expected; in fact he would not have been surprised to have found Abbott and the others sullen and uncommunicative. Instead, here was this dark-haired, rather handsome man, with a charming smile which just showed his white teeth, taking the whole thing into his own hands; Abbott, he thought, was used to command. It was said that he had been a Group Captain; that would explain it.

''And very naturally,'' said Abbott. ''Look here, Inspector, I've killed no one.'' The thought seemed to afford him some amusement. "I can see that if matters are allowed their head things might become awkward, so the utmost frankness is called for on my part."

"I'm glad to hear it," said Foster.

"Then I will start by saying that I heard something of the conversation next door, when you called there. It concerned our boat, didn't it?"

"Yes," said Foster, still more aggrieved.

"I think my brother-in-law has telephoned to the village policeman about that," said Abbott. "I don't mind admitting that I was once rather——"

He broke off because there were footsteps in the hall; a moment later the door opened and Julius came in. He raised a hand in greeting and grinned at Foster with such aplomb that the Inspector was now completely taken aback. Suddenly there was a light burst of laughter, more footsteps, and both women appeared on the scene. Gillian was flushed and looked excited; her sister was much calmer, but there was a glint in her eyes which Foster had not seen when he had first met her. The complete assurance with which all of them greeted him, amounting in Gillian's case to exuberance, was remarkable.

"Tony is about to spill the beans," declared Julius, including Gillian and Anne in his broad grin. "Shall we leave it to him, or shall I handle it?"

"You'd better leave it to Tony," said Anne.

"All right, all right, he's the word-spinner of the family," said Julius.

He struck a wrong note, although Foster did not think the others realized it; 'word-spinner' or 'yarn-spinner' applied with equal force; he got the impression that he was going to be told a carefully rehearsed story, and that the bright atmosphere was being deliberately created for his benefit.

He was not altogether right.

. . . . .

A little after twelve o'clock that morning, Mrs. Kelly had let off her broadside. The whole story, including the fact that Foster had questioned her about them, was poured out into Gillian's startled ears. Anne, who had been washing some smalls, kept her face averted. She went off before the recital was finished, and when Gillian had gone to tell Tony, Julius's bellowing voice sounded from upstairs. Anne and Julius were still touchy, especially with each other. Between Julius and Tony there had been a state of armed peace, and no further outward signs of trouble, and Gillian had been busily intent on preserving that peace, even though Julius obviously vented his ill-temper on Anne.

While the quarrel was at its height, sometimes loud, sometimes carried on in undertones punctuated with roars of anger from Julius, Gillian had told Tony all that Mrs. Kelly had said. Each of them thought immediately of the boat and Castle's warning.

"It's beginning to worry me," Tony said.

"Tony, you *can't* think that they know anything about it!"

"They've been behaving very queerly," Tony said, and then seeing his wife's expression, he drew her to him and kissed her forehead. "I'm sorry, darling. I'm talking nonsense! There must be a simple explanation of it. Supposing we come out with it bluntly, and tell them what's been passing through our minds?"

"It will probably start Julius off," said Gillian.

"We'll have to risk that," said Tony. "We'll wait until they have settled down a bit, and then bring up the matter about the boat, shall we? Luncheon will be a good opportunity."

"All right," said Gillian, doubtfully.

She went back to the kitchen, and Tony began to read what he had been writing that morning. He scanned the pages inattentively, and went over the passages time and time again, until at last he gave it up in despair and pushed the typewritten sheets away from him. There was something queer in the atmosphere, and it was useless to blink at the fact. It would have been kinder to act less sentimentally with Gillian, and not try to pretend that there could be nothing in it. He knew both Julius and Anne very well; there was nothing really new in their behaviour, but it was accentuated—after the quarrel in the study, Anne had been subdued most of the time, and Julius icily polite towards him.

He went upstairs to change his clothes, for it was getting hot, although it had been chilly in the morning. There had been a period of quiet for some time, but now he heard Julius speak again in a high-pitched voice; he was in Anne's bedroom.

"I tell you it's *not* impossible!"

"But——" Anne began.

"For crying out loud!" roared Julius. "Do you think I'm taken in by that pi-faced scribbler? Of course he was capable of it!"

"But Julius, he——"

"Oh, have it your own way!" cried Julius. "I tell you that he's quite capable of anything; it wouldn't surprise me if he committed the murder."

That was not all he said. There was a lot more uttered in a lower voice, but normally Tony would have been able to hear it. Now, however, there were noises in his head, and he stood quite still, his hands clenched, his eyes narrowed so that he could hardly see out of them. His heart was thumping painfully. This fit of rage was greater than any in the past; he did not know how he restrained himself from rushing into the room and storming at Julius. Instead, when the worst had passed he turned and went downstairs, out of the front door and along the drive at a pace which he found uncomfortable. He walked towards the village, and found himself on the cricket field, a pleasant stretch of turf, with a laid table behind the quaint Tudor inn which faced the village green. There he walked up and down for a while, until peace came to his spirit; afterwards he was agitated for a different reason. In such a mood as that which had possessed him, he *was* capable of murder.

He assumed, of course, that Julius was suggesting that he had thrown the body into the river; unlike Foster, he was not even partly right.

.   .   .   .   .

There was no doubt that Anne's nerves were stretched to breaking point. It took little to upset her now, and the paragraph in the paper which she had read just before Mrs. Kelly had pointed to the 'hanging oak' had nearly made her break down in front of Tony. She had been hardly aware of the quarrel in the study, was interested only in talking to Julius. The conversation on the Friday afternoon, however, had been most unsatisfactory; that day's conversation in the studio, and then in her room, whither Julius followed her, began no more auspiciously. It was absurd for Julius to start accusing *Tony*; there was no sense in it. They had argued about it upstairs, and when he had entered her room, just before Tony had come upstairs, he had said:

"I tell you it's *not* impossible!"

"But——" began Anne.

"For crying out loud!" roared Julius. "Do you think I'm taken in by that pi-faced scribbler? Of course he was capable of it!"

"But Julius, he——"

"Oh, have it your own way!" cried Julius. "I tell you that he's quite capable of anything; it wouldn't surprise me if he committed the murder. I——"

"Be quiet!" cried Anne.

Tony heard nothing of that, nor of what followed; Tony was standing outside in the grip of that ungovernable rage, while Julius went on in a quieter voice:

"Oh, you make me sick. Why in the world did you wait until to-day to remember that Tony called at the flat when Lovelace was there?"

"But he couldn't have seen Lovelace!"

"How do you know what he saw? He knew the man, didn't he? He actually introduced Lovelace to me. How do you know what passed between them? How do you know that after you had gone out, leaving Lovelace alone in the flat, he didn't come in and kill him? Don't you tell me that he wouldn't do such a thing. I tell you that there's been murder in his eyes more than once when he's looked at me. His hands have itched as if he would like to strangle me! The man's liable to fits of insanity, if you ask me."

"Don't be absurd, Julius!"

"My dear, trusting, innocent sister," said Julius, in a voice suddenly silky with sarcasm, "I may be a fool in some respects. I may not be a genius. I may be a lazy good-for-nothing who has caused you a great deal of heartbreak. But—*I am not a congenital idiot!*" He hissed the last words, stepping forward and glaring into Anne's eyes. "Have the goodness to admit that, my dear. I am not entirely witless. Tony knew Lovelace. You left Lovelace in the flat alone, shortly after Tony had called on some trivial excuse about the moving. Tony might have had a better reason for wanting to kill him than you or I dream of. Oh, don't misunderstand me, *I*'m not going to accuse him of it. It wouldn't do, but it certainly wouldn't surprise me.'' Suddenly he threw back his head and roared with laughter. ''Here's a pretty situation! We worry ourselves stiff and risk getting hanged for a murder which Tony Abbott committed. That's rich! That's——''

''I am beginning to think that you are a worse beast than I thought,'' said Anne, in cutting tones, ''and I knew you were bad enough.''

When she resorted to biting sarcasm, she always silenced him, for he was a creature of moods and could not be relied on to be the same for five minutes on end. He stood in front of her, shamefaced, and mopped his forehead. She saw the little beads of perspiration there and on his upper lip.

''Well, you've got to admit that he could have done it,'' he said, aggrievedly.

''I don't believe it is possible,'' said Anne. ''It's true that he knew Lovelace, but as far as we know they were friendly enough. He hadn't any reason to hate Lovelace, as we had.'' She was speaking in a soft voice, as if she were trying hard to force herself to contemplate dangerous circumstances, and not to let herself lose her composure. Everything she did and said, everything she thought, was the result of considerable effort. The strain was telling on her; even in the past ten days she had lost weight, and there were crow's-feet about her eyes which had not been there a few weeks before.

''You mean we don't know that he had any reason to hate Lovelace,'' said Julius, but he did not return to the attack on Tony immediately. ''What are we going to do, that's what I want to know. I think it's time we started making sure that even if they find out that our boat was used, they can't blame it on to us. Supposing we complained that the boat had been used by someone else——''

''Tony and Gillian know that it hasn't, and they won't lie,'' said Anne.

''Oh, no, they're too smug for words! But how can they tell whether the boat's been used? It may surprise you, my dear sister, to know that I am always first up in the mornings in this household. It is not unusual for me to walk in the garden before breakfast. It is quite possible that I might notice what your remarkable Tony does not.''

''It would have to be remarked upon at breakfast time,'' said Anne.

''Not at all, my dear,'' said Julius, his voice syrupy again. ''Not at all. We now have Mrs. Kelly's story about the finding of the sack in the river and therefore we know that a boat was used—we didn't before. There is no reason why I should not pretend to be horrified by the possibility that our boat was used.'' He stared at her with narrowed eyes, and she watched him closely.

He was certainly no fool, and there were times when he was brilliant. She could almost see his mind working, and she waited patiently.

"I think I see a way in which we can present a happy and united front to the police," he said at last, "and make the others rejoice at a change of heart on my part. It will demand great magnanimity, my dear, and I have no liking for it—there are times when I would like to knock my hypocritical brother-in-law through the wall. However, we must study the family interest first, mustn't we? Here is the situation as I see it. In order to save ourselves, and because we lost our heads—let us admit it, my dear!—we have put ourselves in a position of acute danger. The police will find it hard to believe that we took the body from London and dumped it into the river simply because we were innocent but afraid that the murder would be laid at our door."

Anne said: "Why don't you say what you mean? *I* made you do that."

"My dear sister, although, as I said, I am not brilliant, I have a rudimentary intelligence. Possibly I was drunk when I agreed to help in the conspiracy, but I have never seriously doubted that it was the wise thing to do, even when I have been sober—I *am* sober most of the time, you know. Both of us were shocked when we first realized what had happened. We were not normal. We did what we thought was best, and now it appears at least possible that at the same time we saved Tony a great deal of trouble." This time she ignored the barb against Tony. "Let me proceed," went on Julius, with heavy sarcasm. "A united family can, I think, be created if I apologize to Tony for going into his study. His temperament will not allow him to reject the olive branch. Then we need to explain why we have been somewhat on edge during the last few days. We have, you know. Even I admit it. Well, what is the matter with us? This: we knew that the boat was being used by night. We assumed it was for some nefarious purpose. We had reason to believe that Tony and Gillian were using it. As it was used again last night, when we know they could not have used it, we are now filled with remorse at our vague suspicions. Do you think they'll bite?" he added, with a touch of anxiety.

"I don't see why not," said Anne, thoughtfully.

"You see! In emergency come to Julius," said Julius, almost childishly pleased. "There is one other thing, my dear, which might cause trouble—that is the fact that the suit-case was lost. I do not think the police have found it, but they may have been lucky. It will be better if we have an answer for all questions before they are actually put to us. So, I will discover in the grounds some oddments of clothing which I will say were packed in that case. I will remember that, in the rush on the day of our arrival, the case was left by the back door—or the front door, it doesn't greatly matter—and that it was stolen. I had completely forgotten about it until I made the discovery in the grounds. How does that appeal, my dear?"

"It sounds all right," said Anne.

"It *is* all right!" declared Julius. "Let us prepare for a sentimental *rapprochement* during luncheon."

. . . . .

Julius was more fortunate than he expected, for when he was going into the grounds with some ties and collars tucked beneath his coat and other oddments in his pockets for him to 'discover,' he overheard a brief exchange between Tony and Gillian. Tony was speaking lightly, as if he did not take it seriously.

"He must be crazy, but he actually said that he wouldn't put it past me. I nearly gate-crashed, and that would have caused a real shindy."

"But it's absolute nonsense!" Gillian protested.

"There must be some reason for it," said Tony.

Julius hurried off, very thoughtful.

He made sure that he was not seen at the end of the garden, where the river came over a muddy bank and lapped at the rough grass near the landing-stage. High hedges hid him from the houses, and there was no one on the other side of the river nor in the vicarage garden. There was a muddy pool close to the landing-stage and he dropped the things into it, ground them down under his heel, and then retrieved a few of them. These he took back with him, and there was water dripping from ties and collars and a hair-brush when he went into the kitchen. Gillian and Anne were dishing up lunch.

"What on earth have you found?" demanded Gillian.

"There's some funny business going on around this place," declared Julius. "Some *very* funny business. Where is Tony?"

"Here," said Tony, coming from a cloakroom near the kitchen. "Now what's the trouble?"

He came in slowly, half expecting Julius to make a more public statement of his suspicions, and he was taken aback by Julius's opening sentence, which seemed so sincere that he himself coloured a little.

"Tony, I know I have been pretty bearish during the last few days. I'm sorry. The truth is that I've had something on my mind and it's worried me a great deal." Julius uttered a short laugh. "I was even working myself up into a frame of mind where I was capable of suspecting *you* of funny business."

"Me?" exclaimed Tony, mechanically.

"Yes. The first morning we were here I strolled down the garden and I saw that the boat had been used," said Julius. "I thought you'd been out for an early morning airing, and didn't take much notice of it, of course. Then I saw that it had been out several times afterwards. There were rumours in the village about thieves working after dark, from the river. Oh, I know it was crazy," he added, looking shamefaced, "but once or twice I saw you coming up the garden fairly early in the morning, and—

well, especially after the row about old Castle's book, I wanted to believe the worst of you."

"Oh," said Tony, out of his depths.

"Then this morning Mrs. Kelly was blabbing about a body in the river," Julius went on with a short laugh. "Like a damned fool I mentioned my earlier suspicions to Anne, and when she saw what I was driving at, she nearly bit my head off!" He gave a rueful smile. "I started to put in some heavy thinking. As a matter of fact the boat was out last night, and I happen to know you didn't take it out, because I was awake and I would have heard you had you gone out after the rest of us had gone to bed. I *stayed* awake, to find out," he added, with another sheepish smile. "One way and another, I've been a pretty lousy specimen, old chap. I'm damnably sorry."

"Oh, forget it," said Tony, awkwardly.

"I'm afraid we can't dismiss it as easily as that," said Julius, seriously. He held up the muddy articles. "I've just found these, in the garden—they'd been thrown away. I remember they were packed in a case which I'd borrowed from you a few days before we moved."

"Oh, *that's* where the case went!" exclaimed Tony. "I remember now."

"I also remember that I put it down out of the removal van—the foreman was a swine of a fellow, and I rather lost my temper with him. I forgot about the case until I found these things. I distinctly remember putting it by the back door," went on Julius, "and presumably I left it there over-night, and it was stolen. Why anyone should want to steal the case and throw away the contents I just don't know, but there it is. I think it would be wise to tell the police, don't you?"

"I do," said Tony.

"Surely that can wait until after lunch," said Gillian, who had been cooking. "It's getting cold now."

"Oh, there's no hurry for half-an-hour," said Julius. "I'll dump these things in a shed," he added. "Can you spare a moment, Tony?"

As Gillian turned to the stove to dish up, she felt flushed but relieved. She had been afraid that Tony's calmness, after the spasm which he had just admitted having, would be a brittle one, liable to break. Now there were no fears of that, for he was so made that he could never refuse to accept an apology. This one, so frank and open-handed, and uttered in Julius's humblest manner, might go a long way towards healing the breach for good. She felt angry that Julius had harboured such absurd suspicions, but it did not really surprise her; he was capable of pondering any tortuous notions. Probably Julius had taken Tony into the garden to put the finishing touch to his apology; she would know as soon as they returned.

She was right; Julius was talking in a confidential undertone in the little potting-shed where he was putting the 'recovered' oddments.

"I don't mind admitting, Tony, that it worried me no end.

You're a secretive kind of customer, you know, and when you flared up at me in the study the other day I jumped to the conclusion that you had something to hide in there. I can see now that it was quite unforgivable—my behaviour, I mean. I don't know what came over me.''

"Well, you can forget that, anyhow,'' said Tony.

"That's very sporting of you, old chap. As a matter of fact it wasn't until Anne really let herself go—she's got a soft spot for you, you know!—that I pulled myself up. Er—earlier this morning I'd been inventing all manner of wild theories. You know the police have been watching the house—or else the vicarage—don't you?''

"I've seen two or three men about, and the constable has been within sight most of the morning,'' said Tony. "I did wonder if it were connected with the murder. As a matter of fact——'' it was his turn to appear, and to feel, sheepish. "I'd noticed that the boat had been out once or twice, and I rather thought that you——''

Julius stared, and then guffawed with laughter.

"What a precious pair of fools we are!''

"I'm beginning to think so,'' admitted Tony. "I can't say that I went as far as you did, but—well, let's wash it out, Julius. If the police have some curious ideas about us we can soon put that straight. The stealing of the case is a funny business, isn't it?''

"Yes. It looks as if someone's picked on us to help them out of a jam,'' said Julius. "I'll let the police know about the boat after lunch—do you think we need mention the case?''

"I think they'll come to see us,'' said Tony, "and we can mention the case then.''

"That's a good idea,'' said Julius.

During lunch there was a more genial atmosphere than at any meal since the first breakfast, when Gillian had wrongly thought that they were off to a good start. There was a complete absence of bickering and sly digs. To improve the situation, Anne's fiancé had sent a telegram postponing his visit indefinitely because of his mother's illness; Anne did not seem to mind, and Julius was obviously delighted. Tony and Gillian admitted to each other that they felt greatly relieved, and even when they saw the police car drive up, and Anne and Julius pointed out Foster, they were not unduly worried. The loud voices from the vicarage had rather startled them, but nothing that Agnes Blackshaw did and said surprised them. It was a good thing, thought Tony, that Julius had already telephoned to the sergeant in the village about the mystery of the boat.

As it happened, Tony was alone in the drawing-room when Foster came along the drive, and in a mood almost of elation he prepared to welcome the Inspector.

CHAPTER 12

INSPECTOR FOSTER IS BOTHERED

FOSTER returned to his headquarters in a very puzzled frame of mind. He was disappointed in some ways, relieved in others. The theory he had built up appeared to be demolished, but he was by no means satisfied that he had heard all the truth from the people at 'Spindles.' For one thing, Julius Stafford had shown a new aspect of himself; his geniality and good-humour had been remarkable. All of them appeared to have been hugging some delightful secret, and Foster could not rid himself of a feeling that they had conspired to confuse and outwit him. For the Abbotts he admitted a definite liking, and he rather liked Anne Stafford. He could not make up his mind about Julius.

All of these things had been subservient, for a while, to Mrs. Castle's condition, and he was still worried about her. Before he left 'Spindles,' Anderson had gone, and Castle had not been in any shape for talking. As soon as the Abbotts learned what had happened they hurried next door, and Foster found himself out in the cold. He left Sharp and the other plain-clothes man on duty.

The first thing he did was to telephone Anderson.

"I don't think I can commit myself," said Anderson, frankly. "I was astonished to hear that she had walked down the stairs without assistance—I did not think she would ever have the use of her legs again. I'm getting another opinion, of course. She was still unconscious when I left, and if she comes round to-day I think she may have considerable pain. I've given the district nurse instructions to inject morphia if it seems necessary, and there isn't much else I can do."

"What about this second opinion?" asked Foster.

"It will have to be someone from London," said Anderson, with a short laugh. "Castle can't afford it, of course, but——"

"I can," said Foster.

Anderson was silent for a moment, and then he said:

"You're a good chap, Foster. I was thinking of footing the bill myself, and introducing Trevelyan—if I can get him to come down—as a friend. Shall we split his fee?"

"All right," said Foster. "You don't think there's any immediate danger, then?"

"I can't see where it can come from," said Anderson. "Still, it's a new development as far as I'm concerned. There's no doubt that Trevelyan is the right man, although whether he'll come is a different matter."

"Isn't he a consultant pathologist to the Yard?" asked Foster, suddenly.

"Now you come to mention it, I think he is."

"Leave it to me," said Foster, suddenly more cheerful. "If he comes down here to have a look at our *corpus*, you can get him to look at Mrs. Castle as a matter of professional interest, probably at a nominal fee."

"Good idea," said Anderson. "See what you can do."

Saturday afternoon was not a good time for such endeavours, but two hours later a telephone call from the Yard brought the hoped-for news; Sir Alexander Trevelyan would come to Milton the following day, and Superintendent Folly would accompany him. The fact that Folly was coming puzzled Foster; the Superintendent had a big reputation, and he rarely left London.

That information finally sent Foster to the Chief Constable. He found Harrington in the club-house at Milton Downs Golf Course, warm and pleased with himself after a round which he had done inside his handicap. He was having tea with his wife, a tall, willowy woman who Foster always felt was a little beyond him. He could not understand Mrs. Harrington at all; either she was an intelligent woman who covered her intelligence by a show of light-heartedness, or else she was flippant and feather-brained by nature. She went to join another table after Foster arrived; it was part of her creed to have nothing to do with the more sordid details of her husband's profession.

"You're hunting me out well this time," said Harrington. "Peggy—bring a fresh pot of tea for the Inspector." A waitress hurried off, and Harrington went on: "By the look of you, things haven't gone as well as you hoped."

"Certainly not according to plan," admitted Foster. He lit a cigarette as he marshalled his thoughts. "I can't make up my mind whether the people at 'Spindles' have been pitchforked into this business accidentally, and really know nothing about it, or whether they are an unusually clever lot who are intent on cheating us. I'm glad we called in the Yard, after all—and there is a curious development up there, sir."

"What?" asked Harrington.

"Folly is coming."

"Folly, by George! That's unusual, most unusual. He's got a reputation for not stirring from his office. I wonder what's brought him."

"So do I," said Foster, ruefully. "On the face of it there's nothing to attract him. I'm wondering if the fact that we've suggested that the dead man might be an alien has anything to do with it—Folly did a lot of work on Aliens during the war."

He plunged into a recital of the afternoon's events, including the fact that he had asked for Sir Alexander Trevelyan, and why. Harrington raised no objection, and seemed sympathetic, although he did not know the Castles very well. He was far more interested in the developments at 'Spindles.'

"Well, what do you make of it?" he asked. "Did they realize that you knew their boat had been used when you put men to watch, and try to get a step ahead by reporting an imaginary unknown user?''

"It wouldn't surprise me," said Foster. "But there was something else which makes it seem less likely. Stafford told me that a suit-case which he had borrowed from Abbott was stolen on the day he moved in. He showed me some things which had been taken out of it and were thrown away at the bottom of the garden. I don't think he could know that I'd found the case. Martin is too scared to open his mouth about it, and I took precautions to make sure I wasn't seen carrying it away—in fact I left after dark."

"Hum," said Harrington. "Stafford or Abbott might know that the case was used."

"Unless he thought we had it, he would hardly put up an explanation like that," said Foster. "Still, that's what I mean when I say that I can't make up my mind whether they're being victimized or whether they're putting up a very good show."

To his surprise, Harrington laughed.

"Folly won't stand much nonsense," he said. "Now don't misunderstand me, Foster—but he has a reputation for being merciless and very heavy-handed. I haven't met him," he admitted. "I'm rather looking forward to; he is the lion of Scotland Yard all right. I wonder how you'll get on with him?"

Foster grimaced. "Well, I made my own bed," he said.

"Don't let him be heavy-handed with you," said Harrington. "I'm not going to let my officers be browbeaten—but you know that. If he's really difficult, we might bring Garth in," he added with a sly smile.

Foster was in a good humour when he left the club-house; it was reassuring to be sure that he would have the Chief's firm support. He told himself that he was not even slightly anxious about working with the great Folly, but the truth was that he would be on edge until he discovered what the man was like.

He went back to the office, not expecting to find much there. To his surprise, there was a man waiting for him in the hall, accompanied by Sharp, who should still have been at 'Spindles.' Foster recognized the caller as the manager of a Milton firm of builders. He thought of the bricks, and made a mental note to reprimand Sharp for leaving his post.

Sharp suddenly sneezed three times in quick succession, and buried his face in a handkerchief. His eyes were watery and his voice was thick.

"Sorry, sir," he said. "I came over so faint that I told Grimes to take over, and—t'choo, t'choo, t'choo, sorry sir!" he gasped for breath. "I think I'm running a temperature, sir, I—t'choo!"

"Here, you get off home and send for a doctor," said Foster, in alarm. "You'll have the whole station down with that cold if you sneeze all over the place. Don't report back until you're better."

"Thank you, s—t'choo!" sneezed Sharp, and hurried off.

Wylie, the manager of the building firm, smiled at his departing back. He was a tall, well-dressed man of middle age.

"I went to Bray to see you, Inspector, as they told me you were there, and I persuaded Sharp to come away—I thought he was going to peg out on the spot."

"Oh," said Foster. "Thanks. Well, what can you tell me?"

"It's about this brick," said Wylie, as Foster led the way to his office. "I don't think there's much doubt where it came from, Inspector."

"Where?" asked Foster.

"It's a special brick, much dearer than most used for building in this district," said Wylie, "but old Blackshaw wouldn't have anything but the best—he knew exactly what he wanted, too. We built 'Spindles,' you know." He smiled into Foster's unwinking eyes. "I shall be very surprised if any other builder in the district says he's used that brand. I've been looking up the report from the foreman after 'Spindles' was built. There were a few dozen bricks left, but not enough for any useful purpose, and they were left on the site."

"Oh," said Foster.

"I hope that's what you want," said Wylie.

"Yes, thanks," said Foster. "I suppose they could have been taken away from the site by unauthorized people."

"Obviously," said Wylie, "but I can't see why, unless they were to be used." He smiled, as if he suspected that Foster was trying to be more non-committal than he felt. "Is there anything else I can do for you?"

"Not just now," said Foster, "but you may be called to give evidence. You'll be prepared to, I suppose?"

"I'll swear that bricks of that brand were used in building 'Spindles,' " said Wylie. "I can't do any more than that, of course."

"Of course not," said Foster.

He saw the builder out, then looked thoughtfully at the brick which the man had left on his desk. Everything he needed to prove that the body had left 'Spindles' was now at hand—bricks, suit-case, boat, everything except the sack was associated with the house. It dawned on him that he had not been as thorough as he might have been at 'Spindles,' and he looked at his watch. It was a little after five-fifteen. He telephoned Laura, and when she answered, said:

"I can't get back for an hour or so, old girl. How would you like to bring the infants for a ride as far as Bray?"

"They'd love it," said Laura.

"It won't be too late for Wanda?"

"We'll waive her bedtime rule for one night," said Laura. "Shall we come to the station?"

"No, I'll pick you up in ten minutes or so," said Foster.

Half an hour later, Laura and the three children got out of the car by the village green, and Laura, only a little taller than her eldest daughter, raced with them towards some ducks waddling about the pond, laughing and waving as Foster drove towards 'Spindles.' Grimes and the other men were talking together, and had nothing to report.

Tony was working in the garden, and looked up when he saw the visitor.

"Still at it?" he asked, amiably enough.

"Still on the daily grind," smiled Foster. "There are one or two things I'd like to do—I was rather worried about Mrs. Castle and they slipped my memory. Do you mind if I have a look round the garden?"

"Of course not. Can I be your guide."

"Thanks," said Foster.

"My wife's in the village," said Abbott as he pushed a fork into a bed which he had been clearing, and dusted his hands on a rag, "and I think my brother-in-law is in the last stages of germination."

"Germination?" asked Foster, startled.

"Yes. At any moment weird and wonderful sounds may come from his piano, and by to-morrow we shall probably have to listen to a new masterpiece," said Tony. "He's a curious fellow—I think you ought to know that, Foster. He often does things which no normal human being would dream of doing, and trivial things upset him."

"Defence of a brother-in-law," said Foster, lightly.

"Nonsense! Guidance for the police," said Tony.

They both laughed.

Foster, who had brought a walking stick, poked about the long grass which grew near the river and at the sides of the large garden. Now and again he touched something hard, but it proved to be only a stone. Then, behind some bramble bushes and thick blackthorn, he saw a little shed, not much larger than a dog-kennel. The water had come up to it recently, a nd there was mud on one side. He saw the footprints on a patch harder than the rest, but when he went down on his knees he came to the conclusion that they were not clear enough to give him any help. He forced a way through the brambles towards the little shed, with Tony helping him to hold the thorny branches back.

He found a clearing, and saw that the shed had been approached from the river side several times, for the earth was churned up and branches were broken and trodden down. By the side of the shed was a patch where the grasses were white and delicate-looking—as if they had grown beneath something standing there, out of the light of the sun. Then he saw a part of a brick buried in the ground.

"Is this what you're after?" asked Tony.

"I'm after anything I can find," said Foster.

He was satisfied, after a few minutes' inspection, that a dozen or so bricks had lain at this spot. Then he tried to open the door of the shed. It was fastened with a staple and hasp, the staple a piece of wood recently cut to a point and pushed in; it had jammed tightly. He took a handkerchief from his pocket before he grasped the wood firmly and tugged at it.

"Surely you won't find fingerprints on that," said Tony.

"You never know where you might find 'em," said Foster. "By George, it's tight!" He could not exert much pressure from where he was standing, and some brambles were brushing against his face. Tony held them aside, and at last Foster drew the wooden peg out. The door swung open.

"Look here," said Tony, "you aren't looking for another body, are you?"

"No," said Foster, "but nothing would surprise me." He bent down, peering into the little shed, but it was dark inside and he could not see much. He had not brought a torch with him, and before daylight was let into the place, the bushes would have to be cut down. There was something on the floor near the door, and he put his hand inside and pulled at it.

He took out a piece of sacking; there were other pieces beyond. Some of them looked almost unused, although they were wearing in places.

"The sack!" exclaimed Tony.

Foster snapped: "What do you know about the sack?"

"What I read in the paper," said Tony, promptly.

"The papers say too much," growled Foster.

He examined the sack closely. He could not be sure until he had compared it side by side with the sack taken from the river, but it looked to him as if it were of the same material and manufacture; it was fairly closely woven. Expert opinion would be easy to obtain, and he had certainly justified his second visit.

"Satisfied?" asked Tony.

"Look here, you take this business very lightly, Abbott," said Foster.

Tony shrugged his shoulders. "I can't make myself take it seriously," he said. "It isn't very real to me, you know. A man whom I don't know has been killed—it would be different if I knew him. To tell you the truth I'm extremely interested," he admitted. "I've never seen the police at work before."

Foster had to accept that explanation.

He did not give up his search then, but looked for some of the oddments which Stafford said he had left from the case. He found nothing. The pool where the goods had been discovered was thick with mud, and even Stafford's footprints were vague and confused. It was not likely that they would find any clues to help them there, but he decided to send for a sergeant who was an expert on foot-prints, in the hope that he could get one or two casts.

He told Tony so, and added:

"I'm afraid we're being a bit of a nuisance, but I can't help myself."

"I tell you I'm deeply interested," asseverated Tony. "Do you think he was killed in the grounds?"

"I wouldn't like to go as far as that," said Foster.

He had another look at the boat, which was still tied up to the landing-stage. He had examined it thoroughly in the afternoon, and there was not the slightest trace of blood on it. He toyed with the idea of having it taken downstream, and decided that it would be better to leave it; the people who had used it once might want to use it again, and it would be better to watch the place and give them the opportunity. For the first time he wondered, uneasily, whether he had been wise to let his men stay in such obvious places. His plan to stampede the people at 'Spindles' had been a lamentable failure; it was the kind of thing on which Folly would probably seize as an example of the errors made by country policemen.

They walked back to the gates, and Foster tucked his finds into the boot of his car. He left the wooden peg in the handkerchief.

"If you're going to the village you might give me a lift," said Tony. "I'll just about get to the shop before it shuts—I forgot to ask my wife to get me some tobacco."

"Gladly—hop in," said Foster.

Tony climbed in carefully, and Foster reflected on the poor taste of his invitation; it did not appear to affect Tony, however. It was only half a mile to the village, and when they reached it the sun was shining on the pond and the green, and made gold of the thatched roofs. On the green, still bright from the recent rains, two women were standing by three little girls who were calling the ducks, now swimming sedately in the middle of the pond. One of the women was Gillian. A little way away from them was a poorly dressed boy, who watched the scene gravely.

"Hallo, there's Archibald Kelly," said Tony, smiling. "It looks as if he's attached himself to my wife. Poor kid! He just doesn't know how to mix with the others. Pretty little woman, isn't she?"

Foster laughed. "That's my wife!"

"Oh!" said Tony.

Obviously the two women had been talking together, and Gillian was startled when she learned who the other was. She had been watching the ducks when Mrs. Foster and the family had arrived and, soon afterwards, Archy had come hurrying to her side. He greeted Tony with grave politeness, and then his mother called him. They all looked round, and all of them tried not to smile, for Mrs. Kelly, looking like a football on wheels, was cycling along the road.

"Archy, you *bad* boy! You *wicked* boy!" She peered across the green, then recognized the adults. "It's Mrs. Abbott!" she exclaimed. "Oh, that's orl right, Mrs. Abbott, I fought 'e was playing wiv' strangers." She beamed. "Come along, Archy."

Archy trotted off, watched curiously by the three girls. Tony, on his way to the shop, looked back and thought what a pleasant scene it made. Foster was talking animatedly to Gillian and his wife, and a burst of laughter followed Tony into the shop. Never again would he look on policemen as rather stiff-necked, regulation-bound individuals who only unbent in the quiet of their own homes. His first good impression of Foster increased, and he was attracted by his tiny, vivacious wife.

He bought his tobacco, and rejoined the group. The Fosters drove off, and Tony and Gillian waved until the car was out of sight, for the three children were pressing against the rear window, all trying to wave.

"There's nothing sinister about them," said Tony.

"No," said Gillian. "I like her." She was frowning, in spite of her words. "Darling, is that man trying to attract your attention?"

She looked towards 'The Angler,' outside which a man was standing with his hand half-raised. At first Tony thought it was someone who knew of the interest he was taking in the cricket club— for that news was already all over the village, and there was a notice about a meeting posted outside the inn and the village shop. There was something different about this man, however. He looked as if he were a townsman, dressed in a badly cut blue suit, a shade too bright, and with a cheap trilby at the back of his head. He wore yellow-brown shoes.

"I don't think so," he said. "He's a shifty-looking customer, isn't he?"

"He gives me the creeps," said Gillian.

Halfway to the village they met Maude, and stopped to speak to her. She was dressed in her finery, and confided that she was going to a dance at the village hall. Her round face was glowing, and she did not seem unduly affected by the events at the vicarage; Mrs. Castle, she said, was still asleep. As she went on, Gillian glanced after her—and then she stiffened and put a hand on Tony's arm.

"Darling, that man!"

"What about him?"

"He's following us," said Gillian.

Tony glanced round. The fellow was fifty feet away, walking slowly, and his shoes were creaking.

"Not he!" said Tony. "You're imagining things."

As he spoke, however, the stranger raised a hand and this time there was no doubt that he was beckoning him. Tony waited. Gillian glanced round, and started when she saw one of Foster's policemen standing quite near, certainly within earshot; Tony did not seem worried by the interest of the police, but she did not like it.

The man drew up; his thin features had a furtive look, and when he spoke it was out of the corner of his mouth. He looked up at Tony with a smile that was not far from a leer.

"Reckernise me?" he asked.

"I do not," said Tony, sharply.

"Yer'd better, mister." The man's voice was low-pitched, but penetrating. Gillian could not stop herself from glancing at the policeman, who had come a little nearer and seemed intent on what the stranger was saying.

"What on earth are you talking about?" asked Tony.

"Come orf it, mister," said the little man. "You know me as well's I know you. I wanter word wiv' you?"

"About what?" asked Tony.

"About——" the man took a step nearer and there was a look of great cunning on his face—"about Jerry Lovelace, mister."

"Lovelace?" echoed Tony. "I don't know a man named——"

He stopped abruptly, and caught his breath. Gillian looked at him in surprise, and the policeman drew a little nearer still, while the sharp-faced man gave a titter of a laugh and said:

"I fought yer'd reckernise 'im, mister. Where c'n we 'ave a nice quiet little chat?"

CHAPTER 13

A MAN NAMED LOVELACE

"AND that's all I heard, sir," said the detective-constable who had listened to the conversation on the road from the village. He was sitting in the pleasant lounge of Foster's house, and had a self-important look. "He mentioned the name—a man named Lovelace, Jerry Lovelace. Abbott said he didn't know anyone of that name, and then he caught his breath. He looked as if he could kill the little fellow, sir."

"Aren't you exaggerating?" asked Foster.

"No, sir, I assure you I'm not. He looked real wild, and then he ticked the little man off, sent him off with a flea in his ear all right. I've never known anyone look so surprised, that's a fact. I thought they were going to have a quarrel there and then but the little man was frightened, and I don't blame him, sir. Abbott and his wife walked back to 'Spindles,' and the stranger went to 'The Angler.' I made one or two inquiries at once, sir—or at least, I told Grimes to." ˙

"What did you find out?" asked Foster.

"The little man is named Hibbett," said the policeman, preening himself. "Albert Hibbett, and he's staying at 'The Angler' for the week-end. In the register he's given his address as Clapham, London. I didn't like to go too far, in case you wanted to talk to him yourself, sir. I've told Grimes to keep an eye on him."

"Grimes will need a dozen pairs of eyes if we go on like this," said Foster. "All right, Smith, thanks—you've done very well."

"Anything more I can do, sir?"

"No, I don't think so."

When the man had gone, Foster put in a call to headquarters. He wished more than ever that his favourite sergeant was in Milton; Sharp would be off duty for a few days, and was no great loss, but anyone else might be worse. They were all good, sound fellows, and Foster wondered if he were doing them an injustice as he waited

100

for the operator to answer. Mentally, he went through the names of the men on duty, one of whom would have to be sent to 'The Angler' to keep an eye on the stranger who had expected to get a rise out of Tony Abbott and had certainly not failed.

He was still undecided when the operator said:

"Milshire Police Headquarters."

"This is Chief Inspector Foster," said Foster, and made a last-minute decision. "Put me through to Sergeant Guy."

"Sorry, sir, he's just gone out—there's been an accident in the High Street. Sergeant Buckingham's just come in, sir, will he do?"

"Buckingham!" exclaimed Foster. "Isn't he off duty until Monday?"

"Well, he's here, sir. Shall I put you through?"

"Yes, please," said Foster.

He was greatly cheered, for Buckingham was the man he was so anxious to have with him. The sergeant was a Milshire man who had gained rapid promotion and was ear-marked for the next Inspectorship; he would probably get it if Garth were transferred to one of the coast towns.

Laura came downstairs, and when she saw him, she said:

"Found a golden sovereign, darling?"

"Buck's back," said Foster. "I—hallo, Buckingham? What are you doing back already?"

"I heard what was up, sir," said Buckingham, who sounded eager, "and I thought you might find me useful, so I came straight back. Can I do anything?"

"You can! Come round and see me, will you?"

Buckingham stayed to supper, during which 'shop' was the only topic of conversation. By the time he left for Bray, Buckingham was fully acquainted with the facts of the case; those which were more pertinent but a little obscure he had written down, to study during the evening. He was to watch Albert Hibbett, and Foster had already telephoned for accommodation for him. Hibbett would have recognized the man who had just reported; Buckingham was unknown to everyone at 'Spindles' as well as Hibbett. Foster, still cheerful, thought that it might mark a stage in the investigations; Buckingham would be a reliable assistant and was perhaps the only sergeant on the local force who would not be overawed by the fame of Superintendent Folly.

A little after eleven o'clock, when Laura was upstairs getting ready for bed and he was looking through a magazine, the telephone rang. He heard Laura exclaim in annoyance; late calls often meant that he would have to go out during the night. He was feeling pleasantly tired and hoped that this one was a report; then he heard P.C. Grimes's voice.

"Grimes reporting, sir," said the constable. "A message from Sergeant Buckingham, sir."

"Yes," said Foster.

"The man Hibbett has gone up to 'Spindles,' sir, and is prowling round. Sergeant Buckingham has gone after him. He thought you would like to know, sir.''

"Yes," said Foster. "Yes, thanks. Does your wife make good cocoa, Grimes?''

"*Cocoa*, sir?'' For once Grimes was startled. "Very good, sir, yes.''

"Then ask her to be a good soul and to have a cup ready for me,'' said Foster. "I'll be at your house in half an hour.''

.   .   .   .   .   .

The encounter with the furtive little man had been upsetting for both Gillian and Tony. There was something about the man which had troubled Gillian from the time she caught sight of him, and Tony had not improved matters by the way he had behaved. What was worse, he had said nothing to her about it, but she had seen his face go pale and his eyes harden—as happened sometimes when he was furiously angry. These moods of intense anger were worrying in themselves; Snub Savory had told her that Tony admitted how badly they affected him, and she could see that he was fighting to keep his composure. She did not worry him with questions, however, but the rest of the walk home, and the first half-hour in 'Spindles,' were uncomfortable. The only relief was that neither Anne nor Julius was downstairs. Now and again there was a furious burst of sound from the piano, the same tune over and over again, with slight variations; Julius was obviously in the throes of composition. At such times Anne was always at hand with suggestions which her brother often used but rarely acknowledged.

They had supper together. Anne came down for some sandwiches, and then went upstairs. Tony lit his pipe, stood up, and said:

"Let's go to the study, Gill.''

"If you want to work, I'll wash up, and——''

"I want to talk,'' said Tony. "We can lock ourselves in there, if needs be, without arousing comment.'' He rested a hand on her arm, and, in better spirits, she went with him. He settled down at his desk and she in the hide armchair, and then he smiled.

"That little customer gave me a shock.''

"I know," said Gillian.

"I don't ever remember seeing him before," said Tony, "and for the moment I'd forgotten that Lovelace ever existed. There was some talk a few years ago, that he had been sent to a German concentration camp—he was in Germany before war broke out, and I think they suspected him of spying. And well they might! He was one of the nastiest pieces of work you're ever likely to meet.'' He seemed to be talking to himself as much as to Gillian, and his voice was low-pitched. "I liked him once—in fact we were good friends, and he handled some of my work for me before I met Snub. He wasn't an agent, but a music publisher with contacts all over the place, and he wasn't a bad judge of books as well as music.''

Gillian did not interrupt.

"As a matter of fact he published some of Julius's early work," went on Tony. "That was on my recommendation, although I often wished I hadn't let myself do it. It's hard to believe that I knew Julius before I knew you, isn't it? I've known him for ten years, and he's almost a stranger!"

Gillian said nothing.

"Well, as I say, Lovelace handled some of my articles and stories," said Tony, "and he placed several of them in England. It wasn't until I happened to pick up an American magazine and see one of my stories, under a different name, that I began to think he might be a bit of a rogue. I taxed him with it. He tried to pretend that someone in the States had been pirating the stories, but——"

"Pirating?" asked Gillian.

"Call it selling for profit without the author's permission or knowledge," said Tony, rather absently. "I made some inquiries, and it proved that Lovelace had been doing the same thing with the work of other writers. Goodness knows why, for he had a decent income from his legitimate business and a host of contacts. I suppose there are some people who can't keep straight." He was silent for a while, and Gillian kept quite still, watching his face and seeing the shadows in his eyes. The recollections caused him pain, and she did not think it was because Lovelace had been found out. He sighed, and straightened up, then went on more briskly. "I was young, you know. I hadn't much money. The proceeds from those American sales would have made a world of difference to me. I suppose, in all, he robbed me that way of three hundred pounds over a period of eighteen months or so. Like a fool I went to see him at a time when the story was being spread by everyone who had suffered. He wasn't in a mood to apologize—he knew that he would either be boycotted and cold-shouldered altogether, or else that some of the more angry victims or perhaps one or two people with the interests of the business at heart, would prosecute. Do you know what that unpleasant fellow outside reminded me about?"

"No," said Gillian, to fill the gap.

Tony said: "He reminded me of something I have almost forgotten. These damnable outbursts of temper. It came back vividly as he stood there. I remember going into Lovelace's office, in a grim, determined mood, intent on making him pay me for the stories he had sold. He sneered at me. I flew at him."

Tony stopped again.

The room was very quiet. Tony's face was set, and his eyes were so narrowed that Gillian could not see their expression, but she understood the mental torment which he was undergoing. These paroxysms had not been started by the crash, but had grown worse, perhaps been reborn, because of it.

Suddenly the quiet was broken by an outburst on the piano; it did not sound loud in the room, but it broke the spell, and Tony sat up more briskly.

"Well, that's that part finished," he said. "I haven't talked

much to you about it, but I fancy you had a word with Snub."
He smiled. "Quite rightly, darling. I'm glad you did. To complete
the story, I can remember from boyhood having a temper which
all my relatives said would lead me into serious trouble. My father
taught me to check it. He was a lovable man," added Tony, with
a reminiscent smile. "My mother and the others were inclined to
answer temper with temper, but not dad. He reasoned with me,
persuaded me to stand quite still and not move whenever anything
happened to upset me, and after a while I was able to control not
only paroxysms of violence—I would fling my toys or food all over
the place at one time—but also the temper itself. By the time
I went away to school I was fairly normal, and I'd forgotten the
evil urge when I started to write. The first outburst came that day
in Lovelace's office. It might have been serious, for I think I would
have strangled the man. One of his secretaries, a badly frightened
girl, hit me over the head with a ruler, and I've never stopped being
grateful to her. Then, while I was recovering and Lovelace was
getting up—oh, I had him on the floor—in came a policeman."
Gillian gasped.
"A plain-clothes man, of course, an elderly, rather acid-tongued
fellow," said Tony. "He saw that there had been trouble and
probably heard the shouting, but he did not ask me any questions,
and I doubt whether he got much out of Lovelace. He had come
to see Lovelace about complaints that other people had lodged
against him. Eventually the matter was dropped, although there
was talk of action, and of course Lovelace faded out of music
publishing and agency work. He went to Germany and, as I said,
there were rumours that he had been interned as a spy."
"You haven't seen him since?" asked Gillian.
"No. I was so ashamed of the way I'd behaved that I would
play no part in the plans to prosecute him," said Tony. "In fact
I don't think more than half-a-dozen people knew that I had been
one of those to suffer."
Gillian said: "Tony, did Julius lose anything?"
She spoke tensely, and the meaning of her words was clear.
Tony answered her quietly.
"I am quite sure that he did not. Although Lovelace went out
of business, they were good friends. I think that Julius was one
of the few people who believed in Lovelace. I never heard him
say a word against him, and he often defended him in my hearing.
I kept quiet, of course. I didn't see that the man could do him
any harm, and I was determined not to take any further part."
"I'm glad," said Gillian. "Just for a moment——"
Tony laughed.
"You're getting as bad as Julius himself! I suppose it's crossed
your mind that the dead man might be Lovelace?"
"Yes. Hasn't it crossed yours?"
"I suppose it has," admitted Tony, "but I think that would be
stretching coincidence too far. Let's forget it," he went on. "I've
got it out of my system, thanks to you. I don't think Julius will

come down again to-night, so let's spread ourselves in the lounge, shall we? There's a Beethoven concert, I think—or have we just missed it?''

"It's started," said Gillian, "but we'll hear most of it."

The concert finished before the nine o'clock news. Gillian went to make some coffee, Tony listened to the news, then switched off and picked up a book. He intended to get to bed early, but he lost himself in the book, and Gillian was content to knit and read. It was nearly eleven before Tony yawned and put the book down.

"Hallo, who's going to wear navy blue?" he demanded.

Gillian smiled. "It's a jumper for Archy—I suppose I should say a jersey. The poor little chap is short of clothes, and I think Mrs. Kelly spends most of her spare time in the bar at Riversmeet. It's curious about her and Archy, isn't it? I can't imagine him being her son."

"Let's not get involved in other mysteries," said Tony. "And let's get to bed. All is silent upstairs, Julius is probably prostrate and Anne smoothing his fevered brow!"

He went along to the bathroom and Gillian to the bedroom. As he squeezed toothpaste on to his brush, with the door ajar, he was thinking of the way she had listened to him, without interruption. She had been able to understand his feelings more clearly than anyone else could have done, with the possible exception of Snub Savory.

He was wrong about Julius; the piano started off again, and he thought ruefully that they might be in for an all-night session.

Then he heard a scream.

It came in a lull in the music, and he heard it quite clearly, then thought he heard his name called. He dropped the brush and rushed out of the room towards the bedroom, with the froth from the toothpaste at his lips. He heard a thud. Then the piano went off into wild movement, drowning the sounds on this floor, but he saw shadows on the wall, shadows of struggling people. Next, he heard *Gillian* gasp his name.

He rushed into the room.

Gillian was standing near the wardrobe, struggling with the little man whom they had met outside. The fellow had one hand over her mouth, and with the other he gripped her wrists. There was a livid look on the foxy face, and fear in the little eyes.

Tony said nothing, but leapt at him.

The man saw him coming and released Gillian, uttering a high-pitched scream and putting up his hands, for there seemed madness in Tony's eyes—and froth from the toothpaste at his lips. Tony struck the fellow on the side of the head and sent him reeling against the wardrobe. Gillian staggered away. Tony reached the man again and put his hands about his throat and began to throttle him. The face in front of his eyes seemed to be going round and round, and changing colour. He saw the man's tongue pushing between his lips. He heard a shout, and then felt something beating at his head and shoulders, but he did not let go. He felt his thumbs embedded in the man's neck . . .

"Tony!" screamed Gillian. "Tony! Tony! Tony!"

CHAPTER 14

ATTEMPTED MURDER

SERGEANT BUCKINGHAM first heard the screaming as he was examining a downstairs window and found that it was unlatched. He lost no time, but opened the window and climbed in. He found himself in a small cloakroom, which led into the hall. The piano was playing, but he thought he heard shouts and hurrying footsteps. He hurried upstairs, and as he turned into the main passage he heard a woman scream:

"Tony! Tony!"

A little way along a door was open, and light streamed into the passage. Buckingham raced along, and when he reached the room he saw a woman standing over a man and beating at his head and shoulders with her clenched fists. The man had his hands about Hibbett's neck; Hibbett's face was mottled, his tongue was protruding and his eyes were starting from his head; he was obviously unconscious.

Buckingham thrust Gillian on one side, and drove his fist into Tony's face. The blow was so powerful that Tony lost his footing and released his grip. As he fell, Buckingham saw his white face and glittering eyes, and the froth at his lips. The sergeant prepared for a renewal of the attack, but Tony leaned against the wall and stared at him, the glitter fading from his eyes.

Buckingham snapped: "Get hot-water bottles, quickly."

He lifted Hibbett to one of the twin beds, then began to apply artificial respiration, watching Tony all the time, not certain that the man would not fly at him. No one else came in. After a few minutes Buckingham felt that the danger from Tony was past, and concentrated on Hibbett. The man's tongue was no longer protruding, but his eyes were very prominent.

After ten minutes, Buckingham, who was perspiring freely, stopped for a moment.

"All right, I'll take over," said Tony.

"You——" began Buckingham.

"Don't be a fool," said Tony, sharply. "I won't hurt him."

Buckingham let him begin to work, and was soon satisfied that he was accomplished in the art of applying artificial respiration. He worked steadily, and by the time Gillian returned to the room Hibbett was breathing noisily. Buckingham took off the man's shoes, and when Tony stopped work, bundled him into the bed, piled blankets on him, and inserted the hot-water bottles.

"He'll be all right," he said. "A lucky thing for you." He stared at Tony.

"Yes," said Tony, crisply. "Who are you and what are you doing here?"

Buckingham showed his card, and repeated: "It was certainly a lucky thing for you. I was downstairs and heard the shouting, so I broke in."

"I see," said Tony. "Thanks." He brushed his hair from his forehead and smiled wanly at his wife. "Can you make some coffee, Gill?"

"Yes," she said, and hurried out. She suspected that he wanted a few minutes alone with the policeman, and it was not a time to insist on being present.

Hibbett was breathing wheezily, but was in no danger. His face was a purplish red, and his lips were open. Buckingham looked from him to Tony, waiting for him to speak; Tony kept silent, and offered cigarettes.

"No, thank you," said Buckingham. He was a tall, well-built man, with attractive curly hair, a snub nose and very full lips—lips which were almost negroid, and which even in his most serious moments curved as if about to break into a smile. "Are you Mr. Abbott?"

"Yes."

"What happened?"

"I was in the bathroom and I heard my wife cry out," said Tony. "I hurried here and saw this man trying to prevent her from calling for help. I flew at him."

"You flew at him all right," said Buckingham. "You very nearly killed him. Who is he?"

"I don't know him."

"You don't *know* him!" echoed Buckingham, sceptically.

"To the best of my knowledge I have never seen him before to-night," said Tony. "He stopped me in the road and said that he knew me, and asked for an interview. I disliked his manner and I told him to clear off. That's all I can tell you about him."

"I see," said Buckingham. He took out his cigarette-case, and was dismayed to find it empty. Tony offered his again. "I shouldn't smoke on duty," said Buckingham, but he accepted a cigarette and a light. "Thank you." He looked curiously at Tony, who now seemed calm and self-possessed; it was difficult to believe he was the same man who had been so intent on throttling Hibbett. "I must telephone headquarters," he said.

"I suppose so. The telephone is in the hall."

"I think I'll get someone to telephone for me," said Buckingham. "Call Grimes, the local policeman, please. Ask him to telephone Chief Inspector Foster and request him to come here, and then ask Grimes to come to this room."

"I won't do that fellow any more harm," said Tony. "I've done enough for one night, I think. You'll be quite safe to go yourself."

"I'd rather not chance it," said Buckingham.

Tony shrugged, and went downstairs.

He was surprised to hear Foster's voice when he rang the local policeman's cottage. He passed on the message, and Foster made no comment but said that he would come at once. Gillian was coming out of the kitchen with a tray of coffee on which were three cups.

"You'd better make it four," said Tony. "Foster is on his way." He went with her into the kitchen, but there was a restraint between them, and he could not break it. Neither of them spoke until they were halfway up the stairs, and then Gillian said:

"Tony, I——"

"It's all right, my sweet," said Tony, gripping her arm. "I know what you're feeling and I know what a fool I was, but believe me I saw red in real earnest when I saw the little swine manhandling you. Don't worry, it will work out all right. If this policeman fellow thinks we are in a huddle, he will jump to conclusions."

"I suppose so," said Gillian. "You'd better wash your face, Tony. You've got some toothpaste on your lips."

"Have I?" asked Tony.

When he got to the bathroom he saw the toothbrush on the floor, and the coating of dried paste on his lips. It did not occur to him that he had looked like a maniac as he rushed into the bedroom, but he washed quickly and went back to Buckingham. The piano was being banged upstairs, and now and again Julius started to sing. Apparently he and Anne knew nothing of the incident.

As he turned into the bedroom there was a ring at the front door bell.

"I'll go," he said.

He admitted Foster and Grimes, who stood in the hall trying to efface himself while Foster looked at Tony inquiringly.

"As you've gathered, we have had a spot of bother," said Tony. "I'm afraid that your man upstairs thinks it is attempted murder."

"By whom and on whom?" asked Foster.

"By me. On a man whom I've never seen before."

"Oh," said Foster. He did not entirely succeed in hiding his surprise. "Was it attempted murder?" he asked, rather heavily.

"No. The man was attacking my wife. I attacked him. I might well have killed him," Tony went on. "I don't think I would have let go of him if your man hadn't been on the spot."

"Oh," said Foster again. "Where is he now?"

"Upstairs," said Tony.

Foster found it strange to walk beside this calm, self-possessed man, who spoke almost with humour of the unusual situation. Tony did not speak again, and they entered the bedroom, where Gillian was pouring out coffee. She too seemed composed. Buckingham was stubbing out a cigarette on a table by the bed where Hibbett lay.

"Will you have some coffee?" asked Gillian.

"No thanks," said Foster. "I've just had some cocoa." The sight of Buckingham was reassuring; he would get a good report. He called Grimes, who had followed him as far as the passage, and made arrangements quickly. Hibbett obviously did not need a doctor, so he left Grimes with the man and led the others out. On Tony's suggestion they went to the study. Buckingham sat at the desk with a pencil and notebook, and Foster asked Gillian for her story. She told it clearly: She had gone into the bedroom and opened the wardrobe door to get a hanger for her dress. The little man had been inside, and when she screamed, he jumped at her. She pointed to the red marks under her chin, where the man's fingers had gripped her. There was a small tear on the shoulder of her dress, where a button had pulled out, and it was obvious that there had been a struggle of some kind. Foster appeared to accept her story at its face value, and asked Tony for his. Tony told it as clearly as his wife had done hers, but with more restraint.

Foster said: "Having dragged the man off your wife, Mr. Abbott, why didn't you call enough?"

"I wasn't quite myself," said Tony.

"You remember trying to throttle him?"

"Of course."

"You were beside yourself with anger—is that it?"

"Yes."

"How long did this fit of rage last?" asked Foster.

"Not very long after your man hit me." Tony rubbed his chin, and looked at Buckingham with a smile. "I've never welcomed being punched like that before!"

"When did you realize that it was a good thing for you?" asked Foster, dryly.

"Very soon after it happened," said Tony. "Inspector, I don't want to evade your questions. I want to tell you the truth as simply as I can. You know what caused me to attack the man. I can only tell you that once I started to grip his throat, I had no thought except to make a job of it. It would be folly to pretend otherwise. If your man hadn't interfered, I think I would have killed him."

"I see," said Foster. Buckingham was writing quickly, and Foster looked at Tony for a few seconds to give his man time to get everything down. Then: "Have you ever seen Hibbett before?"

"Hibbett?" asked Tony. "Is that his name?"

"It's the name he has given here," said Foster. "Do you know him?"

"No."

"Earlier this evening, I was told of an encounter you had with him in the road outside here," said Foster. "I had a detailed report. The man said that you knew him as well as he knew you. At the time you appeared to lose your temper with him, and he went off. That is not corroborative evidence for your present statement, Mr. Abbott."

"I can't help that," said Tony. "I'm telling you the truth."

"I see. When Hibbett spoke to you, he mentioned the name of a man—and it was that other name which appeared to make you lose your temper," said Foster. "The name was Lovelace. Who is this Lovelace?"

"A man whom I once knew in business."

"Yet you told Hibbett that you knew no such man."

"It is six or seven years since I had dealings with Lovelace," said Tony. "I had almost forgotten the man's existence—and it isn't unusual to be unable to call to mind even a once familiar name, after a lapse of time."

"I see," said Foster. "What were your relations with Lovelace?"

"I don't see what that has to do with it," said Tony.

"It might have a great deal. What were your relations with Lovelace, Mr. Abbott?"

"Unfriendly," said Tony.

"Why?"

Gillian said: "Tony, need you answer questions like this?"

Foster could have smacked her. He thought that Abbott was on the point of making a full statement, but now he saw the way the man's expression altered, as if all he had needed was a little moral support. Tony looked at his wife with a grateful smile, and then back at Foster, shaking his head.

"I don't think I need," he said. "I will gladly tell you about my relations with Lovelace if you can show me that they are relevant to the point at issue," he said. "At the moment I imagine you are more interested in my relations, which are non-existent, with the man you say is Hibbett."

Foster managed to hide his vexation as he said:

"Very well, Mr. Abbott, but at all times frankness with the police is advisable. Have you heard the name Hibbett before?"

"Not to my knowledge."

"It doesn't strike a chord in your memory, as Lovelace did?"

"No."

"You have had a good opportunity of seeing the man at close quarters, now. Are you sure that his face is unfamiliar?"

"Quite sure!"

"I see." Foster turned to Gillian. "Do you know Hibbett?"

"Of course not," said Gillian. "I'd never seen him until to-night, when I thought he was trying to attract Tony's attention."

"Thank you," said Foster.

He was inclined to believe most of the story, but he saw the flaws in it. It was as well that someone else would be able to question them the next day, for he might be subconsciously biased in their favour. The stories appeared to be detailed, but there might be collusion. The torn dress and the red mark under Gillian's chin might have been caused when she had tried to drag her husband from Hibbett. There was more satisfaction in the fact that he had now good reason to pursue his inquiries inside the house; a charge of attempted murder might not be necessary, but it was a good opportunity to gain admission whenever he wanted to. He wished that the attack had concerned Stafford, and that thought made him ask:

"Where is Mr. Stafford?"

"Upstairs in the studio," said Tony, "and Miss Stafford is with him there."

"Isn't it strange that they heard nothing?"

"No," said Tony. "Julius is composing, and the noise of the piano would probably drown any sound from the floor below. Haven't you heard him?" he added.

"Yes," said Foster, with a smile. "I suppose that is possible, but I would like a word with him."

"Must you interrupt him now?" asked Gillian.

"Yes," said Foster, crisply. He had not yet forgiven her, although now he thought that if there were anything which they wanted to hold back, it might be a good thing for them to do so; he believed that they knew Hibbett, and were lying in that respect. If it could be proved, he would be able to exert greater pressure on them. A complete and straightforward story, which could be checked and corroborated, was not exactly what he wanted at this juncture. "Buckingham, go up for Mr. and Miss Stafford, please," he said.

"Let me go," said Gillian. "If a stranger goes, Julius might lose his temper, and——" she broke off, at the rather tense smile on Foster's face. "Well, that wouldn't be unreasonable," she snapped. "Nothing is more exasperating than to be interrupted when you are working, especially such work as his!"

"I think we shall have to risk another show of temper," said Foster, dryly, "but I will draw it on my own head. You stay here, please."

Tony shrugged, Gillian looked angry, and Foster went upstairs briskly. The piano was silent. When he reached the second floor, which was new to him, he saw a closed door, the only one on the landing; and he thought he heard voices. He listened outside for a moment, but could not distinguish the words. Without tapping, he opened the door.

He stood on the threshold, astonished.

There was a grand piano in the centre of the room, and the top was littered with blank music sheets; others littered the floor. Some of those had been written on, some had been screwed up, some torn into several pieces. On the piano was a bottle of whisky and a glass, which were standing on some brown paper. There were music racks all round the room, and in one corner was a settee.

Julius Stafford was lying on the settee, with his head propped up on cushions. He was flushed, and his eyes were closed. Anne Stafford was sitting on a pouffe by his side, bathing his forehead. She had heard the door open, and looked round.

"Oh!" she gasped.

She went so white and stood up so abruptly that Foster was astonished, and his surprise at the scene took the edge off his sense of perception.

111

"You—you quite startled me," said Anne, with a catch in her voice. "What on earth are you doing here at this time of night?"

"I am on official business," said Foster.

There was something in the woman's manner which held his interest; she was not only surprised, she was frightened. She stood rigid, with her hands clenched, staring at him fixedly. Her eyes were wide open and bright. Foster felt instinctively that if he could find the right question he might start a landslide, but he could not imagine what that question could be.

Then Julius opened his eyes.

Foster shifted his gaze towards the composer. Julius wore yellow corduroys and a pink shirt, open at the neck. His hair was ruffled and damp at the front and sides, and his forehead also looked damp. There was a smell of eau-de-Cologne in the room, with a faint odour of whisky.

"What the devil do *you* want?" demanded Julius, sitting up with a start. "My hat, have we got to be plagued with policemen day *and* night?" He swung his legs from the settee, pushed Anne aside, and advanced threateningly, looking an odd mixture of boyishness and toughness. "Well, what d'you want?" he shouted.

"There will be no advantage in losing your temper," said Foster, coldly. The feeling that if he asked the right question he would create consternation in these two people grew stronger, and he sought desperately for one. If he flung one of the names at them—'Do you know Hibbett?' or 'Do you know Lovelace?' it might work, but there was no time to lose.

"What do you know of Albert Hibbett?" he demanded.

He knew almost as soon as the name was out of his mouth that he had picked a loser. Anne relaxed, and Julius stared at him, wide-eyed.

"Never heard of the fellow. Who is he?" Julius still sounded aggressive.

"He is a friend of——" began Foster.

He was about to say 'Lovelace,' in the hope that it would start something, but he was interrupted by a shout from downstairs. This time it was Grimes, and there was something in the man's voice which sounded an alarm. Foster hurried to the landing and saw Grimes standing in the middle of the landing below, dishevelled and wild-eyed.

"Sir! Sir!" cried Grimes. "Inspector——"

"What is it?" called Foster, hurrying down the stairs.

"What's the matter up there?" boomed Buckingham, from the hall.

Grimes gasped: "He's got away, sir. Hibbett. He—I——"

"*Where?*" roared Buckingham. "Which way did he go?"

"Out of the window," said Grimes. "He——"

"After him!" roared Buckingham.

Foster saw his sergeant rush to the front door, leaving it wide open. He disappeared round the side of the house. Grimes was almost distraught, and Foster did not harass the man, but went into the bedroom. The window was wide open and the curtains were blowing inwards. On the floor near the wall was a hot-water bottle, with water leaking from it. The bedclothes were off the bed, and Grimes's helmet lay on its side near the hot-water bottle.

"It's too late!" wailed Grimes.

Foster hesitated for a moment. He saw Tony hurry in Buckingham's wake, and decided to see whether he could get out of the window to the ground without much trouble. It was just possible that he would be able to see the man from the window and guide the others to him. It was moonlight, but clouds were scudding across the sky, and it was not bright. There were no lights from the vicarage, but he could see the yellow glow from the front door of 'Spindles.' Along the drive a man, presumably Buckingham, was moving behind an electric torch. Almost immediately beneath the window was Tony, with another torch.

"What the devil's happening here to-night?" roared Julius, and Foster turned and saw the man striding into the room. His sister was passing the door on her way downstairs.

"I'll explain later," said Foster.

"You'll explain *now*!" snapped Julius.

"Oh, don't be a fool!" said Foster, and pushed past him.

Poor Grimes was halfway down the stairs, but Foster caught up with the man, who was almost in tears. Foster gave his arm a friendly squeeze.

"Don't let this upset you, Grimes. What happened?"

"He—he came round, sir," said Grimes, trying to steady his voice, "and complained that his foot was hurting. I—I thought he looked so ill that there wasn't any danger. I didn't give anything else a thought. I pushed the clothes back at the foot of the bed, so as to keep the rest of him warm, and he poked his foot into my eye. Then he hit me with the hot-water bottle, sir—it caught me on the back of the head and nearly knocked me out. Proper dazed for a minute, I was. When I saw him going out of the window I shouted, but he threw a pillow at me." Grimes wiped the perspiration from his face. "I can't tell you *how* sorry I am, sir."

"I'm sure you are," said Foster. "Do you feel well enough to have a look round for him?"

"I'm all right now," said Grimes, "but I don't think we'll see *him* again to-night."

"I'll put a general call out for him," said Foster.

While he telephoned headquarters, he could see Gillian, Anne and Julius talking in the study. Gillian was doing most of the talking. He thought that the others were genuinely surprised, and after that scene in the studio he saw nothing remarkable in that. They had been more like lovers; now he came to think of it, Anne Stafford had a rather motherly way with the man, like some wives with their husbands.

"I suppose they *are* brother and sister," mused Foster.

113

He gave instructions for a general call to be put out for Hibbett, and when he finished telephoning, went towards the study.

Julius was asking: "What was the little tyke like?"

Gillian gave a fair description of Hibbett. Foster would have interrupted then, but he saw Julius start, as if he had realized something unpleasant. Julius and Anne shot quick glances at each other, and then made an obvious effort to appear unperturbed. Once again Foster felt that if he could put the right question, he would be able to learn a great deal. They were both worked up, but a few hours' rest would probably enable them to regain their nerve. He went forward determinedly, calling from the passage:

"Oh, Stafford. Do you know a man named Lovelace?"

"Lovelace?" asked Julius, in a steady voice.

"*Love*lace?" echoed Anne; her voice was not quite so steady, but there was nothing to go on.

"Do you?" asked Foster, sharply.

"I used to know a Jerry Lovelace," said Julius, with the same studied calm. "We were very good friends, Foster. He did a lot of business for me. Useful fellow. Why?"

"Hibbett—the man who has escaped—mentioned the name."

"Well, fancy that," said Julius, with a sneer.

'The day will come when you'll change your tone, my man,' Foster thought, but he was aware of the weakness of his position and he did not pursue that line of inquiry. Buckingham and Tony returned from their fruitless search, but Grimes remained outside for some time. Before he returned there was another visitor—Castle, wrapped in a dressing-gown and looking even more gaunt than usual, with his hair on end and his eyes dulled with sleep. He came from the gap in the hedge, and the first the others heard of him was a challenge from Grimes. Then the vicar entered the hall.

"I heard movements and wondered if I could be any help," he said, looking curiously about him.

"No, we're all right," said Tony. "I do hope that we haven't disturbed Mrs. Castle."

"She's not come round yet," said Castle. He looked unhappy, and was obviously trying to restrain his curiosity. It got the better of him, however, and he asked: "Has there been some trouble?"

" 'Spindles' has been burgled," said Foster, quickly.

"Oh! I hope you've not lost anything?" Castle looked at Tony and Gillian. "I thought those burglaries were finished," he added, uncomfortably. "Perhaps you'll be able to catch the fellow now, Inspector."

"I'll certainly try," said Foster.

Tony and Gillian felt grateful for his bland answer to Castle's question. Tony walked back with the vicar, and when he returned Foster, Buckingham and Grimes were in the hall together. He suspected that he had been given an opportunity to escape. Gillian was sitting in his study, with Anne, and Julius had gone upstairs.

Tony looked at the three policemen with a rueful smile.

"Well, what are you going to do with me?" he inquired.

"Nothing at the moment," said Foster. "I hope you won't go from here during the night or until further notice, Mr. Abbott. We shall have to make further inquiries, of course. On the strength of your statement, I don't see any reason for taking immediate action."

"That's considerate of you," said Tony.

"I hope you appreciate it," said Foster.

He left with the others. Tony watched them walk along the drive, and then closed and bolted the door. He stood in the hall alone, with a hand at his forehead and a tormented expression in his eyes. The relief had come and gone; now he recalled that paroxysm, the mad fury in which he had nearly choked the life out of Hibbett. The thought of what he might do in these fits of rage was frightening in itself. He had no inclination to plead extenuating circumstances; he should never have gone so far—he could easily have dealt with Hibbett, who was a puny creature.

Now and again he recalled Julius's talk with Anne; if the police thought along these lines, he might be accused of the murder of the unknown man. Did the fact that Foster had harped on Lovelace mean that the body had been identified?

Anne came out of the study.

"Good-night, Tony," she said. "Don't worry too much."

"I'm all right," mumbled Tony.

He felt exhausted when he got upstairs. Gillian was subdued, and that was not surprising. She made the bed and took the hot-water bottle to the bathroom, for it was leaking badly. When she returned he was in bed, sitting up on his pillows and looking pale and forlorn.

"I'm beginning to wonder whether I'm sane," he said, in a harsh voice. "Gill——"

"My sweet, don't torment yourself," said Gillian, in distress. "It's been a horrible night, but no one could blame you for what you did. We ought to be thankful that it's no worse."

"Yes," said Tony, and after a moment's silence, he repeated: "Yes. I wonder what the devil Hibbett wanted? I don't know of such a man in connection with Lovelace, and I think I would have remembered by now if I'd ever seen him before. What on earth could he want with me?" he added, helplessly.

It was the question in his mind when at last he fell asleep.

CHAPTER 15

SUPERINTENDENT FOLLY

THE London train was due in at half-past one. Foster and Buckingham waited on the platform from five-and-twenty past, and Foster began to fidget when the train was late. The porter told him it would not be long, and he smoked another cigarette, saying nothing; there was so little to say.

There was no news of Hibbett, although all the county police had been warned, and even further afield a watch was being kept for the man. Foster had telephoned Scotland Yard the previous night, giving a description of him, and also mentioned Lovelace. He did not doubt that Folly would be fully acquainted with the latest details.

Buckingham and Grimes had been relieved just after dawn; nothing had happened at 'Spindles,' and before he left for the station, Foster had been told that all four residents had been seen during the morning. He had made a full report to Harrington, who had said little and was obviously sorry that the case had taken a turn for the worse just before Folly's arrival; had they detained Hibbett, there would have been a very different complexion on the whole business.

A porter passed and touched his cap.

"It won't be a few minutes now, sir, it's past the junction."

"Thanks," said Foster. He tossed away his half-smoked cigarette, and grimaced at Buckingham. "We're a fine pair to be meeting a man like Folly," he said. "You look half-asleep, and I feel washed-out. He'll rate us as a couple of country bumpkins right enough."

"Then we'll teach him better," said Buckingham.

Foster laughed. "That's the spirit! Ah, here's the train."

It came snorting into the station, and porters crowded the edge of the platform. Milton was a junction for several seaside resorts, and the station was larger than the size of the town warranted. Foster scanned the ranks of the descending passengers eagerly, especially those who came out of the first-class carriages. He had seen a newspaper photograph of Folly, and was led to expect a big man. According to Anderson, Trevelyan, the surgeon, was tall and thin.

When most of the passengers were on the platform and the rush for taxis began, and when Foster was beginning to think that Folly had missed the train, a tall, thin man came out of a first-class carriage. He was carrying a brief-case, and laughing. Then his companion appeared, and squeezed himself through the doorway. It was no easy task, for he was abnormally fat, and as tall as the man whom Foster took to be Trevelyan.

As he stood on the platform, Superintendent Folly opened his mouth in a wide yawn, and the sun, shining through the glass roof, glinted on gold teeth. Belatedly Folly covered his mouth, while Trevelyan looked round for a porter. One hurried up, and Foster approached slowly, anxious to size up the man from Scotland Yard. Buckingham was staring wide-eyed, as if he could not believe that this could be the legendary Superintendent.

Folly yawned again, and the sound could be heard ten yards away. Although he was so fat, his well-cut suit made him look well-groomed and compact. He was wearing a black Homburg hat, which made his head look massive. His heavy jowl half-covered his collar and tie. His well-shod feet were absurdly small for so large a man, and created the illusion that a slight push would send him over.

None of those things were so remarkable as his face.

He was not bad looking, although his features were embedded in flesh. He was tanned a golden brown, had a little mouth which appeared to pout, and a prominent nose. His eyes fascinated Foster, for the lids drooped and he looked half-asleep.

"You said *I* looked tired," whispered Buckingham. "He looks dead beat! He's yawning again!"

"Come on," said Foster.

A porter was getting the luggage out of the carriage, and as Foster approached the third huge pigskin suit-case with the initials F.F. was piled on the trolley. Beside them, Trevelyan's one small case looked insignificant. As Foster drew up, Folly spoke in a deep, penetrating voice which suited the man perfectly.

"I knew there would be no one to meet us. There never is. All the decent hotels will have finished serving lunch. We shall be faced with police station sandwiches. I know of only one sort of sandwich worse than those obtainable at a railway station. It is obtainable at country police stations."

Foster took the bull by the horns.

"You're wrong on two counts," he said. "I'm here to meet you and I've reserved a table at the best hotel in Milton."

Folly looked at him; the idea that he was tired or that his eyes were sleepy was an illusion. They were very bright and shrewd, penetrating and deceptive. He stared at Foster for an appreciable time, until Foster began to feel uncomfortable; then he smiled. It made him look almost cherubic, and the flash of gold teeth robbed his face of the portentous solemnity which it assumed in repose.

"I am delighted to hear that, Inspector—you are Inspector Foster?" When Foster nodded, he went on: "All that remains to be proved is the quality of the best hotel in Milton. I warn you, I am hungry. I may say I am famished. Sir Alexander Trevelyan is equally hungry. Who is to be the fourth? Colonel Harrington?"

"He wants me to convey his regrets," said Foster, "but he is engaged until this evening. Sergeant Buckingham will be with us."

"Sergeant Buckingham," said Folly. He turned towards Buckingham, who blushed and looked boyish. Folly fixed his gaze on the fair, curly hair, and smiled again. "Good sergeants are the backbone of the police force," he declared. "The only trouble is that when they are really good they are promoted, and then they become members of the detective hierarchy, and forget they are policemen. I wish the word detective had never been invented. Do you know Sir Alexander?"

"Only by reputation," said Foster, faintly.

"Good physicians are ruined when they become pathologists,"

117

declared Folly. "You see here the ruin of one of our most promising physicians." He smiled again. "Trev, this is Chief Inspector Foster and Sergeant Buckingham, and they are men of worth or they would not have thought of my lunch."

"Unless they've heard all your reputation," said Trevelyan.

He was a younger man than Foster had expected, probably not much more than forty. He seemed mildly amused by the Superintendent, and they were obviously old friends. With the luggage trundling ahead of them, they walked along the platform, Folly talking to Buckingham in his deep undertones, Foster with the pathologist. It was so entirely different from what Foster had expected that Trevelyan did all the talking—chiefly to the effect that the surest way to make Folly happy was to look after his inner man.

The luggage was put into the car, and Folly stood looking at it with his head on one side.

"Obviously you do not cater for fat men," he said. "Perhaps I'd better sit on the bonnet."

"I'll walk on," volunteered Buckingham. "There will be room for you in the back then, sir."

Folly regarded him severely.

"That is unkind. If the axle can stand the strain, I can."

"Get in, Freddie," said Trevelyan.

Buckingham gulped, and Foster turned his face away; to hear such a man as Folly called 'Freddie' was almost more than they could bear. A little crowd gathered at a discreet distance, and watched Folly climbing into the car. It was a fourteen horse-power, with a large family body, but there was a moment when it looked as if Folly would be defeated. As he disappeared inside at last, two small boys raised a cheer. Folly glared at them out of the window, and then chuckled.

"I hope you have plenty of room, sergeant," he said as Buckingham climbed in after him.

"I'll manage," said Buckingham.

Foster was light-hearted as he drove to the 'White Horse,' and nothing that happened during the excellent luncheon depressed him. He would get on well with Folly, who was very different from his reputation. Trevelyan was a likeable man, too, and the immediate future promised well. Not once during luncheon did they talk of the case in hand, and Folly drew Buckingham out, obviously trying to judge his mettle; Foster thought he was satisfied, and felt pleased because Folly seemed to assume that he did not need testing. Immediately after lunch, Buckingham left the dining-room, and Folly stared after him.

"Useful man, Foster. Doesn't look a bit like a man with grandiose ideas. Where's he gone?"

"He'll be back in a moment," said Foster. "I can serve some good coffee in my office, or if you'd prefer to come to my house we can talk there—I've all the papers ready."

"Let us sit here for a while," said Folly. "Who wants papers? I am not interested in papers. Show me people. The more people

118

the better. Bad people and good people. Trevelyan will tell you
that my hobby is people. In spite of my long experience, I still
have some faith in human nature. True, it is a remarkable thing.
The most promising and attractive people are often the rogues.
I have never really succeeded in preventing myself from being biased
in favour of a decent fellow. Take Abbott, now.''

Foster stared at him in amazement.

"Do you know Abbott?"

"Not personally. I have made inquiries and talked to people
who do know him. I am shortly to retire," announced Folly.
"This may be my last case. Consequently, like all good policemen,
I am thinking of writing my memoirs. They will be astounding.
Immediately I knew that Abbott, an author, was concerned in this
case, I discovered the name of his agent. I visited this agent to
discuss my memoirs." Not once during this statement did Folly
smile, and his eyes were half hidden by the heavy lids. "In discussing my memoirs, I discussed promising young authors. My
experience does not follow the accepted rule that authors invariably
talk a great deal about themselves. They have no need to. What
their publishers do not say for them, their agents do. I also visited
his publishers, who Savory suggested—Savory is his agent—were
just the people for my as yet non-existent memoirs. They were
enthusiastic about my book, but not particularly so about Abbott's
work. They like Abbott, however; everyone likes Abbott. So,
Abbott is the man to watch.

"Stafford is in a different category," continued Folly. "Few
people have a good word for him. Even those people who publish
his music are unenthusiastic about the man, but they rave about
his music. I don't know an F sharp from an A flat, but I know
that Stafford is considered a remarkable composer. You must
expect eccentricity from a man whose business acquaintances are
foolish enough to encourage him with the idea that he is a genius.
However, even that is better than dealing with a man who *is* a
genius. Do you like Abbott?" he asked, unexpectedly.

"I like what I've seen of him," said Foster.

"And I like what I have heard of him," declared Folly.
"I imagine that our opinions of Stafford also coincide. My
assumption is that Abbott's wife is a pretty, plump, sensible woman
whose loyalty to her husband is unwavering."

"I wouldn't say she was plump," said Foster.

Folly cocked an eyebrow at Trevelyan with a comical gesture.

"Inspector Foster obviously believes in studying the woman to
assess the man. Very sound. Concerning Anne Stafford, Foster.
Do we agree on her, I wonder? A woman with a mission, and the
mission is the preservation and glorification of her brother's so-
called genius, the fostering of all the children born of his labours;
not perverted—don't misunderstand me—not even abnormal, but
fiercely devoted to the man's ability rather than to the man himself,
her self-imposed task to shelter him from storm and trial, a Martha
who rarely thinks of herself. Yes?"

"I think it fits," said Foster, cautiously. "I don't know her well. But how on earth did you——"

Folly held up his hand.

"Do you tell others how you work? Do you allow them to learn the secrets of your success? Certainly not. I, however, do. I am untroubled by the fear that you will copy my methods. No one could do so without inviting disaster. I would not like to tell you how many times I have been severely reprimanded for *not* conforming to the police manual. I should be a sergeant. At heart I am a sergeant. I am only a C.I.D. officer because the fatter I became, the less comfortable it was to walk the streets, and I had to do something about it. What was I saying? Oh, yes, about Anne Stafford. You must know, Foster, that people like Stafford have many friends and more acquaintances, hangers-on many of them, who will gladly talk. The relationship between the Staffords is well known. Anne is an admirable woman. She would probably make an excellent wife *or* mother, but she will almost certainly die holding her brother's hand. I can tell you that she is engaged to a man named Barr, whose parents disapprove. So they should. She is probably thinking of marriage so as to provide her brother with money. Stafford is a spendthrift, always hard up.

"As for how I learned about her that was not at all difficult," Folly continued. "Three times in four years Julius Stafford has been detained for motoring offences—or other trivial offences, I am not sure what—and each time she bailed him out. Each time, I understand, she showed a great concern for him. If she were to be taken away from him for a few months, it would make or break him—and he has been used to leaning on her for so long that it would probably break him." Folly smiled, and he looked beatific. "Now if we could detain her for a week or two—but I am drivelling! You do not want to hear me drivel, but want to solve this case and allow me to take the kudos. I know! It is always the same. The generosity and lack of jealousy on the part of provincial police officers is a glowing tribute to their sense of duty. Because I dislike trading on their good nature, I always try to avoid coming away from London." He laughed. "All right, Foster, all right, I'll be serious. We mustn't take this matter too much to heart, you know. What's gone wrong?"

Foster gulped. "So you've guessed that?"

"Guessed? My dear fellow, it was written all over you. If you had things nicely together, you would have waited for me in the office and received me with terrible formality."

Foster laughed. "That's not true, but something has gone wrong. Perhaps you've seen the reports I telephoned. A man named Hibbett——"

"Not Hibbett. Welch."

Foster gaped, and then said: "I wish someone had warned me about you. You're not safe."

Folly chuckled. "A simple business. Hibbett, as he called himself, is not unknown to us in London. Nor is his *alias* unknown.

He is a confidence trickster, a card-sharper, a very thorough-going rogue. He has been out of prison for two years. and that is probably two years too long. Such a man cannot keep away from crime. He is as the bread-and-butter of a policeman's life, easy to arrest, easy to convict, easy to watch. When his kind is non-existent we shall not need a police force but a system of automatic traffic control, together with a few scientists like Trevelyan here. I was very glad that Hibbett appeared on the scene, because he is known to have visited the Staffords' Chelsea flat.''

''Good Lord!'' exclaimed Foster.

''It is true, and not necessarily surprising. Did I mention that he is not above a little blackmail and certainly not beyond committing crimes with violence? A *most* unpleasant creature. As he has been out of prison for so long it is obvious that he has committed none of the more obvious crimes. Therefore, he has been conning with unusual cleverness, which I do not believe, or he has been extorting blackmail, which I can believe and which I think is likely. The Abbotts, according to your admirably clear report, deny knowing him.''

''Yes,'' said Foster.

''Any self-respecting person would deny knowing Hibbett, *alias* Welch,'' declared Folly. ''If they are being blackmailed by him there is even more reason for them denying their knowledge. That report of yours, now. It impressed and amused me. You would not commit yourself to opinions—most unusual in reports from country policemen. However, there is always that faculty called reading between the lines. I have it. You think it possible that Hibbett, as we will continue to call him for the time being, was blackmailing the Abbotts. You think it possible that he was found in the room, that Abbott deliberately attacked him, intending to commit murder, or else was driven to it by some extortionate demand that nearly turned him insane. Isn't that so?''

''It's obviously possible,'' said Foster.

''Yes. The Abbotts would stick to each other and tell the same story. The necessary thing is to watch them and to find out what they are like together. If the man has committed some crime of which the woman knows, she will probably feel bitter about it. Shocked. Idol with feet of clay, if you follow me. To the general public she would present a brave front, and perhaps be even more than usually cheerful. One might say exuberant. She—ah! I have scored a bull,'' declared Folly, complacently. ''Well, is she too high-spirited?''

''At one time, all of them were,'' said Foster. ''In my first report——''

''I remember it clearly. You are referring to the time when you first met them. That is not exactly what I mean. We must get a third-party's opinion of the relationship between the author and his wife. Trevelyan, here, might get it from this clergyman, Castle—we shall see. I fear I have digressed,'' continued Folly. ''No, thank you, I will not have another cigarette. I have my

121

heroes, and I try to emulate them.'' He took out a cigar case and stuck a cigar into his mouth, screwing up his features until he looked almost incredibly like Winston Churchill. ''A match, Trev, if you please—*thank* you.''

''I wish Buckingham hadn't gone out,'' said Foster, glancing at the door. ''He shouldn't have missed this.''

''I have been wondering why he has denied himself this unusual opportunity to inspect one of the more curious mammals at close quarters,'' said Folly. ''He is probably trying to solve the problem before he has to sit in the back of the car with me again. Concerning Hibbett's visit to the Staffords' Chelsea flat, now. It happened on the afternoon of Thursday—I beg your pardon, Tuesday—May the 11th. Yes, Foster, you are right—the day before the removal from Chelsea. You know that Stafford is not unacquainted with the police force, and consequently the police on duty in Chelsea are not unacquainted with him or his flat. Moreover, the noise which came from his attic while he was in the throes of composition reached the Chelsea Police Station whenever they were at their loudest. I have heard complaints from neighbours saying that, during the war, it drowned the sound of the flying-bombs. The Chelsea house where the Staffords lived, then, is not unknown to the local police. Forgive me if I repeat myself, I want Trevelyan to understand.'' He shot the doctor a sly glance, and Trevelyan grimaced at him. ''When Hibbett called there it was reported. The policeman who saw and recognized him, a most intelligent man whom I must persuade not to apply for transfer to the C.I.D. branch, kept observation. Shortly after Hibbett arrived, Abbott called. He went upstairs, came out again in a few minutes, had tea at a nearby café, and then went back, after Anne Stafford had returned—both Staffords were out when Hibbett and Abbott arrived. This was at a time when the Staffords were out. Hibbett left after half an hour. Abbott then left. It was some time before Stafford himself returned, and he was in a very advanced stage of intoxication. It was a very fortunate thing,'' he added, softly, ''that an accident had taken place in Whitehall Place soon after Stafford left his club. Otherwise there would have been no excuse for asking you to send a man to 'Spindles' so early—I am very glad you called in person, Foster. That must have been inspiration.''

Foster said: ''Confound it—*excuse* for sending me out there?''

Folly looked smug.

''That is the word I used. I was delighted when I had your report. It was both factual and interesting, and so brief! You see, Foster, a short while before Hibbett and Abbott—curious similarity of consonants in those names, isn't there?—visited Chelsea, another man was seen to enter that house. Yes, you're right. Lovelace is the name.'' He beamed. ''Don't say it, Foster! Pretend not to be surprised. By keeping a poker face I have for many years impressed on my superiors my infallibility and my great cunning, whereas in fact I am the simplest of creatures. Lovelace went to Chelsea. He was not seen to come out. The next morning there was a hurried removal—I have ascertained that by an urgent request the removal was put forward two days. *Why*, I wonder? Where is Lovelace?'' He bellowed the question. ''Where is the morgue?''

He pushed his chair back and rose majestically to his feet. Foster, a little dazed, followed him to the door with Trevelyan. As they reached it Buckingham appeared, a little flushed as if he had been hurrying. He winked at Foster, who did not notice it. There was a great disappointment in store for Buckingham, in fact, for outside was a Daimler—the largest taxi in Milton, which he had obtained after much trouble to house Folly. Folly simply said: ''Is this our car?'' and climbed in, falling heavily onto the seat. Not until the others had got in and they were settled—with Buckingham next to the driver, looking mortified—did Folly speak again.

''Trevelyan knows Lovelace,'' he said. ''That is why I agreed to bring him. We shall soon know whether Lovelace was murdered. Hurry, driver!''

CHAPTER 16

SUPERINTENDENT FOLLY IS SAD

TREVELYAN identified the body after a close scrutiny. The features were unrecognizable, but the scar on the neck and the short little fingers were sure indications, and there were other small pointers which enabled him to be quite sure.

During the examination in the cold, clammy morgue, Folly talked in loud undertones to Foster and Buckingham, explaining that Lovelace had been in Germany until the end of the war, had been suspected of spying for the Allies and beaten up terribly, but allowed to live for some obscure reason.

''Did he work for us?'' asked Foster.

''Not officially,'' said Folly. ''Whether he was moved to try to find out information while in Germany, before being interned, I don't know. Judging from the man's reputation, I should say that it was unlikely. It's more likely that he offended some high German official and the suspicions were imaginary, just an excuse for making him suffer. Be that as it may, it does not affect our work.''

''I don't quite follow you,'' said Foster.

Folly raised his eyebrows.

''Indeed? Think again, Foster! You might imagine that such an eminent investigator as myself would only stir from his comfortable London office on a matter of great importance. You might think that Lovelace's sojourn in Germany has something to do with the interest which I am showing in him. I, however, am not interested in his past except in so far as it affects his murder.''

To hear the man talking now, thought Foster, it was hard to imagine that he had a scrap of humour in him. "You may conceivably have some fantastic notion that I am here because I want to find out whether Lovelace was killed by an Englishman or a vengeful German."

"*What?*" exclaimed Buckingham.

Folly turned a baleful eye on him.

"Why make such noise in a chamber of death, sergeant? It is not respectful. Is it not a fact that such notions have passed through your mind, Foster?"

"Vaguely, and I rejected the possibility," said Foster, firmly.

"So you rejected the possibility," said Folly, in a vast whisper. "You imagine that I have come to Milton—which is doubtless a charming little country town, but I have no use for charm and little for the country—to investigate the murder of a man when a dozen other officers could do it as efficiently. Well, well! I am disappointed in you."

Foster grinned. "That's too bad. Do you think he might have been killed by a vengeful German?"

"I did once," said Folly.

Buckingham had recovered from the rebuff and was staring wide-eyed at the fat man. Foster could not make up his mind whether Folly was being serious, or whether this was another example of his frolicsome humour.

"Really," said Foster.

"Really!" mimicked Folly. "Really! Come, Foster. You doubt my word. You need not. Lovelace came from Germany not many weeks ago. We did not discover it until a few days before he visited the Chelsea flat. We learned it when we arrested a German who called himself a refugee and was in fact a gentleman wanted very badly by the authorities. In an effort to save himself—a vain effort, I may say—this German told us why he had come to England. It was to seek out Lovelace, who had contrived to bring into the country a small parcel—that is the technical term—of jewels which certain Nazi runaways wanted in order to finance their future activities. I understand that a man who has been responsible for butchering tens of thousands of people was intent on buying a cattle farm in the Argentine. Most suitable! Lovelace stole the jewels which were to have financed the purchase. Naturally the victims of the robbery were angry. Also, they were almost without means. A desperate venture was launched, no less than an effort to regain the diamonds from Lovelace. All of these things, you understand, I knew when your first report reached me. I may say that had you not asked for the co-operation of Scotland Yard, I would have persuaded the Home Office to allow me to come down here. Then the fat would have been in the fire," he added with an unexpected grin. "No luncheon parties and outsize taxis for Superintendent Folly then!" He glanced at Buckingham. "I am not unmindful of your concern for my comfort, Sergeant!"

"Good!" said Buckingham, feelingly.

"Must you digress?" demanded Foster.

"Can a cyclone change its own course? Neither can I. You are interested in these jewels. You may well be. Immediately the story was known, a widespread search was made for Lovelace. He was traced to an apartment house in Bloomsbury. Some jewels were found there. There may be others, and might be a motive for his murder. These are the reasons for my especial interest in the case. At one time I thought that other Huns might be after Lovelace's blood, but I no longer think so. This is a local business, as one might say. Outside his Bloomsbury quarters," went on Folly with heavy sarcasm, "there waited two men who are persuaded to call themselves detectives. They made their presence known only too clearly. Lovelace did not return. He was next seen going to the Staffords' flat. Then he disappeared—or, rather, he failed to reappear. Had any other man been in charge of the investigations, I have no doubt that the Staffords and the Abbotts would have been closely questioned about him. However, there was no evidence that he was dead. There was ample evidence that he had visited other people whom he had known before the war with the sole purpose of begging a few pounds. We were charitable. We assumed that was what he had gone to Chelsea for, although of course we kept an open mind.

"In my experience," went on Folly, "it is a waste of time to investigate the murder of a man if his body is missing. By interrogating the people who might have killed him, including Hibbett, we would have warned them. I succeeded in persuading my superiors to wait until the body was discovered. There appeared a reasonable hope that this was the body, and your prompt recourse to Scotland Yard gave me much pleasure, Foster, *very* much pleasure. True, the fact that it is naked creates a problem—we must find the clothes. However, let me say again, I am *quite* sure that the motive for his murder was nothing to do with his flight from Germany or the man who pursued him.* I looked upon this case, with justification, I think, as one in which I had prior rights. I rarely leave London, but I was interested not only in the murder of this remarkable man, but also in a county police force which, before it had made reasonably sure that there were no prospects of making an arrest, asked for our assistance. Such people, I thought, deserved the best that I can give them. So here I am. I said just now that I was disappointed in Sergeant Buckingham; that was momentary annoyance, I am not disappointed in anything I have found here—least of all in the body. Have I told you how Trevelyan came to know him?"

"No," said Foster.

"That was remiss of me. Lovelace was involved in an accident before we knew that he was in the country—he used an *alias.* He was taken to the London Hospital, to which Trevelyan is a consultant. He was suffering from concussion and shock which had temporarily deprived him of the use of his nether limbs. That, as Trevelyan would say, was right up his street. You may come to

* Foster later discovered that Folly was quite right.

125

know that Trevelyan has the most careful mind in Great Britain. I have never known a man who observes so clearly and remembers so vividly. He examined Lovelace and came to the conclusion, which proved right, that the paralysis was temporary, and the man recovered in a comparatively few days. Two days after he had been discharged from hospital we arrested the Hun who was looking for him. A description of Lovelace was soon circulated, and Trevelyan saw it—he does a great deal of police work. Are you satisfied, Foster?''

''Quite,'' said Foster.

''That's more than I am,'' said Folly. ''I want to know who killed Lovelace, and why.''

''What are you going to do next?'' asked Foster.

''Meet the people involved,'' declared Folly. ''There is no other course open to me.''

. . . . .

Gillian and Tony were alone most of that Sunday. They went to church in the morning, and walked back with Castle, who was obviously worried about his wife, and who had appeared distracted in church. That was a pity, because the little church had been crowded, in comparison with other Sundays. Castle admitted, on the way back, that it was not due to him, but to local curiosity about the people at 'Spindles.'

''So you see,'' he said, ''you have found a way of filling my church for me, Abbott! I wish I had been able to take advantage of the opportunity, but——''

''Try not to worry too much,'' said Tony.

''From what you have told me,'' said Castle, ''it is you who have so much to worry about. Abbott, please believe me when I say that if there is anything at all I can do to help you, I am only too ready. Just say the word.''

''I will, thanks very much,'' said Tony, appreciatively.

He had found it a relief to tell the vicar what had happened, to admit to the rage which had nearly made him kill Hibbett; in spite of his own preoccupation, there was something about Castle which inspired confidence. The composure which he had felt after Foster's arrival the previous night had gone. He had slept badly, was irritable with Gillian, and had to exert himself to behave normally. Only grim determination had enabled him to sit through the service with half Bray gawking at him, but he was glad that he had gone. As he turned into 'Spindles,' in full view of the other half of Bray, which had been waiting in the road from the church, and most of whom were gathered within a hundred yards of the house, he was not so much on edge.

''I half expected to see Foster's car,'' he said to Gillian.

''I was half afraid that we would,'' said Gillian.

There were two or three policemen in plain-clothes near the house, and P.C. Grimes was standing there leaning on his bicycle; he saluted respectfully as they passed him. It was a relief to get inside. Tony went to his study, Gillian went to prepare the cold lunch which, by mutual agreement, they had on Sundays. Anne came down to say that Julius had a splitting headache and proposed to spend the day in bed. She took her own lunch up to Julius's room.

Towards the middle of the afternoon a Daimler pulled up outside 'Spindles.' Gillian and Tony were in the drawing-room, and they looked out of the window. They saw an enormous man walk along the drive with Foster and Buckingham, and they saw Anderson with another stranger going next door.

"I think I know what this means," said Tony, slowly.

"What?" asked Gillian.

"Foster's called in Scotland Yard," said Tony, narrowing his eyes. "Yes, that's Folly—Superintendent Folly, the big man of the C.I.D." He smiled mirthlessly. "They don't mean to lose much time!"

"How do you know who it is?" asked Gillian.

"I've seen him in court once or twice," said Tony. "Police courts and criminal courts are part of my stock-in-trade. Oh, well. Folly can be a bit of a brute, by all accounts."

Folly, however, set himself out to be pleasant. He greeted them in a booming voice, bowed gallantly to Gillian, lowered himself onto a settee, and congratulated them on having a piece of furniture large enough for him. Then he proceeded to declare how deeply he sympathized with Tony in his predicament. It was natural that a man should lose his temper when his wife was attacked by a villain like Hibbett. It was a great pity that the circumstances made it necessary for him to help Inspector Foster to prosecute his inquiries into the murder of the man found in the river—an acquaintance, it was now known, of Hibbett. Did Tony know a man named Welch?

Foster listened admiringly.

Whatever Tony had been thinking, he certainly could not have been prepared for the casual utterance of Hibbett's real name. Foster watched Tony closely, and although Folly looked half asleep, that was an illusion. Tony, however, showed no reaction at all.

"No," he said. "Is that the dead man?"

"Obviously you do not know Welch," said Folly. "He is, I have every reason to believe, very much alive." He went on to talk about the bricks and the use of the boat, and to ask questions so blatantly intended to encourage Tony to implicate Julius and Anne, that Tony began to wonder whether Folly's reputation was all deserved. It was a curious fact, said Folly, that Julius Stafford had brought forward the day of moving, was it not? Did Tony know why? That was a pity, a great pity. Had they noticed anything peculiar about the behaviour of the Staffords? No? That was also a great pity. Was Mr. Abbott seriously asking him to believe that in the ten days or so that they had been in Bray, Julius had behaved like a normal man? What? He rarely behaved like a normal man? Then why had Mr. Abbott denied that there was anything peculiar in his behaviour? What? It would be considered peculiar in other people, but not in Julius Stafford. Surely this was asking too much of a simple policeman to believe. Stafford was temperamental, was he? Simple policemen had little time for temperament. A genius? He had heard it suggested, but he had grave suspicions of most people who claimed to be so brilliant. Where was Stafford now? In bed with a headache. How sad! And his sister? Keeping him company. How kind!

By the end of half an hour, it seemed clear to Tony and Gillian that Folly had some reason to suspect Julius. He did nothing at all to try to hide his suspicions, and waxed more and more sarcastic until, with a sudden heave, he rose from the settee and said:

"Foster, lead me to this remarkable musician!"

"He doesn't know his room," said Gillian.

"Then, please, be good enough to direct him," said Folly, majestically. He listened to Gillian's directions, and then stalked to the door. He waited for Buckingham to open it, and stepped into the passage. Then he turned round and squeezed himself into the room again. Something in his manner was forbidding; the man was capable of creating whatever atmosphere he wanted. He spoke softly, staring at Tony.

"Oh, Mr. Abbott, there is one other thing. Seven years ago—in April—you made a violent assault upon the person of a man named Lovelace, Jeremiah Lovelace. Is that not a fact?"

Tony stood quite still. Gillian caught her breath. Foster was out of his depth, but he kept his face expressionless. It was astonishing that in a few seconds Folly had not only charged the atmosphere with tension, but had blasted through Tony's composure with a statement which was obviously made with full knowledge of the facts.

Tony said: "I——"

"Did you or did you not make a violent assault upon Lovelace?" roared Folly.

"I——"

"Answer me, sir!"

Tony raised a clenched hand and began to lose his colour. Buckingham was reminded vividly of the way he had looked the night before, and took an involuntary step forward. There was a moment of high-tension silence before Tony relaxed and said quietly:

"When you stop behaving like an ill-bred oaf, I'll answer your questions. Not before."

"Ill-bred—*oaf*," breathed Folly. "You have the impertinence to stand there, sir, and to talk to me in that fashion? To try to hide your guilty conscience by such trivial methods. Pshaw, sir!"

He paused, and no one spoke. He took a step forward, smiled with exaggerated politeness, bowed slightly before Tony, and said in a honeyed voice:

"Mr. Abbott, be good enough, please, to tell me whether you once made a violent assault upon Jeremiah Lovelace."

128

"We quarrelled, yes," said Tony.

"So you quarrelled. You quarrelled! You have the impudence to say that you quarrelled when you tried to murder the man in exactly the same way as you tried to murder Hibbett last night. Do not attempt to deny it! It is the truth! Buckingham saved you from the gallows for Hibbett's murder, but other men have been murdered. You——"

"Don't!" cried Gillian.

"Have the goodness not to interrupt, madam!" thundered Folly. "Abbott, the police have long memories. A policeman saw Lovelace immediately after your dastardly attack on him! At Lovelace's urgent request no action was taken; you were not charged with assault. You were fortunate. Only a generous man like Jeremiah Lovelace would have refused to lay a most serious charge against you."

Tony said: "Lovelace was about as generous as Uriah Heep."

"So you dislike him? You have a grudge against him?"

"I have had nothing to do with him for seven years," said Tony, deliberately.

"In that seven years you have nursed your grudge. He cheated you, according to your lights. He robbed you. You conceived a violent hatred for him and you attempted to kill him. That attempt failed. You thereupon determined to bide your time. You nursed your grudge, I say! You worked out a scheme of revenge, most terrible revenge, and——"

Tony said: "You're talking absolute nonsense."

Halfway through the man's bellowed statements he had felt on the point of losing his temper completely, and had fought desperately to retain his composure. Then suddenly something in Folly's manner struck him as comical. There was no evidence of tension in his voice when he spoke, but he managed to stem the flood of Folly's extravagances.

"I see," said Folly, quietly again. "I am an ill-bred oaf and I talk nonsense. *Most* illuminating. Perhaps I shall be able to revise your opinion of me, Mr. Abbott. Do you deny that you once attacked Lovelace?"

"No."

"*Thank* you, Mr. Abbott. I congratulate you on the revival of your most convenient memory. Yesterday you were asked, most civilly, whether you had any reason to dislike this Jeremiah Lovelace. You refused to tell the truth. *Why*, Mr. Abbott?"

"The questions were not justified," said Tony.

"I see." Folly uttered a baying laugh. "So Inspector Foster is now the victim of your superior mind. A mere policeman, Mr. Abbott, and policemen are ill-bred oafs who spend their time talking nonsense. How nice to go through life so convinced of one's superiority."

"Until ten minutes ago," said Tony, cuttingly, "I had a good opinion of the police."

"Until——" began Folly. He stared, gulped, and flushed. His eyes widened and they seemed to flash. Tony thought that the man was about to burst into a raging anger, but abruptly Folly turned on his heel. He contrived to sail through the doorway without jamming himself, and disappeared into the passage. Buckingham followed him and when Foster joined them Folly was covering his mouth with his hand, and heaving; he looked convulsed. He waved his free hand towards the door, and Buckingham closed it hastily. There were tears in Folly's eyes, and Foster stood looking at him in sheer amazement.

"Beautiful!" Folly wheezed, at last. "Oh, my! Damn it, Foster, the man's a treasure! I haven't been spoken to like that for ten years. Then the man went to Dartmoor for seven, to repent." He wiped his eyes, and went on in a loud voice in spite of his precaution with the door. "A worthy opponent, Mr. Abbott! Did you observe him closely? Did you see how, at one stage, he was about to lose his self-control—or appeared to be. Did you see how neatly he prevented himself, how differently he acted? Foster, I tell you that Anthony John Abbott is a *very* clever man. Fits of rage—*pshaw!*"

"Surely——" began Foster.

"I have great doubts about the genuineness of those fits of rage," said Folly, in a voice so loud that Buckingham waved agitatedly to him, but was ignored. "Think how convincing a defence it would be if he were to say that he has suffered from these paroxysms for many years, that he was not responsible for what he did during them. Think how it would affect a jury. Oh, it would not surprise me if Mr. Abbott is not cunning as well as clever, and convinced that even if the crime is traced to him he will not suffer the consequences." He pulled Foster towards him and beckoned Buckingham. "He has heard me express my doubts, of course. I think he is probably in there fuming, and his wife is pleading with him not to come out and rate me again. He may be clever; he may be cunning; he is certainly worried. You see how it is done, Buckingham? Come, now, let us see Stafford."

He led the way up the stairs.

Tony and Gillian were standing in the big, odd-shaped room looking at each other, white-faced. Hardly a word that the Superintendent had said had been lost, although they had not heard his last-minute whisper.

Gillian said: "Tony, it—it must be Lovelace who's dead."

"It looks like it."

"And—and they bring up a thing that happened seven years ago. It's damnable!"

"We ought to have expected it," said Tony. He was rubbing his hands together, and they were moist. "Folly probably knows, or thinks he knows, a lot more. If I could be sure that I hadn't done some crazy thing I wouldn't care a hoot, but——"

"Don't, Tony!"

"But I might have done," said Tony, and drew in his breath.
"I might have done."

* * * *

Superintendent Folly's face was quite expressionless when he
reached Julius's bedroom and stood outside. He held up a hand
for silence, and the others stood on either side of him, rather like
boys obeying the behest of a headmaster. There was no trace of
laughter on the Superintendent's face, and he seemed to have forgotten what he had said downstairs.

There was no sound in the room.

"Open the door," he whispered.

Foster would have knocked, but he decided to let Folly have
his head, and opened the door. There was no sound. He stepped
inside, and saw a rumpled bed and an untidy room, but no one
was there.

"Curious," said Folly. He stepped across the room and put
a hand on the bed. "Cold," he said. "Not been slept in for some
hours, I imagine. Perhaps the genius is in labour again. Do you
know the way to his studio?"

"Yes," said Foster.

"More stairs," said Folly, and sighed.

He did not have to go upstairs then, however, for Anne's door
opened at that moment. All of them looked round, and saw her
come from her room. She was dressed in black, and it heightened
the pallor of her cheeks. She stared at them in surprise, and was
the first to speak.

"What are you doing in my brother's room?"

"We are in the passage outside his room," said Folly, with
exaggerated accuracy. "We are policemen, madam, with every
right to search this house. Where is your brother? You are,
presumably, Miss Anne Stafford?"

She ignored the last words, and said: "He's in his room."
She hurried towards them and disappeared into the room, pulling
up short when she saw the empty bed. She turned round without
a word, pushed past them and raced up the stairs to the studio.

"After her!" hissed Folly.

Foster was already on the stairs, and he reached the studio a
yard or two behind her. Again she stood quite still for a second,
staring about the untidy, deserted room. When she turned her face
was chalk white.

"What have you done with him?"

"We're looking for him," said Foster.

"Why must you hound him like this?" cried Anne. "Why
can't you leave him alone? *Where is he?*"

"Now, please," said Foster. "We want a word with him and
expected to find him up here."

"I left him asleep," said Anne. She pushed past him again and
went downstairs, hurried into his room and looked into the wardrobe.
Folly followed her into the room and watched her closely. She

pushed aside several suits, obviously looking for a particular one. Then she turned round, and her eyes looked heavy with dread.

"He's gone away," she said in a toneless voice. "He's gone away."

"How disappointing," said Folly, absurdly peevish. "I particularly wanted to see him. Perhaps *you* can answer my questions, Miss Stafford."

CHAPTER 17

THE LULL

FOSTER expected a series of questions in the high-handed manner which Folly had used with Tony; he was disappointed, for Folly treated Anne with great courtesy, and there was little point in any of his questions. He mentioned Lovelace, but did not ask whether she had seen the man recently.

As they went downstairs leaving Anne in Julius's room, Folly said quietly:

"The girl's thunderstruck. She must be watched. I don't think she really heard what I said; I could have got nothing out of her. If I'd asked leading questions she would have remembered them afterwards, and been warned. Felt sorry for her—nearly as sorry as I did for Gillian Abbott. Not a very nice case, Foster, there are some pleasant people involved. I never like it when we have to deal with decent, ordinary people who have been driven to commit some crime. Someone here *has* committed a crime, you know. Not necessarily the murder of Lovelace, although it is beginning to look like that, I must say. However, Hibbett could have been a party to it, and they may have moved the body under duress."

"So you think they brought it from Chelsea?"

"Someone brought it here, put it in the boat, and dumped it in the river," said Folly. "It could have been someone unknown to everyone here, but it isn't likely. Too many undercurrents of fear. Buckingham! Have you telephoned headquarters and asked for a watch to be kept for Julius Stafford?"

"Why, no, I——"

"Then what are you waiting for, man? We want to see him, don't we? That's two of them have got away from here. It looks as if your men outside want jerking up, Foster. I suppose one of them might have followed him."

"There'll be trouble if they didn't," said Foster. "I'll go and see them."

He did not think it was likely that Julius had been seen to leave the house, however, or one of the watching men would have reported. There was still a curious crowd hovering about the gates, and the road leading to 'Spindles' was full of people. In five minutes Foster knew that Julius had not been seen to leave by the front gates; Grimes, in fact, went further, and swore that the man had not gone out that way. There was a plain-clothes man at the back, who had seen nothing.

"He can't have disappeared into thin air," said Foster.

He was standing by the side of the house, immediately opposite the gap in the hedge which led to the vicarage. He heard Trevelyan's voice alternating with Castle's, but he was too preoccupied to notice the relief in Castle's tones. He looked round; there was a side door from 'Spindles,' and a man could have left by that and, in a few steps, got behind the untrimmed laurels near the gap in the fence.

"That's probably how he went out," said Foster.

He went into the vicarage garden through the gap. Castle was by the drive gates, still talking to Trevelyan, and Anderson came hurrying out of the house. He looked surprised to see Foster in the garden.

"Looking for something?" he asked.

"Yes. Have you seen Stafford?"

"No," said Anderson, frowning. "Has he run away?"

"He's gone out," said Foster.

"Well, he can't have gone far," said Anderson. "He was in his bedroom when we came here, I noticed him looking out of the window—it was an upstairs room, so I suppose it was his bedroom."

"Thanks," said Foster. "Is there anyone at the back, do you know?"

"Probably the maid's there," said Anderson. "Mrs. Blackshaw is in her room—she appears to have kept to it since the shindy the other night. I must hurry," he added, and then turned back. "Oh, Trevelyan has good news of Mrs. Castle. She'll probably be able to walk in a few weeks' time."

"Splendid!" said Foster.

He spoke mechanically as he went to the rear of the vicarage. Maude was sitting in a deck-chair on the back lawn, and she looked up with a start. Her face was flushed and her eyes were heavy with sleep. At the best of times she was not a good witness, and now she was thoroughly confused. She had seen no one, she said, and it was her afternoon off. Foster gave her up, and went to the end of the garden. In places the hedge was so thick that it was impossible to see the garden next door, but in other places there was a clear view of the river, the landing-stage and the boat. The plain-clothes man who had been on duty at the back was in sight, but there was no reason to believe that he had been interested in the vicarage garden. Foster went to the end of it. There was no hedge for the last few yards, and it was possible to step from one garden to the other; that was doubtless how Mrs. Blackshaw had seen the damp boat. He stood looking along the river. On the tow-path, on the other side, were several families dressed in their Sunday best, and obviously they were interested in 'Spindles.' Since everyone in the village had seen Julius Stafford by now, there was no reasonable chance of his having escaped without being noticed. Foster sighed; he had no desire to question person after person, and try to sort out the conflicting statements which would undoubtedly be made.

Grimes came up, looking thoroughly miserable.

"Can I help, sir?"

"I'm thinking of striking while the iron's hot," said Foster. "We'll go to the other side and find out whether he was seen, and we'll use 'Spindles' boat. Come on."

Grimes took the oars, and the little crowd congregated near the bank for which he was heading. Foster started to question them as if addressing a meeting. Two or three said they thought they had seen Stafford (Foster himself had not mentioned names) but there was no general agreement. Then one old man said:

"Tell 'ee who I did see, Inspector."

"Who?" asked Foster.

"That young feller who writes for the paper."

Foster said sharply: "Do you mean Lancing, of the *Milshire News?*"

"Aye, that's un," said the old man. "Running, he was, I thought he'd fall in afore he finished, but he never." The man sounded regretful. "Running that way, he was," he declared, and pointed towards Riversmeet."

"This looks promising," said Foster. "Pull over to the other side a moment." He thanked the crowd, and then waited until he was close enough to the other bank to speak to the watching plain-clothes man in normal tones. "Go and tell Superintendent Folly that I think I'm on to something," he said. Then to Grimes: "Now let's see how fast you can row, Grimes!"

Grimes certainly put his back into it, and within five minutes he was perspiring freely. He took off his helmet, perched it between his feet, and then bent to the oars again. The little boat skimmed the quiet river, and Riversmeet soon came into sight. Old Martin was standing by his garden gate, and his face darkened when he saw who was coming. He did not move away, however, and Foster called:

"Have you seen Mr. Lancing, of the *Milshire News?*"

"Why, that's a funny thing," said Old Martin, obviously relieved. "I see him a little while back, now—crossing the bridge, he was. Run along the road and then he went into the caffee an' come out on a bike. Rode like mad, he did."

"Good, thanks," said Foster.

There was no point in continuing the chase, but there was every reason to hope that Lancing had seen Stafford and was on his heels. Foster took a turn at the oars, but it was stiffer going against the current, and before they were halfway back Grimes took over again. They were away from 'Spindles' for an hour in all.

Only the plain-clothes man was in the garden. They left him to tie up the boat, and hurried to the house. Folly was sitting on a garden seat, smoking a cigar, and his face was screwed up in Churchillian fashion. Buckingham was still in the house.

"Taking the air?" asked Foster.

"Waiting for a country policeman," said Folly, heavily.

"I thought I had a chance of catching up with Stafford," said Foster, "and I think we'll have some news of him soon; a local newspaper-man was seen hurrying towards Riversmeet—that's the next village."

"I know it is," said Folly.

"Brilliant, aren't you?" said Foster, with a touch of acerbity. He felt sore because his men had let Stafford go, and Folly's sarcasm seemed to have a barb.

"I am a simple person, as I repeatedly tell you," said Folly. "I am also too old to go chasing about the country in search of a man who is bound to be found sooner or later." He grinned suddenly. "All right, Foster, all right—it hasn't turned out as I hoped it would. I think there's going to be more disappointment in store. I think we shall have to wait a few days before anything turns up."

"Oh," said Foster. "Why?"

"There's a change in the atmosphere," said Folly. "Don't ask me to explain myself at every touch and turn, confound you! Let's get back." He led the way to the waiting taxi, telling them that Anderson and Trevelyan had already gone back in the doctor's car. There was some excitement in the medical profession, he declared, over a patient next door. He gave the impression that he did not see why Trevelyan should interest himself in anything but the case.

When they were settled back in the car, he said:

"I've talked to Anne Stafford again—only for a few minutes. That girl is living under a great strain, as great as Anthony Abbott's. It's a very nasty business and I'm a little frightened about what we might find. This thing goes back a long time, I'm sure of that. Abbott might be frightened because he suffers from these fits, or whatever you like to call 'em, but that's only a surmise. The girl is in a different category. She has been living on tenterhooks for a long time. She's nervous and highly strung. It's because of that damned brother of hers, of course."

"Perhaps she thinks he killed Lovelace."

"Perhaps. You should examine the evidence." He grinned puckishly. "That's hard—you haven't seen it, so how could you? Lovelace entered the Chelsea house at four-thirty in the afternoon. Stafford was seen to go out at three-fifteen, was at his club at four o'clock, and didn't leave—according to the evidence so far obtained —until nearly seven. Abbott called about five o'clock, and Anne also went back to the flat soon afterwards. Hibbett called, too. They're the known facts. If Lovelace was killed at Chelsea, and I think he was, we must narrow the issue down, on the available evidence, to Abbott, Anne Stafford or Hibbett. All of them, for one reason or another, are capable of doing it. Of course, there may be flaws in the evidence. We'll see."

Foster asked: "What did Anne Stafford say?"

"What you'd expect: That there is nothing unusual in her

135

brother going off without telling her why or where he's going. The Abbotts agree—he's often gone off for a week or ten days, and they've never known where, and never had an explanation from him. So we meet with another factor which I think we shall have to accept—Julius Stafford disappears for short periods, usually prior to an outburst of composition. The difference this time appears to be that he went off during it. His genius was not working," he added, with a grimace. "He was dissatisfied with his work. She says he collapsed last night, that's how it was you found her bathing his forehead with eau-de-Cologne. To-day, he had a headache which laid him prostrate—quite usual, also, and probably not simulated. Then he went off. It *might* be because he saw us coming, but it might be that he's gone off because he's got into the habit of it. We want to find out where he's gone, but I don't think it will be easy."

"Why are you so pessimistic?" asked Foster.

"Nothing pessimistic about that," said Folly. "People who go away without leaving a trace or an address *are* hard to find. Hibbett will be hard to find, unless he goes to a place where our fellows know him. Take my word for it, Foster, we're going to have a few days peace and quiet. How would you like to come up to London?"

"Why?" asked Foster, cautiously.

"To acquaint yourself with the evidence which you can only obtain in London," said Folly, and added with a grin: "You could see a show or two, you know. London isn't dull. Have you ever been to Scotland Yard?"

"Only twice, for flying visits," said Foster.

"Come up with me and I'll show you round," said Folly. "Don't ask me why, but I think we're going to get results in London before anything else happens down here. We've done some good work. It won't do the Abbotts or Anne Stafford any harm to have a week to think about the situation. If they're guilty, they'll do something silly to betray themselves—or else they'll get worked up to such a pitch that when we come again they'll be easy meat. If they're innocent—"he shrugged his shoulders. "Well, it won't make any difference."

"I'm not a bit sure that you're right," said Foster.

"Please yourself," said Folly, "but if I had a fine, upstanding sergeant like Buckingham here to do my work for me, I would take advantage of my seniority and come up to London. What's the trouble? Don't you think your Chief Constable will like the idea?"

"I don't think he'll mind," said Foster.

"All right, then—take the chance which I offer you. If you're worried about the return of Stafford or Hibbett, I'll promise you that I'll come back with you as soon as we hear they've turned up here again."

"It might be a good thing," admitted Foster, slowly.

"It will."

"I'll have a word with Colonel Harrington," said Foster. "He may think that you're wrong to go back, you know. He expects great things of you."

"He won't get 'em if I stay down here," said Folly. "The scene has changed." He sat back, drawing at his cigar, and they drove through the outskirts of Milton to the police station. Foster was mildly amused when he saw the men on duty stiffen to attention at the sight of Folly, who sailed past them with his head high and the cigar jutting from the corner of his mouth.

Foster was puzzled by Folly's insistence about London, and by no means sure that the man was right, but the thought of a trip to town attracted him. He only wished he could take Laura. He was thinking of the suggestion while he talked over the points of the case which were now established, and he realized with a sense of shock that he had accepted the identification of the murdered man without the slightest excitement. Folly was the chief cause of that; he was fascinated by the man's behaviour. Folly was a *poseur* but he had a touch of brilliance and a characteristic essential to a good detective—patience. It seemed almost as if he wanted a respite.

A late tea was served from the canteen. Folly applied himself to it with the single-mindedness which he had shown at lunch, and talked about anything but the case. They were finishing the meal when the telephone rang, and Folly scowled at it.

"I never talk on the telephone when I'm eating," he said. "That's a good rule—I recommend it. No calls while at meals."

"This might be Lancing," said Foster.

It was Lancing, whose voice held a mingling of excitement and disappointment. He had been at 'Spindles' in the hope of getting an interview with Folly, and had noticed Julius Stafford leaving by the side door; there had been something furtive about Stafford, Lancing said, and he had followed hot-foot. The man had gone upstream for a few hundred yards, to the bridge nearest Bray, and then hurried along the tow-path, dodging into the trees whenever he saw a crowd by the river. He had crossed the bridge at Riversmeet and caught a local bus which ran to a neighbouring town. Lancing had not wanted to be seen following him, and had borrowed a bicycle from Symes at the café. The bus stopped frequently and there had been a chance of catching it, or at least getting to its terminus soon after it. In fact he had arrived ten minutes behind the bus. The driver and conductor had noticed Stafford, who had gone to the railway station.

"And that's where I lost him completely," said Lancing. "I'm speaking from the station now. There hasn't been a train out for nearly an hour, so he couldn't have travelled by train, and presumably he's in the town somewhere. Can I do anything while I'm here, Foster."

"I'll telephone the local police, I think," said Foster. "You might as well get back."

"All right," said Lancing. "I say, can you fix an interview with Folly for me? He looks a tartar—what is he like?"

"He's terrible," said Foster. "He does nothing but eat. He probably regards newspaper-men as the bane of his life, but he'll be at home with me until a quarter to eight, I think, and if you care to look in I'll give you an introduction." He was grinning at Folly, who glared back.

"Good man," said Lancing. "Thanks."

"Strange as it may seem," declared Folly as Foster replaced the receiver, "I do not look down on reporters. I find them useful, intelligent people, and I am always glad to talk to them. What does your particular reporter imagine he is, though? A policeman?"

"Lancing's very good," said Foster. "He knows where Stafford went." He laughed at Folly's expression, put through a call to the neighbouring town's police, and then put out a general call—not to detain, but to report if Julius Stafford were seen. That done, he sat back in his chair and looked at Folly, whose eyes were so narrowed that he looked asleep.

"I'll give you ten to one, in sixpences, that Stafford doesn't show up for several days," said Folly, opening his eyes suddenly. "We might get Hibbett before then, but I don't really think it's likely. *Must* I come out with you and see this newspaper-man?" he demanded. "I am looking forward to a quiet evening at the 'White Horse,' interrupted only by your Chief Constable—I suppose he will be gracious enough to meet me."

Foster smiled. "He wants you to dine with him at eight—didn't I tell you? And before that we're going to my house. If I didn't show you off to my wife, she'd never forgive me."

"If you insist," said Folly, with a long-suffering sigh. "One thing I beg of you. Leave it until the children have been put to bed. I have a niece whose chief joy in life is to have me standing by the side of the bath while her three-year-old son giggles at me. I know that I am a subject of humour," continued Folly, "but strange children may look elsewhere for their bath-time amusements."

"On Sundays mine are always bathed in the morning," said Foster, "but how did you know that I had a family?"

"Children please you," said Folly. "I noticed you smiling at them at 'Spindles,' whereas Buckingham, who presumably is a single man, was sorely tempted to clout them and tell them to get out of the way." He laughed. "Of course, Foster, I'll be delighted to meet your wife. Send Buckingham on ahead, to warn her what to expect. I have had enough of excited females this afternoon."

So it happened that Superintendent Folly, who was a bachelor, and Foster watched the three children at their evening meal, and before long Folly was telling them a story about a big, bad man in a boat. When Laura came downstairs after tucking them in bed she said:

"They won't go to sleep for hours, after that."

"Do 'em good," said Folly. "I don't like machine-made children. I don't like anything that's machine made. Funny the Abbotts haven't any children, isn't it?"

Foster laughed. "They've only been married two years."

138

"I've a curious impression that they're a childless couple," said Folly. "I—now, Mrs. Foster, what have I done to deserve a look like that?"

"I'm beginning to think you *are* uncanny," declared Laura. Standing by his side, she looked elfin. "Yesterday afternoon, when I was talking to Mrs. Abbott, she told me that she was afraid she wouldn't be able to have children. It troubled her, I know; they both want a family. It's the result of an old operation, I gathered."

"Curious," said Folly. "Was it the first time you'd met her?"

"Yes. She had no idea who I was. I think I caught her at a moment when she was feeling rather wistful and low—she was watching the children. She has a way with them. There was a little boy standing by, her charwoman's son, and she looked at him longingly. Of course I may be making a mountain out of a molehill," said Laura, "but that was the impression I got."

"A very good impression," said Folly. "Curious fact that she should unburden herself to a stranger. Only people who can't confide in friends usually do that, except the incurably garrulous, and Mrs. Abbott isn't one of those. Evidence that she was feeling some kind of strain even then—prepared to take her hair down in front of a complete stranger. Curious indeed," declared Folly. "Mark my words, young Foster. The people at 'Spindles' are in a hot-bed of emotional strain. All of 'em. There'll be an explosion there one day. Even if they get away with this business, and we pin it on Hibbett—which I'm inclined to think is most likely— there'll be trouble. Last people in the world who should try to live together. Oh, well—we'll see."

"So you think it was Hibbett," said Foster.

"I think nothing of the kind! I said I'm inclined to think he's most likely. Possibly he killed the man and skipped out, leaving the body for the Staffords to get rid of. Nasty shock for them, especially if they had quarrelled with the man or otherwise had a good reason for wanting him dead. People like the Staffords might well rush into some silly business such as hiding the body instead of calling the police and being frank. They can't help doing the wrong thing. Emotional instability, you see."

"That would let Abbott out," said Foster.

"Nonsense!" roared Folly. He looked at Laura with comical dismay. "Is your husband always as dull as this? It lets no one out. We've still three suspects. Suffering goldfish, Foster, I said it was a *possibility*. Possibilities don't rule anything out!"

Thereafter he behaved more like an ordinary man, became a firm favourite with Laura, and was gracious when Lancing called.

. . . . .

He had left behind him at 'Spindles' an atmosphere which was almost unbearable. Tony and Gillian would have stood up to it better had Anne been normal, but she was obviously beside herself with worry. She had been collected enough when she had told Folly that it was quite customary for Julius to go away for a few days at a time, but usually he let her know that he was going. Now she was obviously terrified lest anything happened to him, but she would not say what she thought might happen. Although she went up to her room and did not come down again, the fact that she was in such a state affected the others. Tony was pre-occupied with his own particular anxiety, and Gillian found the situation quite beyond her: Tony could not bring himself to talk; Anne would not. There were policemen and villagers within sight all the time, even on the other side of the river. She got no peace of mind when she went into the garden, and she was soon back.

Tony had watched her from the porch, and now he stood up and put an arm about her waist as they went inside.

"Try to take it easier, darling. I know it's difficult, but if we look at it the reasonable way, we've got to admit that it's most unlikely that in a fit of rage about which I have completely for-gotten, I killed Lovelace. In fact it's fantastic. I suppose you know," he added, slowly, "that it's fairly certain that he was killed at Chelsea, and that's why Julius and Anne hurried down here."

"Of course I do," said Gillian. She caught her breath. "Tony, Julius is my brother. Anne——"

It cleared the air a little when, quiet-voiced, they discussed seriously the possibility that Julius or Anne had killed Lovelace. They were so absorbed in their conversation that they did not hear the car draw up outside, nor the footsteps on the drive as the car went off. When there came a knock at the front door they broke off, and Tony said wearily:

"Oh, Lord! More policemen and questions."

"I'll go," said Gillian.

She walked sharply to the door; he heard her fumbling with the catch, and the squeak as the door opened. He made a mental note to oil the hinges. Then the mental note and everything else was forgotten, for Gillian cried:

"Snub!"

"Hallo, my poppet!" came the deep, laughing voice of Snub Savory. "Here you are then, all at home like a dutiful housewife, and looking very pretty, although I say so myself. Spare a kiss for your best man. Ah! I was, remember."

Tony limped to the hall, his eyes glowing.

"Snub, why the dickens didn't you let us know?"

"Complaints, complaints, that's all I ever get from authors," said Snub. He was a youthful-looking man, rather below medium height, and very well dressed. His homely face, always good natured, was wreathed in smiles. His fair, curly hair was thin, and he had a small bald patch. He put down a suit-case and advanced, clasping his hands together and looking about him. "Not at all bad, not at all bad. The muse should be busy here—how's work, you scoundrel? You probably haven't written a line since you've been here—all you've been doing is reading manuscripts for other people, which is kind but unprofitable."

"Is it any good?" asked Tony.

"The Castle thing? We'll talk about that later." Snub looked from one to the other, and frowned slightly. "Have I come in the middle of a lovers' tiff?" he demanded.

"No," said Tony. "We're having a spot of bother, but it'll work out. You've got to be the best listener in the country for the next few hours."

"After you've made me a cup of tea, I hope," said Snub.

It was a great relief to see him and talk to him. His level-headed common sense was always soothing, and Tony had found that he was rarely at a loss, no matter how difficult the situation. It was characteristic of the man that he did not seem surprised or horrified, and discussed the situation quietly and practically. By the time supper was ready both of them felt very much happier, and that in spite of the fact that Anne called out in a muffled voice that she did not want any supper, only to be left alone.

Snub stayed until Wednesday morning.

The days passed surprisingly quickly, and with no interruptions. It was Castle who told them that Foster had gone to London with Superintendent Folly—a hasty snippet of information given while Castle was waiting for the local bus to take him into Milton to get a prescription for his wife. She was now conscious and in some pain but remarkably cheerful, although she had not yet been told that the pain might be nothing more than the return of life to her legs. Twice they had called at the vicarage, each time finding that Castle was in the village; Snub's opinion of his book was the same as Tony's, and it was ironic that the opportunity to see Castle about it did not come while he was there. Castle had forgotten everything else in the new hope about his wife.

Policemen still watched the house, but they had no visitors. Anne was more herself on Monday, apologized for having made a fool of herself, but remained pale-faced and jumpy. Whenever she heard tradesmen on the drive she went hastily to the window. There was no news from Julius, and, as far as they knew, none about Hibbett.

Tony saw several of the villagers about the cricket club, and by Wednesday morning, when he saw Snub off at the station, he felt that he could really become enthusiastic about it. The fact that the policemen had been to London suggested that they expected to find the solution there; so, at least, he tried to convince himself.

He was standing by the bookstall at the station after Snub's train had gone, when another train came in. His bus back to the village left from the station. It was not due out for half an hour, and he always found it possible to while away the time looking at books. He glanced up, for no particular reason, and then gaped towards the ticket barrier, through which Julius was passing.

confound it, I'm out of change," he said. "Pay the cabby for me, will you?"

'So he's broke,' thought Tony, as he obliged. Julius was striding up the drive, calling something which Tony could not catch. The driver grinned.

"Did he make that up hisself, sir?"

"Yes," said Tony.

"I heard there was a composer down these parts," said the cabby. "I likes music, I could listen to it for hours. Wonderful, I calls it. All out of his own head, too.. Thanks, Guv'nor." He touched his cap and drove off, and Tony walked leisurely towards the house.

Inside, Julius was standing in the hall, and shouting:

"Shake a leg, there! Anne—where are you, Pet? Sweetie Pie, come and welcome your great big prodigal brother! Pet! Sweetie Pie!"

When Tony reached the hall Anne was coming down the stairs and Gillian was approaching from the kitchen. Gillian was frowning, and obviously she did not intend to give her brother a warm welcome. It was difficult to assess Anne's thoughts. She walked slowly, and he saw that she was dressed in black, which she seemed to prefer these days, almost as if she were in mourning. Her face was white, and she looked very thin; there was something almost tragic in her expression. Her complexion was transparent, and her eyes had an unnatural glow.

"Hallo, old girl!" cried Julius. "It's done the trick! I've got exactly what I wanted!" He stepped forward and as Anne reached the last few steps, lifted her by the waist and held her high. Even then, her expression did not change. "Come on!" he adjured when he set her down again. "Don't be angry with your favourite brother, Pet. I tell you it's worked again."

Anne said: "Why did you go, then of all times?"

"Pooh, if you're thinking about the police and their interfering insolence, I'm not going to allow myself to be dictated to by them," said Julius. "And I'll soon tell them so, and send 'em off with a flea in their ear if they come worrying us again. Cheer up, Pet! I tell you that I've got something for which the world is waiting." He took off his hat and flung it towards Gillian, who was standing and staring severely at him. "Catch, Sweetie Pie, and go and make your clever brother a cup of coffee—I haven't had anything since morning tea, I just had to get back to that piano. I'll race you, Pet!"

He went tearing up the stairs.

Anne watched him, and then began to follow. At the landing she looked down. She was smiling faintly, and Tony got the impression that a great load had been lifted off her shoulders. For some reason he thought of her fiancé. She had received a long letter from him at breakfast, opened it, glanced quickly at it, and then put it aside. She was just not interested in Teddy Barr.

She disappeared, but before Tony and Gillian had spoken there

144

was a crash on the piano, and suddenly Julius began to play with a wild abandon the air which he had been humming. It was fascinating. They stood looking upwards, without speaking, holding hands. The whole house rang with the music, and there was no doubt that it had a touch of genius; it would capture the public imagination like nothing Julius had done before. It was as if in the few days of his absence he had matured and grown in stature and understanding.

Gillian said, slowly: "It *is* good."

"It ought to make his fortune," said Tony. Reluctantly, he led her to the kitchen. "I suppose we'd better get him a cup of coffee, and keep him in a good humour. He really has the most infernal nerve! He probably feels exalted, knowing what he's got running through his mind. The trouble will come when he falls to earth, as he's bound to when this spasm is over. Then he probably won't be so light-hearted or so ready to jeer at the police. I know one thing," he added, slowly.

"What's that?"

"He can't have anything much on his conscience," said Tony.

.   .   .   .   .

It had been an exciting, exhausting and in some ways incredible few days for Inspector Mark Foster. Folly went to his head like strong wine. He seemed to go to everyone's head, for he had enthralled Harrington when they had dined at his home on the Sunday evening, and Harrington had not hesitated to give Foster permission to go to London, leaving Garth in control of local investigations, with Buckingham to help him. On the journey to London Foster had wondered how Garth would take it, but from the moment he had stepped out of the train at Waterloo all anxieties of that nature dropped away from him.

Taxi-drivers, newspaper-sellers and porters all seemed to know Folly, all touched their foreheads and grinned knowingly.

They went straight to his office, and in fifteen hectic minutes Folly made sure that all the necessary inquiries had gone out, up and down the country, for Hibbett and Julius; then he had roared through the open door of his office for a cup of tea and a sandwich; he had already eaten a heavy breakfast and stuffed himself with apples on the journey. He had an office which he shared with his Chief Inspector, who was out, and there were several easy chairs. He settled Foster in one, and then proceeded to tell him the story of Scotland Yard, as he put it. He seemed to have no further interest in the case in hand, but was intent on describing exactly how the Yard system worked. From time to time—after the tea had come in—other men entered, were introduced, asked Folly a question or two about some other case, and then went out. Folly gave his answers like an expert on the Brains Trust, without hesitating and with full assurance. It was an experience which Foster would not have missed for a fortune. He was obviously popular with the men as well as with his equals.

He thrust open the door of the bathroom. There was an enormous pearl-shaped bath, with steps leading down to it, and handles so that he could pull himself up without difficulty. It was positively sumptuous, and on the glass shelves on one wall, beneath a specially lighted mirror, were a dozen white pots of creams and emulsions.

"Cleanliness," said Folly, with the air of a man about to deliver himself of a profound statement, "is next to godliness. Like it?"

"It's wonderful!"

"Then don't snigger, confound you! Talking of godliness, are you?"

"Am I what?"

"Godly. Not an impertinent question," said Folly. "I'd like to know. One needs to know everything about a man before one can understand his actions and his mental processes. I've told you before, the first essential in police work is understanding people. I don't pay much attention to Trevelyan and his fancy name for it—people and their habits, thoughts, prejudices and work. Get to know your man is the first principle of police work, even with little rats like Hibbett. Well, are you?"

"Not excessively so," said Foster, cautiously. "I mean, I don't go to church regularly. My wife——"

"Curious fact that many men think that their wives can stand proxy for them in church," said Folly. "Not a thing I've ever been able to understand, it's one of the little mysteries of life. Take the religious lives of the people in this case, now. Hibbett—absolutely *nil*. Julius Stafford—he worships at the twin altars of music and himself, but he does not, as far as I can discover, acknowledge his Maker. That rules out any question of *high-minded* crime on his part. Anne Stafford—indifferent for the most part, and High Church when she thinks of it. Nothing personal in her religion, except in so far as it affects her brother, whom she worships. She would be prepared, I feel sure, to commit murder to save him from hurt or to preserve him and his work for posterity. High-minded possibilities in Anne Stafford. The Abbotts—you've got to lump them together. Low Church, with a bent towards Nonconformity, particularly as far as Abbott is concerned. Genuine Christian convictions in both cases. It affects their lives—considerate to others, helpful where they can be—look at the way Abbott gets on with that man Castle, for instance. And his interest in village affairs. I rule Gillian Abbott out as a possible murderer, *absolutely*," went on Folly, firmly. "I put Abbott high on the lists of suspects, because he might have committed murder for a very high-souled reason about which we know nothing at all. There are also, of course, these fits of rage of his. I've already cast some doubt on their genuineness. The fact remains that they might be genuine, in which case his religious convictions would have no influence on his actions when in the grip of such a rage. I was having a word with Trevelyan about it," he added. "They're not impossible. It isn't even impossible for Abbott to do something in such a mood

148

and afterwards be completely unaware of what he has done. Not likely, and I don't want to believe that happened, for it's the kind of case which is extremely difficult to handle—we'd have to face opposition witnesses in the medical category, and when experts fall out it always confuses a jury's mind. Or should it be minds?"

"I don't know," said Foster. "Have you any firm opinions about who killed Lovelace?"

"No. Preferences, which you might call prejudices. It often turns out that the most likely murderer is the last one who will do it. See text books. I think Hibbett stands as high as any of them, as I told you. He's not above murder—he would probably like to wipe out half a dozen policemen, for instance!—but the question is whether he could screw up his courage enough to do it. Alternatively, of course, he might have flown into a rage, and what people do when they completely lose their tempers is incredible. The way Lovelace was hacked about points to someone who really went berserk. You yourself pointed out that if he were sliced up to conceal his identity there would have been no need to cut his shoulders and neck. Lovelace, I think, was sitting in a chair—remember the deeper wounds were high, and they grew more shallow further down, suggesting downward strokes with a knife or sword. Where was I? Yes, sitting in a chair when someone just went wild and slashed him mercilessly. Another curious thing you haven't mentioned—the weapon."

"It might have been a carving knife, and they're two a penny," said Foster.

"The literal mind. You're right, of course. It would be more important if the body had been fresh for us; as it is we're never likely to be able to fit the weapon to the wounds. Well, we'd better sleep on it. Do you snore?"

"Sometimes, so my wife says," said Foster.

"Good! So do I."

"Who told you?" asked Foster, and was astonished at the deep laughter which the sally brought forth.

He spent Tuesday morning at the flat, going through the files and trying to weigh up everything to be learnt from them as well as all that Folly had said. He could not see any further through the mass of evidence, and was disappointed when Folly telephoned to tell him that nothing had been seen of Julius Stafford or Hibbett. He lunched alone, for Folly had to attend a conference, and then walked to the Yard. It was pleasant to be recognized by the men on duty and C.I.D. officers who walked the stone corridors.

He heard Folly's voice, booming as if with some excitement.

"*Where?* Are you sure? . . . What time? . . . Don't you dare lose him until I come down!" The receiver was banged down, and a bell rang somewhere nearby. Foster turned into the office as a messenger came hurrying from a room opposite. "Just in time!" roared Folly. "Nearly left you behind—messenger! My car, my usual driver, petrol for a hundred and fifty miles at least, better make it two hundred. Hibbett," he flung at Foster. "Village in Sussex, not so very far from Milton—curious fact emerges, the village is on the same railway line served by the station from which Julius Stafford probably travelled. Often wondered why he went there to catch a train, not to Milton. We may stay the night. Don't talk for a minute, I've got to clear one or two little things up.''

He spoke into the telephone to several different people, a few words here, a few sentences there, and he gave Foster the impression of being in charge of a dozen different cases. The clearness of his mind was a revelation, and as Foster walked with him along the corridor he felt humble in the presence of a master. The impression remained with him, although he did not voice it.

A Buick was waiting outside, with a driver in plain-clothes.

''Grateful populace lets me travel in comfort sometimes, you see,'' said Folly. ''This thing was being overhauled on Saturday, that's why I had to come by train. Generally I avoid train travelling. Absurd corridors! Not large enough for a child to pass along. Hallo, Yule!'' He smiled at the driver. ''This is Chief Inspector Foster, of the Milshire Police, and you'd better get on his right side, he's a holy terror when he's roused.''

Yule smiled, and winked almost imperceptibly at Foster.

''That's enough of that,'' said Folly. ''We're going to Appleby, a village seven miles this side of Brighton. The 'Horse and Hounds' public-house. Do you know it?''

''Yes, sir,'' said Yule.

''Astonishing fellow, Yule,'' said Folly, sinking back in the car. ''He's a teetotaller—I believe he preaches at temperance meetings!—and he knows every pub in Southern England. I've never caught him out yet, anyhow.''

''When was Hibbett seen at Appleby?'' asked Foster.

''Half an hour before I was telephoned. He spent the night there—using a different name, neither Welch nor Hibbett. That's a good thing to know, it means that he's really frightened. Curious fact emerges,'' added Folly. ''He's a townsman. A cockney. He hates the country. Yet he visits Bray and then he visits Appleby. Not for love of the green grass or the twittering of birds, you can be sure of that.''

They sped through London and the suburbs, then took the Brighton road. Folly was deep in thought, and Foster was wondering whether the forthcoming interview with Hibbett would bring them to the end of the case. He admitted hoping that it would; he did not want to harass Tony Abbott any further if it could be avoided. Yet he was not optimistic, and was surprised to find himself almost depressed.

CHAPTER 19

HIBBETT CORNERED

APPLEBY was a straggling village which gave an impression that it envied Brighton, its majestic neighbour, which was visible from the hill on which the village was built. There were several made-up roads, and small modern houses and bungalows. The main street was wide and had terraces of shops on either side. A few thatched cottages and old buildings were almost hidden by the ugliness of red and yellow brick and cement-faced buildings. Folly pulled a face when he saw it, and muttered something under his breath.

Yule turned a corner and pulled into the yard of an old hostelry. It was larger than Foster had expected, and much older than most of the buildings in the village, and it had undeniable charm.

"That's better," said Folly. "If we must go to the country let it be the country, not an outcrop of suburbia. That looks like the local watchdog," he added, seeing a man standing near the front entrance of the 'Horse and Hounds'; the man was tall, rather ungainly, and red in the face, for he was unable to move out of the sun and watch both back and front entrances of the inn. Folly's guess was on the mark, and the man looked startled when the car pulled up alongside him.

Folly opened the door.

"Is Hibbett still here?"

"Yes, sir," said the man, more startled than ever. "I—who are you, sir?"

"Superintendent Folly," said Folly, grandly. "What room number?"

"Seven, sir."

"Thank you."

"Excuse me, sir, but I think Inspector Wright is in Room 11, he expects you, sir, he——"

"Ah, yes," said Folly. "Thank you." He led the way to the hotel, pushing through the swing doors, and murmuring under his breath: "You see—Inspector Wright is waiting for me. Doesn't trust me on my own. It's better not to upset the local people, they're very touchy." He grinned. "Coming to Room 11, or going to watch Room 7?"

"I'd better come with you," said Foster.

It was immediately obvious that Inspector Wright was not a man who would understand Folly. He was a smaller edition of Garth, with little humour and a great sense of his own importance. He was long-winded, too, as he told Folly that Hibbett had been traced thanks to the keenness of one of his men, and that a careful check had been kept on his movements.

"Has he left the pub since you located him?" asked Folly.

"No, not once."

"Fat lot of movements, then," said Folly.

"I should have said that we have been checking his movements since he arrived here on Sunday evening," said Wright, flushing. "You would like to know where he's been, I presume?"

"Please," said Folly. He looked half asleep, but his hands were fidgeting in his pockets.

"Hibbett *alias* Welch, *alias* Webster, the name by which he has registered here," said Wright, solemnly, "arrived here at 7.30 p.m.

on Sunday, May 23rd. He did not leave the hotel until 10.15 p.m. on Monday, May 24th.'' Folly began to snap his fingers softly. "He went to the hamlet of Geeves, two miles south-west of Appleby, where he visited Geeves Cottage. The owner of Geeves Cottage is an old man who has lived in the district for many years, and has an extremely odd reputation.''

"Odd?'' barked Folly.

"That is so. He is eccentric, *most* eccentric. One might almost say that he is a hermit,'' declared Wright. "Nothing is known against him, although during the war there were times when he was suspected of signalling to German aircraft. The charges, made by his neighbours, were all investigated and proved to be groundless. The suspicions were aroused because he was extremely critical of the war, and called himself a pacifist. Even at the height of his unpopularity he was vehement in his defence of the German race.''

"Hum,'' said Folly, his fingers now still.

"I have not had time to get a full report ready for you about Professor Gimbert——''

"Professor?'' interjected Folly.

"That is what he calls himself—Professor of Music.''

"Well, well!'' said Folly. "Remarkable how music crops up in this business, isn't it, Foster? An eccentric Professor of Music. Gimbert, Gimbert, the name is familiar—*Foster!* Have you seen it lately.''

"It does sound familiar,'' admitted Foster. "I——''

"Man, man, you read the dossier after I did,'' said Folly, his eyes glowing. "Think! Julius Stafford studied music in Prague and Vienna and London. His London maestro was Professor——''

"Gimbert!'' exclaimed Foster.

"That's all very well, I put it in your lap,'' said Folly. "Well, we are making discoveries. Professor Gimbert—Inspector, you've some very brilliant men down here, that has been proved by what you have already discovered.'' Incredible though it was, Wright preened himself. "I wonder if you would be good enough to find out whether a man answering the description of Julius Stafford has been to Geeves recently, or at any time, for that matter. Stafford is the man who——''

"I have the description here,'' said Wright. "It is about the same case, is it not?''

"Yes,'' said Folly.

"It isn't likely that he has been there, or I would have heard about it,'' said Wright. "I will make inquiries immediately.''

"Look here, this is really urgent,'' said Folly. "I don't think we ought to leave it to a local constable, we want someone with a really acute mind. I wonder if you'd mind going to Geeves immediately, Inspector, using my car, and making the inquiries in person. I should feel much happier if I knew you were on the job, I would really. Stafford is far more important than Hibbett; we really wanted Hibbett in the hope that he would tell us where to find Stafford.''

152

He was so earnest that Foster almost believed him, and Inspector Wright stood up immediately and said that he quite appreciated the situation and would gladly go to Geeves himself. Would he have the pleasure of meeting the Superintendent there a little later?

"If you haven't telephoned a message to me here, I'll come out as soon as I've had a few words with Hibbett," said Folly. "You're more than good, Inspector." He waited until Wright was hurrying away, out of earshot, and then he grinned at Foster. "That's got rid of him; now we can tackle Hibbett on our own."

"You heartless ruffian!" exclaimed Foster.

"Now, now! Ill-bred oaf is the current term of abuse. Terrible fellow, Wright. *Terrible!* Well, let's get to Room 7."

The passages of the 'Horse and Hounds' were narrow and gloomy. At a landing a little way from Room 11 there was a dull electric light, which made the brass numbers of the nearby doors give off a faint gleam. There were heavy oak beams in the walls and the ceilings, and the floorboards creaked as Folly walked to the landing and peered at the door numbers. Somewhere in the hotel a radio was on, and the strident notes of a saxophone came along the passage. Passing traffic was audible, and the footsteps of people in the street could also be heard through an open window on the landing. Apart from these things, however, the hotel was very quiet.

"Room 7," whispered Folly. "Be careful, the man must know that he is being watched. He *might* be desperate. That's why I didn't want Wright here."

He did not tap on the door, but turned the handle cautiously and then tried to open it; it was locked or bolted. He muttered an imprecation, and stood back. Foster thought he was contemplating flinging himself at the door, which looked flimsy enough for him to break down in a single effort. Instead he clenched his fist and hammered on the door with a vigour which made it shake and seem to shake the floor.

There was no answer.

"If Wright's let him go——" began Folly.

"Hush!" Foster stood with his ear close to the door. "I can hear him moving."

"Good!" Folly thundered on the door again. "Hibbett! Welch! Webster!" The names echoed up and down the passage. "Open this door immediately!"

The door opened almost on his words.

Foster was taken completely by surprise, in spite of Folly's warning, and even Folly seemed unprepared for what followed. The door was pulled open sharply, and Hibbett appeared, holding a thick stick above his head. He struck savagely at Folly, catching him on the shoulders, and then he flung himself at Foster. His toe-cap cracked on Foster's shin and made him gasp with pain. He staggered against Folly, who was off his balance, and the fat man thudded against the wall. Foster made a despairing effort to grab Hibbett's sleeve; he touched it, but Hibbett wrenched himself away and flew along the passage.

"Hurry!" roared Folly.

Foster turned, but when he put his right foot to the ground there was a stab of pain along his leg, and he nearly fell. He saw Hibbett disappear at the end of the stairs. He tried again, but it was impossible to do more than limp forward. He heard Folly's heavy breathing, and when he reached the next doorway, Folly snapped:

"Let me pass!"

Foster moved into the doorway. Folly squeezed past him, and then Foster watched a truly impressive sight—the Superintendent was running. The whole floor seemed to shake, but Folly went with commendable speed, and hurried down the stairs with the nimbleness of a man half his weight. Foster limped to the head of the stairs and reached them in time to see Folly disappearing through the front door. Several people were staring at him in pop-eyed amazement. Doors were opening on the same floor, and curious eyes were turned towards Foster. Filled with mortification, he limped down the stairs. His leg was more painful with every step, and he thought that it was bleeding. When he reached the hall a man hurried from the manager's office, full of importance, and began to ask questions. Foster said, wearily:

"Wait a few minutes, please."

He felt sick with pain, and that enraged him. He sat down on a chair in the lobby, and pulled up his trouser-leg. A woman standing near gasped, for his leg was bleeding freely; little red streams were trickling down to his sock. He dabbed at it with a handkerchief, and saw a mark the shape of the toe-cap; he suspected that Hibbett wore steel on the edge of his shoes, for nothing else could have made quite such an ugly wound as that. The sight of it even silenced the manager, except that he sent a maid for a first-aid dressing. The little lobby was crowded with a dozen people, all of them giving advice on how to treat the wound. Foster was feeling better now that he was sitting down, and his head was clearer. He knew that he would limp for several days, and he harboured evil thoughts of Hibbett.

Shouting outside had diminished; he could picture Folly running wildly, with the red-faced man also in pursuit.

Then someone opened the door, and gasped:

"Look!"

There was a rush for the door, and Foster was left well behind. His trouser-leg fell over the wound, and made him gasp, but determinedly he limped into the little reception office and stared out of the tiny window into the courtyard.

Folly was crouching, massive and alert, a few yards in front of Hibbett, who was just visible. The red-faced man and three others formed a half-circle about the little fellow, who was standing against the wall with the stick raised. Folly went forward a pace; the others did the same. Hibbett shouted something incoherently and brandished the stick. The little half-circle of men closed in slowly and remorselessly, and the wildness in Hibbett's eyes increased.

Folly got within three yards of him before he moved again.

He chose the hard way, and launched himself against Folly like a tiny battering ram against a massive wall. For a moment he disappeared from sight. Then Foster, who was looking sideways towards the scene, saw that Hibbett had gone at Folly like a goat, head downwards and aiming for his most vulnerable part—his stomach. The other men closed on him quickly, but Folly was bowled over, and went down, his legs raised high into the air. Hibbett had kept his balance, and dodged to one side. He tripped up one man and struck another savagely over the face with his stick. Then he raced towards the entrance, but he was still several yards away when three policemen appeared, their truncheons drawn.

Foster had to admire the man's tactics.

Hibbett doubled back on his tracks, going within a foot of the helpless Folly, who was trying to pick himself up; the scene would have been indescribably comic in any other circumstances. The red-faced man lunged forward, and received the stick on the tip of his nose. He fell back.

"He's coming here!" screamed a woman.

Foster swung round, nearly fell again but forced himself to push his way through the crowd towards the stairs. There were several doors leading out of the hall, but as the crowd surged sideways, most of them were blocked—only the stairs and the passage running alongside them were easily accessible to Hibbett, who burst through the doorway, still swinging the stick and with the wildness in his eyes. His lips were open and slobbering, and he was gasping for breath. He was not yet finished, however. He saw only one man standing by the stairs and raced towards them, striking out with the stick to try to keep Foster away. Several men in the crowd came forward, but they were reluctant to get too near; it was a token attempt to assist more than serious endeavour.

Foster swept his arm round; the stick caught him a powerful crack just below the elbow, but the impact loosened it from Hibbett's grasp. It fell. Foster flung himself at the man, who was trying to get down the passage. For a moment it looked as if he would succeed, but Foster managed to fling out an arm and grab his coat-tails. It was the last straw which broke Hibbett's back; he was almost exhausted, and when pulled up he dropped to the floor, taking in great gulps of air and no longer showing fight. The men who had been so chary of advancing now came forward boldly.

"Get back, please," said Foster.

His leg was extremely painful, but he meant to consolidate his own capture of the aggressive little man. As he stood over Hibbett, who seemed genuinely exhausted, the doors were pushed open and Folly appeared. He was dishevelled and dusty, and his hair was rumpled. There was a bright light in his eyes, and his lips were set.

"Did you lose him?" he demanded of the crowd in general. Then he pushed his way forward, and saw Hibbett and Foster.

He glanced at Foster and gave a tight-lipped smile. "Excellent!" he said. "Combination does it, you see. So, Mr. Hibbett-Welch-Webster, you are so frightened of the police that you will commit assault in an effort to get away. *You!*" He swung round suddenly as the red-faced man and a uniformed policeman entered the hall. "Take him upstairs to his room, away from the gawking crowd."

One or two murmurs of indignation followed the words, which Foster felt were well deserved. The red-faced man came forward quickly, and said to Hibbett:

"Let's have no more of it. Get up."

When Hibbett did not immediately obey, the man jerked him to his feet by his collar, and then hustled him up the stairs. He could have made two of Hibbett, who seemed to be helpless in his grasp, and once or twice Hibbett's feet actually left the floor. Folly watched with a grim smile, and said:

"Come along, Foster. I—what on earth is this?"

A maid appeared, carrying a bowl of water, a towel, and a small box marked with a red cross. Foster explained briefly, and Folly said:

"Give them to me, my girl."

He took the bowl in one hand, draped the towel over his arm and tucked the box beneath it, and then walked upstairs, beckoning Foster to follow him. Soon they were in Hibbett's bedroom. The red-faced man was standing over him, and Hibbett was sitting back in the only easy chair.

"Stand up!" roared Folly.

Hibbett gulped, and scrambled to his feet.

"You, sir," said Folly, to the red-faced man. "Are you proficient in first-aid?"

"Why—why yes, sir."

"Then be good enough to bathe Inspector Foster's leg. Take Hibbett's chair, Foster, you need it far more than he does—*at the moment*," he added, grimly.

Hibbett backed to the fireplace. His furtive face was set in fear, and his eyes were wide open and terrified. Now and again he drew in his breath, making a little hissing noise because of the saliva at his lips. His trousers were torn, his collar and tie were halfway round his neck, and his hands were bleeding at the knuckles. He did not move his gaze from Folly. The red-faced man tried to give full attention to his task, but kept glancing up at Folly, who was truly terrifying in the few minutes of silence which he imposed while he stood glaring at the prisoner.

He broke the silence abruptly.

"Albert Hibbett, *alias* Albert Welch, *alias* Albert Webster, I hereby charge you with the wilful murder of Jeremiah Lovelace, at 18a Bliss Street, Chelsea, and I warn you that anything you may say may be used in evidence." The words were clipped, and seemed to be forced from him. Then: "Well, sir?" he thundered. "What have you to say?"

Hibbett gasped: "I—I never, it wasn't me, it wasn't me!"

156

"Nonsense!" boomed Folly.

"He was dead when I got there," gasped Hibbett. "Abbott killed 'im, mister, Abbott killed 'im, there was blood on 'is 'ands an' face an' blood on 'is clothes—Abbott killed 'im!"

CHAPTER 20

HIBBETT'S EVIDENCE

"I SEE," said Folly, heavily. "You wish to save your own neck. Naturally, you would rather see another man hanged. You will not succeed. Your lies will not serve you."

"I tell yer it's true," gasped Hibbett. His eyes were staring, and he took a step forward with his hands outstretched. "Lovelace was dead when I got to the flat, that's Gawd's truth."

"Let us have no blasphemy," said Folly, harshly.

"It's Gawd's truth, I tell yer! I went ter see Lovelace, I knew 'e was there." Hibbett gulped. "'E owed me some money, Folly, 'e owed me a pony, I wanted ter git it aht've 'im. I went upstairs. The door was open, I never broke in. I got inside an' Abbott was standin' there wiv' a knife in 'is 'ands, it's Gawd's truth! All over blood 'e was. An' Lovelace—*Gawd!*" Hibbett covered his face with his hands. "I got aht quick, I knoo you ruddy narks would try an' pin it onter me, I got aht quick."

Folly said: "And you would have me believe that you went into the flat with no intention other than to get your debt repaid— a debt of money—and saw Mr. Abbott standing with a knife in his hand, and covered in blood. *Most* interestin', Hibbett. But it is a lie!" he thundered. "You were in that flat for twenty minutes! You were seen to enter and to leave!"

"I wasn't in the flat all the time," gasped Hibbett. "I was too scared, Folly. I—I was leggin' it aht when I 'eard some one else comin' up the stairs. I dodged into the bog an' 'id for a bit, that's what I did; that's why I was in the 'ouse for twenty minutes."

"Who came upstairs?" asked Folly.

"I dunno. It was someone 'oo went to a flat below, it's a big 'ouse. I just waited until Abbott left——"

"Abbott was seen to leave the house, and he had no blood on his clothes," said Folly. "He might have changed had it been his own flat, but it was not. He could have washed the blood off his hands and face, but not off his clothes. Come, Hibbett. You are lying. Admit it."

"I tell yer I'm not!" cried Hibbett. "It's Gawd's truth, Folly. I knoo the narks would try ter pin it on me——"

He began to tremble from head to foot.

The red-faced man had given up all pretence of bathing Foster's leg, but when Folly glanced round at him he dipped the sponge

157

into the water quickly, and dabbed it on the wound so vigorously that Foster winced. The pain in his leg was trifling compared with the issues now at stake, however. He found it hard to disbelieve the man, and yet it was obvious that Hibbett did not expect to be believed. The man was completely broken, and Foster was prepared for another demonstration of Folly's bullying methods; he did not get it. Folly spoke quietly and seemed to have some sympathy for the man, almost as if he too were inclined to believe him. He asked question after question, each one to the point. He put the same query in several different ways, and he tried trick questions, all uttered in the quiet, reasoning voice which Foster agreed was his best method of interrogation just now. He failed to shake Hibbett's story. It was elaborated at some length, but the essentials were the same. He said that Abbott had looked like a madman—just as he had when he had attacked him at 'Spindles'; there had even been froth at his lips. Folly, for some reason, hammered at that point for a long time, and Hibbett was adamant; there had been froth at Abbott's lips. He himself had been frightened, partly because he was on the spot just after a murder, partly because of the knife in Abbott's hand. He had slunk out of the room and hidden until he heard Abbott go downstairs. He did not remember what Abbott had been dressed in, he only remembered that there had been blood all over the floor, over Abbott's face and waistcoat, and over his hands. He told the same story so often, and with such little variation, that despite his sickening sense of dismay, Foster found it increasingly convincing.

Folly tried another tack; why had Hibbett gone to see Abbott?

Hibbett made no bones about admitting that he had gone to tell Abbott that he had seen the whole thing, and to extort blackmail. He seemed relieved to have to make the admission, as if he realized that it would lend colour to his story. He did not know whether Abbott had recognized him, or even noticed him at Chelsea; he was sure that Abbott had realized that afterwards, and believed that was the reason for the attack on him at 'Spindles.' It was true, he admitted, that he had been hiding in the wardrobe, and Mrs. Abbott had seen him, but it wasn't true that he had grappled with her; he had run to the door, and then Abbott had rushed in and attacked him.

"Why were you hiding in the wardrobe?" asked Folly.

Hibbett answered readily; he wanted to hear the conversation between the Abbotts when they were getting ready for bed. It would probably tell him whether Abbott did know what he had come for; the more he went on, the more Hibbett emphasized his intention of blackmailing Abbott; blackmail seemed to him a trivial crime.

"Now tell me why you went to see Lovelace," said Folly.

There was no hesitation about that, either; Lovelace had known him seven years before, and had visited him just after his return to England. He had some jewels with him, and he wanted money for them. He knew that Hibbett was a man who could sell 'hot' stuff; Hibbett imagined that the jewels had been stolen, and had taken the two stones which Lovelace had given him to a well-known East End jeweller. He had got two hundred pounds for them, and Lovelace had promised him a commission of fifty pounds. When he had first seen Lovelace after selling the gems, Lovelace had been in a frantic hurry, snatched the money, and hurried off. Hibbett thought that he was being bilked. He went to see Lovelace at his Bloomsbury lodging-house, but the police had been waiting there. Hibbett had watched from a distance. Lovelace had come along, seen the waiting police, and hurried off again. He had gone to another rooming-house and, two days afterwards, had gone to Bliss Street. There Hibbett, thinking the Chelsea house less likely to be watched by the police, had made his effort to get his commission on the sale.

"I know one fing," Hibbett said. "Lovelace 'ad that cash on 'im, I know 'e 'ad."

"How can you know such a thing?" demanded Folly. "You have probably told me a hotch-potch of lies. Why add an unnecessary one?"

"It's the truth, Folly. 'E 'ad the cash, 'e was leanin' forward in 'is chair, an' 'is coat was open; 'e had 'is wallet 'arf aht've 'is pocket, an' I could see the cash. Most've it was there, that's a fact. I *saw* it, I tell yer!"

"I see," said Folly. "Had you ever seen Abbott before?"

"A long time ago, I knew 'im by sight, Folly."

"If you must give me a name, call me Superintendent," said Folly, with unexpected touchiness. "When did you see Abbott before?"

"Years ago, Fol—years ago. 'E 'ad a row wiv' Lovelace, an' Lovelace give me the job o' watchin' 'im, in case 'e 'ad anuvver go at 'im. 'E never, though. Soon arterwards Lovelace 'opped it. I never see 'im again until the day 'e brought me the sparklers."

"And what was the name of the buyer of stolen jewels whom you patronized?" asked Folly, heavily.

"Listen, Folly, I can't squeal——"

"There is no crime under the sun too mean or too beastly not to attract you," said Folly, bitingly. "Your life may depend on the evidence of this purveyor of stolen gems whom you profess to be so anxious to protect. His name, Hibbett!"

Hibbett muttered: "Old Sam—Old Sam Frazer."

"Well, well," said Folly, in a cooing voice; obviously the statement delighted him. "Old Sam Frazer—he will be *very* pleased to give evidence on your behalf, I am sure. He has succeeded in escaping the attention of the police for as many years as I can remember. Excellent, Hibbett! I am almost disposed to feel grateful to you. You have not forgotten, I trust, that you are under charge, and that what you have said can be used in evidence."

"I never croaked him," Hibbett said. "I don't care wot you get me for except murder. I never killed 'im."

"I hope not," said Folly. "For the sake of your miserable neck, I hope not." He looked at the red-faced man, who was now

159

standing idly by; he had put a pad of lint over the wound and stuck it down with adhesive tape. "What is your name and rank?"

"Sergeant Winn, sir."

"Thank you, sergeant. Take this man downstairs. Have him removed under strong escort to Brighton Police Station, if you please. From there I shall probably indent for him to be transferred to Milton." He reached the door, seemed about to open it, and then swung round swiftly. "A moment! Hibbett, listen to me! Why did you visit Professor Gimbert?"

"G-G-Gimbert!" faltered Hibbett.

"That is the name. Make no mistake, Hibbett, your movements have been most carefully watched. You may imagine that you have evaded the police, but no man ever made a greater mistake if that is what you think. Come, now! Why did you visit Gimbert? Out with it!"

"I——" Hibbett gulped. "He——"

"Hurry, man! I have not all day to waste!"

"He's a friend of—of Lovelace's."

"I *see*," said Folly, with impressive scorn. "You visited Professor Gimbert because he was a friend—was, do you understand, not is—of Lovelace. I suppose you came to bring the sad tidings of his death? Or perhaps you came to collect a donation for a wreath for his funeral. Do not treat me like a fool, sir! Why did you visit Gimbert?"

"I've told you!"

"I do not believe you."

Folly spent ten minutes trying to make the man admit that he was lying, but he failed. He grew soft-voiced towards the end, but no matter how sarcastic he became, he could not shift Hibbett from his statement: he had come to see Gimbert simply to tell him that Lovelace was dead.

"I think you are a fool," said Folly at last. "The truth will be discovered. I think you will hang for Lovelace's murder, Hibbett, and all your lies will make it worse for you."

"I never killed 'im," asserverated Hibbett, but the spirit had gone from him and his voice was lifeless.

"All right, all right," said Folly. He glared at the man, and then snapped: "Was Lovelace fully dressed when you saw him dead with Abbott standing over him?"

"Why—why, yes."

"You are sure?"

"O' course I'm sure. I told yer abaht 'is wallet——"

"So you did," murmured Folly. "So you did. What kind of clothes was he wearing?"

"Just—just clothes."

"Come, man! Try to use what little intelligence you possess. Were they light or dark? Did he wear an overcoat? Were they of good or poor quality? You appear to have registered every detail of the scene on your mind, including the froth on Abbott's lips; you must have seen the clothes."

He did not get a really satisfactory answer. As far as Hibbett recalled, Lovelace had been wearing a grey suit and no overcoat, but he said that he could give no further details. Folly gave it up, and turned away abruptly.

"All right, Sergeant Winn," he said, "Take the man away."

He opened the door as the man gripped Hibbett's arm firmly and led him outside. Then he closed the door, stepped to the window, and glanced into the teeming High Street. The noises from the street were loud and varied, and a man was crying: 'Piper! piper!'

"The place is nearly a suburb of London," said Folly, as if in disgust.

He lit a cigar as he sat at the head of the bed, leaning against the pillows. Foster stood up and tried his leg; it was very tender, and he would not be able to walk far. Questions filled his mind, but Folly looked absorbed in his own thoughts and there was no telling what harm an interruption might cause at that juncture. The waiting grew oppressive. His thoughts turned to the Abbotts, particularly to Gillian; it was surprising that she had made such an impression on him, although he had met her so rarely. It was no use pretending; there had been a ring of truth in all that Hibbett had said.

"I must telephone!" exclaimed Folly, explosively. "Wait here!"

He hurried downstairs, and Foster heard him booming a request for the telephone, not a penny-in-the-slot machine. Several people answered at once. Folly boomed replies, and a door slammed. People began to walk about the hotel, talking with subdued excitement. He saw a crowd gathered on the pavement opposite his window, and sighed heavily.

After a long interval, Folly came upstairs. His cigar had gone out, and he relit it with great care.

"I have sent someone to interview Frazer, and to try to get the numbers of the notes with which he paid for the diamonds. If he confirms the story, then we shall have no option but to arrest Abbott. I frightened Hibbett with the charge, of course, but after his exertions he was ready to talk freely. I have never heard a man and wished so fervently that I could disbelieve him, but scepticism in the present circumstances is against my better judgment. We will stay here, I think, until I get information from the Yard. We'll have a look round here," he added, lapsing into the vernacular unexpectedly. "It isn't a bad pub, as pubs go. Don't get up," he added, as Foster moved. "Here, rest your leg on this chair." He pushed an upright chair into a convenient position, turned to a dressing-table, and then said: "I *knew* there was something the matter. I've had no tea. Can you reach the bell-push behind you? Thanks," he added, as Foster pressed the bell-push. "I do not think we shall get very much from this room." He opened cases, putting them on the dressing-table and taking each article of apparel out separately and shaking it to make sure that nothing was concealed. "Motive!" he exploded, suddenly. "Motive, Foster. We haven't got a good one."

"Against Abbott?"

"Naturally."

"The money," said Foster, tentatively.

"Don't be a fool. A hundred and fifty pounds would not tempt Abbott. It would tempt few people enough to make them commit murder. In any case, even if Abbott killed him, it was not for the sake of what he could steal."

"You seem very sure of that," said Foster.

"I feel sure. I am liable to err, of course, but it is not in character. Even——" he stopped speaking and gave more attention to the search, but Foster took him up quickly:

"You were going to say that Abbott wouldn't do murder for a couple of hundred pounds—Lovelace hadn't paid Hibbett, remember—or for any other jewels which he had on him. Hibbett was sure he had more jewels."

"Yes. We knew he had. It is an obtrusive element. I am anxious not to give it an exaggerated importance. Some murders are committed for profit, but the majority are crimes of passion. We will only know the whole truth when we know the motive—but this is not a kindergarten class, you are not Inspector Wright."

He was oddly human, thought Foster, and liked the man more because of it. They were both depressed because they had testimony of a kind which might damn Abbott; both of them realized that the counsel for the defence could pour scorn on Hibbett's veracity, and he would be a poor witness, but when Abbott was charged, other things and other witnesses would probably emerge.

A maid brought in tea—a poor tea, with stale bread and butter, stewed tea, and some bright yellow cakes at which Folly stared in disgust, though that did not prevent him from eating them. He broke one of his rules, too, for he was halfway through the meal when he said abruptly:

"We should detain Abbott forthwith. We should telephone to your headquarters and arrange it. The question I am asking myself is whether, in the absence of a known motive, we are justified in holding our hands a little longer. If we set the robbery motive aside, and I intend to do so as far as Abbott is concerned—I repeat, I am liable to err—then we have to fall back on something which I dislike intensely. That is, murder during a paroxysm of ungovernable rage. We may not believe in these fits, but that is all we could offer as a motive for the moment. It is not good enough. My opinion is that when we know the true motive, we shall know the murderer—not before. Only maniacs murder without motive."

"The house is being watched," Foster reminded him. "Abbott isn't likely to get away."

"We thought the same of Stafford," Folly reminded him. "Your men will be more careful, of course, but a determined man can usually find a means of getting away, if only for a while. I am not worried about Abbott trying to escape, however. If he did this thing, he will know that flight would heighten suspicions. No. I am worried in case he should do further violence. Does anyone else know that he killed Lovelace—I will correct myself—if he did kill Lovelace, does anyone else know it? Remember that he tried to kill Hibbett and the most likely motive for that was because he knew Hibbett had seen him at Chelsea.''

"His clothes——''

"Hush!'' said Folly. "He could have carried a clean coat under his arm, if he went prepared to kill. He could have borrowed one of Stafford's and replaced it at 'Spindles,' so that Stafford would not know it was missing. We haven't searched his wardrobe, have we? We should have done; we want Lovelace's clothes too.'' He popped a piece of cake into his mouth and took a gulp of tea. "We can't afford to take the risk, Foster. We must detain Abbott, I fear. We can then make a thorough search of 'Spindles.' We had better do it ourselves, and go there across country to-night. I will go and telephone.''

"I suppose you're right,'' said Foster.

"You know I am right. We will wait for information about old Sam Frazer, after I have telephoned to Colonel Harrington, go out and interview this unpopular Professor Gimbert and see Wright again, and then——'' he paused, and grimaced. "I am a thought-less fellow, Foster. *You* must telephone Harrington. It's your privilege. Unless,'' he added with a faint smile, "you would rather not take the responsibility of asking for Abbott's arrest.''

"I'll take it,'' said Foster, "but I won't like coming upstairs again from the telephone.''

"Then I will make the call,'' said Folly, "and see that you have the full blame—or credit!''

He was downstairs for some time, and when he returned he was brisk and confident. As he had reached the manager's office a call had come from Scotland Yard, confirming old Sam Frazer's purchase of two small diamonds from Hibbett; Frazer did not know the numbers of the notes and denied knowing that the gems had been stolen, said Folly, and added with a grin:

"But we'll have the old so-and-so this time. If we get nothing else out of it, that'll be a reward enough. You ought to meet old Sam Frazer, Foster. Most cunning and most charming crook in the country.'' He laughed. "Well, let's get out and see the Professor.''

"Have you arranged about Abbott's arrest?''

"Oh, no, not yet,'' said Folly, with a puckish grin. "Your amiable Chief Constable is out, playing golf I expect, and I can hardly go over his head, can I? I asked the fellow who answered me to make sure that the house was watched very closely. You'll want some help to get downstairs, I expect—come along.''

The arm with which he supported Foster as they went down-stairs was firm, not flabby. Foster noticed it absently, as he reflected on the unexpected humanity of this huge man, and the way he snatched at an excuse to postpone Abbott's arrest. Folly was complaining that in order to get rid of Wright he had sacrificed his car and would now have to fit into a dilapidated taxi, and they were waiting for one in the lobby, peered at from all doors and windows, when Foster said:

"It's a queer thing that we're both so reluctant to detain Abbott. I thought I'd succeeded in cutting out sentiment, but——"

"*Sentiment*," breathed Folly.

"Why, yes." Foster stared at him.

"My dear, good fellow!" said Folly. "Oh, my dear chap! *Sentiment*. On duty, I have permitted no sentiment for seventeen years. The last time I allowed it to interfere with policy the fellow punched me in the stomach and nearly choked the life out of me. Sentiment? Come, Foster, grow up—it is not for such a trivial reason that I am reluctant to detain Abbott. I hoped you would see better than that—I really did. I'm disappointed in you." He looked aggrieved.

"Then why——" began Foster.

"Don't!" cried Folly. "Don't complete my disillusionment. Let me explain before you ask the question. My dear fellow, I've actually told you once. We have no motive, or none that will satisfy a jury. We might get one, but that is neither here nor there. It is eleven years since I made an arrest without getting a conviction. Eleven years! On that occasion only a defending counsel with a golden tongue and a witness who was a proved liar and was discredited when he was telling the truth, defeated me. No, Foster, not sentiment: *policy*. Ah, this would appear to be the taxi, at least it is a large one. Your Sergeant Buckingham is not the only man with a sense of proportion, you see."

The journey to Geeves, which took a little over ten minutes, was a silent one. Foster now hardly knew what to make of the Yard man; and he had an uncomfortable feeling that he had fallen low in Folly's estimation.

The hamlet consisted of half-a-dozen small cottages, a large house standing on a hill, bleak and forbidding, and a little church which looked as if it were crumbling with age. The whole place had a forlorn appearance. It was on a by-road, out of sight and sound of the great highway leading to the coast, and lay in a hollow. Outside a cottage which stood by itself, a hundred yards or so away from the others, was Folly's Buick. Yule was standing by it, and when the newcomers got out of their car he looked at Folly and gave an expressive shrug of his shoulders.

"How much progress has Inspector Wright made, Yule, do you know?"

"Not much, sir," said Yule. "He came out to get something from the car just now, and he looked hot and bothered."

"What could he get from my car?" demanded Folly.

"He'd left his case in it, sir."

"He'd left his case!" echoed Folly. "He'd left—Foster, I ask you to be of service to me. If I appear to be on the point of losing

164

my temper, cause a distraction. I am quite sure that I shall need moral support in dealing with Inspector Wright.''

He made his majestic way along a weedy gravel path. The small garden was neglected, and the cottage looked as if it were unoccupied. Two windows were broken and boarded up, and the woodwork had not been painted for many years. They drew within a few yards of the front door, which was ajar, when Folly stopped.

''Hush, my friend!''

Foster was glad to put his weight on one leg. He heard Wright's voice, and the hectoring tone made him grimace and made Folly frown.

''Did you or did you *not* see this man Stafford?'' demanded Wright. ''I warn you, Professor, you must be frank with the police.''

''It isn't what he says, it's how he says it,'' murmured Folly. ''He sounds like a crow with laryngitis. I——'' he stopped, and into his eyes there sprang an expression of delight, while Foster stood staring at the cottage.

Wright's words were cut short or else drowned by the sudden playing of a piano; and as the music came from that old cottage, the whole place seemed transformed. For a man who declared that he could not tell an A flat from an F sharp, Folly was remarkably impressed, and he was still smiling when he touched Foster's arm and led the way to the front door.

CHAPTER 21

THE PROFESSOR

THE front room of Geeves Cottage was in unspeakable confusion. Oddments of clothing, crockery and cutlery were piled on a small table near the window, and in one corner was a heap of empty food tins. A cup and saucer, incredibly dirty, stood on the narrow mantelshelf. Odd pieces of furniture, many of them broken and useless, littered the room, with torn pieces of paper, more paper screwed up in balls, odd shoes and, in an untidy heap, a pile of newspapers and magazines. This in itself would have been astonishing, but it was not all.

Filling half the room was a grand piano. It was highly polished, and did not appear to have a scratch on it. Black as ebony, it stood there amid the dirt and confusion, and at the keys sat a little old man with a long, grey beard, dressed in a skirted coat which was much too large for him, flannel trousers and carpet slippers.

He must have seen the door open, but did not stop playing. Now the music was soft and persuasive, with a haunting quality, a touch of mastery which made Foster forget the state of the room

165

and look towards the player. Professor Gimbert appeared to be smiling. His eyes were narrowed, and his head held high.

By his side, looking flustered, red and angry, was Inspector Wright, who stared at the newcomers with obvious dismay.

"I——" he began.

"*Hush!*" said Folly, in a penetrating whisper.

Wright gulped, and stood at attention. Folly approached the piano and stood where the old man could not fail to see him, gazing at the long fingers which caressed the keys. The hands were veined and spotted with brown, the hands of a very old man; but the movement of the fingers, the gentleness of their touch, proved that they were as good as ever they had been for their main purpose.

At last the old man stopped. He looked vaguely before him for a few seconds, then sighed and opened his eyes wide. Now there was no doubt that he was smiling.

"It is consoling to meet a man of understanding," he said. "You are very welcome, sir, whoever you are." He had a soft, rather quavering voice; Foster thought that he was at least eighty years old.

"It is exhilarating, Professor, to hear such playing," said Folly, in a voice which was full with something approaching awe. "Remarkable! I am sorry, deeply sorry, that I had to interrupt you. Forgive me, please. I am Superintendent Folly, of New Scotland Yard. My companion is Inspector Foster, of the Milshire Police."

"Well, well," murmured Gimbert. "Three eminent policemen in my humble cottage. I am proud to have you here, Superintendent."

"That's a different story from what you told me," said Wright, in a strangled voice. "You said——"

"That I disliked your manner, my dear Inspector—*and* I still do," said Gimbert. "That does not alter the fact that you *are* an eminent policeman. Does it, Superintendent?" Gimbert's voice was so gentle that it was hardly possible to believe that the irony was intended.

"Indeed it doesn't," said Folly, as if he were still under the influence of the music. Foster was trying to recall where he had heard it before, and believed it was one of Stafford's lesser-known pieces. "I dislike worrying you, Professor. Inspector Wright has told you why we have to, I think."

"He was inquiring about an old pupil of mine," said the Professor. "A most promising pupil, one of the most promising to pass through my hands. Julius Stafford. He has lived up to his promise, too, that in itself is a rare thing. Do you think that he has committed some crime, Superintendent?"

"He might be able to help us to solve one," said Folly.

"I see. That is a different matter, although you probably hope to make me answer the questions by pretending that there is no danger for Julius Stafford. Superintendent, I am an old man. My days are numbered. I have lived for music—forgive this embarrassing sentiment, please—and nothing but music. The things of the world do not interest me. Crime? What *is* crime? There are different opinions. In my view, the major crime is the debasement of music. Some modern music—'' he shuddered—''deserves capital punishment. My life is music, Superintendent. If a man has it in his being, then whatever else he does, whatever life he leads, counts as less than nothing so far as I am concerned. Believe me, I am serious.''

''I've no doubt of that,'' said Folly. ''Has Stafford been to see you recently?''

''Yes. He——''

''Why didn't you tell me that?'' snapped Wright.

Gimbert turned his faded eyes towards him.

''I am an old man, as I have said and as must be obvious, Inspector. I am querulous and obstinate, like most old men, and I took a dislike to you. Don't blame yourself. I dislike a great number of eminent people, and often like disreputable characters—*you* have quite taken my fancy, Superintendent.''

Folly smiled. ''I am disreputable, yes. Ask anyone at Scotland Yard—or ask Inspector Foster here. When did Stafford come?''

''On Monday morning.''

''How long did he stay?''

''Until an hour before Inspector Wright called,'' said Gimbert, gently.

''An hour!'' exclaimed Wright. ''We'll get him!''

''So he *has* become suspected of some crime,'' murmured Gimbert.

''We want his evidence,'' said Folly. ''He is accused of nothing. That is the sober truth. Why did he come to see you?'' He shot a withering glance at Wright, who was fidgeting and trying to attract his attention, and brought a smile to the old man's lips, which were visible through his thin beard.

''He wanted mental refreshment,'' said Gimbert. ''It is not surprising, Superintendent. He gets little sympathy and less understanding from his friends and relatives. His mind is a delicate creative organism and there are times when its smooth working is interrupted by the people about him, people who, no matter how good their intentions, misunderstand, abuse and perhaps condemn him, and make his life miserable. So he came to me for refreshment, as he has often come before and will, I hope, often come again. I am afraid of what will happen to him when I am dead,'' added Gimbert, gently. ''He is utterly dependent on me—*utterly* dependent. There is some satisfaction, Superintendent, in knowing that a man of rare genius is lost without one. It gives me great joy to see him when he comes, and I only wish that he would come more frequently. What crime do you lay at his door, please? Do not name some trifling thing; I am sufficiently well acquainted with the affairs of the world to know that only a crime of exceptional gravity would cause you three gentlemen to congregate in the village of Geeves. Is it the murder of Lovelace?''

''How did you——'' began Wright.

"A moment, Professor!" Folly turned to look at the local Inspector, and his face was so pale, his eyes flashing so angrily, that at great pain to himself, Foster kicked his shin. Folly opened and closed his mouth. His eyebrows were in one straight line, and seemed to have no parting between them. He coughed, and then said in a remarkably thin voice:

"Inspector Wright, if Mr. Stafford was here a little more than an hour ago——"

"We ought to be combing the district for him!" stormed Wright, his voice growing even harsher.

"You are perfectly right," said Folly, and he looked positively ashamed. "I must confess that the Professor's music—I might almost say magic—has unbalanced me. We should be searching for Stafford now, or at least, one of us should, and Inspector Foster is incapacitated. In any case, this is your district, Inspector, and I hesitate to do anything without your participation. Do you feel that you can——"

Wright was already near the door, and he broke in abruptly:

"May I use your car again?"

"Gladly, gladly! But wait! There is a taxi outside, the one in which we came. That would enable me to travel back in greater comfort. Perhaps you will use——"

Wright opened the door and half-ran along the weed-strewn path. At the gate, Yule and the taxi-driver were talking. Wright called to them, and the taxi-driver hurried to his wheel. Folly uttered a sharp exclamation, and said:

"He is empty-handed—the addle-pated fool! His case, Foster, where is it? He'll be coming back for it unless—ah, thank you, Professor, thank you a thousand times. Foster, will you—but of course, you cannot hurry. Move aside, please." He took the brief case from the old man's hand and squeezed through the door, then ran along the path; he was surprisingly graceful. He bellowed in a voice loud enough to sound above the snort of the taxi's engine. Yule came hurrying towards him, took the case, and carried it to Wright. Folly stood quite still, and when the car moved off he raised his right hand and waved. He went further. He kissed his hand to the disappearing car, and turned slowly.

"The Superintendent is a remarkable man," murmured Gimbert.

"How remarkable we don't yet know," said Foster.

He felt no inclination to ask questions before Folly returned, breathing hard, but with his cheeks a more natural colour. He beamed at Foster.

"Thank you, my dear fellow. I nearly insulted the man. Now, Professor, I assure you that Inspector Foster is a man of deep understanding, not unlike myself." His eyes twinkled. "You were asking me whether Stafford was wanted for the murder of Lovelace. I will be frank with you. He is wanted for questioning in connection with the murder of Lovelace. Of course, that man's name has not yet been mentioned in the newspapers. I, however, see nothing remarkable in your knowledge of it." That was by way of a valediction

168

for Inspector Wright. "Hibbett, *alias* Welch, *alias* Webster, told you."

Gimbert said: "Is he a man of three names? I know him as Welch. Yes, he told me. He also told me a remarkable story, Superintendent. He said that he knew who murdered Lovelace. He had a preposterous suggestion to make. He told me that Julius Stafford would come under suspicion, but that his own evidence would assuredly establish the fact of Julius's innocence. He even went so far as to ask for a certain sum of money, for which he promised to give himself up to the police and to tell his story."

"Did he receive the money?" asked Folly.

"He did not," said Gimbert. "Even if I had as much as he wanted, I would not give it to a rogue." He smiled. "Or at least, not a rogue who is also a philistine. Welch—or Hibbett—once told me that his favourite instruments are the piano accordion and the saxophone."

"My dear sir!" gasped Folly, distressed.

"So you can imagine that he got little sympathy from me, Superintendent. Of course, had I thought it possible that you would seriously suspect Julius, or that he was in real danger, I might have listened more readily to the man. However, such a possibility is non-existent. True, I was a little afraid that I had judged the circumstances wrongly when I met Inspector Wright, but you have put my mind at rest."

"One performs these small services," said Folly, modestly. "Tell me, maestro, why are you so confident that Julius Stafford will not be suspected?"

Gimbert looked at him, his faded eyes quite gay, and without altering the direction of his gaze he began to play softly, a merry little air which seemed to dance and flicker about the room.

"Lovelace and Julius were very close friends. It has greatly distressed Julius to know that Lovelace was abroad. At one time I think I can safely say that Lovelace and I were the main sources of Julius's inspiration. A man does not kill the source of his inspiration. Lovelace, you see, was one of the few men prepared to put up with Julius's waywardness, his excesses of temperament, and the fact that he was a fool where money was concerned. I will be quite frank, Superintendent. I had no love for Lovelace; I disliked the man. He was a charlatan. On the other hand he had a good effect on Julius and so I bore with him. It was a distressing thing when he left England. I did not know he was back until Julius told me that Lovelace had been to see him. He also told me that he was afraid that something had happened to the man. He was in very low spirits. I cheered him up as best I could, of course, and I was glad when my influence succeeded in making him turn to his work. In a matter of hours there was a transformation."

"I see," said Folly. "Did Stafford say when Lovelace came to see him?"

"No, Superintendent." Gimbert stopped playing, and turned round on the stool. "That is really all I can tell you—except one thing. A week ago I received a parcel. Occasionally pupils who remember me with gratitude send me a small parcel of delicacies, but they are few and far between. You will, perhaps, wonder why I prefer to live the life of a hermit down here, instead of taking what you might think is my rightful place in the world to which I belong. The answer is simple, Superintendent. I grew weary of the commercialism which has eaten like a growing cancer into the minds of men who should love music. Money—contracts—always more money and more favourable contracts!'' His eyes were suddenly angry. ''I would not take part in the mad scramble! What do the *rewards* matter if the conscience is free and a man has the knowledge that he is giving all that is in him to his art? *Nothing*, Superintendent! That is why Julius is my favourite pupil. He likes money—only a fool would not. But he did not sacrifice the spark of genius in him for the sake of it. It was, and is, a secondary consideration. I am afraid,'' continued Gimbert, apologetically, ''that I am revealing my feelings too much, Superintendent. I was talking about a parcel. It was so large that I thought I was back at school and that someone had sent me a tuckbox!'' He chuckled. ''Alas, it was only a parcel of old clothes.''

''Clothes!'' exclaimed Foster.

''Yes. Come with me,'' said Gimbert.

He swung himself from the stool and walked with firm steps to the kitchen door. It was a tiny room, even more dirty and chaotic than the first. Outside was a lean-to with glass on two sides, a few overgrown ferns in cracked flower-pots on a shelf almost bare of paint, and a collection of buckets and brushes on which cobwebs were thick and dust thicker. On the shelf was a large brown paper parcel. The string had been cut, and several loose ends hung down. The paper had been pushed back to its original folds, and when Gimbert pulled it open again it revealed a grey suit, a collar and tie, a pair of shoes and socks, a shirt, vest and trunks. Folly checked these things carefully, lifting one garment at a time. The trousers, coat and waistcoat were neatly folded.

''I was grateful at first,'' said the Professor, ''and then I examined the shirt, Superintendent. You see the stains?''

''Yes,'' said Folly.

They were on the front of the shirt, dark brown in colour, and the material was stiff and dry. There were also stains on the collar and the tie, but it was on the waistcoat and trousers that most of the blood had fallen, so that the material was like a board. There was a faintly unpleasant smell, too—that of dried blood when it was too hot. Gimbert watched Folly touch each article, and there was a faint smile in his eyes, but Foster, watching the man covertly, thought he looked a little wary, as if afraid that his story of how he had come by the clothes would be doubted.

Folly examined the paper wrapping, the postmark and the stamps. A thick inner sheet of corrugated paper was also stained, and it was obvious that the clothes—and undoubtedly these were the things which Lovelace had been wearing—had been packed up while the blood was still wet upon them.

No one spoke; but the atmosphere was tense, and Folly's breathing was very laboured. He spread the clothes out along the bench after putting a sheet of paper on it, and then he picked up the coat. He took a wallet from the inside breast pocket, and unexpectedly he handed it to Foster, without speaking. Foster opened it and shook the contents out on to the brown paper; there was a thick wad of one-pound notes, held together by a rubber band, and several loose ten-shilling notes. Apart from that there appeared nothing of interest. Folly was going through the pockets quickly, and placed his finds by the side of the notes. A handkerchief, folded neatly; a newspaper cutting; a whole sheet torn from a newspaper; a pen-knife; a cheap cigarette-case with half-a-dozen cigarettes; a box of matches, and a lighter. That finished the coat. Folly said nothing, and went through the waistcoat. He drew out a heavy watch, a pocket-comb and some book-matches. He glanced at Foster before he picked up the trousers. Silver and copper, a yale key, and two trouser-buttons came from the side pockets; only the hip and fob pockets remained. It was clear that Folly hoped to make a find; something in the way in which he worked fascinated Foster and seemed to hypnotize Gimbert.

Folly took something out; it was another match-box, inside the fob pocket, which had been buttoned. Foster felt a sharp sense of disappointment, but that disappeared and his excitement increased as Folly pushed the box open and some cotton-wool came into sight. Gently the fat man took out the cotton-wool and unfolded it. Something sparkled. Next moment the contents lay revealed: four scintillating diamonds, each larger than a pea, lay on the palm of Folly's hand.

After a long, tense silence, Gimbert spoke in a high-pitched, wondering voice.

"Good gracious me!"

"You were sent a very handsome present, after all," said Folly. "A *very* handsome present. I will not ask you whether there was a letter enclosed, or an address. There was nothing, of course. Also, the profit motive has gone. Professor Gimbert, do you know a man called Anthony John Abbott?"

"You mean Julius's brother-in-law?" asked Gimbert. "I have never met him, Superintendent, but he has written to me once or twice. Why?"

CHAPTER 22

ARREST

FOLLY countered with another question: why had Tony Abbott written to him? Gimbert, who seemed to understand that a great deal depended on his answer, turned from the little lean-to and led the way back into the first room. He opened a drawer in a table by the window. It was crammed full of letters, most of them still in their envelopes, and several fell to the floor. Foster picked them up. Gimbert began to run through the letters, putting them aside swiftly, until he picked up an envelope, old and faded, addressed in a firm masculine hand.

"See for yourself," he said.

Folly took the letter out, and Gimbert began to rummage through the rest. Foster stood beside the fat man, and saw the date on the envelope—July, 1938. They read the letter together, and there was nothing startling in it; it was simply a request for Gimbert to read through a manuscript which had music as a theme. Gimbert found the second letter, dated August, 1938; it was shorter, and said simply that he had received Gimbert's post-card and was sorry that the Professor could not do the work suggested.

"Is that all?" asked Folly.

"Yes, Superintendent."

"Do you know why he asked you to do the work?"

"I can only imagine, Superintendent, that he had learned from one of my old pupils that I was in great need and, being a generously-minded man—that is the impression I have always obtained from Julius—he thought that I might welcome the few guineas which such a task would earn. So few people understand that I *prefer* to live like this, you see. I have enough money for my simple needs."

"I see," said Folly. "Have you heard from Abbott since 1938?"

"No, never."

"You are sure he had never visited you?"

"I am quite sure," said Gimbert.

"Thank you, Professor. You have been a great help. I will take these clothes and the money and jewels with me, of course—you lay no claim to them, I suppose?"

"None at all," Gimbert assured him.

"Good! I will try to avoid calling you in evidence," said Folly, "but I cannot guarantee that I will succeed. However, be sure I will do my best to save you from a journey and the unwanted publicity. And thank you very much indeed, Professor, for your courtesy and frankness. Ready, Foster?"

"Yes," said Foster, and turned towards the door.

"A moment!" said Folly, unexpectedly. He turned and smiled at the Professor, his expression friendly and appealing. "I beg one favour of you, Professor. I was enthralled by the tune which you played as I came in. It would be gracious of you to play it again. Am I asking too much?"

"I will gladly do so," said Gimbert. "The day may come when you will hear it too often, I am afraid—it is one of those things which will become a great favourite throughout the country, and it will always be played on the wireless. It is not, in my opinion, a great composition, although it has a great deal to commend it and its popular appeal will be greater than anything Julius has ever done.''

''Did Stafford compose it?'' said Folly, as if startled.

''I can show you the music sheets where he made the first scores,'' said Gimbert, looking towards the heap of papers in one corner. ''It is the thing which gave his tormented spirit the relief which it so badly needed.''

He began to play, softly at first, and then with increased tempo, until once again Foster was unaware of the poverty-stricken appearance of the room and the incongruity of the piano standing amidst the rubbish and confusion. Before it was finished, however, Foster noticed a strange thing; Folly's hands were moving, his fingers rubbing the seams of his trousers; it was an indication that he felt impatient. He had wanted to get something which Gimbert had failed to give him, and now he was forcing himself to hear the piece out, although he wanted to be on his way.

The last note was still echoing through the room when Folly opened the door.

''*Thank* you, Professor. Delightful. What a great loss to our concert platforms! Good-bye for the present, my dear maestro, good-bye for the present!''

He went hurrying along the path, carrying the parcel, and Foster limped after him, trying to hurry. Folly was already waiting in the car, and Yule was at the wheel, when Foster reached it. Folly gave him a helping hand, and then put an arm out of a window and waved to Gimbert, who was standing in the doorway of his cottage. Then he dropped back in his seat, and the springs clanged.

Foster said: ''I thought you couldn't tell one note of music from another.''

''I can't,'' said Folly, abruptly. ''Hush!''

Foster sat back, trying to make the man out. It was difficult to give his attention to the case, even to Gimbert's story, and the discovery of the clothes, now on the floor in front of him. Folly took all his attention. If he were tone-deaf as he pretended, he had acted most convincingly at the cottage. It was probable, of course, that he had wanted to disarm the old man, and had chosen the obvious course, but Foster could not help thinking that there was something else on his mind. His impatience, after he himself had asked for the piece to be played, should convey a great deal; it did not.

They were in the outskirts of Appleby before Folly spoke.

''We are making progress of a kind,'' he said. ''We have further evidence against Abbott, although we still have no motive. The fact that he knew the address means that he could have parcelled up those clothes and sent them to Gimbert. It would be a sensible thing, if he wished to implicate his brother-in-law. I wonder if that does, in fact, give us a motive.''

Foster stared at him in bewilderment. Folly leaned forward and tapped the glass partition between him and Yule, and when Yule opened it he said: ''Pull up to the side of the road, Yule,

I want a little more time before I meet the terrifying Wright again. Under the shade of a tree, if you please. Now, Foster. Don't look dumbfounded—you look too much like Wright!'' He was not smiling. ''We know of no reason why Abbott should wish to murder Lovelace. There might be a reason why he should wish to murder his brother-in-law. If he could succeed in making a case against Stafford, and get him hanged, that would be murder.''

''Nonsense!'' snapped Foster.

''Nothing of the kind! You are making the sentimental approach —that Abbott is not a man to do such a thing. I tell you, Foster, that there are deep emotions hidden beneath this ugly business. Abbott is capable of a high-minded crime, there is no doubt of that. He might believe that there is a good reason for being rid of Stafford.''

''You just don't believe it,'' said Foster, flatly.

''Indeed? I submit it as a considered possibility,'' said Folly, huffily. ''However, let us turn to the things that even you will admit. Hibbett is cleared of suspicion of the actual murder. He might conceivably be an accessory; but he did not kill Lovelace and was not alone with the man immediately after his death.''

''Otherwise the wallet would have been empty, and the diamonds gone.''

''Good! We must admit, then, that if he is freed of suspicion of the actual murder; there is a greater likelihood that his story is true—his evidence against Abbott, I mean. There is further indication that he spoke the truth. With his knowledge he saw a way of extorting money from Stafford, or from Gimbert on Stafford's behalf. Being an employee of Lovelace's, he knew of the remarkable relationship between master and pupil. He has the twisted kind of mind which would made him do exactly what he attempted. He is shrewd enough to know that if he admitted that he tried to use the murder of Lovelace as a lever with which to obtain money, he would be making himself an accessory after the fact, possibly damning himself as the actual killer. So he pretended that he simply went to tell Gimbert that Lovelace was dead. The case against Abbott strengthens. Would you like to telephone the man and warn him that he will shortly be under arrest?''

''Don't be a fool,'' said Foster.

''It is not my habit. You are such a lover of sentiment that I thought you would like the opportunity.'' The sarcasm oozed from the fat man. ''It is now well into the evening. I do not think that we shall find Stafford to-night, but I think he might return to 'Spindles' to-morrow. I also think that it will be better to arrest Abbott when Stafford is at hand. Have you any objection?''

''No,'' said Foster.

''Thank you. It means, of course, that we give Abbott another opportunity to run away, but I cannot convince myself that he will take it. As I said before, I think he might conceivably commit another murder in the hope of saving himself. The risk is not negligible, but I think we can allow it to remain for another twelve

174

hours. Shall we return to London and travel to Milton to-morrow, or shall we go there to-night?"

"I'm quite prepared to leave it to you," said Foster.

"Thank you." Folly smiled, suddenly. "I'm sorry, Foster, I shouldn't have snapped at you. You may be quite right in thinking that the suggestive motive against Abbott is fantastic. However, *nothing* in my experience is too fantastic when such people are involved. Remember that Abbott is a writer, a quieter type altogether than Stafford, but a writer. Some, not by any means all, but some of his kind think they live as a divine right. Abbott may be one of those. Remember, also, that we know that he and Stafford have quarrelled and are often on bad terms. Remember that this is an involved, ingenious business, and that Abbott writes stories which are involved and ingenious; he might possibly be making capital out of his writing experience."

"Confound it, he doesn't write crime stories!" protested Foster.

"Study his work," said Folly. "I have done so. They are unremarkable novels. The standard of his writing is high—I have an expert's opinion on that—but the stories themselves are artificial. He would probably write extremely good crime stories. He uses the wrong medium. Oh, he has the mind to conceive something on these lines, have no doubt of that. Also remember that we are dealing only in possibilities; because we have what appears to be unanswerable evidence against Abbott, we must allow our imagination to have free play where the motive is concerned. Well, that's enough for now."

"Shouldn't we look at the contents of the wallet?"

"Need we?" asked Folly. "What—oh, I follow you, you have remembered the newspaper cuttings. Yes."

He took them out. One was about a recital of Stafford's early work, another, much smaller, was from a provincial paper. Folly widened his eyes.

"Well! Take nothing for granted. You were wise to be interested in these."

"What——" began Foster.

"Lovelace was interested in *Anne* Stafford," said Folly. "This is about her engagement to Mr. Edward Barr, younger son of Colonel and Mrs. Edward Barr, of High Lodge, Warwickshire. Now why should Lovelace be so interested in Anne's affairs?"

"I give up," said Foster.

"For the moment only, I hope. Well, let us see whether by any chance Wright *has* found Stafford."

All that Inspector Wright could tell them was that Stafford had caught a train to London, from Brighton, about the time when they had all reached Geeves. Wright was obviously feeling bitter and angry, but Folly flattered him and before they left for London the local Inspector was in a reasonably good mood. Folly looked sour when he got away from the man, but cheered up on the way to London; he was sure that if Stafford went as far as Victoria he would be seen by men watching the station.

He was right; at Scotland Yard there was a report that Stafford had reached Victoria and gone to a hotel in Buckingham Palace Gate; the hotel was being watched. Folly decided to be satisfied with that, but before he took Foster to his flat he telephoned Milton and, winking broadly at Foster, spoke to Garth and asked him to take especial care that night, to make sure that no one left 'Spindles.'

"Now we can relax," he said, as he replaced the receiver. "By George, I'm hungry! Terrible tea we had, wasn't it? Come along, let's see what we can find."

.   .   .   .   .

In spite of their annoyance with Julius, it was difficult for the Abbotts to be ill-tempered that Wednesday afternoon. It was a fine day, with just enough wind to prevent it from being too hot. Anne had completely recovered, and looked younger and gayer. Julius was positively sunny, and humming his tune over and over again, occasionally going upstairs and playing it over, but satisfied now that, in a burst of wild energy, he had completed the score. Somehow the change affected Gillian and Tony; fears receded, although they did not go completely. The near presence of the police did not harass them as much as it had done.

Towards the middle of the afternoon Tony was working in the garden, gravely watched by Archy Kelly who had been allowed to spend the afternoon at 'Spindles,' when he saw Castle and Anderson arrive in the doctor's car. Soon afterwards Anderson left. Before long, Castle appeared at the gap in the hedge, and when Tony saw his expression, his own heart rose.

"Good news?" he asked.

"So good that I can hardly believe it is true," said Castle, stepping through the gap. "Mildred is in very little pain, now, and she can stand without assistance. It is a miracle, Abbott, and I shall never cease thanking God for the fate that brought you here."

"Oh, I had nothing to do——"

"And I shall never stop trying to help you in the unhappy circumstances which surround you," said Castle, quietly. "I know you must find them very harassing. I do wish there were something I could do to help you. It's a most difficult situation even for me," he added, with a grave smile. "If Agnes had not burst out as she did I doubt whether Mildred would have come downstairs and precipitated the crisis which for her has had such happy results. On the other hand——"

It was Tony's turn to interrupt.

"I don't think the story about the boat would have made any difference; please don't let it worry you. We're trying to forget about it," he added, with forced cheerfulness. "It won't be surprising if the police go away and we see nothing of them again. It's almost certain that they are busy on the case in London. Let's talk about something much more cheerful—your manuscript, for instance."

"I'm afraid I set too much store by that and by your very

generous remarks," said Castle. "Don't hesitate to tell me the worst. I can stand it."

"I don't think there is any worst," said Tony. "My agent agrees with me that after a little pruning it will find a publisher without any difficulty, and might be a reasonable success."

"*Seri*ously?" Castle gasped. "But of course, you would not joke about such a matter." Although he was less elated than when Tony had discussed it with him before, there was a glow of deep pleasure in his eyes. "I can rely on fifty pounds, you say?"

"Quite definitely," said Tony.

"Then as soon as Mildred is able to walk more freely, I can send her away for a month or two," said Castle. "It could not have been more opportune. You know, Abbott, if it had not been for you, I doubt whether I would have plucked up the courage to show it to anyone. It's hard to believe, even now, that it might appear as a book, actually printed and published. I wonder if I have been a little too harsh in some of the things I have said about ritual, and——"

Tony smiled. "I think that's where it needs the pruning. Let me get it. Snub left his notes with the MS., and it's on my desk."

They went to his study together, and then strolled back to the vicarage. Castle was obviously eager to read the suggestions which Snub had made, and Tony left him, made more cheerful by the man's obvious pleasure and the joy he was feeling. The whole situation had taken a marked turn for the better. If Julius and Anne retained their new cheerfulness life would be much easier, and the only thing remaining was to see the last of the police. He felt remarkably calm and composed, and it seemed impossible now that he could ever be subject to those tempestuous outbursts of rage. It was nonsense to think that he might have killed Lovelace without remembering it. Apparently the man had been cut about badly, and there had been no blood on any of his clothes. He might have had a brainstorm for a few minutes, even for half an hour, but it would have passed before he had time to clean his clothes, and in a brainstorm he wouldn't have thought of doing that. The absence of the chief policemen encouraged the belief that they had found a different trail, probably starting from the man Hibbett.

He sat back in his study chair and looked out of the window. Gillian was coming from the village with a shopping basket over her arm, and Archy had gone to meet her. He was a lovable little chap, and his mother showed less concern for him now—she allowed him to come whenever he wanted, and he seemed to haunt the house. Gillian was getting very fond of him, perhaps too fond. Tony set that thought aside and reflected that he might soon be encouraged to read better books than the comics; it would have to be a slow process, of course. The difficulty was to decide whether it would be justifiable to try to educate him. He might suffer the more if Mrs. Kelly suddenly stopped him from coming to 'Spindles'; she was unpredictable in some ways.

Gillian called out through the window.

to have a few words with you and your friends. Be good enough to ask them all to come down here.''

''What——'' began Tony.

''You will understand my reason in good time,'' said Folly, very heavily. ''Come, sir! I am not here to waste my time!'' He glared at Tony, who was annoyed but turned and called out to Gillian. Then he shouted for Anne and Julius. They appeared at the head of the stairs, and when he saw the police Julius's face darkened. He came heavily down the stairs.

Abbott ignored him as Grimes came up to report about the fire. Folly nodded, and the information seemed to make him thoughtful. In a clear, rather hectoring voice, he said:

''Presumably there was something in the study which someone wishes to destroy. However, we need not worry about that now. The study can be searched when we have gone—Sharp will be able to do that, won't he?''

''Of course,'' said Foster.

''Good!''

All this time Julius had been approaching slowly. He stood in front of Folly, eyed him insolently up and down, and then said in a tone of deliberate insult :

''So you're back, you fat slug! I've been waiting for this opportunity. When are you going to remove your men from my garden?''

''When I consider it safe,'' said Folly, as sharply. ''I want neither obstruction nor insolence, sir.''

''Who the devil do you think you are?'' bellowed Julius.

''Julius, don't——'' began Gillian.

''Do not interfere with the rampaging creature,'' said Folly, scornfully. ''Let him bellow and let him abuse me. It will make no difference.'' He turned his baleful eyes on Julius. ''What I think I am, sir, is everyone's business. I am an officer of the law, here in the course of his duty, which is to arrest a man for a cold-blooded and brutal crime. Have you anything more to say?''

''You must be mad!'' gasped Julius.

''If anyone is mad, it is not I,'' said Folly. ''This way, if you please.'' He led the way to the study, and the others followed him, Foster bringing up the rear. He looked from one to the other. Julius flushed and angry, and a little uneasy; Gillian flushed, charming and pretty, wearing a pair of gardening gloves, and with some dust on her nose; Tony, pale but quite composed, and giving the impression that he feared the coming interview; Anne calmer than any of them, and looking a little exalted—she was a curious person, Foster thought as he watched them all; Gimbert probably did not know how she worked and slaved for her brother.

''Well, get on with it,'' growled Julius.

''You do well to remind me that I must make haste,'' said Folly. ''You are aware, I think, that Jeremiah Lovelace, known to all of you, met his death at the hands of a callous and brutal murderer. He was murdered in your flat at Chelsea, Stafford. He was, sir!'' His voice grew suddenly loud, and he pointed a quivering finger at Julius. ''His body was put in a trunk or similar capacious receptacle and brought here. It was taken from here and dropped into the river. Every single action had all the evidence of careful, cunning premeditation. Well, sir!'' His voice echoed about the room. ''Why did you drop the body into the river?''

Julius said: ''It's a lie. I didn't——''

''So you deny it,'' breathed Folly. ''Very well. The body *was* removed from this house. It was——'' he broke off and turned suddenly to Tony with one of those unpredictable changes which made him so dangerous. ''Anthony John Abbott, it is my duty to arrest you for the wilful murder of Jeremiah Lovelace. Anything you say may be used in evidence. Tell me, why did you kill him?''

CHAPTER 23

SOME OF THE TRUTH

''IF I killed him,'' said Tony, very quietly, ''I remember nothing about it, Superintendent.''

''Remarkable!'' sneered Folly. ''Are you calling yourself a homicidal maniac?''

''I——''

''It's madness!'' cried Gillian. She stood with her hands clenched and raised, and her cheeks drained of colour. ''It's madness, he couldn't have——''

''I greatly regret causing you pain, Mrs. Abbott,'' said Folly, in a surprisingly gentle voice. ''I do not wish you or anyone to imagine that I enjoy this task which, in duty bound, I must perform. However, murder has been committed and I have evidence that it was committed by your husband. I can remind you that there is such a thing as a defence in English criminal law. Killing can be justified, if the provocation is strong enough—if, for instance, it was a matter of self-defence. Was it, Mr. Abbott?''

''I know nothing at all about it,'' said Tony.

''So you insist on that story,'' said Folly, with a sigh. ''I am sorry. It will be useless as evidence in your defence. Now I have an equally grave duty to discharge. You had accomplices in the disposal of the body. Your wife, perhaps, or your brother- and sister-in-law. Be frank, please. The truth must come out. It will come out eventually. By lies and deception you will only postpone the inevitable.''

Tony said: ''I am not lying. I did not bring the body here, I did not know that there was a body. I did not take it out in the boat, nor dump it, and I am quite sure that my wife did not.''

Folly stared at him levelly.

"You, sir, do not appear to realize that if your sister had a motive for killing Lovelace, and obviously she had, although she will not be frank about it as to the reason, you probably *shared* that motive."

"It isn't true," said Anne, in a flat voice. "Julius liked Lovelace. Only I knew that he—he was always a bad influence. He——"

"My dear Miss Stafford, Lovelace had been out of the country for seven years! Be plausible, if you can't be truthful."

"I'm telling you the truth," said Anne. "I don't know who killed Lovelace. *I* didn't, and Julius was out all the afternoon. I don't believe Tony did, and Tony certainly didn't ask me to move the body. I—I was frightened, Julius was drunk. I persuaded him to help me——"

"Pet——" began Julius in a strangled voice.

She ignored the interruption, and continued, giving each detail of their actions. She even told of Julius's idea of putting the contents of Tony's suit-case in the garden, to make the story of third-party intervention more plausible. Quietly, inexorably, the story built itself up, until all the truth was known from the moment she and Julius had left the Chelsea flat. When at last she finished she looked at Julius as if she were asking him to forgive her. No one else spoke, and she went on in a tone almost of desperation: "I began it; I persuaded Julius to help me. He knew——" she broke off again, and Julius said:

"Oh, Pet, Pet!"

Folly moved to a chair and sat on the arm; he had to lean one hand on the other side, to prevent it from tipping up. His face had no expression, but Foster thought he was thoroughly satisfied.

"Thank you very much, Miss Stafford," he said. "I am grateful for your frankness. It is much the wisest course. Won't you please round it off by telling me *why* you had a motive for killing Lovelace. The present story about that won't do, you know, it just won't do. I can assure you of one thing; no one will be punished for a crime he or she did not commit. I have already made it plain that I have evidence, reliable evidence, to justify the arrest of your brother-in-law. The same remark applies to him, however. I will be frank with you; a third party *might* have committed this murder. We shall not necessarily consider the case finished with this one arrest. Much remains to be discovered, your reason for wishing to see Lovelace dead is one of them. Please, Miss Stafford." His voice was gentle and pleading. "Why was Lovelace interested in your engagement to Mr. Barr?"

"I——" began Anne.

"Pet!" cried Julius, in an anguished voice.

"It's no use," said Anne, "it's just no use, it will all come out eventually. I had a very good reason for wanting Jeremiah Lovelace dead. He—he was my husband."

. . . . .

It was Julius who took up the story; a strangely subdued Julius, who spoke quietly and with apparent frankness, admitting that all

184

Anne had said was true. He had once been very friendly with Lovelace, but the man had proved a thorough-going rogue. Anne had married him after an elopement nine years before, and left him within a few weeks. Thereafter, said Julius, he had remained friendly with the man, and for Anne's sake, taken his side when he had been accused of fraud. Now Anne was engaged again; she had become engaged when Lovelace had been missing in Germany for years, and she had assumed that he was dead. The shock of seeing him alive had been great.

All that could be required in the way of a motive was there, as convincing a motive as any jury could expect.

"Only it applies to the wrong person," Folly said.

He and Foster were in a downstairs office at the police station; Foster found stairs difficult to mount, so a small room had been put at his disposal and an extra large armchair brought in for his use at the behest of Sergeant Buckingham, who had been off duty that day because he had been watching 'Spindles' the previous night, but who had hurried back as soon as he heard that Foster and Folly had returned. Now he sat in a corner, his eager eyes on Folly.

"The wrong person," Folly said. "The woman had every reason in the world for wishing to kill Lovelace. She had the opportunity. With such a motive, she would not be influenced by his money or the diamonds. She knew Gimbert's address and could have packed up the clothes and sent them to him."

"That's a curious thing," said Foster. "I can't understand why they took the trouble to strip the body. You didn't ask them that, either. There were several questions you could have asked."

"Always keep something up your sleeve," said Folly, with an absent smile. "Always, if possible, know the answer to a question before you put it to your man. It gives you confidence, you know. We'll keep the matter of the clothes to ourselves for a little while. You're quite right, there must be a good reason for it. Well, what do you think of things generally?"

"That perhaps we were premature in arresting Abbott," said Foster.

"Obvious kind of remark," said Folly, with a touch of acerbity. "However, you forget one thing, my lad—one most important thing. Anne Stafford did not feel that she could stand by and allow Tony to be accused, and the case against him strengthened by our version of the disposal of the body. Had we not arrested Abbott we would not have heard her story. It's really very bad," he added with a scowl. "We should have found out that Lovelace was married. I thought we knew everything about him. That goes to show that you can't be too thorough. Now if we could shake Hibbett's story, if we could——" he paused, leaned back and closed his eyes.

He sat like that for a long time, before he sat up sharply.

"I think we can!" he cried. "I'm sure we can! Foster, a fig for your sentiment! You didn't take to Julius Stafford, nor did I! Yet here was a man prepared to help his sister when there was a lot of risk involved. A man who kept silent when a word from him would have started us on the right trail. A man who is largely dependent on her, I grant you, so there might have been a selfish motive. However, if he would do so much to save her, would he not go even further? *He* was at Geeves. *Hibbett* was at Geeves. We have not yet proved a meeting, but one could have taken place after dark. Gimbert told Julius of Hibbett's visit and suggestion. Supposing Julius, seeing a golden opportunity for clearing his sister, put Hibbett up to the story about Abbott—gave him money, I mean, for telling it. Hibbett may have been violent to lend colour to his story. Possible?''

"I suppose so," said Foster.

"What do you mean, suppose so?" demanded Folly. "How about you, Buckingham. Are you feeling bright to-night?"

"If you ask me——" said Buckingham, and paused.

"I am asking you, man!"

"Well, Julius Stafford isn't a chap likely to be moved for the sake of someone else," said Buckingham. "As you advise, sir, the people come first—what kind of people, and how their minds work." He paused, as if he expected to bring a storm upon his head, but as Folly kept silent he went on. "Stafford would want to save his sister, all right, but he wouldn't go to all that trouble just for that. No, sir! He might have done it if he wanted to frame Abbott." He gave another pause, but was met with silence, and he dabbed his forehead. "Well, it isn't impossible," he said, defensively. "We know they're bad friends, and we don't know what else there is behind it. He might have wanted to get rid of Abbott. He used Abbott's suit-case for the bricks, Abbott's trunk for the body; he pretended—according to what we've been told— that he suspected that Abbott had used the boat——"

"Careful, Buckingham. You're doing well, don't spoil it—that trick is over and done with. He's admitted using the boat himself."

"I know he has," said Buckingham, "but only because he had to. I'm putting up a case suggesting he wanted to frame Abbott *although he knew his sister had killed Lovelace.*"

"Even I have seen that possibility," admitted Folly. "Go on. What other pointers are there to such an ingenious frame-up?"

"Sending the clothes to Gimbert could be one," said Buckingham. "The fact that the body was stripped is a puzzle, isn't it? All right, then—Stafford knew that Abbott had Gimbert's address. He'd guess we'd find out. So he sent them to the old man. It wasn't likely that we'd think him or his sister did that, it'd look too obvious."

"Not bad," said Folly. "Not bad at all."

"Well," said Buckingham, spiritedly, "I think it's as good as any theory we've had yet, anyhow!"

"Perhaps it is. Well, what else is there? That fire—according to Grimes, Mrs. Kelly might have left a firelighter in the study after laying the fire. It *might* have been an accident. Then the clothes— Foster, how long will your fingerprint people be with the paper and label on that parcel of clothes? You did ask 'em to go over it, didn't you?"

"Yes," said Foster, and nodded to Buckingham, who went out at once. There was silence until Foster admitted that it seemed to get more involved as they went on. He was still sceptical of the wisdom of arresting Abbott, and made that very clear. Folly grunted, but made no comment. Buckingham was away for some time, and Foster stirred impatiently.

"I wish we'd stayed and searched 'Spindles' ourselves, you know," he said. "Sharp's a sound man, but——"

Folly said: "We left four men there, and we brought Abbott away. So the attacking force is outnumbered! What do you hope they'll find?"

"If Abbott killed him, something happened to the clothes he was wearing," said Foster. "If Anne Stafford did, something happened to her clothes—we've often agreed that there must have been a lot of blood. I——" he broke off, for the telephone rang. He lifted the receiver. "Yes," he said. "Yes . . . what's that, Sharp?" His voice rose. "Where . . . behind the books in his study. . . . Yes, bring it out at once."

He replaced the receiver, and looked into Folly's eager eyes.

"A blood-stained coat, shirt and tie were stuffed behind the books in Abbott's study," he said. "Yes, Abbott's—they've found his name-tabs on them."

"Well, bless my Aunt Sophia!" exclaimed Folly. "As obvious as that. Now we know why he tried to set fire to the room!" He heard the door open and turned his head quickly. "Ah, Buckingham! Results?"

"That paper and label, sir," said Buckingham, and paused.

"Well, Go on, man, go on!"

"They're covered with Abbott's fingerprints," said Buckingham, slowly, and almost reluctantly.

. . . . .

"Well," said Folly, after a long pause. "Now perhaps you two clever gentlemen will admit that the arrest of Abbott was fully justified, and perhaps delayed too long. He might have destroyed those clothes."

"If Abbott was clever enough to plan this crime, he would have got rid of the clothes before this!" snapped Foster.

"Nonsense, man! What are you, counsel for the defence? If Abbott committed it he wasn't clever, he was just a bungling fool. It's only clever if someone else did and is trying to frame him. Well, Buckingham? Perhaps you think Julius Stafford applied Abbott's fingerprints to the paper. If we could only find a motive against Abbott!" he cried, and for once he really looked put out. "I'm almost inclined to fall back on his ungovernable rage. He killed him, then realized with horror what he'd done. Then he lost his head. You did tell Sharp to bring those clothes out here quickly, didn't you?"

"Yes," said Foster.

"They can't come too quickly for me," said Folly. "I wonder what Abbott will say when he sees them?" Unexpectedly, he laughed. "You know, Foster, on the whole, I *like* this case."

"That's more than I do," said Foster, lugubriously.

It was a little more than half an hour before Sharp arrived with the coat, shirt, collar and tie. In the interval little had been said in the downstairs room, but as soon as Sharp entered Folly heaved himself to his feet and, with a purposeful look in his eye, he took them, beckoned Foster, and then strode towards the waiting-room where Abbott was being detained. He waited for Foster to catch up with him, and then flung open the door.

Tony was standing by the window, smoking. A policeman in uniform got up from a hard chair, trying to look disinterested. Folly waved him aside, and strode up to Abbott, waving the clothes in his face.

"Well, Abbott! Your clothes. Bloodstained. Behind the books in your book-case. *Your* clothes, I tell you—the clothes you were wearing on the day you killed Lovelace. Stop pretending, man. *Why* did you kill him? Can't you see that the motive is your only hope? If it were good enough, you might save yourself from hanging."

Tony took the coat, looked at it for a long time, and then returned Folly's gaze with one which was quite steady.

"Yes, they're mine," he said, "and I was wearing them that day. I hadn't missed them. You know, Folly, I've never denied killing Lovelace. I've only said that if I did I remember nothing about it. Until this moment I was terribly afraid that I attacked him as I did Hibbett. Now, thank God, I know that I didn't."

Folly actually gaped.

"I might have killed Lovelace," said Tony, "but if I did I came away and left him there and knew nothing about it. I know for certain that I did not discover bloodstains on my clothes and did not hide them away. I'm very glad you found them, Inspector. The question I suggest you apply yourself to now is—who put them there?"

CHAPTER 24

SUPERINTENDENT FOLLY IS AGITATED

"Yes, I agree with you," said Folly, half an hour afterwards. "He was as cool as a cucumber, and very much to the point. Who did put them there? He reminded us that Hibbett broke into the house, and might have gone to the wardrobe before he was caught and taken the clothes downstairs, after daubing blood on them. True, Hibbett had to work fast and had the luck if he chanced upon the right suit, but it's a good point. On the whole, Abbott came out

188

of it very well. Of course, I've told you from the first that he might have thought up this paroxysm of blind rage as an alibi, and we've no proof that he isn't bluffing well now. On the other hand, we can certainly have another go at Hibbett, on the strength of what we know. Pity we didn't bring that little scoundrel with us, but we can soon put that right.''

He spoke abruptly, and showed some signs of agitation. Foster did not find it difficult to guess why; whatever the Superintendent's good qualities, he was vain, even though he acknowledged and laughed at his own vanity; so, thought Foster, he was now afraid that he had arrested the wrong man and would be agitated inwardly, although he might show it very little until he found out the truth.

Foster nodded to the telephone.

"You'll bring him down to-night, won't you?"

"Yes," said Folly. "Yes." He stood up, but did not go immediately to the telephone; he stared at Foster. "You know, Foster, something is missing. I can't tell you what, but something is missing. The big trouble in this case is that too much has come too quickly. From the moment you discovered where the body was dropped into the river, we have made continual progress, and our setbacks have been remarkably few. Now, tumbling over each other in their eagerness, come the items of evidence against Abbott —all except that elusive motive.''

"I thought you were so anxious to make it Abbott," said Foster, a trifle sourly.

"My dear fellow, *please* don't wilfully misunderstand me," said Folly, querulously. "If I had my choice I would make it someone other than Abbott. I can't help it if things point his way. All I want is the murderer. Foster, what is on your mind? You are annoyed with me. That irritates and harasses me, for I value your good opinion. Until now, I have had it. What has gone wrong? What shakes your faith in me?'' He sounded like an aggrieved old man, and still further surprised Foster.

"On the evidence which we got at 'Spindles',"' said Foster, "you should have detained Anne Stafford. She had opportunity and motive, and is certainly an accessory.''

"Yes, yes, I know. We needn't be in a hurry to detain her, though. Abbott was enough for our immediate purpose.'' He was still agitated, for his fingers were rubbing the seams of his trousers.

"Enough for——" began Foster.

"Oh, my dear fellow, *please* use your mind. There were four people at 'Spindles,' all of whom might be involved. There was Hibbett, as an outsider, and my early favourite. The fact that the jewels and money remained in the clothes rules him out, except as an accessory. The man's rapacity is too well known for us to consider anything else—why *must* I repeat these obvious things? While the other four remained together they could close formation, conspire and confer to their hearts' delight, and possibly outwit us.

189

Now their ranks are open—I've told you so once. The first result was the truth about the removal of the body; the second, the reason why they were too frightened to tell the truth when they were in London. Oh, have no doubt about it, that's what happened. First, they were afraid that her unfortunate marriage would be discovered; and even if it weren't, the scandal of the murder would deter her fiancé. He is a wealthy young man whose parents oppose the marriage, and whose absence from 'Spindles' proves one of two things: either he was asked to come, and refused, or Anne did not wish for his presence. However, we didn't get *all* the truth. When Anne Stafford broke down I watched Abbott, watched him closely. I expected a confession, I freely admit it. I thought that he would see the danger into which his sister-in-law had placed herself and, knowing the truth, that he would save her. That is the way his mind would work. More than anything else, Foster, I am troubled by his attitude when she implicated herself so completely. He is not a man to allow anyone else to suffer for his sins.''

''He isn't the man who killed Lovelace,'' said Foster, firmly. He stared into Folly's eyes, and went on: ''Call it sentiment if you like, but I think we've got the wrong man.''

''All right, all right—that doesn't matter, it would only matter if he were about to be hanged. We must assume that one of the four was guilty. I thought an arrest would force a confession. It provided, instead, a most unsatisfactory anti-climax. Don't keep reminding me that I may have made a howler, *please*.''

''I only want you to admit it,'' said Foster, relievedly.

''Only a fool would refuse to do so. Whatever my faults, I am not a fool. Hum! We want to see Hibbett again, and—I *think* we'll send for that steward fellow at the National Club. The fellow who told us that Stafford had been there all the afternoon. Yes! If he was lying he will have time to repent on a journey in the company of a police officer.'' He stepped to the telephone and called the Yard, and while he was waiting for the call to come through, he went on: ''I'm not happy about the case. Don't remind me that I said I liked it; I do. It is a teaser. Every now and again, however, I get worried by the possibility that there will be another crime. *Something* remains beneath the surface. It may be the real motive. Ah!'' He broke off as the telephone rang, and gave instructions to his own office. Hibbett and the steward were to be brought down by road as quickly as possible. He gave precise instructions as to how the matter of the steward was to be handled, and then rang off.

''Well, what now?'' asked Foster.

''Food,'' said Folly. ''You never seem to think of it. I *can't* think on an empty stomach.''

''Oh, I don't know,'' said Foster. ''You ought to try, one day.''

The remark put Folly in a surprisingly good humour, but he remained on edge, and again broke his rule of not discussing business during a meal, which was sent in from the *White Horse*. In the course of it Harrington came in, and Folly took the opportunity of going over every inch of the case, as he put it, and examining all doubtful points closely. When they got back to headquarters, Folly snapped his fingers.

"Fool!" he cried. "No, not you, Colonel—me, this time." He took out a notebook and turned over the pages quickly. "Savory, Savory, private telephone number—ah!" He put in a call to Snub Savory's home, and while he waited for it to come through, he said: "The man knows Abbott as well as anyone. It will be interesting to find out if he knows Hibbett. Curious fact, you know—Abbott hasn't asked for legal aid. Most guilty people demand it immediately. I——" he broke off at a tap at the door, and asked innocently: "D'you mind seeing anyone?"

"Come in," called Harrington, and a constable opened the door. "Well?" said Folly, but the constable ignored him and looked at Harrington.

"A Mr. Savory called, sir, and asked to see you or Chief Inspector Foster."

"Ah-ah!" exclaimed Folly. "He gets here before we send for him. Curious eagerness." He cancelled the call to London, and was standing by the telephone when Snub came in.

The agent looked agitated; his curly hair was dishevelled, there were smuts on his face, and for once the turned-up nose and eyes failed to suggest that he was about to burst into laughter.

Harrington was standing up. "Good-evening, Mr. Savory."

Snub said: "Good-evening. Since when has it become the fashion to make arrests on a serious charge without giving the accused an opportunity to send for legal aid?"

"Nonsense!" boomed Folly. "No aid asked for. The opportunity remains." He looked ready for a verbal battle. "Have you brought legal aid for your client, sir?"

"I have arranged for legal aid for my friend," said Savory, abruptly. "I wish to see him, at once and alone."

"I am afraid——" began Harrington.

"I beg you, Colonel, to permit it," said Folly, with an elaborate bow. "I, at least, have no desire to prevent Mr. Savory conspiring with Mr. Abbott to defeat the ends of justice." He sneered at Savory.

"Any man who seriously thinks Tony Abbott capable of murder ought to be in a lunatic asylum," said Savory.

"You are offensive, sir!"

"Or else he is a fool," said Savory. "Folly, this isn't like you, you're usually very sound. If you're putting Tony and Gillian through purgatory with the idea of making your real suspect feel secure, it's one of your beastliest tricks."

"I am acting on the strength of the evidence," said Folly, aggressively. "Overwhelming evidence."

"What motive have you got?" demanded Savory.

"That, sir——"

The telephone bell rang, and Folly seemed glad of the opportunity

to turn away. "Hallo!" he boomed. "This is . . . Yes, Buckingham, yes? . . . speak more quietly, man, I am not deaf . . .
What!" he roared. "We will come at once. No, don't bring
her here, stay there!" He banged down the receiver and swung
round. "Anne Stafford has confessed to the murder," he said.
"No, Savory, I will not release Abbott until the confession is proved
genuine. You may come with us if you wish. Your interview with
Abbott is indefinitely postponed—isn't it, Colonel?"

"Yes," said Harrington.

"Thank you. You perceive, Savory, a united police front.
Come, gentlemen, to 'Spindles'! *Not* you, Mr. Savory, in *our*
transport."

.   .   .   .   .

As dusk fell over the countryside a mist rose from the river and
crept sluggishly towards 'Spindles' and the vicarage, blotting out
the ground and the hedges and gradually rising above the trees.
It concealed all movement and muffled all sound. Its effect was
felt inside 'Spindles'; it seemed to worsen the plight of the three
people who were there under police surveillance. Sergeant Buckingham and two plain-clothes men watched from the hall and
landing, making sure that no one moved without their knowledge.
There was little desire on anyone's part to move, however. Anne
was in a mood which had started with an exchange of words with
Julius and grown into hysteria which she was not able to control.
In the course of it she had flung that confession at Sergeant Buckingham, who was startled but gratified, and since then she had sat
in the great, odd-shaped drawing-room, staring into the empty fireplace, with her hands clasped about her arms as if she were
cold.

Julius was sitting in an armchair, but he did not look at ease.
Occasionally he broke the awful, oppressive silence, but if Anne
answered at all, it was in monosyllables. He did not address Gillian,
who was torn between a great relief at the importance of the confession to Tony, and horror at the thought that Anne might be
hanged. The fact that Lovelace had been murdered did not worry
her; of them all, she alone had never known the man. Her concern
was for the living, and as she sat and watched first Anne, then
Julius, the cold, clammy hand of fear took hold of her.

Policemen were on duty outside.

Chief Inspector Garth, having been given strict instructions from
Harrington to make sure that none of the occupants of 'Spindles'
could escape again, had gone to excess, sending six men in addition
to P.C. Grimes. On Foster's return he had gone away, to tell his
wife bitterly that now he had made sure none of the suspects could
escape Foster would step in and make the arrest. None of the
seven policemen who stood or walked about the garden of 'Spindles'
as the mist crept further from the river and got into their clothes
and down their necks and up their sleeves, making them clammy,
cold and uncomfortable, were thinking about Garth. At first they

had been intent on their task to make sure no one stirred without being noticed. Now, in the wet darkness, they began to move about more briskly, and their attention was apt to wander. It was impossible to see more than five or six yards, and not always as far as that. With the darkness the mist became thicker, too. All sound had ceased. 'Spindles' was like a house of death.

* * * * *

There was a faint glow of light from the vicarage study, and inside the room there was turmoil. The untidiness had become absolute disorder, and Castle was on his knees, peering beneath his desk, breathing heavily and with an expression akin to dismay. He stood up, pushed his hands distractedly through his hair, and muttered: "It can't have been stolen. That's impossible!" He looked in places which he had already searched several times, but found no trace of what he wanted—his precious manuscript. It had been on his desk when Mildred had called him, and he had hurried upstairs to sit with her while the police were in 'Spindles.' Together they had watched Tony Abbott being taken away, and seen Gillian standing on the porch with a dreary, hopeless expression on her face. Castle had gone to offer comfort, but had quickly seen that there was no desire to see or talk to him in that house, where the shadow of Blackshaw's corpse hanging from the tree seemed all-pervading.

So Castle had come back, gone to tell Mildred, and come downstairs, only to be distracted by three unexpected callers from the village. When he had turned to look at the manuscript and Snub Savory's suggestions, it was not on his desk. He had turned the room upside-down, had interviewed Maude twice and Agnes once, all fruitlessly. Suddenly he heard Agnes's footsteps in the passage, and she opened the door abruptly.

"Well," she said, "have you found it?"

"No. Agnes, are you *sure* you haven't been tidying up in here?"

"Tidying up!" she exclaimed. "It would take me a week! But *I* can tell you where to find your daft book, if only ye'll believe me."

"Where?" snapped Castle.

"At 'Spindles'," she hissed. "That home of thieves and murderers! To think that *my* house has ever known such evil folk. My house!"

"That's enough!" cried Castle. "You're not sane, woman!"

When she had flounced off with an ugly look in her eyes he repented the outburst, but when he went to find her and to apologize, she had gone out. All Maude could say, wringing her red hands, was that she had looked like a creature possessed of the Devil and had gone into the misty darkness without hat or coat, muttering blasphemies to herself. Castle then went into the garden, but realized it was hopeless to expect to find her, and returned to make another futile search of the study, growing more agitated and alarmed. It was such a senseless thing to steal; and to suspect anyone from 'Spindles' was ridiculous—ridiculous.

Yet—there *was* evil in that house.

. . . . .

A mile out of Milton, Superintendent Folly had been seized with another idea. Apologizing extravagantly to the Colonel, he had stopped the car by a telephone kiosk and hurried to it, spent ten minutes fuming and fussing—so it seemed to Harrington and Foster —but at last returned with a seraphic smile on his face. As he climbed into the big car, he grunted:

"I really am sorry, Colonel. Forgetful of me. I've sent for Abbott." He beamed and rested a hand on Harrington's knee. "You don't mind, I trust?"

"I don't have to mind," said Harrington, good-naturedly.

"You're very good. I think it will be wise to have them all together. I have also sent for Professor Gimbert."

"That old man!" exclaimed Foster, startled.

"He will not like travelling, I feel sure, but the more I think about him the less happy I am about his story. Stafford went to see him, followed by Hibbett. We may have been told the truth; on the other hand, Gimbert, a self-confessed moron in all matters except music, might have held back something of importance. Normally I do not like gathering all suspects and witnesses together. It is poor technique—this is work, not stagecraft. However, with your permission, my dear Colonel, I will do it."

"Granted," said Harrington, straight-faced.

Folly laughed. "I don't know what it is about you people in Milshire, Colonel, but I will say you are after my own heart. Even Foster here, sceptical though he often is, is a treasure. Ever thought of applying for a transfer for Scotland Yard, Foster?"

"Now that's enough," said Harrington.

They were approaching Riversmeet when the mist first closed upon them, and the silent Yule slowed down to five miles an hour. Twice cyclists loomed up in front of him, narrowly avoiding a collision, each time when Folly was expressing his agitation and annoyance at the slow pace; Yule was unimpressed. It took three-quarters of an hour to cover the two miles from Riversmeet to 'Spindles,' where Yule pulled up and said decisively:

"I don't think I ought to try turning into the drive, sir."

"Confound it, there is a long walk!" said Folly, aggrievedly.

"That's better than knocking the car about, sir," said Yule, firmly.

Grimes loomed out of the mist when they approached the gate, but had nothing to report. There had been some talking in the vicarage, where something appeared to be missing, but not a sound had come from 'Spindles.' Grimes explained carefully where the men were stationed, and then they left him disappearing in the mist. They had been heard, for the door was opened and the bright hall light shone on Buckingham's fair head.

"Well?" said Folly, sharply.

194

"No change, sir," said Buckingham.

"Have you questioned the woman?"

"No, sir, I thought it better left to my superiors."

"Thoughtful fellow," said Folly, affably. "Where are they? In the drawing-room." His voice was loud. "All right, there's no hurry, I'll see them a little later. Don't let anyone—anyone, you understand, especially that loud-mouthed musical wonder— leave the room." He started up the stairs, and Foster grimaced but followed slowly. Folly and Harrington turned into a doorway, after Folly had looked into several rooms, and Foster found to his astonishment that Folly was in the bathroom, examining various toilet articles.

"I could tell them something about bathrooms," grunted Folly. "Hum. Three different makes—Buckingham! Pop downstairs and ask Mrs. Abbott what toothpaste her husband uses."

"Toothpaste?" echoed Foster, and then added: "You scoundrel, you know Buckingham's downstairs. But why——"

"Are you serious?" asked Harrington, and when he was convinced of that he volunteered to get the information. He returned quickly and reported that Abbott used *Kolno*. Folly picked up a yellow tube, eyed it narrowly, and asked whether Harrington or Foster used the stuff. Foster said that he had done. "What's it like?" asked Folly.

Foster gave a long-suffering sigh.

"The flavour is pleasant, with a little peppermint. The consistency——"

"This is not a joke," said Folly. "Never mind, here's an unused toothbrush." He tore the cellophane wrapping off a brush, damped it after reading the instructions, and squeezed out a little paste. Then, solemnly, he brushed his teeth; in a few seconds the froth from the paste was over his lips and a little was on the tip of his nose. "Good!" he said, and rinsed out his mouth and beamed. He dried off the brush and put it in his pocket. "Now let's have a look at the studio," he said.

The studio had been tidied up, but all the music scores had been preserved, some of them crumpled but straightened out. "I wish I knew more about this stuff," said Folly. "It looks as if this is the work Stafford started on—what's it like, Foster?"

Foster took several sheets and scanned them, humming to himself. Folly began to frown. "Either you're terrible or it's tripe," he said.

"It isn't very good," said Foster, "but there's nothing surprising in that. It's been discarded."

"*Hum!* No report that anything of interest was found up here, is there? No. All right, now for the study." He led the way downstairs, and turned into the narrow passage which led to the study. Being segregated from the rest of the house, it was not visible from any of the vantage points from which the police were watching.

Halfway along the passage, Folly sniffed, and Foster thought that he smelt burning. Folly suddenly broke into a run, a senseless thing since it was only three steps to the door, and opened it. It jammed for a moment, then sagged—and a billow of smoke poured into the passage.

"*Another!*" cried Folly. "Not Abbott this time!" He dashed into the room, where flames were flickering near the window. Harrington called for Buckingham, while Folly switched on the light and began to tread on paper and carpet which were burning or smouldering. He began to choke, and soon Foster was doubled up with a paroxysm. Buckingham rushed into the sitting-room and asked whether there was a fire-extinguisher; there was not. He called for other men and they brought buckets and bowls of water. It was useless now to try to keep Gillian from the study, and Julius came with her; only Anne remained in the drawing-room. The smoke was thick and curled about the window, billowing whenever there was a slight puff of wind. The curtains were alight halfway up, but smouldered rather than burned. Gradually the men subdued the fire, but the carpet was sopping wet, one chair was ruined, and the woodwork of the windows was scorched. Smuts floated everywhere and the room was filled with the acrid smell of burning.

On the floor were dozens of pieces of loose paper, charred or yellow and brown; the writing on some sheets was indecipherable. Folly stood in the middle of the room, smuts and wisps of smoke floating about his head, reading a sheet of paper covered with a neat hand.

"Anyone recognize this?" he asked.

"It's probably some of Abbott's work," said Foster.

"It concerns church organization. Was your husband interested so deeply, Mrs. Abbott, that he——"

Gillian was staring at the paper, and spoke as if she had not heard the question.

"That's the *vicar's* manuscript! But Tony gave it him back."

"Bring the vicar here!" snapped Folly, and he looked at Buckingham with a truly terrifying scowl. "And find an answer, if you can, to this question: how was this fire started when the house is supposed to be watched so closely? It is disgraceful! I—what's that?"

He broke off, for from outside there came a high-pitched, almost maniacal scream; it stopped, then started again, and all but Folly and Foster stood rooted to the spot.

CHAPTER 25

THE FIRES EXPLAINED

CASTLE came hurrying from the vicarage, roused by the screams. Mildred Castle was at her window, calling out in alarm, and her husband shouted to reassure her. The light from the study window and from Mildred's room cast a faint glow about the garden between the two houses, and in the glow a policeman was seen struggling with a woman who was tearing at him, trying to get away, and giving vent to those awful screams. It was Buckingham who climbed through the window and slapped her face, and so succeeded in stopping her.

"And who in the name of goodness is this?" demanded Folly, in his mildest voice.

Foster said: "It's Mrs. Blackshaw. Agnes Blackshaw."

"I saw her crouching outside the study window, sir," said the policeman; he was Grimes. "I thought I saw a flicker of light and came along to investigate. Then I saw you come into the room, sir, so I concentrated on her. She was doubled up with laughter, silent laughter. She isn't——"

"That will do, constable, thank you." Folly stared at the woman, and then at Castle, who came in great distress through the gap in the hedge. "Bring her into the house," he said, and in a few minutes she was in the blackened, scorched room. There was an ugly glitter in her eyes as she looked at Folly, but her chief interest appeared to be in Gillian, at whom she glared and shook a fist. Castle was standing by the door, looking helplessly about him; and suddenly he caught sight of a page of his manuscript. He picked it up, stared at it, and went very pale.

Folly stepped forward, took Agnes's arm, and sniffed at her hand. He dropped it as if it were red hot, and backed away as she struck at him. She was trembling from head to foot and looked like a witch, with her hair dishevelled and her clothes ruffled and soiled with black; one sleeve of her long, grey dress was singed.

Folly said: "You have been handling paraffin or firelighters. Did you begin this fire, ma'am?" The question, uttered so mildly, seemed absurdly short of what was required; and yet it was effective, for she cried in sudden fury:

"Yes, I did, and I would again! This is my house, my house, my house! Now thieves and murderers live in it, it is besmirched with their foul touch, fit only to be burned down, burned, burned, *burned!*" Her voice broke, but she stood glaring at him; just then, at least, she was not sane.

"Did you start an earlier fire?" asked Folly, in the same soft voice.

"Some fool put it out," she cried, "some fool put it out! But it did not matter, I came again." She lowered her voice and looked at Castle with an expression of great cunning. "It gave me a chance to undo more evil. You, Henry, have lent yourself to the devil himself!"

"Agnes——" said Castle in a broken voice, and he glanced towards the window. As he did so Gillian seemed to come to life; she thought of Mildred Castle in her room alone, and she turned to the door; then she looked back at Folly. "I must go to the vicarage," she said, and when Folly raised no objection she hurried

197

out. They could hear her calling from the garden, and heard her enter the front door of the vicarage. For a while there had been silence, with Agnes glaring at her brother-in-law, who looked suddenly old and broken.

"So your brother-in-law has lent himself to the devil," said Folly, encouragingly.

"Please——" began Castle.

Agnes screamed: "Ever since the murderers came to 'Spindles' he has befriended them—befriended people who have blood on their hands! Oh, I know them for what they are, I know the evil that is in them—and in you, Henry! I took your book! I read the terrible things you have said about the Church, the terrible lies you have written, *so I destroyed it!* I set it alight and here it is—*look, look, look!*" She stabbed her quivering finger in a dozen directions towards pages which were mostly burned, while Castle stepped to her side and rested a hand on her shoulder. She tried to fling it off; he would not let her, but held her firmly.

Suddenly she began to cry.

.   .   .   .   .

Folly admitted that the first weakening of the evidence against Tony had come; he did not sound displeased. He saw how easy it was for Agnes to come through the gap in the hedge to the window of the study; and he examined the overgrown trees and bushes which practically hid the study from sight. He spared a moment to congratulate Grimes on his speedy action, thus making up for much of the misfortune which the constable had suffered. He raised no objection to Castle taking Agnes away, but asked the vicar to send Gillian back. She came promptly, less troubled now, for she had shared something of her burden with Mildred Castle. Julius, very subdued, had contributed nothing to the conversation, and Anne was still sitting with her hands clasping her arms, staring into the empty fireplace.

A car drew up outside, and was followed by a second and a third. Abbott was brought in by Sergeant Sharp; he looked for Gillian, and his eyes lighted up; Folly did not stop her going to him. Then Savory came in; he had lost no time in getting a taxi. Immediately afterwards two plain-clothes men from Scotland Yard brought Hibbett in. There was also a tall, thin-faced man with a stoop, who looked about him bewilderedly but did not seem alarmed. His arrival brought the first look of animation to Julius's face.

"What the devil are you doing here, Bright?"

"The police asked me to come," said the thin man.

"Mr. Bright," said Folly, to the room at large, "is a steward at the National Club. We may require his evidence this evening." He looked at each man in turn, his lips curling when he saw the frightened look on Hibbett's face.

Foster, sitting on the arm of a chair with his injured leg stretched out in front of him, expected Folly to start on Hibbett. There was, he knew, the possibility that the Yard man would wait until Professor

Gimbert arrived, but that would not be for some hours; he would hardly keep Harrington waiting for so long. There was no knowing to what lengths Folly would go, however. The fat man continued to look about him with a baleful stare, as if he hoped that by keeping silent among all the people gathered together, he would force someone else to speak.

No one did.

Julius stood by Anne's side; she was looking at Folly, her face haggard and her eyes dull. Tony and Gillian stood near them. Hibbett and Bright were in the middle of the room, and the police were by the windows and doors.

Abruptly, Folly said: "Abbott, come with me, please."

Tony joined him. Folly sent Harrington a bright smile and assured him that he would not keep him waiting long. Breathing heavily, he led the way upstairs. Tony did not speak as they hurried along to the bathroom, but he looked puzzled.

Folly said: "Abbott, I am quite serious. Your life might depend on what happens in the next few minutes. I want you to follow my instructions carefully. You recall the evening when you attacked Hibbett?"

"Yes."

"You told me that you were brushing your teeth when you heard a scream. I want you to brush them now, please."

Tony stared, then shrugged his shoulders and obeyed. He was halfway through, and the frothy *Kolno* was thick about his lips, when Folly snapped:

"That is enough! Come, please." He gripped Tony's arm and hustled him down the stairs, and Tony was too bewildered to protest. A policeman outside the door stared. Folly brushed him aside, and said: "Follow me." He strode into the room, and Tony followed. Harrington gaped and Foster raised his hands helplessly. Folly led Tony across the room to Hibbett, and his voice grew suddenly thunderous:

"Hibbett! Is this how Abbott looked when he attacked you? Don't lie to me, man, is this how he looked?"

"He—his eyes were glaring," Hibbett gasped.

"But he was frothing at the lips in this way?"

"Yes, yes!" Hibbett backed away, as if afraid that another attack would come, but Tony stood still and Folly raised his voice to an unprecedented pitch.

"Very well, sir! Is this how he looked, with froth on his lips, when you saw him at Chelsea? Answer me? Is it? *Is* it?"

"Yes!" cried Hibbett.

"Thank you," said Folly, in a cooing voice. "Thank you. You are a brazen liar, Hibbett. That is now proved. The froth is the chemical reaction after using *Kolno* toothpaste. I do not believe that Abbott brushed his teeth immediately after slicing Lovelace's face. You elaborated your story too much. *Hibbett!* You saw someone standing over Lovelace, with the blood streaming from the terrible wounds in his face and neck, you saw the blood dripping from the knife, but you did not see Abbott? *Whom did you see? Whom——*"

"Stop!" screamed Anne. "Stop! He saw me, I was standing there, I saw him, he was frightened and ran away. I've told you that I killed Lovelace because I wanted to marry again, because——" she broke off, and her lips were trembling, her hands were rubbing against one another in the agony of her confession.

"I see," said Folly, and he looked at her with an expression which was almost of commiseration. "You know the penalty, Miss Stafford. You know the consequences, and yet you stand by your story—that you killed Lovelace."

"I tell you I did! He maddened me, he——"

"And after killing him, you took off his clothes."

"Yes!"

"Where did you send them?"

"I—I sent them to—to a friend of my brother's."

"Name him, please."

"To Professor Gimbert."

"Why?"

"I—I believed he would help me; I meant to go to see him but I didn't get the chance."

"I see. What did you do with your own blood-stained clothes?"

"I burned them in—in the fireplace at Chelsea."

"I see. I inspected the ashes, but saw no trace of burned cloth," said Folly.

"I cleaned it out, and we burnt some papers afterwards. Ask Julius, he will tell you—we burned some papers. Julius, didn't we? Answer me, Julius?"

"Yes," said Julius, with an effort. "Yes, we did."

"We make progress," said Folly. He still looked at Anne. "You have told me that you went out for an hour and came back and found the dead body. So that is a lie. You killed him and, when you realized what you had done, with great cunning and heartlessness you tried to make it appear that your brother-in-law, Mr. Abbott, had committed the crime."

"I—yes, I did, but I couldn't keep it up!"

"I see. Where did you get the paper in which to wrap the clothes which you sent to Professor Gimbert?"

"It was in the flat. I—Julius had just received a big parcel of music; I tore off the label and—and——"

"When Mr. Abbott came in and saw you in a different room, you gave him the paper and the label, and made sure that he handled it freely, so that his fingerprints were on it. You then used gloves when tying up the parcel. Is that right?"

"Yes!"

"Look here," began Tony.

"Quiet, sir, please! Let us continue, Miss Stafford. You prompted your brother to put the body in Mr. Abbott's trunk, to use his suit-case——"

200

"They happened to be handy, that's all, they happened to be handy. I—I didn't realize that it would—would help."

"I see. You were not such a thorough-going scoundrel as you might have been, Miss Stafford. Let us proceed to the next step in the course of your remarkable crime. You took some clothes belonging to Mr. Abbott, stained them with blood, and hid them behind the book-case in his room. Isn't that right?"

She stared at him, and then gasped:

"Yes. Oh, God, don't torment me! I've confessed, I couldn't go on with it. Tony, I couldn't let them hang you!"

"A point in your favour, certainly," said Folly. "Well, gentlemen, we know now how the crime was committed, and how cleverly it was made to appear that Mr. Abbott had committed the murder. Now all that remains to be obtained is the corroborative evidence. *Hibbett!*"

Hibbett raised his hands, glanced desperately at Anne, opened his lips—and then stopped as Julius roared:

"You little swine, if you say a word against her I'll kill you with my own hands! Folly, don't listen to her, she's lying to you! Abbott killed Lovelace, she's trying to save him. *Ever since he married Gillian Anne's been in love with him.* Anne, my pet, don't lie for him any more, tell the truth!" He went down on his knees beside her. "Don't sacrifice yourself for him, he's too worthless, he's——"

Tony said: "It's fantastic! If Anne really——"

"Be quiet!" snapped Folly. "Come along, Miss Stafford. Is it true that you love Anthony Abbott, your sister's husband? Is it true that you have reached the supreme height of devotion, and you are prepared to sacrifice your life to save that of a man whom you love? Come, please! Let us not continue this tragic drama for a moment longer than we must. Is it true that between you and Mr. Abbott there has been deep, requited love? If that is so, it would not be hard to understand why he killed Lovelace: *to save you.* He would take the risk for your sake, you for his. A story of great devotion. Let us have the truth now, please."

Gillian was staring at Tony, her hands clenched. To Foster, Harrington and the others, it was a fantastic scene; in the centre of the room Anne and Julius, Julius kneeling with his arms about her, her face white and her eyes bright with unshed tears.

Savory broke the long silence.

"I am quite sure that your notion is fantastic, Folly. Tony is devoted to Gillian."

"Hold your tongue, sir, or I will have you put out!" cried Folly. "You will not save a profitable client that way! Miss Stafford, I beg you to tell the truth, the whole truth. Is it possible that Lovelace attacked Abbott, that he was killed in self-defence? That is not a crime, you know." His voice tapered off and left another silence; but it did something to Anne, who raised her head and stared at him with dawning hope in her eyes.

"Yes," she said, in a strangled voice. "Yes, that's what happened, Lovelace—Lovelace had a gun!"

"Now why didn't you tell us that before?" asked Folly, gently. "Why didn't you admit everything from the beginning, Miss Stafford? There would have been no danger." He waited, and then he smiled gently, and squeezed Tony's arm. "You didn't tell us that, you know, because it isn't true. None of it is true, Neither your confession nor your evidence against Tony Abbott. You——"

He broke off and swung round, for at that moment of all moments there was a tap at the door. His eyes were stormy and his hand was clenched and raised when a scared-looking policeman poked his head round the door and said:

"Telephone for Superintendent Folly, please. It's from Brighton."

"Colonel! Foster! I charge you not to allow a word to be uttered while I am absent." Folly strode out, leaving a silent gathering in the large, bare room.

CHAPTER 26

MOTIVE

No one spoke while he was gone. He left the door open and they could hear his voice, raised in mostly monosyllabic questions; and then they heard the ting of the receiver being replaced and his heavy footsteps on the hall floor. He stopped outside the room for a moment, then slowly pushed the door open. Every eye was turned towards him, and, as if conscious of being the centre of the stage, he approached the middle of the room slowly, one hand at his chin, the other pressed tightly against the seam of his trousers. He stood in front of Anne and Julius, and after a long time he spoke in a soft voice.

"Miss Stafford, you are an accessory after the fact of murder. I am sorry. I shall do all in my power to make your ordeal easy for you. I have never, in all my long experience, come into contact with a woman who is so utterly devoid of self-interest and who is prepared to go to such great lengths of self-sacrifice. I shall not add to your mental torment by asking you to speak again. You have done all that any human being could do to deceive the police, and for a splendid motive. It is a motive which others might feel was misguided, but in your opinion it was sufficient to justify everything which you have done." He stared at her, holding out a hand, as if pleading with her. Then, without altering the tone of his voice, he went on: "I hoped to bring another witness here to-night. I sent for him. I have just learned that he is dead. I speak of

202

Professor Gimbert, who, unable to stand the strain of being interviewed, and to face the full exposure of this long-established train of deceit and double-dealing, died of heart-failure soon after I sent a man to fetch him. Professor Gimbert,'' he repeated, and then his voice hardened and he turned to Julius. ''Well, sir—what will you do *now?* Where will you get your inspiration?''

Julius, on his knees, stared up at him.

All the colour had gone from his cheeks and he was trembling. His eyes were staring, there was no doubt that he had received a terrible shock. He licked his lips, tried to speak, failed, and licked his lips again.

''Julius Stafford,'' said Folly, in a hard, even voice, ''you murdered Jeremiah Lovelace because he knew that you have never in all your life composed a piece of music worthy of being played. *Professor Gimbert composed them for you.''* He swung round, and in the hush that followed, pointed a quivering finger towards Hibbett and roared: ''You saw Stafford! He bribed you to name Abbott! You, Bright! Stafford paid you well to say that he had been at the club all that afternoon, whereas in fact he was away for an hour or more. Stafford! You did all those things to which your sister, to save you, confessed so freely, even to sending the clothes to Gimbert, although she did not know where they had gone! I have described exactly what happened, but *you* killed Lovelace, because he could and would have told the world that you are a fraud, a failure, a scoundrel. You returned to the Chelsea house, gained entry by the back door, and——''

It was Foster, so placed that he could see Julius's hand at Anne's waist, who caused the sensation which followed. He sprang forward, a hop rather than a jump, and struck Julius's hand as it reached his mouth. Two little pills flew from his grasp; one struck Folly in the face, the other hit the wall and dropped onto the fireplace. Julius jumped to his feet, striking out wildly, but Foster needed no help, for by the time Buckingham had joined him Julius was leaning back against the wall with a trickle of blood at his lips. Folly, solemnly and almost portentously, uttered the formal words of the charge and arrest.

Inside five minutes, both Hibbett and Bright were making statements that would hang Julius. Hibbett had gone so far as to take away Julius's blood-stained clothes, and burn them.

. . . . .

There was not room for all the police to return to Milton on the first journey, and Foster elected to stay behind. Anne had been taken away, but so far Folly had not preferred a charge against her, although one would be inevitable. Savory also remained behind, smiling now, looking rather pugnaciously at Foster and patting Gillian's hand from time to time. For an awful moment, Gillian confessed, she had thought Folly meant what he said when he had talked of Anne's love for Tony. She still was white, but her relief outweighed her anxiety for Anne.

"Folly always said that the motive was more important than anything else in this case," declared Foster. He still felt a little bewildered, and he was sitting with his leg up. "He wasn't far wrong. I don't think he is often wrong."

"He was about Tony!" declared Gillian, heatedly.

"I'm not at all sure about that," said Foster. "I think he believed that an arrest would start much heart-searching, but he will probably never admit that he was convinced you were innocent, Abbott. That toothpaste experiment was a touch of genius—I wondered if he were off his head at first! And for a man who doesn't understand music," he added, "he didn't do so badly."

"Had you suspected the truth about Julius?" asked Savory.

"Not for a moment," admitted Foster. "Folly showed much interest in the sheets of half-written music at Gimbert's cottage, and I remember wondering why he asked Gimbert to play him a piece and then got impatient before it was finished. I don't need telling now: he had some idea of the truth then, and hoped to trap Gimbert into something that might be construed into an admission. He failed—he gets impatient quickly when anything doesn't go as he wants it."

"I got impatient with him," said Savory.

Foster laughed. "I wouldn't like to have to work with him for long at a time. He must be a trial to his juniors at Scotland Yard, but it's been an experience I wouldn't have missed for the world."

Gillian said: "I still find it hard to believe that Julius was such a complete fraud."

"You needn't," said Savory, decisively. "I'd never dreamed of it, but I know he turned out some atrocious stuff as well as some that was very good—Gimbert's was the good. I wonder if we shall ever know why Gimbert let his work be signed and credited to another man?"

"Probably not," said Tony, slowly. "Well, we do know why Julius went off without telling anyone where he was going, and why Anne was so worked up and worried. She suspected the truth, I've no doubt. Will it go very hard with her, Foster?"

"I doubt it," said Foster. "She will be found guilty of being an accessory after the fact, of course, but it doesn't always mean a death sentence, nor necessarily a life sentence. She must have known practically all that happened, including the fact that Julius was the murderer, although from what I can gather she never let him know what she suspected—or knew."

"No wonder she wasn't herself!" exclaimed Gillian. "Inspector, how can we help her?"

"Get legal advice——"

"I'd hired Pendelton for you, Tony," said Savory, "so he can take over."

"Good!" said Tony. He frowned thoughtfully, but there was a faint smile at his lips. "Well, Folly is certainly a remarkable man. The way he led her into 'admitting' that she knew exactly how I had been framed deceived me completely; I thought she had done it. The fact that Julius did doesn't surprise me," he added, "and yet—will Pendelton take Julius's defence, too?"

"It will hardly be a defence," said Foster.

"Perhaps not, but—well, I think we ought to do the best we can for him. Can we afford it, Snub?"

"Just about," said Savory. "What an astonishing fellow you are! If the man had had his way you would have been hanged."

"Never mind that," said Tony. "I'll see Pendelton when he gets here—he might be able to plead insanity. Confound it, no man who is sane could plan a thing like that. I wonder why he actually killed Lovelace when he did?"

Foster said: "Lovelace wasn't a very nice specimen, as you know. It's probable that he saw two excellent ways to make an easy living by blackmail—first, holding the marriage over Anne's head; second, threatening to betray Julius to the world. The second threat undoubtedly made Julius go wild; he was very vain, of course, and terrified of being shown up. Folly timed the announcement of Gimbert's death perfectly; Julius's resistance just broke down."

"Yes. The only thing——" began Tony.

He broke off as the door opened and Buckingham appeared. The sergeant's face had a puzzled look, and he beckoned Foster, who limped towards him. Buckingham's whisper reached the ears of the others.

"There's a car just arrived from Brighton," said Buckingham. "I can't understand it—an Inspector named Wright is in it, with— *Gimbert*."

Foster gasped: "What? I——"

He stared along the hall, and could just see Professor Gimbert coming in behind the self-important Wright. Foster hurried along as best he could, while Gillian, Tony and Savory stared at each other. Savory broke the silence by saying:

"The damned scoundrel! He lied about Gimbert's death so as to break Julius! I wonder if we can hear what's being said?"

They went to the door, and heard Foster speaking as levelly as he could while struggling with his surprise. They could just see Gimbert standing and looking at Foster with a gentle smile, as Foster explained that Folly had gone into Milton; then there was a shout from outside, and Folly burst into the hall. He was puffing heavily, and held his hand up to enjoin silence. Tony and the others made no bones about going forward, intent on catching every word.

Gimbert spoke next. "Well, Superintendent, now you have uprooted me, perhaps you will explain why."

"Yes," said Folly, and he took a deep breath. "Gladly, Professor. I wanted your evidence to convict Julius Stafford of the murder of Lovelace. You were to supply the motive. You were to admit that Stafford's name is given to your compositions. However, your evidence will be superfluous. Stafford has admitted

205

it. He has not, however, said *why* you connived at this fraud. You are under no obligation to talk. Nothing you say can affect the issue. However, you can satisfy my curiosity, Professor.''

Gimbert watched him closely without a change of expression. When Folly stopped the old man kept silence, but a smile dawned and slowly broadened. Folly made no effort to persuade him, and the waiting seemed to be prolonged unbearably.

"That is very simple," Gimbert said at last. "I have no wish for fame, money, notoriety, for the pleasures of the world and the adulation of fools. I wished to live alone with my work; I did not wish to rob the world of the products of my mind, however, and at first I helped Julius to correct his own work. Gradually I fell into the habit of writing everything for him—or nearly everything," he added, "the foolish fellow would insist on publishing some of his own compositions. There is no crime in what I did, I hope— not even by your strict standard, Superintendent. I permitted—nay, I encouraged—him to do it. You have found out, I suppose, that Lovelace knew, and proposed to blackmail Julius?''

"Yes," said Folly.

"And also that Welch, or Hibbett as I believe you call him, was Lovelace's messenger. I told you the truth about Hibbett, Superintendent. In fact I told you the whole truth—except that I pretended I did not know who sent me Lovelace's clothes.''

"Ah! Who did?'' asked Folly.

"Julius," said Gimbert. "He asked me to leave them un- touched until the police arrived. I wonder why?''

"He hoped it would help to forge the chain of evidence against his brother-in-law," said Folly. "That was why he stripped the body. It was not a sudden idea, this blaming the murder on to you, Abbott. However, I am convinced that his sister knew nothing about it. I understand, now, that he even pretended that he really suspected her, and he would have let her hang. Bah! The man is utterly vile. *He* will hang. Oh, a small thing. The blood on your clothes was rabbit's blood, Abbott; perhaps that would have saved you. Professor, you will need a new stooge. Thank you for coming—oh, Inspector Wright, I have booked rooms in Milton for you and Professor Gimbert; you will find them extremely com- fortable, I'm sure.'' He ushered them out, and on the porch muttered a request to Wright to get Gimbert's statement in writing. Then he turned back, and surveyed the little crowd in the hall. He was smiling as he said:

"It is well-ended. Foster, forgive my little trick about Gimbert's 'death.' When I was in the telephone booth I was arranging to be telephoned as if from Brighton—I wanted Stafford to think a call was from there, to wear his nerves. "Abbott, forgive me. The evidence was strong. One must act on evidence, even if one is not always convinced. Foster was a staunch champion, you should be grateful. If you take my advice, you will consult a specialist about your dangerous temper. Mrs. Abbott, I will do all I can to ease the ordeal through which your sister must go.

Believe me, please. Oh, one thing. Do you wish to make a charge against Agnes Blackshaw?''

''No,'' said Tony, promptly.

''You are very forgiving. Her first effort at fire-raising nearly got you hanged. There is one thing I have been wanting to ask: was Castle's manuscript good? It is such a shame if it was, and I am hoping that it was piffle, and therefore best destroyed.''

''Unfortunately——'' began Tony.

''Destroyed?'' asked Snub Savory, sharply.

Tony told him what had happened, but he could not understand Snub's cheerful smile as he heard the story. When he had finished, Snub chuckled and rubbed his hands together.

''I knew I was wise,'' he said. ''No one ever takes a copy of a hand-written manuscript, so I had it typed. I've three copies in the office, and copies of my notes, too. We'd better tell the old chap, hadn't we?''

.   .   .   .   .

Some time later, while Julius was awaiting trial with his sister—on whose behalf a Mr. Edward Barr was working furiously—a letter reached the Rev. Harry Castle, and within five minutes of opening it he was rushing through the gap in the hedge, calling Tony's name. Tony looked out of the window of the redecorated study. Mildred Castle was standing by the window of her room, well on the way to recovery, and smiling happily. Castle waved the letter, and Tony recognized the familiar Savory letter-heading.

''He's sold it to the first firm he offered it to,'' cried Castle, almost incoherent. ''And seventy-five pounds advance on royalties, Tony. Oh, my dear chap, I can't thank you enough, I really can't! It's miraculous.'' He turned and shouted: ''Isn't it, Mildred? Miraculous!''

''Yes!'' called Mildred.

''You wrote it, you know,'' said Tony, as Gillian hurried from the house to congratulate the vicar. Castle calmed down, but was still excited, and for once he was able to talk about his sister-in-law without sounding too grave. At Anderson's urgent request, he had allowed her to go into a private home; for Anderson assured him that while she lived near 'Spindles' she might become homicidal.

Gillian went in to see Mildred Castle, and the vicar and Tony stood talking for a while. Tony had been wondering whether to leave 'Spindles,' but he had decided to stay, although it was rather too large for them. The cricket club was in being again—that very afternoon there was a match with Milton 'A' Eleven—and now the conversation turned towards it.

Suddenly, Archy Kelly turned into the drive gates, alone, and carrying a letter gravely in front of him.

''Grand little chap, that,'' said Castle. ''You've made a difference to him, too. Mrs. Kelly is a good-hearted woman, but how she ever gave birth to such a child I just don't know. I hear she is going back to London.''

"No!" exclaimed Tony. He stared at Archy, and then glanced at Mrs. Castle's window. He thought of how much Gillian had come to care for the child, and how her affection was greater because there was no hope at all of children of their own. He forced himself to smile as Archy came up.

"Good-morning, Archy."

"Good-morning," said Archy, gravely, and touched his forehead twice—once for the vicar. "Please, Mr. Abbott, my mummy has gone away, and she asked me to give you this."

'This,' to Tony's surprise, was a typewritten letter in an envelope addressed to Mrs. Kelly. Tony opened it, and as he read his eyes began to shine.

"Dear Madam,

"With reference to our interview, I can inform you that to the best of my knowledge, after making full inquiries, Mr. and Mrs. Abbott would make excellent foster-parents for your grandchild. The fact that his mother is dead and the father unknown does, of course, mean that the responsibility rests with you, as the only known surviving relative. I suggest . . ."

There was much more; it was obvious that Mrs. Kelly had seen a golden opportunity of finding a home for Archy, and had made sure that there would be no legal obstacles. Written at the foot of the letter in an untidy hand were the words: "*I do hope you can take 'im, Mrs. Abbott. His muvver wasn't married, she got killed by a buzz-bomb . . . please, Mrs. Abbott.*"

"Gill!" cried Tony, almost incoherently. "Gill! Archy, come with——" he stopped, raised Archy in his arms and limped eagerly towards the vicarage, the letter fluttering in his hand.

THE END